"Engrossing. . . . Smith's characters are so real you not only know what they look and sound like, you feel the wind as they pass."　　　　*—Seattle Times* on *Kingdom River*

"Mixing politics and ferocious military action, this should grab historical fiction fans as well as postapocalyptic-adventure buffs."　　　*—Booklist* (starred review) on *Kingdom River*

"Smith blends a keen insight into human nature and its motivations with a gift for storytelling in a saga that should appeal to fans of postapocalyptic and survival fiction."
　　　　　　　　　—Library Journal on *Kingdom River*

"A strong plot, memorable characters and a setting both intelligently imagined and artfully invoked. The future he depicts is so well thought out that it seems almost inevitable. The author recounts [events] with authority, elegance, and, frequently, poetic grace."
　　　　　　　—The Cleveland Plain Dealer on *Snowfall*

"Smith's thriller focuses on groups of people kicked backwards down the stairs of knowledge and discovery, trying to maintain a society in the face of starvation and invasion."
　　　　　　　　　　—Publishers Weekly on *Snowfall*

"[A] beautiful, compulsively readable novel [with a] Robert-E.-Howard-meets-Jack-London vibe."
　　　　　　　　　　　　—SciFi.com on *Snowfall*

By Mitchell Smith
from Forge Books

THE SNOWFALL TRILOGY

Snowfall
Kingdom River
Moonrise

MOONRISE

BOOK THREE OF THE SNOWFALL TRILOGY

MITCHELL SMITH

 A TOM DOHERTY ASSOCIATES BOOK

NEW YORK

This is a work of fiction. All the characters and events portrayed in this book are either products of the author's imagination or are used fictitiously.

MOONRISE

A Tor Book
Published by Tom Doherty Associates, LLC
175 Fifth Avenue
New York, NY 10010

www.tor.com

Tor® is a registered trademark of Tom Doherty Associates, LLC.

ISBN 0-765-34059-3
EAN 978-0765-34059-7

First edition: February 2004
First mass market edition: February 2005

Printed in the United States of America

0 9 8 7 6 5 4 3 2 1

TO LINDA

My Lord lives still, in his son—the child with strangers, but alive.

LAST WORDS OF MICHAEL RAZUMOV,
KHANATE CHANCELLOR, AT HIS EXECUTION

Do the seasons warm? Perhaps a very little, though the wall of ice still stands across the continent, the seas lie shrunken, and Lord Winter rules more than eight Warm-time months each year.

If Warm-times do come again, I will not see them, since I am dying, and so leaving the service of the Achieving King. And, after all, I have seen enough. I cannot believe in the Shadow World, though I wish to, for there my friends would be waiting for me. My dear Catania, and Newton—sad, reluctant ruler. Dangerous Jack Monroe . . . my Gardens Lady Bongiorno, and the late great Queen of Kingdom River. They have seemed too grand, too vivid for death's idiot emptiness.

I have not been so grand, so vivid. Still, I will miss my breakfasts.

NOTE FOUND IN THE DESK OF
NECKLESS PETER WILSON, LORD LIBRARIAN AT ISLAND.
FILED IN THE DAILY BOOK BY HER HONOR,
THE LADY PORTIA-DOCTOR.

Knowledge of one's self—a study often unrewarding as a southern songbird's battering at its own reflection. Futile as complaining of cold in a world gone to cold for six hundred years, thanks to treacherous Jupiter's altered orbit.

I have seen persons cry, of course, and found it odd. . . . No longer. Imagine my startlement, imagine the sudden pain in my eyes as tears, hot tears in my rooms carved from ice, came welling at the news that Small-Sam Monroe, an old—May I call him friend? I believe I may. —When news came to me that he and his queen had perished in a storm on the Gulf Entire. Their ship, aptly named *Unfortunate*, had foundered.

I had seen him last—he was not yet called the Achieving King—almost twenty years before. Only his first great victories were behind him. Still to come were the campaigns against Manu Ek-Tam in Map-California, and the organizing of the Great Rule of North Map-Mexico, Middle Kingdom, and the West. . . . Young, stocky, and strong, with beautiful eyes in a fighting man's grim face, he'd kissed me good-bye (our only kiss), and helped me up onto the occa's back—a stupid and inferior occa, sent up by my Second-cousin Louis from Map-McAllen.

The Made-beast had been sent to save me weeks of Walking-in-air back to New England—to which, I'd thought then, I'd been so foolishly recalled. Thought that, and wrongly, since my order home was to an appointment of infinitely greater honor than even that of Ambassadress to a Kingdom certain to grow greater.

The occa had grunted, groaned, flapped up from Island's East battlement into the freezing river wind . . . then sailed its first wide ascending spiral. It was the last I saw of Sam Monroe, looking up in the company of his officers, all still dressed in their wedding finery, leathers, jewels, and velvets, their veteran sword-scored armor polished to shining.

I have been to weddings, since—Boston taking contractual matters very seriously and in celebration, so we march through frozen Cambridge singing—but have been to no such wedding as Sam Monroe's and his Princess Rachel, where sadness and joy were so mingled that the ceremony seemed the very mirror of our lives.

FROM <u>EARLY YEARS,</u> THE MEMOIRS OF PATIENCE (NEARLY-LODGE) RILEY

MOONRISE

Someone chased with a sense of humor.

A hunting horn winded along the river's bank. The hoofbeats following those notes came cracking through the last of Lord Winter's failing snow and puddle ice, fell softer over mud. Someone called—perhaps a name, perhaps an order.

These were Heavy Cavalry reservists, unsuited to rough-country chasing, which was certainly why Bajazet was still alive. Light Cavalry, Light Infantry, would have filtered here and there until they had him.

It was a blessing of both Blue Sky and Lady Weather to have gifted him with terror enough to smother sorrow, so he could lie trembling beneath a frozen log, fallen to rot years before, thinking more of staying alive than remembering the king, his Second-father, and his Second-mother, Queen Rachel. Remembering Newton—named for a royal grandfather—and his brother in all but blood.

It seemed to Bajazet, lying hunched in puddled ice under frozen wood, that the true world had been taken from him, with only this desperate dreamed one left. And the taking accomplished in only a day. He heard the hunting horn again . . . but distant.

Newton, a year younger, but bigger, stronger, kinder—older in every important way—had seemed indestructible as the king had seemed indestructible. Prince Newton, only nineteen years old, but already with endless hours spent in tedious councils, and study with ancient Wilson, while Bajazet, even quite young, was amusing himself in Natchez brothels . . . also amusing himself puncturing, though not murdering, less accomplished swordsmen—husbands, for the most part. This, until the king, one day, came into the *salle*, gestured the bowing Master aside, chose two fighting rapiers from the rack . . . tossed one to Bajazet—and attacked to wound or kill him.

They'd fought across the slippery oil-puddled floor, until the king parried a desperate thrust in *quarte*, reposted . . . and, during what had seemed recovery, reversed and ran Bajazet through the left shoulder. Then, the king had stepped in to disarm—breaking Bajazet's right wrist—and while stepping out, had kicked him in the groin so he fell, curled in three agonies.

Portia-doctor had done wonders with a short slender iron rod, heated to only dull red. Then done more wonders with a wrist-splint, and very gradual exercise—Queen Rachel coming, anxious, to stroke Bajazet's forehead, leave imperial chocolate candies, and a kitten for company. Newton coming to make jokes . . . play checkers and chess. So that after the so-short summer, Bajazet—then barely eighteen, after all—had been left with only rapier memories, and an occasional ache in his left shoulder. The wrist was good as ever.

Healed, he'd encountered the king in the West Glass Garden. Sam Monroe had smiled. "Lessons learned, Baj?"

"Yes, sir."

"And what lessons were they?"

". . . That there is always someone better. And only luck prevents the meeting."

"And?"

"Dueling is one thing. Fighting is another."

". . . And?"

"A decisive blow may be struck in retreat."

"And . . .?"

"Pain is too important to be suffered or inflicted without good cause."

Then, the king had gathered Bajazet into his arms as if he were still a child, and hugged him hard before letting him go. Strong arms, and the scent of leather and chewing tobacco. "Your

First-father," the king had said, "—the Lord Toghrul, would have been proud of you."

And on the first day of Lord Winter's festival, the king had given Bajazet a sword—a rapier made by Guild-master Rollins himself, its blade (of imperial *wootz* steel) folded and hammered again until even Rollins had lost count of the doing, so the slender double-edge, slightly sharper than a barber's best razor, and needle pointed, could with great effort be bent into a curve—to then spring humming, perfectly straight. The sword's grip was wound with twisted silver wire, its coiled guard forged of simple steel. A fighting instrument, its only decoration a cursive along the base of the blade—*WITH GOOD CAUSE*.

This weapon, its belted black-leather scabbard matched with that for a long left-hand dagger as finely made, was the only thing of value Bajazet had with him under the frozen log.—And if he hadn't already been up and dressed for before-dawn's hunt breakfast when men in Cooper livery came kicking through the lodge doors, he would have had to flee naked out the upstairs window and down the wooden fire-ladder—Old Noel Purse shouting, *Run . . . RUN!* amid the noise of steel on steel, breakfast tables toppling, the screams of dying men.

Naked, Bajazet would himself have died in the icy day he'd been hunted through East-bank woods. But, up early for pig sausage and fried chicken-eggs when treachery came calling, he'd snatched up his sword-belt, then run in imperial cotton underthings, buckskin jerkin and trousers, wool stockings, fine half-boots, and a pocket knife with a folding blade. A long wool cloak as well—plucking that from a wall peg the only thoughtful act of a frantic scurry down the corridor from his chamber to the window and its fire-ladder, while a few brave men bled for him below. His only thoughtful act . . .

If he'd always been alone in the world—unknown, unknowing First-father or Second-father—he would not be weeping now, for shame. Shame at imagining what Toghrul Khan, what Sam Monroe would have thought of him scrambling along the hall, breathless as a girl, then half-falling down the ladder to run into the woods—the formidable duelist, the dangerous boy, proved only a Lord of Cowards, and a fool.

Old Noel Purse had said, "Better not," at the notion of going to the hunting camp. Had said, "Better not," but hadn't explained. Bajazet had assumed it was thought unseemly, with the king and Queen Rachel lost for only months. . . . But his brother—crowned Newton-the-Second only weeks before—had said, "Nonsense; I know you loved them," and turned back to a desk half-buried in paper-work.

"Can't I be of some help . . .?" had been Bajazet's only and casual offer.

Newton had turned again to smile at him. "And I'll need your help, Baj. I'd be a fool to waste the son of Toghrul Khan. . . . But for now, one of us at least should be without care. So go hunting, for the both of us."

It was . . . unbearable to remember. As the royal family's affectionate adoption of a baby boy—sent by the Kipchak chancellor to save him from Manu Ek-Tam, the would-be khan—as *that* was unbearable to remember. All memories that could be ended by simply standing up out of mud and ice from under a rotting log, and shouting until green-armored cavalrymen heard him and came riding. Then, out sword, and an end to it.

Only anger prevented him. Anger at himself—even more than at Gareth Cooper—for carelessness in not considering what opportunity must have been seen after the king's death, with Newton only nineteen, and kinder than most at Island. A kind and thoughtful prince. Too kind . . . too thoughtful. The king had held the river lords down, the Sayres, DeVanes . . . and Coopers. Had held New England to caution as well. Boston and its Made-creatures stepping lightly in country of the King's Rule.

Newton should have caught up those reins at his crowning, set the bit hard at once—with his adopted brother to help him. But Newton had been young, thoughtful, and kind. And his brother had gone hunting.

And now, was hunted . . . and deserved to be. It didn't occur to Bajazet to even wonder if Newton were still alive. Cooper and his friends—known also as friends of Boston—would have made no such blunder. As they must also have considered Newton's brother, and found him worthy of at least casual killing.

. . . He lay beneath his icy log into the evening, and made no noise, though his nose ran from weeping, his empty stomach muttered as glass-hours went by. Lying huddled there, Bajazet found that the rapier thrust, broken wrist, and bruised balls of almost two years before, had been no pain at all compared to the loss of loved ones.

Daylight faded slowly to nearly dark, so he lay safer though aching with cold, heard no hunting horns, and dreamed an uneasy dream of being warm and fed. A celebration, a shifting remembrance of Tom MacAffee's welcome dinner, Boston's Ambassador sent to Island after years of none, and bad feelings. . . . The food at Bajazet's place, set on hammered silver, was lamb-chops, roasted carrots, and potatoes. He saw this clearly, and seemed to eat, but—distracted by MacAffee's laughter—somehow never quite chewed and swallowed, though he tried to keep his mind to it. In his dream, he did consider how clever Boston had been to send a fat and cheery man to represent so frozen and grim a state, its nastiness born in palaces of ice.

Bajazet dreamed, but was filled by no dream food, warmed not at all by the six great iron Franklins rumbling down the dining hall. He did watch the king and Queen Rachel, and stole glances at Newton, sitting beside him, with great attention, as if to be certain of remembering them, though his dream offered no reason for it.

. . . From the colors and confusion of that lamp-lit banquet, Bajazet woke—trembling with cold, sick with hunger—to the odor of leaf-mold, wet wood, and soaked snow. The evening wind, come with fading light, hissed in the trees. That wind mentioned death as it passed over, so—with lying still and dying the alternative—he rolled stiffly out onto frozen mud, sheathed rapier tangling his legs, and tugged folds of his cloak free of skim-ice. He managed up onto all fours, crawled a little way cramped and sore as if badly beaten . . . then, grunting like an old man with the effort, staggered to his feet to stand hunched, shivering in darkness.

"What . . .?" Bajazet asked aloud, as if his First and Second fathers both lived, and stood under the trees, listening. They listened, perhaps, but didn't answer him.

What should be done? What could be done, but run or die— and more likely run *then* die?

His First-father would likely have said, "Surprise is the mother of victories." But what surprise was possible, now? The hunters would hunt again in morning light—and be surprised only by how long it had taken to catch and kill him.

"Lessons learned?" His Second-father had asked in the Glass Garden.

Among the answers: a decisive blow may be struck in retreat.

Feeling faint, Bajazet leaned against a birch for strength, and felt that unless he attempted *something*, sorrow and shame would kill him, sure as the cavalrymen. He would fail, and wish to fail, and the horsemen or the cold would catch him. —Why not, instead of certain losing, at least attend his fathers' lessons?

"Something," he said to the tree. "Something surprising . . . and attempted by a man in retreat." He'd called himself a man, to the birch, and supposed now he would have to be one while he lasted, and no longer only a young prince, the king's ward, and in so many ways still a boy.

He stroked the tree's sheeted bark as if the birch were a friend, and cared for him. "Good-bye," he said to it, imagined a poem about the dignity of its stillness, so superior to mens' foolish motions . . . then found the dog star through the birch's branches, and began to walk west, back toward the river, the way he'd come. It seemed a strange and foolish thing to do, to pay a debt of honor owed only to the dead, and himself.

* * *

He was walking, hurrying, hooded cloak wrapped tight against the wind, before he was clear in his purpose. Still, it seemed certain the way he'd come was the way to go . . . go quickly as he could, back through frozen tangle as darkness began to grow deeper.

Gareth Cooper—no doubt swiftly crowned *King* Gareth now—was a tall, slender man, as his father had been, stooped, prone to illness and not strong, though Coopers had always been strong enough in purpose. A reedy man, whose wife had died of crab-cancer years before. . . . Now, a new king—by treachery— and with only one child. One son and heir to prove a dynasty to the river lords and other magnates of the Great Rule along the Mississippi, south into North Map-Mexico, and west to the Ocean Pacific.

Bajazet, barely twenty years old and an improbable successor, would not have been important enough for the king to come kill him . . . but perhaps slightly too important for some liveried captain's responsibility. Who better, then, to deal with the last of family business, than the king's only son?

It certainly seemed possible, even likely. Bajazet, trusting in the first hints of cloudy moonlight for his footing, trotted back through the woods as if cold and hunger were sufficient sustenance. He traveled as certain of direction as if back-tracking the lingering scent of his own terror the day before. Moving fast, ducking through tangles, then running full out where occasional clearings widened to shallow snow and wind-burned grasses, he traveled due west through evening into deeper night, short-cutting all the meandering ways he'd fled—and cowered here and there to hide.

In this forest, standing back from the river's east bank, there was only one place—the Lodge—suited to house a new Prince of the Rule as he directed a hunt. . . . No doubt young Mark Cooper's people had scrubbed the blood from the dining-room flooring, washed it off white plaster walls, mopped it from the stair risers where Purse's men had stood and died to give Bajazet his mo-ments running.

Mark Cooper—a playmate since childhood, plumper than most of his family, lazy, and amiable even as a little boy. *Seeming* lazy and amiable, cautious of a fierce father . . . an even fiercer grandfather while that unpleasant old man had lived.

Could Mark have always been called a friend? Yes.

* * *

After what must have been at least six glass-hours of woods-running, of dodging sudden trees, scrambling over fallen logs . . . of exhausted stumbles, scrapes and scratches from frozen branches as he'd shoved and wrestled through to the next clear-ing, Bajazet smelled at last the smoke of camp.

And as he came nearer, heard horses whinny . . . heard the quieting noise and banter of troopers—the last of their patrols long since ridden in, their mounts grained and tended. The men, now also fed, would be settling into sleep at the fires, weary after riding the long day, and into night.

Bajazet paused at the edge of the lodge clearing, stood shadowed under the branch-broken crescent moon, and took deep recovering breaths. He was shivering with weariness and cold. . . . There seemed to be no sentries posted, except for two men standing a distance to the left, talking, by the lodge front's wide half-log steps.

No reason for many guards to be posted, after all. . . . A hound was yodeling in the kennels, interested in these stranger cavalrymen come to camp.

The hounds hadn't been set after him, the whole chase. It must have been thought they weren't to be trusted to track and pull down one of their accustomed masters. And true, there wasn't a soft-eyed scent-hound or brute mastiff there that Bajazet hadn't played with as a puppy. Even more than Newton, he'd had a way with them.

"You don't respect him," he'd said once to his brother, concerning a hound's stubborn disobedience.

Newton had smiled. "I find men difficult enough to respect, Baj. I don't have enough left for even an amiable dog." Though, as was Newton's way, he was more patient thereafter.

. . . The kennel quieted after a time. The lodge camp quieted. Only a fire's hiss and crackle, only an owl far away, only the night wind sounded through the trees as Bajazet walked cloaked into camp as if he were a forester with ordinary business there—had perhaps been out to john trench, and was coming back to coarse blanket and pack pillow. Though the two men at the lodge's steps, if they'd noticed, might have wondered why he strolled around to the back of the building, where no fires burned.

Bajazet threw back the cloak's hood, managed his scabbarded rapier clear, and climbed the fire-ladder back up the way he'd come, a coward fleeing, the morning before. The climb—a dozen rungs up a simple ladder—was surprisingly difficult; he had to stop once to rest, and hung there, very tired.

The window was swung closed, its leaded squares of glass giving blurred vision down an empty corridor lit by two whale-oil lamps hung to ceiling hooks by fine brass chains.

Odd, that he'd never noticed such detail. It all seemed new, not quite the lamp-lit hallway it had been. He'd left the memory of it behind, as he fled.

Bajazet drew his dagger, slid the long, slender blade between window frame and jamb . . . and forced it, levering just beneath the simple catch. It was wonderful how the knife spoke to him through its grip, the steel reporting angle and effort . . . mentioning its limits, but not seriously.

Bajazet felt the latch at the blade's top edge, and lifted it.

The window squeaked and swung wide. He threw a leg over and was in, stood in indoor warmth for a moment, smelled roasted meat, and suddenly felt sick. The heat seemed furnace heat, so he swayed, wanting to lie down. He closed his eyes, breathed deep . . . and felt a little better. Then, his eyes open, he walked as through a dream down the long corridor to his chamber. And, as he lifted the door latch, felt certain as Floating-Jesus who he would find. He stepped in, and closed the door behind him.

Mark Cooper, awake in this small hour as if by appointment, stood startled before the sideboard and a tray of food, barefoot in a bed-robe of velveted maroon.

"... *Baj!* ... Thank Lady Weather! I thought these idiots might have killed you." Great relief on young Mark's face. Great relief. "I just got out here, late, and put a stop to it. No reason for you to be involved in this at all." Mark took a step forward, then a step back as Bajazet came to him. ". . . My father. My father has ordered things—"

"Newton?"

A nod from sad Mark Cooper. "I'm just so sorry, Baj. Dad . . . I never thought he'd *do* something like this!"

"Pedro, and the others?"

"Well . . . I don't know about all of them. But Darry killed three of our people—my father's men. It was all just a real *tragedy.*" He shook his head. "Terrible . . ."

Perhaps it was hunger that so sharpened a person's eyes. Sharpened his ears as well. Bajazet heard Mark's voice subtly uncertain as a banjar's slightly warped by having been brought indoors directly on a winter evening. The voice, like that instrument's, was almost true, but not quite. Cooper's eyes, still the mild blue of his childhood, had shifted, just slightly, toward the door—for escape, for what help might come to him if he had time to shout, if a slant-eyed, dark-eyed fugitive, grimed with mud and smelling like a forest creature gone to earth, weren't standing so close, his hand on the hilt of his long left-hand dagger.

Bajazet saw the food on the sideboard was still steaming, brought up not long ago. A hot meal now seemed as good a reason as revenge. As good a reason as leaving Gareth Cooper with no heir to his stolen throne.

"You'll be safe, Baj." The heir, frightened, and barefoot in his bed-robe. "Really. I promise, absolutely."

"And will also bring Newton back to life?" Bajazet drew the left-hand dagger as he reached to cover Mark's mouth with his right hand, stepped in, and thrust him deep, three swift times with rapid soft punching sounds—into the gut, the liver, and through the heart's gristle.

Mark stood on his toes with the long blade still in him, arching away, squealing into the muffling hand like a girl in her pleasure. Then fell forward, staring, slumped into Bajazet . . . clutched his cloak, and seemed to slip down forever as the steel slid out of him. . . . He settled onto the floor, grunting, turned on his side with urine staining his robe, and took slow steps there as if walking through a tilted world. Then liquid caught and rattled in his throat.

Bajazet, staggering as if his dagger had turned to strike at him, as if the whole of the last day and night had turned to strike at him, stumbled to the sideboard, and wiped his blade carefully on a fine linen napkin. He sheathed it, then took up slices of venison from a serving platter, folded them together dripping gravy and red juices, and crammed them into his mouth. . . . Chewing seemed to take too long; he bolted the meat like a hunting dog, drank barley beer from a small silver pitcher only to aid in swallowing . . . then gathered and swallowed more venison, gravy running down his fingers, spattering on fine figured wood and linen. Tears also; he cried as he ate, and supposed it was because he was still young, and though he'd injured men in foolish duels, had never killed a man before.

As Mark Cooper was certainly killed, since now he was still and silent, and smelled of shit.

Bajazet crammed and ate until he ached, drank more beer to ease it down . . . remembering Mark as a small boy, a playmate always amiable, biddable, so often looking surprised at what the great world offered childhood. . . . Bajazet chewed rye-bread rolls and little roasted potatoes, though they seemed to have no taste at all.

So much gobbling finally made him feel faint, and he had to go sit on the room's cot, bow his head . . . take deep breaths to keep from vomiting. He sat sick, as Mark lay at ease in a rich sticky pond, keeping him company.

"I hope you lied to me, about being sorry," Bajazet said, though now that seemed to make no sense. Perhaps Mark would have understood it. . . . There was the strongest urge to lie down on the cot, the room so warm with its little stove in the corner. The strongest urge to do that, and sleep, so that waking later might prove all a dream, and Noel Purse come in and say, "Are we hunting, Baj? Or sleeping the fucking day away?"

It seemed stupid to stand, but he did. Stupid to search his own locker for his small leather pack, with its flint-and-steel, spare southern-cotton shirt, ball of useful rawhide cord . . . also a red-checked bandanna, and yesterday-morning's hunter's ration of pemmican, river-biscuit, and little round of hard cheese. A canteen—why in the world did Warm-time copybooks call water flasks *canteens*? . . . Strap pack and so forth on over his cloak. And take what else? What else, and why anything, only to run again?

After thinking for what seemed a long time—Mark lying patient on the floor—Bajazet also chose his recurved bow and a quiver of fine broadhead shafts, shouldered them, then cautiously opened the door to no voices from below . . . and only soft snoring from another chamber. He stepped into the corridor, closed the door behind him, and walked what seemed a long way down to the familiar window . . . clambered out to the familiar fire-ladder—the bow's curved upper arm knocking on the window's frame—then climbed carefully down. More burdened now . . . and less.

The camp's ground, when he reached it, seemed the first thing in a while solid and real. Real as the chase to come, that would make a poor joke of the hunt before. Now it would be the new king who pursued—a king bereft of his son and that son's future. A king with now no dynasty possible, no continuance. Gareth Cooper would chase, if necessary, to the Smoking Mountains . . . would have to, or be seen weak as well as lacking any heir.

Bajazet, belly overfull to aching, strolled through firelit darkness—waved once to the two men still talking a long bow-shot away, standing casual guard by the lodge's entrance.

Two dead men, soon enough, when the king—pigeoned the news—came to the lodge and asked who had stood watch while his son was murdered. . . . Some huntsmen, of course, some militia would continue to cast, seeking his trace. But the full hunt would now await the king's coming—a two-days' sail up from Island. Bajazet would have at least that advantage.

He walked on . . . walked out of camp, ducked into forest and was gone. Gone running into the last of night, fleeing east and alone through dark, still, and frozen woods.

He'd slept till near midday, when the hounds woke him, casting uncertain and far away.

Uncertain, since they must be following the scent of clothes taken from his chamber's press, then echoed on boot-prints into the woods. Their master's scent, and never before that of prey. So, fragile and reluctant trailing—and thank Lady Weather, or they would have him in a day's running. The foresters, those fine trackers, were more dangerous.

Bajazet had slept on his belly like an exhausted child—the stems of winter-killed grass were printed across his right cheek. He sat up, then stood, and shook frost-beads and dead leaves from his cloak. . . . He'd certainly heard the hounds, but then had lost their yodels. They'd be Warm-time miles behind him, west, down a small stream's valley. He'd slept the last of night and half the day beneath a budding alder—and had had to, or stagger in circles and drop to be found as they came on behind him.

"I killed him," he said aloud, and saw Mark's eyes again, astonished as he sank down. There was satisfaction to waking to that memory, though he supposed it would be better not to dwell on it, draw pleasure from the killing to chew on as spotted cattle chewed to swallow their mouthfuls twice. Better not to dwell on that with pleasure . . . and also not to talk aloud too often, since he had no good advice to give himself—nor encouragement, either.

So the hounds, poor followers—but the chase was not yet in full cry. When King Gareth came, it would be with fresh hounds, foresters, and at least a troop of the Army-United's regular Light Cavalry. Those hunters would be difficult to lose.

Likely impossible to lose, though the chase took them days, weeks. A new king—a traitor king—his only son murdered, could not afford to return to the river, the river lords, and other greats of the Great Rule, without the killer's fire-dried heart dangling from the Helmet of Joy.

A long, long chase then, and an almost certain end to it. —And if not that end, then what? An escape into deep and deeper wilderness, peopled with savages—and worse than savages, Boston's made-creatures gone feral? And so to an even meaner death?

Bajazet kicked a shit-hole with his boot heel, swung his cloak off, unlaced his buckskins, lowered them and under-drawers, and squatted for necessity . . . then used damp leaves to clean himself, and kicked the place covered. He laced his trousers, then reached up to lift his sword-belt, pack, bow and quiver from the low alder branches he'd hung them from the night before. He buckled the sword-belt, then drew on his cloak, strapped his leather pack to his back, and shouldered the quiver and unstrung bow.

The hounds again. Still distant, several Warm-time miles to the west.

Bajazet walked . . . then jog-trotted east along the narrow stream. He didn't know its name, so as he traveled, named it Confusion—and after a while, his night stiffness easing with the exercise, used it as such. He sat, and took his boots and thick stockings off. Then, holding them high, ran to splash down into the icy water . . . and out and up the opposite bank. Ran a little way angling north—then back the way he'd come and into the stream again . . . jumping, slipping, stepping from sand to rock to shingle, forging upstream until his legs, in soaked buckskins, ached with effort and freezing water, and his toes were bruised and bleeding from stubbing on stones.

He climbed out the opposite bank again, trembling with cold, cloak-hem dripping, sat to dry his feet in the cloak's hood . . . then put on stockings and boots to run again, angling north until the sounds of the stream were lost behind him, and only his footfalls broke the woods' silence.

He ran while he could—when the close trees and tangled brush allowed it—then, very tired, breathing like a Festival runner, he stopped and bent by a berry bush, hands propped on his knees, to catch his breath.

"I should have taken a horse," he said aloud—then remembered not to do that, and was silent. He saw himself—Mark Cooper dead—walking to the horse-lines past snoring troopers, choosing some shifting charger (a tall hot-hided roan) amid the warmth and odor of other horses. Unclipping its halter tether, and leading it away, stamping, snorting, to jump swinging up onto its bare back . . . knee it to a trot, then kick it galloping out of camp, leaving shouts and flaring torches behind.

Bajazet imagined that so well, he looked behind him as if the horse were there, tethered to a tree while he rested from hard riding.

Of course, hoof-marks would have been easier for pursuers to track . . . and stealing one would have required passing many snoring troopers to get to the horses. Careless guard of the new king's son, perhaps, with no danger expected. Careless guard of a regiment's mounts—never.

Bajazet thought of a bite or two of his pack's pemmican, then decided not. It was startling how empty of game—of any food— these wild woods were. He'd seen nothing, not even a rabbit or squirrel for reason to string his bow. And no time to set and wait out snares. . . . Unless many tribal hunters had come through, the distant sounds of the hunt had been enough to frighten the game away before them. In that way, by hunger, the chase might kill him without ever catching.

. . . On the royal hunts, of course, the foresters had already found game, or driven it, for the family's pleasure. But he was no longer a person privileged. Now, he was *only* a person, and could even be alone and by himself—though he'd many times been almost alone with only a whore for company . . . and with other men's wives. Alone in his chambers at Island, of course, though with Terry Fitz, or Noel, or sad old Ralph-sergeant on duty outside his door. The steward, and the maids. It was Terry he missed most, and was surprised to be missing him. A valet . . . clothes-press, hot irons, and fussing over colors.

Bajazet raised his arms, stretched as well as bow, quiver, and pack allowed, and took a deep breath of cold woods air. There was a pleasure to being only a person, and alone—though a pleasure that would likely be short-lived.

* * *

Time to angle back to the stream. East . . . east would have to be the way, at least for a while. East, and thank Floating-Jesus—or the Forest's Jesus, now—for rising hills and deeper woods, where a troop of Light Cavalry (certain soon to arrive and chase) would find difficult going.

Bajazet settled his gear, canted the scabbarded rapier back out of his way, and trotted—allowing for frequent interfering trees—a long southeastern way, taking direction from a watery sun through graying cloud. His toes hurt. . . . He felt he must someday set bitter loss aside, set the last of cushioned boyhood aside as well, to become a slightly different person, one to whom the panoply, music, and colors of the court would seem odd to remember.

Alone. The king gone, the queen gone—and Colonel Mosten drowned with them. . . . Newton gone. Pedro Darry killed—and certainly others.

And who left alive, who had loved King Sam Monroe? Possibly Master Lauder, who'd seemed so sly. Possibly he and Lord Voss—both in their fifties, now—had survived in North Map-Mexico; the Coopers' arm might not have reached so far. . . . Come to a wall of ice-sheathed bramble, Bajazet had to backtrack, go around to avoid it. —And if Howell Voss still lived, then his wife, Charmian, would be alive as well, and she a fair and dangerous match for her husband. Lauder and the Vosses, formidable people who'd been King Sam's officers and friends.

Bajazet had met the three of them once, come up from the Gulf for Lord Winter's festival. The Vosses, particularly, an impressive pair, both tall and battle-scarred. They'd brought twins with them, of all things—a little boy and girl clumsy and curious as puppies. . . . Lord Howell, one-eyed and seeming to Bajazet old to have fathered young children, had been humorous, and played the banjar once in his Second-mother's solar. His wife, not quite as old—her long black hair, streaked iron-gray, worn loose down her back as if she were a girl—had come up to the *salle* once, and stood watching a lesson, a battle-melee where fifteen of the older boys (and a river lord's odd daughter) half-armored, fought with blunted blades in confused turmoil, divided one group against the other. Lady Voss had watched for a while . . . then, smiling, had left.

After the lesson, the others dismissed, the Master—a grizzled West-bank Major, still quick as a cat—had said to Bajazet, "Be careful around the Lady Charmian Voss, Prince, now and in the future. Careful courtesy, do you understand?"

Bajazet had understood, understood even that year before the king's painful lesson. The lady's smile, though pleasantly amused, had seemed to conceal something grimmer. He'd heard the king, later, discussing those two with Queen Rachel as they went hand-in-hand to dinner. "—Howell and dangerous Charmian, together for loss and lack of other loves," he'd said. "But it seems they suit, after all."

"Suit very well," the queen had said.

. . . Slowed to a walk by thickets, Bajazet paged dripping foliage aside. He could hear the stream again—to the right—returned to after his detour. Odd word; he'd read *detour* in some old copy-book, a seventh copy concerning people using Warm-times' bang-powder guns for robbery.

"Stranger than we can know," Ancient Peter Wilson had said of Warm-times, "—even with a number of their books copied and in our hands. Even using those books' language as our own."

Bajazet came to Confusion's bank, and as he stood resting, heard no hounds calling over the soft sounds of running water. He noticed his hands as if they were a stranger's. Dirty—filthy, really—and a fingernail broken like some sweat-slave's on the Natchez docks. . . . Natchez—not Warm-times' town, of course; that long drowned as the river rose in even the short summers' melt-water off the Wall. Not the same town, though named the same, and likely more than twenty miles east of the old one. But what times he'd had there. . . . Gwendolyn.

"You have slant eyes," speaking while astride him, bending down to observe. "Yes," Bajazet had said. "All Kipchak—except Ancient Wilson says my grandmother was a capture from Bakersfield in Map-California."

"Funny eyes," Gwendolyn had said, and leaned lower to kiss them.

Love, of course. He'd loved her, and loved no other, though fucking where he could. Some whores, of course—and court ladies too—had smiled and passed him by. "You're a pretty boy," Lady Bennet had said to him, "but grown men have a sadness to them that I care for. And besides, my Walter might have you killed—adopted prince, or not."

"What am I to do?" He'd asked Newton—a seventeen-year-old's question to a wiser sixteen-year-old. "I love her."

Newton had thought for an afternoon, then found Bajazet on the foot-ball field. "Talk to our mother."

So grotesque a suggestion, that Bajazet had gone to Ancient Lord Peter Wilson immediately for a better notion. The old man had been napping in a library niche—woke, listened to the inquiry, and said, "Speak to the queen about it."

So, in an agony of embarrassment, Bajazet had gone to Queen Rachel's study the next morning—lingering outside her door while a guardsman watched, amused—then, invited in, had "spilled" as Warm-times had had it. Had "spilled his guts."

"Ah . . ." Queen Rachel had held a little gray dog on her lap, stroking it. "The Up-river girl—Gwen?"

"Gwendolyn," Bajazet had said, deeply mortified. Apparently a person's life was not his own.

"I understand she's very pretty, Baj."

". . . Yes."

"But isn't she . . . professional?"

"That makes—" Bajazet had intended to say, "makes no difference," but couldn't bring himself to do it. He didn't care to see pity in the queen's eyes. See *Poor boy* there.

"Though, of course," the queen said, "—regarding love, that makes no difference."

"No."

"It's so sad, Baj, that while it makes no difference where love is concerned . . ." The little dog had turned on its back to have its belly scratched. "It's so sad that it makes a great deal of difference where *happiness* is concerned."

Bajazet had said nothing. He'd seen wisdom coming, and no way to avoid it.

"Would your pretty Up-river girl be happy here at court? Would she be happy as the ladies turned their backs on her? As men stared her through the rooms?"

"We—"

"Would she be happy knowing she was hurting you? Was injuring you in your world, so you would always be thought a fool and cock-thinker, instead of a serious man?" The little dog had grunted with pleasure. Scratch . . . scratch. "Would she be happy, knowing her children would be subjects of laughter, would come to her, weeping?"

"I don't know."

The queen had put the little dog down. "Never lie to me, Baj, for I held you in my arms as a baby, and would die for you as

I would die for Newton. Besides, lying makes men smaller. It's a coward's trick."

"I suppose . . . I do know."

"Of course you know—and knew before you came to me—that if you love this girl, you will of course protect her from any sorrow that you can. Even at your own cost." The queen had stood. "Now, we will think how best to make your pretty girl both safe, and happy in her life."

And so they had. It became a sort of delicious plot between them, and Bajazet saw the subtle powers of the Crown, even in so small a matter. And by doing secret good for Gwendolyn behind curtain after curtain of the queen's influence, she, who had been only a pretty and tender little whore, became at first one thing better—a very lucky whore who won the First Melt lottery. Then a second thing better as she was invited by the sisterhood of Lady Weather to erase the old, and write the new in good works. And finally—when Bajazet was past eighteen—asked to become an ambitious young magistrate's wife, she ended respectable, safe, and a mother.

"Go," the queen had said to him, summer bowling on the south lawn at Island. "Go back to visit Who-was-your Gwendolyn, and see if your love and care for her is proved."

Bajazet had gone, seen, and found Gwen still fond of him, but gently, distantly, and very happy in her husband, baby, and home.

He'd sailed back down to Island, climbed the North Tower's steps to the queen's solar, and knelt to thank her.

"Mine the advice, Baj," she'd said, raising him up. "But yours the decision."

Bajazet loved the king—had always loved him. But loved the queen even more.

. . . Standing by the little stream Confusion, he found he'd had a few more tears to shed, after all, and wiped them from a grimy face with grimy hands. Then turned east again, and jogged away toward distant softly rounded hills, rising to greater hills—mountains—beyond.

* * *

Three days later, the pemmican, biscuit, and small round of cheese long since eaten, Bajazet bent retching nothing but sourness where the course of Confusion divided—a slighter, foaming little creek come down from eastern hills to join. He'd munched alder buds the night before, and scraped the tender inner bark of a birch for thin sweet jelly.

One of these had knotted his stomach, so he'd walked bent as an old man all morning, making barely a mile over tangled deadfall and windfall while keeping to the small stream's course. The little river had become a friend to him, and Bajazet, who now had no other friend, was afraid to leave it to follow the lesser fork that ran up into the first hills he'd come to.

He'd dreamed, last night, of the Vosses. And in the dream they'd appeared armored from a stand of trees with crowding companies of smiling soldiers, absolutely loyal . . . and bringing a buttered loaf and stove-heated blanket as well.

He tried to vomit again, wiped his mouth, and stood straight with an effort. His small pack—only the canteen, flint and steel, and rawhide cord in it, now—still seemed to weigh his back, the bow and quiver also heavier. The rapier, more and more, was in his way.

He knelt in leaf-mold . . . looked into the stream's swift shallow ice-water. He'd seen fish the day before, had tried to hand-catch them—which he'd seen Ted Atcheson do—and failed. Then he'd thought of a willow branch, rawhide string, a little carved-wood hook, and a dug worm for bait. But the staying there to fish, and waiting . . . waiting, became impossible. Every minute would have been a gift to the pursuing traitor-king—and now, the king pursued. Cavalry trumpets had sounded from the west the day before.

Food . . . woods-meat and game. What had seemed simple, easy enjoyment—hunting with foresters, grooms, guards and friends under the horn's music . . . galloping fields and forest edges behind coursing hounds, when it appeared (and was true enough) that driven deer and wild boar had appointments to meet the king's ward and Second-son—all had proved a different matter alone, on foot, and starving.

What use a fine rapier on rabbit tracks in the last of Lord Winter's snow?—or a beautiful bow where only dubious mushrooms, birch bark, and alder buds were found.

A huntsman had once told Bajazet that a man could catch any grazing creature by steady tracking, steady walking-after, day and night, until the beast grew so weary as to stand, head hanging, to have its throat cut. A tale well enough, that even might be true if the man were fed good meals as he followed, and had a savage's eye for tracking.

But no one had come to Bajazet in the forest with spotted-cow soup steaming in a panniken, a half loaf of oat bread to soak in it. And no one had offered to show him the broken twig, the turned clod, the tree bark touched to indicate a fat young buck—frightened by distant trumpets—had traveled just that way, and only moments before.

Savages . . . These eastern woods had been home to the Redbirds—most gone, now, whittled away many years ago by Middle-Kingdom's East-bank army. And other tribes driven from the wider Mississippi's flooded flatlands back into the forest, then hunted there, as well, to prove and temper regiments' recruits, their fresh formations . . . until only the Map-Appalachian hills and mountains offered refuge.

The old queen was said to have reined that in; King Sam had put a stop to it. But too late for the Redbirds. Now, only bands of Sparrows stooged these woods, and occasional Thrushes down from Map-Kentucky, teeth filed sharp, but settling no lowland villages, presenting no chiefs to discuss matters with anyone. . . . Discussing matters with Kingdoms and Khanates, States and City-towns, had long proved unfortunate for all the tribes.

Bajazet had been told the tribesmen used to take children, when they could, from settlements back from the river. Adopted the strong, killed and ate the weak. "True," a sheriff's sergeant had said, when asked. "But not frequent, now, young sir."

"Not frequent." For the last days, Bajazet had traveled frightened at the notion of meeting savages, as he was frightened of being caught by Cooper's soldiers. . . . Now, though the troopers still concerned him, the hill-tribes didn't. Dazed with hunger, he'd formed what seemed a sensible plan to run from their encountered scouts—shooting as he fled—then circle back to find a dead savage, retrieve his arrow, and carve steaks from the man.

He could smell those steaks smoking on green branches over hot hardwood coals. And why not? That meat had been a long tradition on the river—still supposedly practiced now, though only by some old families at festivals.

Kneeling at the bank's edge, Bajazet bent to thrust his face down into the water—was shocked by its chill, but wakened too, and saw in glimmering reflection the face of a gaunt young man, dark-eyed, stubble-bearded beneath the ten dots tattooed across his cheeks—five dots on the left, five on the right—his long dark hair tied into a pony's tail with a knotted leather string.

Men had—only a week before—bent their backs before those tattooed dots, lowered their eyes and voices, waited to hear what the king's Second-son might wish to have done. . . .

Bajazet considered sleeping by the stream, though there was still daylight. His belly ached; his bones ached with weariness. An hour at practice swordplay, a few hours riding, an evening of dancing at Greeting Parties, or strolling here and there on Island or at the short-summer residence in Memphis—these had proved poor preparation for days of fear, woods-running, and starvation.

"I'm in trouble. . . ." It seemed reasonable to say that aloud. But only seemed reasonable, since the remark appeared to wake trumpets—and Bajazet heard, for the second time, the king's men coming. Two trumpets that began to call back and forth far down the valley like bright-voiced angels. The troopers were well behind him still, miles behind—but their trumpet calls had caught him.

It would be Light Cavalry, now, not liveried bravos or a per-suaded file of local reserve Heavies. It would be a troop, perhaps two, of regulars. —And no shame to them, after all. The Achieving King was dead. His queen was dead. His First-son and heir was dead. There was a new king, now, and orders were always orders . . . .

The trumpets, which should have signaled so grim, affected Bajazet in a different way, as if they sang encouragement, re-minded him of the real and waking world, where weariness and hunger were not unusual.

He stood fairly erect, struck his sore stomach with his fist to put it in its place, and started walking east and up the high run's slope. Up into the first of hills. . . . If he met no edible Thrush savage on the way, perhaps he might string his bow at last, and wait in the hills for a cavalryman to cook and carve.

That notion made him smile; his first smile since Noel Purse, amid the clamor of steel below, had shouted, "*Run.*"

. . . With evening, Lady Weather came sweeping into the foothills on a strong south wind, as if to introduce her Daughter, Summer, not yet come to stay. The treetops bowed and curtsied to it, whispering in breezes, roaring when the gusts came booming.

Weary to stumbling, his cloak bannering about him in the wind, Bajazet climbed a thicket slope, searching for a place to lie to sleep. He felt, as if a soft insistent pressing at his back, those who came behind him. He seemed to sense under his boots the beat of horses' hooves, the soft, swift, moccasined tread of foresters and woods-scouts running before. They would be fed, warmed at fine fires, and made furious with the king's fury, their strength growing with his rage and impatience.

What other end, then, could there be, than the prey captured? But a fighting prey—like bear or wolf or boar—that might still take a huntsman with him when he went.

Climbing the crest of the rise, he saw the eastern hills, under dark wind-driven clouds, heaving up like great soft breasts— strange to the eyes as they were tiring to the legs of a young man raised on a river. Bajazet noticed an eagle's nest almost above him, ragged black, swaying in blown bare branches high at the top of a tall yellow birch.

He bent to brace his hands on his knees to rest a moment, take breaths from the climb—then, as he stood, saw the nest more clearly.

For a moment, so high, it did seem an eagle's nest . . . and with an eagle's white head showing. Then the white head moved, and the nest stirred—and the head was a woman's, her long white hair streaming on the wind, and the nest the gathered folds of a dark-blue coat that she now spread like wings in the gusts.

The woman looked down at him, seemed to be smiling from her height—then, as if the gale had picked her up, as if Lady Weather had lifted her, she rose from the branches—buffeted, swaying in the air—then sailed out and out across the treetops, her greatcoat billowing . . . and away into darkening evening.

Bajazet stood staring as she went. He had seen Boston's Ambassador, MacAffee, Walk-in-air, though only once, when that pleasant fat man had been drunk at Festival. . . . This woman had been another New Englander, one of their very few with the talent-piece in their brains to push the ground away beneath and behind them, so they seemed to fly as birds flew.

Wonderful, just the same, though the white-haired woman almost certainly scouted for the king—known to be likely Boston's creature. She would circle back west, find Gareth Cooper and his troopers, then tell the distance and point the way, smiling.

He should have braced the bow and put an arrow into her—tried the shot, anyway, if she'd stayed for it. How many should haves, would haves, could haves, can a person afford, running for his life? . . . Not many.

She'd seemed to smile at him, looking down from that height. . . . It was odd how cruel smiles could be, grimmer than any frown.

Bajazet gave Warm-times' traditional finger to the air she'd traveled, called out *"Kiss my ass!"*—quoting directly from those ancient people's copybooks—then trotted heavily down the rise's wooded reverse, to make at least a run till full dark.

. . . Two mornings later, he woke, stood, and fainted after a dark dream of a weeping infant—its body swollen huge—lying naked but for a blanket diaper in a cave of glittering ice. A little mother, blue-coated, was attempting to comfort it with caring murmurs, little strokes and pattings at its massive belly.

The dream, the child's cries, rang in Bajazet's head like a cracked bell, and he crawled down to the splashing steep little creek, drank ice-water, and ate a bunch of new grass just sprouting on the shallow bank.

Then he got to his feet, went back to gather his weapons and goods, and ate a little spring beetle off a tree. There was no taste to it, only slight crunching.

He was surprised to find he could walk, though starving, could keep climbing the wooded gradual slopes the creek-branch ran through. —Though he walked poorly, bumping into trees he must have seen, then forgotten. He said, "Excuse me," to one tree he struck fairly hard with his shoulder, trying to move it aside. An apology that made him laugh, though probably it had been just as well to be polite. He was not in a situation to make more enemies.

"Absolutely not," Bajazet said aloud, against his own rule, and was perfectly clear in his mind. Hungry, but perfectly clear in his mind. The encounter with the tree seemed to have helped. And in that clarity, he walked a little better, not staggering, and made sure to travel up-hill, and not down.

At noon, seeing squirrels play through an oak above him, he strung his bow—with some difficulty, since the recurve drew eighty Warm-time pounds. Truth of the matter (a nice old copybook phrase) truth of the matter, it had always been too heavy for him. . . . He set a broadhead to the string—should have used a blunt-tip, but had none—blinked to clear his vision, drew short and trembling, and hoped for luck.

No luck. A missed squirrel, and a lost arrow, the broadhead stuck deep in a thick branch half a hundred feet up. He could not afford lost arrows.

Bajazet pretended he'd killed the squirrel, even mimed skinning it as he walked along . . . mimed roasting it over a small fire, his fingers fluttering for the flames. Then he bit, chewed as if there were hot meat in his mouth, and swallowed.

"And so much for imagination," he said, forgetting sensible silence entirely. . . . As he passed trees, looking for other beetles on their bark, leaves flashed their lighter green with a chill breeze come through. —Then the air vibrated to a man's agonized shriek. Loud . . . loud, and just though the woods.

Bajazet froze in shock, fumbled his bow off his shoulder, knelt to brace it, then slid an arrow from his quiver, and trembling, set it to the string.

The man shrieked again—drew in a loud whooping breath for another scream. All in a voice that might have been an animal's, but was not. It was a sound Bajazet had never heard before.

He began to back away . . . back away. His legs appeared to do that without his asking. Just beyond, the man still shrieked; the trees seemed to shiver with it.

Bajazet half turned to run—then found he feared ignorance even more, the not knowing what might follow and come upon him. Perhaps come upon him in the night. . . . So it seemed he was too frightened even to run. And at least now there would be light to shoot by.

There were no more screams.

He took a shaky breath, then began to walk forward slowly through the trees, walked as if in nightmare, bow half drawn. The daylight seemed to have grown brighter, so every detail appeared perfectly clear.

He crouched, moving under hanging branches—and still seeing so clearly . . . seeing each leaf, each plant-stalk. In shadow beside an elm's rough trunk, he knelt and stared out across a wide clearing, brown-black with winter-killed grass.

Only a bow-shot away, three things were eating—one tugging a loop of blue-white intestine from something in the grass. Yanking, tearing it free. There was a man on the ground—a tribesman, Bajazet could see tattoos down his arms amid the blood. A tribesman still alive, though certainly dying. His hands, his arms were raised out of the grass as if to push the things away. Bleeding hands.

Then one of the eaters bent to the man's head, and bit into it like an apple. Baj heard the sound.

He knew them, knew what they were, though these three—gone feral—wore no harness, no saddles, and their bare mottled skin was scarred by weather and woods-living. They were Boston's riding-creatures, massive, human-headed, four to five times the size of a man, and womb-twisted into huge, squat, four-footed mounts. Bajazet had seen them many times along the boon-docks, ridden by New England's merchants and officials, the creatures' legs grown heavily bent for a springing gait, their arms and hands turned to long fores ending in flat, calloused, broad-fingered pads.

One of them—the one that had tugged free a portion of the man's gut—chewed that and swallowed. It raised its great round head (a head almost perfectly human, gray hair grown shaggy, tangled), sniffed the air, then turned to look across the clearing.

There was no question but it saw Bajazet kneeling in shadow. . . . It stared at him a long moment with wide, idiot eyes a light shade of gray or blue, then smiled and stuck out a flat blood-stained tongue. Stuck its tongue out at him like a naughty child.

Bajazet ran, still clutching bow and arrow. A poor, staggering run, but the very best he could do. He ran back through the trees, then up into the hill's undergrowth, listening . . . expecting to hear great swift four-footed paces coming behind him.

But there was only silence, except for the breezy sounds of an end-of-winter afternoon. Silence when he stumbled to a stop at last by a red-berry bush, bending exhausted, a cramp in his left side.

He caught his breath, then shouldered his bow, quivered the arrow, and hurried on across the brow of the hill—still going east, though making a wide half-circle around the feeding beasts.

As he went, tripping now and then when he glanced, fearful, behind him, it seemed to Bajazet almost a wished-for thing to find a file of cavalry and their furious king, caught up and waiting to kill him, so his death would at least be in human company.

3

Late in after-noon, walking, then trotting unsteadily, then walking again to struggle through underbrush, Bajazet supposed his flight—to someone resting in a warm room after dinner, with a copybook on his lap—might seem a suitable subject for epic poetry. Poetry of a sort. Treachery, murders for a crown, a young prince fleeing through forest . . . meeting monsters. Might very well be a poem, if dirt and desperation, if eating insects were left out of it.

Bajazet recalled Lord Peter—the old librarian peacefully dead and River-buried later in the same year—recalled him smiling after reading Bajazet's epic, skip-rhymed triplets on Kingdom River's flow through history from Warm-times onward. At seventeen, Bajazet had imagined himself a romantic figure, a duelist poet, and bound to be fatal to the ladies.

"I've read worse," the Lord Librarian had said, "—and I've read better, poems made with longing and love, rather than pride in a great stack of rhymes, almost all of them beside the point." Most of the old man's teeth were gone, so his *th*'s, tongued off his palate, sounded odd.

Bajazet, having expected praise—even astonishment—had stood in the library goggling at the insult.

"Of course," the old man had murmured, "—of course, if you believe me mistaken, you'll wish Queen Rachel to read this. There is no one with better judgment of writing's worth."

Bajazet had envisioned killing the withered creature by hitting him with the heaviest possible copybook off his shelves. Failing that, he'd said nothing, turned to stride out of the chamber in dignity.

"Prince Bajazet."

"What?" He turned back at the door.

"You asked me once about your First-father. . . ."

"Yes, I asked once—and was told nothing."

The old man had shifted on his high stool, his bony behind likely no comfort. "Answers, like questions, have their proper times. Do you wish to hear about him now?"

Bajazet had *wished* to tell the time-dried mummy to go to Lady Weather's hell of storms unceasing, but found he couldn't. He'd stood, listening.

The old man had smiled at him, gums almost toothless as a baby's. "As you know, I tutored the Khan Toghrul through his boyhood at Caravanserai. . . . I was fond of him, and found him brilliant beyond all others, though crippled."

"*Crippled . . . ?*"

"Yes. By the necessity to dominate all within his reach, and to extend that reach absolutely. It was a hunger in him, insatiable— and ruled his life as completely as he ruled others. But for that sad hunger, he would have been the greatest man of our age, superior even to the king."

"The king beat him."

"Yes, Sam Monroe defeated him—but only barely, and in alliance with Middle Kingdom. The king has never pretended he was the khan's equal in battle, has never pretended his success against him was not more a matter of good fortune than genius. . . . And in that admission—its self-knowledge and sense of proportion—is revealed all reasons why he *is* the Great Rule's king . . . while your First-father is gone into history."

"But, what was he . . . what was he *like*?"

"Ah . . ." The Lord Librarian had closed his eyes for a moment, remembering. "Toghrul—as a boy, a young man—was serious, but also humorous in a somewhat chilly way. Absolutely confident. He was slender—as you are. Handsome—as you are. But much older for his years; the boy in him quickly vanished. Still, some of those close to your father, loved him; certainly the old khan loved his son, though he seemed puzzled by him on occasion.

So, Toghrul was loved by some, but feared by everyone but his father, one or two old generals, I suppose . . . and of course, your mother."

"My mother . . ."

"I met the Lady Ladu only twice, and in passing—once on a path through the summer garden's brief beds of pansies and so forth. She was short, sturdy, and rather plain. Kipchak chieftains tend to be hawks—their ladies, partridges. She was no beauty, except for her eyes—your eyes, now. Eyes at first black, then seen to be the dark gray of evening. She was said to be very gentle. . . . And of course, soon after your father's death, was murdered, with Chancellor Razumov, for sending the infant-you out of Ek-Tam's reach."

Bajazet had tried to speak . . . say something, but found he couldn't, as if the library's warmth, its grumbling stoves, were smothering him.

"Murders," the old man said, "—that among others, decided the king, your *Second*-father, to go west, defeat that general, and see him disemboweled at Map-Oakland."

The Ancient had smiled his gummy smile. "I know, young lord," he said. "—I know it's easier for me to speak of these things, than for you, a boy, to hear them." Another teetering adjustment on the high stool. Couldn't be comfortable for him. "And I know something more—two things. First, you will be at best a *competent* poet. And second, your First-father's strength and your First-mother's gentleness will always war within you, and to your benefit."

Bajazet had cleared his throat, and said, "Thank you."

The old man had nodded, and lifted the poem's pages. "—And this? To the queen . . . or the stove?"

"Keep warm," Bajazet had said, "—dear and honored sir."

"Keep warm." A courtesy and blessing now poorly returned by Lady Weather, since it began to rain. An end-of-winter rain, but cold, and drifting in soaking curtains through the woods. —Uncomfortable, and lucky, destroying his tracks and his scent for the hounds. It would mean some difficulty and delay for the king's men. . . . Bajazet unfastened his bow-string, coiled it, pushed it down into his pack, and tucked the quiver's soft cover up and over the arrows' fletching.

Then he climbed on through wet woods, water dripping from his cloak's hood, soaking it at his shoulders and down the front. The rapier and dagger sheaths were packed with oiled sheeps' wool; it would keep the steel a good while, even in wet weather— though it was hard to imagine the weapons as useful, should Boston's feral creatures have decided to follow.

. . . By evening, he heard voices calling that he almost recognized, voices barely heard above the rain, the steady patter of water dripping from the trees. He heard the voices, and knew it was a bad thing to be hearing them. There were certainly no familiar voices in the woods.

He looked for things to eat—chewed a while on a leather lacing from his shirt. He looked for mushrooms, for an animal to kill, turning in slow circles sometimes, before walking on . . . and was glad when darkness came, so he could look no longer, and be disappointed.

He stopped walking in a little brambled clearing, out from under the dripping trees. The rain gusts felt better than that constant dripping. He took off bow and quiver, pack and weapons, wrapped himself in the cloak—cold and soaked heavy—and lay down to sleep. Soon, it seemed the rain was a warm rain, lulling, protecting and hiding him.

He dreamed of flying—flying in rain, but that rain cold and blowing, making flying difficult. Dreamed of that, and was pleased it was too dark for hawks to hunt him, too wet for owls.

. . . *I'm up Shit's Creek.* With that so-ancient Warm-time phrase scribbled across his mind, Bajazet woke drenched and shivering to the last of dawn's fog, the beginning of a bright and sunny day. . . . *I am up the creek.* Which left only the question of troubling to stand, or not. Putting on his pack, shouldering bow and quiver, buckling sword-belt on . . . or not.

To lie starving seemed oddly too much trouble, too full of shame and sorrow, so—gasping, unsteady as an old man—he climbed to his feet, staggering under the sodden cloak's frigid weight. He stumbled in half-circles to pick up and sling his pack, bow and quiver—arrow fletching soaked—and with some difficulty, managed the buckle of his weapons' belt. Damned thing . . .

Ready, sure he'd left nothing behind, he started away, bent under his wet cloak's weight. Had to wear it, of course; the wool would warm him, even wet. Had to wear it . . .

Bajazet started up-slope, the thud and jingle of swift pursuing cavalry on his mind. The king would be riding silent, saying nothing, perhaps remembering his son's toddler days. . . . His officers would be silent as well, afraid of him. And out in front a Warm-time mile, foresters—trackers in the mottled green of Lady Weather's short-lived daughter, warm-hearted Summer— would be trotting bent, searching by Confusion's shallow water . . . the woods along the way. And finding confirmation enough.

Awkward shuffling steps were the only ones Bajazet could take as he climbed the apron of an eastern hill. Strides and jog-trotting were as unlikely for him as flight. He imagined coming to some improbable canyon that would bar the way of cavalry and a relentless king, but allow him to stumble past.

"Imagination," he said aloud, then imagined he was being watched. To the right, the narrow creek rattled down, elbowing stones. To the left, brambles and brush . . . several evergreens, now.

He thought he might be being watched from behind—some forester having gone running at the chase's start, running ahead of all others, seeing a capful of gold, a grateful king's tears of thanks and satisfaction. Even an estate, perhaps, in the Clearings in Map-Tennessee. Tribal serf-girls, Finches or Mockers, to come

sullen to his bed . . . then, after a while, calling out, baring their
filed teeth in sudden pleasure.

Bajazet stopped and turned to look back. His hand was on his
rapier's hilt—a gesture only. Any strong man, well fed, could come
to him now and knock him down. Then take him to such a grateful king . . . and the avoiding eyes of cavalry officers as he was
hung by his heels to be carefully skinned, then rolled in a patch
of salt brought from the shores of the Gulf Entire.

Bajazet stood watching the way he'd come . . . and saw only
morning's sunny woods, the light of a warming day flashing dia-
monds off raindrops still hanging in the branches.

He turned to walk again—and saw beneath a bare bramble, the
eye, small and brown, that examined him.

He was almost certain what it was as he leaped for it—a convulsion of speed and strength that surprised him while still in the
air, cloak flapping. A small thing—a young rabbit, frozen still by
the ancient command of the best thing to do when come upon.
And stillness *had* been best, before discerning man.

Bajazet got his left hand on it—hooked its downy brown fur.
Grabbed it as it tried to squirm away, late, an age too late.

The brambles scratched and tore his face and forearms as he
fell into them, the little animal kicking in his grip. He rolled free,
holding the rabbit up. It struggled, peed in terror as he fumbled
for his dagger.

The slender steel was out, and Bajazet knelt trembling in haste,
and cut the little creature's throat. Its soft muzzle opened as he
killed it . . . then skinned it with blade and teeth, licking blood,
spitting out soft tufts of fur.

Groaning with impatience, Bajazet snapped flint and steel into
a handful of his tinder, added shreds of underbark, and knelt puffing for a hasty fire. Its minor flames then only used to dip bloody
pieces in—meager meat, frail bones, a small damp gout of bowel.
All dipped into the fire as for a short blessing, then devoured as
Bajazet, trembling, wept like a child for the little creature, its

smallness, innocence, and sudden dreadful death. He ate, tears tracking down his dirty face, then chewed bloody scraps of fur, chewed and splintered the last tiny bones.

Finished, nothing left but indications on bloody ground, he lay curled on his side in the sun for a sudden snoring nap.

. . . And woke, perhaps only a glass-hour later, to a different world. A world of no half-heard familiar voices, no aching belly, no stumbling or dizziness. In this richer world, that seemed now as complete, as promising as once it had been, he got to his feet with no grunt or groan of effort.

He stamped his small fire out, gathered his goods, turned up-hill and strode away. In this warmer, brighter world, it seemed possible he might live longer . . . might travel and travel—surely shoot an unlucky deer, a wild pig or two—and after several Warm-time weeks, even reach the Ocean Atlantic, beyond the grasp of the most revengeful king. Gareth Cooper could not, after all, chase forever.

So, the little rabbit's life, its reluctant gift, seemed to have re-newed his.

He climbed the hill's sloping shoulder fairly fast, his sodden cloak slowly drying on his back. Climbed until he reached a bare rock knoll, scrambled up it . . . then stood to look behind him down a landscape of valley unfolding from valley, woods along the watercourses just beginning to green into spring. Bajazet felt the oddest longing for the River, many miles west and out of sight, though he supposed its silver might still be seen from these hill's highest crests. . . . Since he'd come to it as a baby, pursued even then—carried from Caravanserai by a Kipchak bowman and his wife, to save him horse-trampling under Lord Ek-Tam's execu-tion carpet—ever since he'd come to it, the Mississippi had flowed through his life, had always been near enough to ride to in half a day, as if always waiting to offer its current's infinite strength for him to lean on.

Standing, watching west, he saw something very small and

bright in forest at the foot of a hill, a winking sparkle—certainly off Light Cavalry's sand-polished mail.

Likely only a troop, no more; the king would want swiftness in the chase, not some trundling array. The horsemen would be in skirmish order, as hounds and woodsmen ranged wet woods to recover his trace.

. . . The glitter faded into green. At that distance, Bajazet had seen no pennants, no banners, though King Gareth's red ensign would be there. They'd have stranger hounds with them, now, and foresters promised much if they tracked him—perhaps promised death if they didn't.

Bajazet climbed off the knoll, and—trotting, then walking, then trotting again—traveled as if the eastward slopes were level ground, and fear was feast enough, with every strength to give him.

That night, drowsing by a small, guarded fire, he heard distant trumpets—or the distant echo of them—sounding *Sleep . . . sleep, you weary soldiers.*

A beautiful call.

* * *

Through the next day to evening, the air grew colder with Lord Winter's northern wind—certainly one of his last.

The wind gusted . . . gusted . . . then gathered strength along hill ridges to come at Bajazet whining like a wolf to tear his warmth away, so he staggered, his frosted breath streaming, cloak flapping as he bent to find shelter in blowing evergreens. There would be no fire; no small fire could live in that wind, and any larger might be seen by the hunters, roll smoke into the air to be noticed for miles.

No fire. By full dark, wrapped in his cloak and curled close as he could crowd under a hemlock's draping branches, hands tucked under his buckskin jerkin and shirt-hem to warm at his belly, Bajazet felt his feet numbing in his boots.

The wind's noise was a deep-throated humming roar as gusts came through the trees. It grew colder . . . a cold seeming deeper still when cloud-mottled moonlight filtered through the evergreen's foliage.

Bajazet huddled, hugged himself, and shivered. It was odd how difficult it was to keep his teeth from chattering like a chilled child's. He thought if he could sleep he might be warmer—and tried, but the wind kept waking him . . . shouting in his ear, stinging, burning the skin of his face beneath the cloak's hood. The night grew still colder, perhaps as cold as Lord Peter Wilson had claimed the great void to be, that held the planets and the stars.

It began to be frightening. Too late now to build a fire—to be marked or not; no fire but a burning forest could live in that wind.

Glass-hours later—the wind still howling in moonlight—he could no longer feel his feet, his face. Then, Bajazet didn't wish to sleep, was afraid he would die if he did. Didn't wish it. Didn't wish it . . . but the cold drove him down.

. . . He woke to a still and frozen world—but was not frozen. Something weighed on him, was tucked under and around him in heavy harsh weave. He started, sat half up amid the hemlock's hanging branches, and found a thick blanket—thick as a thumb, and goat's wool by its oily odor—draped over him. The heavy fabric was frozen stiff as planking, and Bajazet lay for a moment trying to make sense of it, of its being there at all— then wrestled it off, footed it away to roll from under the hemlock and stand trembling . . . the rapier drawn before he'd thought of it, its lean steel swaying in gray dawn's light, seeking an enemy.

"*Who*?!" He swung in a circle, his rapier's blade whispering in the turn through icy air, and drew his left-hand dagger also.

"Who . . .?" Bajazet expected amused foresters—hard men to have chased fast enough through the days, then through a freezing night to catch him. Foresters, and an eager trooper or two. There'd be no killing them all.

Bajazet waited, his morning shadow his only company, and tried to stretch a little on guard, ease stiff muscles for the fight. The left-hand dagger . . . remember the dagger. The Master always reminding—the rapier for flourishing parry and thrust, but the dagger for close and finish. The Master before—the honored Butter—had preached the knife.

Bajazet took deep breaths, eased his shoulders, lowered his points a little off guard to relax his arms and wrists. There was no sound but sunrise breeze through evergreens and a single birch standing alone up the hill. No laughter . . . no moccasin-boots and cavalry boots kicking to him through winter-crumpled leaves and pine needles.

He realized, after a while—when little hedge-birds, gray and brown, flitted casually by . . . then back again—he realized he was alone.

But not alone last night. Blanketed against the cold—but by whom? By that creature seen (or imagined) perching in a tree? But there had seemed (or dreamed) only cruel smiling observation there, not friendship. . . . Bajazet knew of no friend in Eastern forests. Perhaps a single fast-chasing huntsman, ghosting beside, tormenting with a cat's sense of humor until the king's men caught up? Or, more likely, preserving King Gareth's prey at the king's orders, for an extended torturing pursuit . . . to a satisfactory conclusion.

And if so, if Cooper intended the chase prolonged, he would have his wish.

Bajazet sheathed his weapons, crawled under the hemlock to retrieve his pack, bow, and quiver. Then he tugged the cold-stiff blanket out, rolled the thick wool lengthwise with some difficulty, tied each end with lengths of rawhide cord, then draped the blanket over his left shoulder, brought the rolled ends down and across, and tied them together at his right side. It made for some awkwardness with his pack, and the bow and quiver over his right shoulder, but an awkwardness that guarded him from any more of Lord Winter's departing rages.

He was hungry again—the little rabbit's gift of life had worn away—but not too hungry to run. Let the king's game player follow fast, and find a broadhead arrow waiting in the hills.

. . . By dark, a distance east, and down-slope in rough woods where streaks of snow still lingered in trees' shadows, Bajazet lay curled in the mocking gift's thick wool—his empty belly cramped—and stayed awake for a long while, waiting, listening. Then he drifted to sleep and a dream of Susan Clay. In the dream, she did him favors she'd refused before—and fed him, too, or at least offered food he never quite settled to eat. Bread pudding in a blue bowl, with thick, hot, imperial chocolate poured over it.

That must have been an end-of-sleep dream, because he woke to a misty morning, saying "*Shit*," as he realized the pudding was insubstantial and gone.

Bajazet sat up in the blanket—and bumped his head lightly on a small basket dangling just above him off a hickory sapling's limb.

At that tap, he thrashed out of the blanket, got to his knees with his dagger out—and saw nothing moving in the woods, no one standing or crouched. . . . His possibles were as they had been beside him. But there was now that little basket, rough woven of twigs and winter-dried lengths of vine.

Whoever had hung it there had followed all through the day, pacing him through brush and forest along the hill ridges. Had followed, waited until he slept . . . then come to lean over him, and leave the little basket like an Easter lover.

Bajazet got to his feet, stood hunched under close branches, and took the basket down cautiously as if there might be a baby hill-rattler coiled in it.

There were . . . berries. A double handful of blueberries and wild cherries, all winter shriveled, likely gleaned from shrubs that must grow in the hills' deeper valleys.

Bajazet began to eat before he intended to eat—but when he noticed, still could not stop. He picked and chewed—spit out the cherry pits, savored and swallowed little pellets of leathery sweetness while looking around on guard that anyone might come and take these from him.

He ate, swallowed—couldn't stop even to think about this second night-gift until he'd eaten the last, scrabbled a tiny weather-dried blueberry out of the basket's rough bottom.

Finished, he stood staring into the basket as if more food might be found by looking very hard . . . and was angry there wasn't. A bread pudding—or something, if not a pudding. Why not more berries? The sweetness of them. His heart was thumping . . . thumping.

Who had left the little basket hanging? No cruel forester, after all, however gifted in woods-running. . . . And not by the king's wishes, either. Gareth Cooper had no such imagination. Chase, catch, and skin alive, would be his way.

But Bajazet had no friend in the Eastern forests. No friend who was such a perfect ghost of the woods. No friend who wove blankets and baskets, and picked winter-dried fruit.

He set the basket down, gathered his things to travel—then ducked out of the thicket and called, shouting into the woods around him. "Whatever your reasons . . . I'm in your debt, and will repay!" There was no echo. He thought of calling again, giving his name, shouting that he was Bajazet, son of two fathers—both greater men than any the world still held—then decided not. Whoever had warmed and fed him while he shivered and snored would not likely be impressed.

His belly still ached, but less, and more pleasantly. He unlaced and peed against a rotted hickory stump, then laced, buckled his sword-belt under his cloak, and strapped on his pack. He rolled the blanket, shouldered it and his bow and quiver . . . and trotted downhill to the east. The hills were becoming greater hills, mountains; level ground was miles behind him. Let the Ghost of

Woods—likely some half-crazed wanderer—follow if he wished. And call him a friend, for lack of any other.

It seemed to Bajazet he must be a little foolish, himself—foolish to feel an odd enjoyment as he trotted along, ducking leafless vines, leafless branches. Enjoyment in the chase, though he was the hunted, hungry, weary, and frightened. Enjoyment, though all those he'd loved, and who'd loved him, were gone. He felt a shameful flush of pleasure at all burdens of obligation vanished with his old world, and old life—leaving only action. And supposed he felt so, being still young, and knowing no better.

He left that for his reason as he traveled. . . . And though fresh frightened past mid-day—hearing hounds voicing not so far behind him in the hill meadows—was not as unhappy as he might have been.

He trotted and ran, trotted and ran, through the rest of the day—imagining he outpaced any dog or horse. Once he went astride a slight stream, a trickling creek, for half a mile, then cut away straight east again by the arc of the sun . . . then slowed, staggering sometimes, now so weak from hunger.

* * *

Bajazet slept that night deep in brambles—was undisturbed by hounds or trumpets—but woke like a disappointed child at Festival, to no new gift.

He roused subdued, exhausted, no longer befriended, got his weapons and goods together, and crawled out of the brambles—thorns catching, tugging at his rolled blanket, the hem of his cloak.

He was very hungry, and caught himself walking first one way, then another. It was absolutely stupid, since while the hounds might cast and wander, the king and his cavalry troop would not—but sit their horses waiting for the pack to call scent, then ride straight to hounds and after him.

He supposed he might be caught, after all. And though he still felt yesterday's odd pleasure in simply being—felt it a little less.

He put his mind to walking straighter . . . trudged east by the tree-shuttered sun, managing with grunts and groans up a steep slant of saplings growing out of broken stone—then smelled the burned-fat odor of cooking meat.

Weary Bajazet became lively Bajazet then—finished his climb without complaining, and hurried stumbling along shelving gray rock open to the evening sky, a darkening blue, with pale clouds marching away south. . . . He found the fire set in soil at the edge of the stone outcrop. It was a small fire, a neat pyramid, and already almost burned down to coals. A plucked partridge, its split breast smoking, sputtering, leaned into it on a slender peeled branch.

Bajazet didn't call out, didn't care for the time being who'd left this gift and the others. He knelt, lifted the bird and branch from the heat—burning his hands—tore at it and began to eat, burning his mouth.

. . . When there was only a little left, a portion to be reluctantly saved wrapped in his bandanna for the morning, Bajazet stood to stretch, easing cramps from so long squatting—and glanced behind him, looking back as he'd so often done, fearful of seeing the riding beasts, or a hound pack flowing toward him, and distant horsemen.

He looked—and had almost looked away, when he realized what he'd seen through failing light. A man's silhouette, solitary, on the near western ridge. And as he saw, he was seen; no question. Seen standing in the open by a fire's ashes, a fool with a cooked drumstick in his hand. Staring, Bajazet could barely make out the limb of a longbow slung over the man's shoulder. A forester, then, and not following with gifts of blankets or food.

Bajazet turned and ran, pack and rolled blanket jouncing, the piece of partridge still in his hand. He galloped down the eastern edge of the stone shelf, scrambling as it steepened, almost slipping, since he could only steady himself one-handed. The partridge leg he wouldn't lose. He reached the base of the outcrop, and ran again—dodging through a stand of stunted evergreens, paused after that for only a moment to look back . . . found the place on the west ridge, and saw no one there.

The forester, whether alone or with others, would have a choice: follow fast, and bring Bajazet down to be held for the king's pleasure, or hurry back to the column to report the prey in view. —He would, of course, choose the first. Bringing a king encouraging word was one thing; bringing him what a Warm-time copybook had called *the object of the exercise* was another, and meant royal favor.

"In the fucking *open!*" Bajazet called out his stupidity to himself. He'd only had to take the bird and keep going, not squat there on the stone like some suppering sweat-slave for the hunters to come upon.

He deserved to be caught. *In the fucking open!* He ran with the strength the partridge had given, as the little rabbit had given strength before. Ran down into woods on the hill's last eastern slope, and saw nothing but forest and the next hill—a softly rounded mountain, really—rising before him . . . already dusted the faintest green of spring in the evening's last light.

He bit into the bird's leg, chewed it as he ran. It was hide and seek, after all—a game in everything but penalty. Could he wait at the hill's foot, watch to see if the follower grew careless enough to catch a broadhead arrow? He might, if he were less afraid. . . .

By full dark, Bajazet was on the opposite slope of that next, and higher, hill, and like a winter bear, was searching for a den. He thought he might run a little farther, then they would have him—would already have had him, but for the day of rain. The strange hounds were the problem, eager on his trace. If not for them, he might have lost the king's people in the hills.

If not . . . if not.

Clouds had come to blur the light of the rising moon, so Bajazet stumbled into trees, searching. He saw deeper darkness under a slanting fallen trunk . . . and weary, untied his blanket roll by touch, and crawled down and under into close coolness and odor of leaf mold and rotting wood. It was only partial cover; some moonlight filtered past the log's sides. But cover enough. He curled in his blanket, wishing for a comforting dream.

Bajazet dreamed, but found little comfort. There were vague imaginings, conversations with strangers begun but never completed—then a deeper dream of matters brightly colored, a great parade of odd men armed and in formation as soldiers, pacing along. Crowds—many of those people naked, though not so odd—standing silent as they watched; women weeping. The parade marched through a great, vaulted, palace of ice, so all color shimmered and flashed in reflection. A band among the marchers was playing music he'd never heard before.

Someone pressed against him in the crowd, the person's odor faintly canine . . . vulpine.

That person leaned against his arm. Bajazet turned in annoyance—and turned out of his dream. A thing was under the log beside him . . . a hard hand or paw resting on his outstretched arm.

Bajazet sat half up, reaching to his coiled sword-belt for the dagger. He found and fumbled it—struck the side of his face against the log, and gripped fur, his left arm up to guard his throat. Teeth. Teeth shone in moonlight.

He wrestled the thing in shadow, kicked, and writhed out from under the log. The dagger was—he didn't have it. He jammed his forearm into the thing's jaws, and felt clamping then sickening puncture as fangs went in.

Hauling himself back and up, Bajazet tore his arm free, and was on his feet when he was kicked in the groin. . . . It was a great relief, though he bent low in agony, and staggered. A relief it wasn't a riding thing, a wolf or mountain lion who'd come for him in the dark, but only a king's forester—and certain death. But later.

Still doubled over, he heard someone say, "I had to. What a silly." A girl's voice, lisping a little at the *s*.

Bajazet lunged away, and struck his forehead on a tree limb very hard with a cracking impact, so light flashed behind his eyes . . . his knees buckled.

"*Ouch.*" A much deeper voice, almost an echo in it.

"Here . . . here, you silly man." The girl again, tugging at his sleeve, turning him in darkness, leading him back. "We're not bad. Well, Errol is bad, but we're not." . . . "We." Two, three of them at least.

"Your fault." The deep voice. "Clumsy Nancy."

Bajazet heard scrape and striking, saw a small shower of sparks. Another. Then soft puffing breaths.

He stood, dazed, his head hurting badly, the directing grip still on his right sleeve . . . and took an odd comfort, a restfulness in being caught in the night—caught by someone. Perhaps savages.

A single flame . . . then more, blossoming to a little fire by the fallen log.

A beast was bent over it, its broad muzzle lit to soft gold, its eyes reflecting slver circles of light.

Bajazet lost his breath and stepped back, but the grip on his sleeve yanked him to a halt.

"Don't be frightened, young lord."

Bajazet saw a girl, quite small, in blurred detail beside him— large eyes set at a slant, their slit pupils black with gathering of light. A long nose and narrow jaw, her hair falling from a sharp widow's peak to glow dark red in the firelight. She was wearing a sort of South Map-Mexican poncho, a belted hatchet . . . and moccasin-boots. She hadn't bathed recently; there was a musky odor.

Bajazet looked to the fire again—certain he'd been mistaken— and saw not. The creature was hunkered by the flames, watching him. Hunchbacked. It was hunchbacked, and very big, bigger than any man Bajazet had seen, even Festival wrestlers. Silvery whiskers ran down the sides of its face . . . its muzzle. Black-and-silver fur rose in a crest at the top of its head.

"He hurt himself," it said, the deep voice only a little thickened by a wide tongue, a heavy squared lipless mouth beneath a nose too broad and black. There were fangs. . . . And the long heavy handle of a double-bitted ax, blade-edges gleaming, leaned against its arm.

"*Boston*—that's a Boston-made thing!" Bajazet spoke to the girl, or the night, and felt too sick to stand. Blood was running down from his forehead. There was some, sticky, in his left eye.

"Hurt," the big Made-thing said again. It was suprising how well it spoke. Spoke, then crouched silent as the girl was silent . . . both apparently content observing their captive, watching him manage to stand straighter as his groin's pain faded, watching him wipe blood from his eye.

Bajazet had known, as everyone knew, of these sorts of creatures—the riding things, and others—created by Boston-talents in captive tribeswomen's wombs. Lord Peter Wilson had explained how a few New Englanders could use their thoughts, guiding the finest-drawn gossamer threads of glass, to alter the making of babies. ". . . They have inferred—with, I suspect, help from Warm-time copybooks—that there are so-tiny twisted ribbons-of-planning inside only-slightly-less-tiny bits in the juices when men and women come together." The old librarian had nodded to himself.

"—Those little things, *much* too small to see, make what changes Boston wishes, when interferred with—as for instance, by mixing men's comings with those of animals." Lord Peter had made the face of smelling something spoiled. ". . . Some of these changes great, others hardly to be noticed once the child has formed in its mother's belly. It does seem, however, that many of these babies die."

The two in the fire's light were certainly just such creatures. Before, and beside New England's riding-things—tame, and feral—Bajazet had seen only Ambassador MacAffee's disgraceful *occa*, flying his baggage into Island. And only saw that once, before the monster left to return to its home. . . .

Suddenly feeling sick—perhaps frightened sicker—Bajazet went to one knee, retching, vomiting remains of partridge. The Made-girl knelt and held him, cooing. "Oh, poor man. Oh . . . *poor* man." There were no *s*'s in that, no slight lisps.

Empty, taking great choking breaths, he heard the big Made-thing say, "Comes of doing good . . . probably killed him."

"Did not!" With a little snarl. It seemed to Bajazet the girl was quick-tempered, and while he considered that, his head aching savagely, a tide of exhaustion rose within him, and he slid from her arms and lay down in his vomit to rest, not caring whether these two, like the riding-beasts, had a meal in view.

* * *

He woke at sunrise, in a different place—a little ragged clearing of early grass and weeds, so steep on a mountainside that he lay half upright on a spread blanket, his cloak drawn over him.

He was being mopped at; that was what had wakened him. His forehead being dabbed with cold water.

Bajazet turned his head, which hurt him, and saw a woman—a girl—he didn't know . . . then remembered from firelight. She was dirty, smudged with grime as he supposed he must be. Dirty, and not very pretty, with too sharp and bony a face. She was doing something with a little wet cloth . . . touching his forehead where it hurt.

"Stop it." He tried to sit up, and was sorry. His arm hurt as his forehead hurt. He pulled the cloak aside and saw his shirt and jerkin were off, and his left arm had been bitten. Tooth marks, and two blood-crusted punctures.

". . . What the fuck?!" A classic Warm-time inquiry, found in so many copybooks.

"Here." The Made-girl was offering a dark strip of fire-dried meat. Baj took it thoughtlessly as a baby, chewed and munched it—then reached for another. When he finished, she offered a small water-skin, and he swallowed and gulped from that.... Then, no longer quite such a baby, he clambered to his feet—stood swaying, dizzy—and looked for his sword-belt, his bow. At least his trousers were on, and his boots.

The girl sat cross-legged, looking up at him. Startling eyes. They were . . . the pupils were yellow, the irises almost slit as a cat's. Not human eyes.

Bajazet saw his sword-belt neatly coiled in the grass, the sheathed rapier and dagger. He stooped for it, buckled it on, and drew both blades.

The girl sat watching him, and seemed concerned, though not by razor-edged steel. There was a glinting small silver medal—a little three-quarter moon—on a fine silver chain around her neck.

The *other* thing . . . Bajazet spun in a half circle to guard against it, heard giggling behind him—the girl was certainly laughing, and showed a flash of sharp white canine, though she covered her mouth with a narrow hand.

"We won't hurt you," she said.

As she said it, the *We* became evident. The big Made-man stepped hunching out of a greening vine tangle just downhill, as if born from it. Then came loping, wide as a tree, the great double-bitted ax seeming only a hatchet in his hand.

Bajazet looked to his bow and quiver—no time. He stamped to be sure of his footing, and stood on guard.

The creature padded to a stop only Warm-time yards away. It looked more human in sunlight than in firelight, its small brown eyes seeming humorous as a bear's might as it ate short-summer's honey, brushed aside swarming bees. The Made-man was dressed in a loose shirt of woven raw wool—a silver medallion hung tiny against its cloth—and wore rope-belted homespun trousers cut short. Its forearms and hands seemed almost human, though massive, and lumped with muscle, but the legs were very strange—short, thickly bent, and hugely knotted at the knees, as if they might almost bend the other way. . . . The skin on the legs was tufted with black-and-silver hair.

The girl stood. "This is Richard. I am Nancy. And we will be friends."

"Not," the deep, deep voice, "—not until he puts down the points."

"Leave me alone." Bajazet was relieved his voice was steady. "Let me go. I need to go, and have nothing to give you."

"We don't want anything," the girl said. Girl, or something very close to a girl. *Nancy.* He wondered what animal's tiny twisted ribbons had been mixed with a man's, to put into her mother's belly.

"Listen . . ." Bajazet's head ached as if he'd struck it again. "I have nothing to do with you people or your masters—"

"We have no masters," the Made-girl said. "We are not beasts to have masters—or humans to have masters, either. We are *Persons*, though tribesmen call us Moonrise people, since they think we are changed under its light—while they greet sunrise always the same."

"Then listen, whatever you are. The king . . . there are people hunting me. I have to go. I have to go now."

"Yes," the Made-girl said, "—very soon."

Bajazet kept his guard, the weapons' hilts comforting in his hands. "If he catches me here, he'll have you both killed as well. He has soldiers with him."

"One hundred and seventeen," the big Made-man—Richard— said, "with foresters and kennel-men counted."

"Your new King of the Great Rule has chased days too far east," the girl said, "—and with too few. It's a known thing in South Map-Tennessee. All the tribes know it, though they muffle their drums." The girl, Nancy, shook her head, the mane of red hair feathering down her shoulders. "—Why is he so eager in the hunt? It's really . . ." She turned to the Made-man. "Remarkable?"

A nod of the great head. "So perfectly the proper Warm-time word. *Remarkable*."

"We thought it very remarkable," she said to Bajazet, "—that a man of power would do such a foolish thing."

"I killed his only son." It seemed odd he felt ashamed to say it. As odd as standing in a sunny mountain meadow with sword and dagger in his hands . . . speaking with these creatures.

"Ah. Then no longer *remarkable*." Richard had a wonderfully rich voice. . . . The girl had covered her mouth with her hand, as he'd seen sweat-slave tribeswomen do on the river, shocked or surprised.

"Cooper killed my brother—all our friends."

"But it's so *sad*," Nancy said, lisping her *s*'s slightly. "Does he imagine that two young princes dead are better than one?"

"I suppose so, miss." Bajazet had answered as he would have any gently-born young lady—and wondered if he might be dreaming, since it didn't seem a waking sort of conversation.

"We were puzzled," Richard said, "—why he chased and chased. . . . Would you please put down your points?"

Bajazet sheathed sword and dagger, but kept his hands on the hilts. "I'm going to gather my things, now, and go." He bent, picked up his bow and quiver.

"And have you pity for your sad king?" The Made-girl's head cocked to one side in inquiry. She seemed, except for small tender human ears, very like a curious fox. "Your sad king, who has lost his son?"

". . . Pity?" Bajazet's head still ached, pounding slowly to the beat of his heart. His bitten forearm hurt worse. "That fucking traitor is hunting me down!"

"But are you now hunted by a traitor king?" The Made-man squatted oddly in spring grass, his small brown eyes curious. "—Or by a father whose only son is dead?" He did appear more human in daylight. More human, but not human. He was too big, his face too muzzled to be only a face . . . and there was the crest of fur, silver-black, and skin mottled a dark gray. The huge hands, resting on its odd knees, were almost thick as they were broad.

"We are curious," Nancy said, "—whether moral matters are important to princes? They are somewhat important to us, though not to Errol." She came close, peering at Bajazet's forehead. "That was a bad bump." A slightly vulpine odor came with her . . . and a girl's sweet breath. She took his left arm in a small hard-calloused hand, its nails pointed, short, and black, and turned his forearm so the bite mark showed in crusted blood. "—But this has bled very well; not many too-tinies should grow in it."

It seemed to Bajazet she looked better than the Made-man, though still very odd. Small, slender, and angled. Her face— long-jawed, long-nosed—*was* a face, even in daylight, though it was a face people passing by would always turn to see again, with its widow-peaked pelt of long dark-red hair as fine as fur, and eyes yellow as Map South-Mexican lemons. When she'd spoken, her teeth had glinted white in morning light.

"—We've been traveling just north of you, several days." She'd been staring at the bite marks—and suddenly bent her narrow head and began to lick at the wound as a dog might.

"Don't!" Bajazet tried to jerk his arm away, but she held it, looked up and said, "Silly. You're a silly prince."

"Let her do as she wants," Richard rumbled. "It helps healing— her bite, after all—and if you argue, we'll hear about it till the dear moon changes."

So Bajazet, supposing he must be dreaming after all, stood still in storm-cleared sunshine while his injury was licked, its crusted blood mouthed away . . . the girl as attentive as if she performed for love.

Something behind Bajazet clicked its tongue. Startled, he twisted half around, his free hand crossing to his dagger's hilt. Sitting fairly close behind him—and come quietly to do it—a skinny freckled boy, looking no more than eleven or twelve in stained rough-weave shirt and pants, smiled and clicked his tongue again. He wore the same little silver moon-medallion as the others. There were two long knives at his belt.

"That's Errol," Nancy raised her head from his injury. "—Be careful." Though not saying what Bajazet should be careful about. The boy at least *seemed* fully human, smiling, blue-eyed, his dark blond hair, stiff with grease and dirt, falling nearly to his shoulders. He appeared fully human, though as their eyes met, Bajazet found the boy's disturbing; they only watched, offering nothing more. A spider's still, attentive, empty look.

Richard suddenly heaved up to all fours, then stood, massive head cocked. "Dogs," he said.

Nancy let go of Bajazet's arm. "*Dogs*. . . . Prince, now you must run!" She bent, picked up his pack, tossed it to him.

Big Richard brought him his bow and quiver, stood looming over him. He smelled of spoiled meat. "You run, now," he said, his voice so deep there was a sort of humming to it. "—Run fast to the crest of this hill . . . then down its east slope to the valley. A narrow valley, shaded. Go along that, go quickly, and they may not catch you."

Bajazet was happy to do as he was told, was anxious to run, run from these three self-called "Persons" as he ran from the king—but his weary legs resisted, content to keep where he was.

The girl shoved him. "Go! *Run*! We travel just to the north of you."

Then, much later than these Made-things had, Bajazet heard hounds' faint baying below. —All this not a dream then, though stranger than a dream, with these creatures speaking . . . advising him.

But it was as if *in* a dream that he hung bow and quiver at his shoulder, and began to run away from them, on east across the clearing . . . then into underbrush. Remembering too late he'd left his blanket behind, Bajazet scrambled up the mountainside, struggling into his pack's straps. He looked back as he reached a stand of evergreens, and saw the three oddities were gone. No sign of them at all, so they might have been only a starvation vision, if it weren't for his aching forehead . . . the throbbing pain of the girl's fanged bite.

"We travel just to the north of you." As they must have for days, and seen he was fed and kept warm as he was hunted. —They must have had a reason, of course, but Bajazet found he hadn't the strength to consider it. What strength he had must go to his legs, for now there was no question; the yelps of tally-ho echoed through the hills.

Good dogs . . . very good dogs had been brought to the hunt, to keep their tracking only for him, and not for the Made-things whose rich scents must have caused the pack to cast and circle, at least for a while.

But no thinking anymore. No questions . . . no compliments to fine hounds. There was only climbing and running to be done, scurrying, ducking branches, shoving past evergreens . . . then more climbing as the mountain's great rounded crest—already greening with the first breaths of Daughter Summer—still lay high above him.

Bajazet labored up and up. There seemed not enough air in the world for him to breathe, he was so weak and weary. Not enough . . . not enough. He hauled himself from sapling to sapling—then thought he heard a trumpet call. But certainly too near. Perhaps only the call of some other Boston-thing. Certainly not a trumpet, and so near . . .

If he had time, he could stop, unbuckle the damned sword-belt, throw bow and quiver away . . . wrestle the pack off. He could— if he had time—tug off his boots, strip his clothes, and run naked and too fast for anyone or anything to catch, following such swift, bruised feet.

Bajazet staggered along the massive granite round of the mountain's crest. Sunlight sparkled along fractures in the stone. He'd lost count of the lower hills come before, now rising to this.

His breath rattled in his chest like a ruined horse's, and his feet were bleeding in his boots. *Might as well have had the damn things off.* He would have wept if he'd had the time. . . . Now, he wished he hadn't killed the king's son. Then the hunt behind him would have been *pro forma* (was there any fucking word Warmtimes hadn't had?) Would have been *pro*-fucking-*forma*, and not this furious . . . unreasonable chasing.

He thought for a moment—halted crouched, gasping, trying to catch his breath—thought of begging the Mountains' Jesus to somehow save him. But he couldn't bring himself to do it. To plead, then die, was to die twice.

His vanity made him smile as he stumbled on, unsteady boots skidding, scraping on the stone. And another sound on the granite behind him, quick raspings coming. —He surprised himself by how fast he turned, how the rapier came sliding from its scabbard. It *was* surprising, as if the staggering, exhausted Bajazet had been one person, and this—drawn and on guard—was another.

Claws rattling on rock, an ambitious hound came bounding— ah, not pure hound, and therefore the ambition. This a half-breed ripper, with talent enough to scent his way once the pack had found the line, and the weight and jaw and muscle to pull prey down, and kill it.

A big shaggy rust-colored dog, a dog he didn't know. It came for him cleverly and fast, scrambling, not leaping. Seemed to be smiling, its long jaw stretched so wide.

The still-strong Bajazet, the surprising one, met it as he'd been taught to meet a furiously charging swordsman. The rapier's needle point stayed where it was, leveled low on guard. He held it still, and left it there while he bent his wrist and—as the dog came to him—swung his body back and away in a quarter-circle to the right, like an opening door, and out of the line of charge. *In quartata* . . .

The big dog lunged onto the sword's point, foaming, and drove itself deep onto the blade. Bajazet turned away farther, wrist wrenched into agony as the animal tried to turn with him . . . then suddenly shuddered, squatted and began to scream. It was the sound a terribly injured puppy made, betraying the dog's adult and ferocious bulk.

Bajazet yanked . . . yanked the long blade greasily free, and sheathing it still bloody, stumbled away from the noise of arriving hounds, horses' clattering hooves. The riders were shouting as they came.

He managed to run, blindly as an animal, labored east on uneven granite, then along a slope of stone . . . skidded down a steeper pitch—and stepped off the mountain's crest into the air.

. . . Falling, safe from the shouts and snarling behind him, Bajazet would have been happy to continue down through the air to whatever end. But he sailed only twenty or thirty Warm-time feet before striking brush, pitching forward in a cartwheel—sheathed rapier flailing, whipping his leg smartly—then toppling over a sheer edge.

Bajazet fell, struck—didn't try to save himself—but went tumbling and rolling, spinning and falling again until he struck a small fir tree hard. It drove the breath out of him as it drove green foliage into his face, harsh as a punch.

He managed to mumble, "Oh, my God." One of the oldest phrases known. Very ancient.

Managed that, tried to twist away from savage pain in his ribs—and went skidding down and down an endless dirt slope, his face numb, agony lancing along his left side. He no longer . . . no longer wished to be falling.

The oddest thing—seeming so unimportant—something whipped singing past him as he went. An arrow, he supposed, from one the Light Cavalry's odd uneven-armed longbows. Bottom arm shorter . . .

Faint echoing orders far above him. Perhaps "Stop shooting!" The king would want him alive . . . if the mountain *let* him live.

Now it was only slower sliding—a bad bump—then on down

with a sore ass and skinned hands. In a shower of dirt and stones, Bajazet dug in his boot-heels, dug too much, tripped, and did a slow somersault, crashing into alders.

. . . Stopped. He was stopped.

He'd shut his eyes, afraid the branches would blind him. Now, half hanging amid sagging limbs and broken twigs, Bajazet opened them and saw he was almost down the mountain's side. The slope eased through forest below him, down a long descent to a narrow valley, dark in the mountain's shadow.

. . . Trumpets. Those motherfuckers—what a valuable old word—would have found and be riding down a gentler way, to run him to earth at last. At least the dogs hadn't cared to try the pitch after him.

Bajazet no longer felt the pain of his bitten arm, his bruised forehead. Those now seemed quite comfortable, compared to deep bruises, badly scraped skin, and cracked ribs burning with each breath. . . . And there could be no waiting, hanging in the trees like cooling venison. No waiting. No time.

He gritted his teeth, wrestled free of low branches, and had trouble getting his breath; it caught in his throat when the pain came. He clambered to the forest floor—still steep enough—found he could stand, and hobbled down the mountain's wide skirt. The king and his cavalry would be nearly down their easier path, and the long valley—narrow, already shadowed in Daughter Summer's first filmy dress of hazy green—wound away in thick low heather and leafing tangle between looming mountainsides . . . a very long run.

Bajazet attempted a trot from the last of the trees—and found, if he bore the pain, that he was able to almost run, though oddly, with a gimping gait. He followed the valley's little creek—a dark shallow flow that barely wet his boots as he splashed and spattered down it—not to lose the hounds, not to lose the horsemen. It was only the easiest way to go.

He could hurry along, but only twisted slightly to the left, like a very old man with swollen joints. If he didn't turn that way, his side knifed him and took his breath.

He tripped, fell to his hands and knees in icy water, then heaved himself up again and stumbled on. A comic figure, no doubt . . . and a person who seemed to have fled out of himself and his life into a more restful valley, where Boston-made children with foxes' tails came yelping to pace him along. They were curious little things, and came so close he could see each one very clearly, leaping beside him. And there were gray-feathered birds calling his name. He would have answered, but couldn't spare the breath, since—in the other, previous place—running remained very important . . . though the reasons for it were unclear.

Though it was true he ran, now, at less than a trot. A shamble, really, and was making poor progress. The problem was breathing; there wasn't enough air. And also the ribs there on his left side. There were other things . . . complaints, though he couldn't remember them, and none bothered him as much as his legs' cramped agony. That was the most bothersome thing. . . .

He fell again, and with icy water splashing, it came to him freshly that this was a question of being caught and killed.

He got his feet—oh, how difficult that was—knowing the Made-children, the discussing birds, had been imagination. And a trumpet call agreed; the trumpet sang out, *Reality!*

Feeling oddly better, Bajazet stood looking behind him, and saw streaming down the last of a gentler slope, and out into the valley, a troop of fine cavalry—pennants streaming, chain-mail sparkling in the last of mountain light, then shading to soft silver in mountain shadow. Foresters, clinging to stirrup leathers, ran bounding beside.

The hounds, weary, were barely leading the king's big gray. Bajazet could see the dulled gleam of the Helmet of Joy—and thought, even at such distance, he made out the king's white face under its nodding weight of gold and jewelry . . . the spinning confusion of its dangling dried hearts.

Bajazet turned away, and was astounded to find himself running again—hobbling, at least—along the frail creek's bed. Running, though so very poorly, and as clear in his mind as if he studied meter for a poem . . . though now, a poem never to be written. What would its subject have been? —Certainly only one, the subject all poems nested in their bowels. *You have wasted time, that will never come again.*

He stopped and stood swaying, taking deep agonized breaths, the creek's small water stroking his boots. Then turning carefully, because of his ribs, he drew rapier and dagger.

Eleven dogs. He could count them as they came splashing down the shallow stream. How sad, that such simple sweetness as theirs should be turned sour. . . . Of course, the same might be said of the cavalrymen. Dogs and soldiers, their honor taken for the use of clever men. Men with much to answer for. . . .

Now he saw the king's face clearly—and saw the king, coming galloping, see his. A glance shared by two of the blood of clever men, users of decent dogs and honest soldiers. The king's fury certainly in his face—but that other, also.

Bajazet supposed even this shallow water would slow him, fighting—as time now seemed to slow to single echoing heartbeats, with all motions ponderous though seen wonderfully clearly. But he liked the idea of dying in running water, as if the little creek might drift some streamers of his blood away to a sort of safety.

A man—an officer—had ridden up beside the king. Cooper gestured him sharply back and spurred along the creek, shouting. The dogs came leaping before him, seemed pleased with the water, soothing to worn pads.

Bajazet braced himself as heartbeats and time suddenly moved much faster—saw the first dog who'd reach him, and drifted the rapier's point that way. "Don't forget the dagger." The Master'd told him that many times, advice handed down from *the* Master. "Don't be so fucking sword-proud!"

First dog's here. Lean into your steel.

The dog—a red-hound bitch—was up and in the air when a javelin came hissing, and saved her from the rapier's point.

Bajazet stood amid a storm of spears sleeting from left and right as the dogs died—were struck, pierced, knocked kicking in agony along the creek. Not one hound, not one had come to him . . . nor any javelin, either.

He was left standing alive amid screaming dying dogs as the king reined in, stallion skidding in a sheet of shallow water. . . . And tufts, tops, and branches of the valley's greening brush—having been fastened to conceal and decorate a thousand painted men—rose in long green waves that rolled like surf down upon the king and his cavalry.

5

Bajazet stood rooted in riffling water, saw the chain-mailed troop deploy to a single shouted order, dividing its double column to left and right—and on a single order after, charge to either side to meet the ambush directly.

It was instantly and perfectly done. Something in Bajazet approved of it—and caused him to take a few steps toward the fighting as if these were still his country's troopers, and his place with them, the long hunt forgotten.

A lean man with a scraggled beard—naked but for a necklace of withered human fingers, and with feather-patterned tattoos beneath the gleam of smeared animal fat—stepped into the creek and held the shaft of a short stabbing-spear across Bajazet's chest to halt him.

The man, who seemed a Sparrow tribesmen, smiled. What teeth he had were filed to points. "Stand still," he said, in book-English with a throaty rattle to it. "—to avoid an accident."

Bajazet stood still, his drawn rapier and dagger drooping in his hands as vase-weary flowers might. The smiling man paid no attention to them.

The troopers had charged, struck the tribesmen pouring down . . . and were foundering in that flood of spears, broad-axes, bush-knives, and hatchets hurled spinning.

The tribesmen killed horses first, then the riders as they sank— sabers slashing—into the warriors' tattooed currents.

The officers and foresters had gathered around the king, were attempting to escort him back down the valley. But they melted . . . melted under a storm of steel that wore them away one by one, though lacing the tribesmen with blood. —Bajazet could still see the king, see the king's gray destrier in that shambles. He thought Cooper had his longsword out . . . was striking with it.

There were, no doubt, good reasons for Bajazet to have watched the end, to have seen the River's men, the River's new king—a traitor beyond question—brought down and butchered. But those reasons were apparently not good enough. He closed his eyes, stood blind, and only listened to the slowly fading sounds of shouts, shrieks of agony, the silvery ring of fighting-steel. . . . And, after a long while, silence except for distant quiet conversation, and a wounded man begging for his mother.

. . . When he opened his eyes, the warning tribesman was gone, and Bajazet's legs—strong enough to have carried him many miles of forest and hills for many days—now became too weak to stand on, and he sat by the stream in sparse, damp spring grass, feeling sick with relief at this rescue—if it was to be a rescue. The hill tribes had no cause to love him for his own sake—perhaps less cause to love him for either of his fathers'.

The morning—its sky's clear vibrating blue barely streaked with yesterday's clouds—seemed extraordinarily important, its every detail perfectly etched, its breeze the perfection of air. He was, perhaps, to live . . . and so young, possibly live for years. He bowed his head in his hands and breathed . . . breathed, felt his heart stroking gently in his chest as if making him promises . . . promises of a future.

Gentle fingers touched, stroked the side of his face. "Poor, tired . . . *tired* prince," the Made-girl, Nancy, said.

Bajazet raised his head, and saw the narrow valley lying thick with dead and dying. A slaughtered horse, a black, dammed the little stream so it murmured, trickling to left and right.

"Not hurt with any new hurt?" The Made-girl knelt beside him, narrow head tilted in inquiry, watching him with lemon-yellow eyes.

"I have no new hurts," Bajazet said, and though his side ached, and he felt many sore scrapes and deep bruises from falling down the mountainside, told the truth.

. . . Unsteady, he got to his feet, and fumbled to sheathe steel in a valley where all steel was streaked with blood and other matter.

Then he followed Nancy up into the valley's brush, past drifts of tribesmen—all already summer-naked to please Lady Weather's daughter, their greased furs left piled in distant village huts. White-skinned, brown-skinned, and black, some were leaping in celebration, whirling, chirping and trilling their totems' calls. Tall men with grease-plaited hair, feather-tattooed, they seemed starved of everything but ropy muscle, restless movement, and scarred ferocity. They smelled of wood smoke.

Guided up the valley's northern slope to a small clearing almost private with budding thicket, Bajazet saw his gift blanket once again, lying unrolled on the ground—went to it, and fell onto its thick leaf-scattered warmth. Then the world and all its sorrows seemed to roll away beneath him, so both screams of a tortured prisoner, and shouts of celebration, faded into sleep.

* * *

. . . He woke in cool misty morning—wakened by calls below, along the valley's little stream. He'd slept yesterday's noon, afternoon, and all the night away.

"Oh, for a great bow." A deep, deep voice. The big Made-man, Richard, stood massive past Bajazet's blanket, staring down the valley toward the calls, the shouting. Seen from behind, Richard might have been a festival bear, dressed in huge shirt and pantaloons, and trained perhaps to dance slow measures. "A great bow," he said.

Bajazet saw the boy—Errol?—also standing, watching . . . and got up himself, though slowly and with difficulty, he was so sore and stiff. His left side was very tender—ribs badly bruised, but apparently not broken—and his arm hurt, where the girl had bitten him.

All this pain, of course, spoke of life and living, so Bajazet felt wonderfully well.

Standing, staring down the valley, he saw an oddness. Spears were fountaining up . . . hundreds of them being thrown high in the air. Some the short, stabbing assags, others—light javelins—being hurled remarkably high.

"There," Richard rumbled, and Bajazet saw a fluttering thing sailing up the valley's air. A cloak or coat was flapping in the wind. Sheaves of spears, and a few hurled hatchets, rose to meet it . . . almost reached . . . then fell short.

The Made-girl, Nancy, came running through a shrub tangle—bounding through it, really, beast-blood perhaps revealed in that light, swift, ease of movement. "The Boston person—from the River!" She took Bajazet's jerkin hem and hauled at him. "Come! Come and hide!"

He went with her a few steps, then stopped despite her tugging. A woods-wise man might conceal himself in this thick scrub from anyone on the ground, even from troopers on horseback—as the tribesmen had shown—but not from a creature flying over.

"No use," he said, and the girl let go. "And I doubt he cares to search for me."

And that seemed so, for the flying person—though not, supposedly, flying, but rather spurning the ground away and behind him by the trick of a talent-piece in his brain—that person patrolled up the valley, then back down it again, apparently observing the scattered ruin of the king's troopers. The ruin of the king. . . . And all the way up and back, the futile spears rose to almost catch him.

"Oh," Richard said again, "—oh, for a great bow."

And, as if the sailor had heard and taken notice, he swerved up the valley's northern slope in a long, slow, curving path through the air. . . . Bajazet could clearly see, even at the distance, the long dark-blue coat-tails flapping in the slow wind of passage . . . the broad-brim blue hat set firmly on the man's head.

"I know him," he said. "Tom MacAffee. Ambassador from New England."

"Yes," Nancy said, "we know of him. All-Irish, and sent from

Boston to be cruel." She made a face, which made her face seem odder. "—He is who helped your foolish new king to be a king."

"And how would you know this?"

"We know because a Boston Person told us so—and we know because the king expected this MacAffee to help hunting you from high, and was angry he was late coming up-river. . . . The officers said that in camp." The Made-girl cupped a small ear, an ear like any girl's, to illustrate listening. "—So their soldiers heard and said it also. From the soldiers, to the foresters. From the foresters, to the sweat-slaves—and those spoke of it when shoveling shit along john trench, while a half-breed Sparrow listened." The girl's lip lifted from a white canine. "We are not all as foolish as princes."

Bajazet had already begun to set this oddity straight—had his mouth open to do it—when he recalled Noel Purse, years before, on a Westfield hunt, advising him and Newton how to go on with the ladies. "Don't argue with 'em. You do, an' lose—you lose. You do an' win—still, you lose."

Newton had looked concerned at this bad news. "But Guard-Captain, there has to be a way . . ."

"Oh, there is, Prince—agree."

With this grim advice, Newton and Bajazet had ridden thoughtful through Westfield woods, wild boar forgotten.

"Well," Bajazet said to the Made-girl, "—at times, I have been foolish."

Noel Purse was instantly proved correct. Nancy smiled, looking almost pretty. "Oh, as princes go, I suppose you're better than most." That slight lisp there on all the s's.

Richard began to pace heavily a few steps to the left, then to the right. Bajazet had seen caged snow-tigers, caged bears, pace in just that way at Island, though not muttering, "Has Mountain Jesus no lightning for that Boston thing?"

Again, it seemed as if the man Walking-in-air had heard—for suddenly as he'd swerved across the valley, he turned his curving course to fly almost directly to them.

"Beneath the blanket!" Nancy yanking at Bajazet's jerkin again.

He pulled free of her—tired of being tugged at, handled, dealt with. "I won't hide beneath a blanket—and doubt there's any need to." It was wonderful what salvation and a good night's sleep accomplished, even for the very sore and starving.

Ambassador MacAffee appeared to be surveying the ground as he came. Bajazet saw his hat tilt as he stared down left, then right. A single spear—thrown very hard—came suddenly up and nearly to him, so he seemed to hop in the air like a magical rabbit, and the javelin flew under.

Hands clapped in appreciation of the throw, or the avoidance. Bajazet saw the boy—Errol—standing back by the little clearing's edge. He was watching the Boston man with almost an idiot's attention, mouth slack . . . half open.

Then the Ambassador to Middle Kingdom, the cheerful and merry Master MacAffee—swung over them like a kite . . . hovered a moment, then a moment more. A light, curved scimitar was sheathed at his belt. Bajazet saw the man's ruddy face under the blue hat's broad brim . . . the ruddy face, and bright-blue eyes visible even at that height.

Bajazet saw—was seen—and received a sudden look of fury, instantly smoothed to smiling. Boston's ambassador sagged in the air for an instant, apparently having lost concentration, then rose and hovered over.

"Good morning, Prince!" he called, rocking a little in the morning breeze. "I *so* regret my lateness. I see you've survived politics—and found friends . . . of a sort."

Now regretting his bow, left lying by the blanket unstrung, Bajazet considered what the Made-girl had mentioned, and shouted, "You seem to have lost *your* friend, MacAffee!"

The ambassador, hanging high in the air, the rising sun bright over his left shoulder, confirmed that with an amused shrug, and called down, "Oh, Boston can always find friends who wish a crown. They sprout like spring onions along your river!"

"Then they will go as this traitor king has gone!" Bajazet's heart was pounding so he seemed to shake with it. "—As you will go, you fat dog, if you come down!"

MacAffee shook his head, smiled—then suddenly swung around in a swift half circle that made Bajazet dizzy to watch. He'd drawn his scimitar; sunlight glowed along the curved steel.

Tribesmen were shouting again, along the valley's little stream.

Bajazet turned . . . and saw a distant motion through the air—but no hundreds of futile javelins rising toward it, no hurled hatchets. It might have been the ancient American totem-eagle sailing, white-headed, wings spread. Then the sun caught dark blue, the wings of an open greatcoat, and long white hair streaming.

What flew—or Walked-in-air—swerved nearer . . . nearer . . . then near, coat billowing in the wind, and Bajazet saw it was the Boston-woman who'd watched him from a tree.

She called something, but the breeze took it away.

"*Exile!*" Master MacAffee shouted at her. "—*Condemned by town council!*" And drifted sideways through the air—sliding toward her, first slowly, then faster.

"He'll kill her!" The Made-girl, Nancy, slid her hatchet from her belt—leaned far back, then threw it with a harsh grunt of effort. It spun thrumming, and surprisingly high . . . but still short and behind the ambassador as he went sailing. "He'll kill our friend!"

"No use," Richard said.

The Boston woman—sitting erect, legs crossed—flew to meet the ambassador, her paper-white hair bannering out behind her. She wore black boots, blue trousers, and white blouse beneath her open blue coat—and seemed, from Bajazet's sun-dazzled sight of her, to be smiling. She lifted a slim-bladed scimitar from her lap—and struck MacAffee's stroke clanging aside as they came together.

Then the air sang with sharp steel's music as they turned and turned together like mating hawks, but winged in blue. Tribesmen were running up from the creek, calling to each other as they came—until there was a growing crowd shifting Warm-time yards this way and that, beneath the fighters in the air.

Bajazet, jostled by wiry naked men smelling of smoke, roasted horse meat, and dried blood, still could hear faint grunts of effort above him. The scimitars wove bright ribbons of motion to *ring ring ring* . . . while both air-walkers dipped and fell to rise again.

Bajazet saw the woman fought with a two-hand grip, and she spun full around, sometimes—first one way, then the reverse as she struck. . . . Whirled one way again as he watched, began to turn back—then didn't, so MacAffee, anticipating, guarding wrong, was suddenly back-slashed across the belly, flew staggering back and back in the sun's glare, a dark silhouette that seemed to bow . . . bow deeply . . . then slowly somersaulted forward.

MacAffee fell from his height . . . fell in a fat flutter of blue and spattering red . . . and was caught, as if by arrangement, on the tribesmen's spears.

The Made-boy, Errol, hummed a three-note tune.

* * *

The Boston-woman, her weapon wiped and sheathed, sailed down after the fight—only lightly sliced along her forearm—to leaps and roars of congratulation by the file-toothed men. Dwarfed in their crowding as she retrieved her opponent's fallen sword, then its scabbard, she treated them like noisy children—presenting that slender scimitar in pretend thrusts and blows, so the men danced away in mock terror, laughing. In celebration, the tribesmen then stamped and trampled the dead ambassador into a muddy red mess with one half-open eye.

. . . When the warriors quieted, began to drift away, the Boston-woman pushed through lingerers the little distance to the Made-peoples' clearing—looked Bajazet up and down, then held out her hand. Though she was small and neatly collected as a girl, she seemed at least in her forties. Her face was marked with a faint web of fine wrinkles, and her hair fell prematurely white past her shoulders. But her eyes seemed of no age, and black as a moonless night. . . . Blood had trickled down her wrist.

"Patience Nearly-Lodge Riley," she said, gripped his hand surprisingly hard, and noticed him noticing her bleeding. "Twenty years ago, he couldn't have touched me. . . . So, you're Toghrul's boy—and, I'm sure, his image, though somewhat worn after your long run." She let his hand go. "Your First-father and I might have met—did you know that?" An oddly merry smile. "I believe something of that sort was planned by the Faculty. And if we'd met, I suppose he would have fallen in love with me—since I was very beautiful, and clever. . . ."

The Boston-woman then turned away and called, with copybook obscenities, to a lounging, tall, naked Sparrow with a fine-feathered necklace and an ax. . . . They walked away together, the Boston-woman's wide-brim blue hat hanging down her back on a plaited cord.

Bajazet sat by the fire awkwardly, and with a grunt of discomfort from stone-rasped skin and bruised muscles. "A 'friend'?" he said to the Made-girl. "—That Boston-woman?"

"She *is* a friend." Nancy slightly lisping her *is* as she watched the Boston-woman go. "And a Person, made as we were made, only more subtly—you know that Warm-time word, Prince?"

"Yes."

Richard, sitting beside the fire. "I consider myself an *extremely* subtle creation—of juice mainly of a Boston breeder, but partly of a grizzled bear, placed within a certain woman Shrike."

"Have you Persons on your great river?" The Made-girl cocked her head for Bajazet's answer.

" 'Persons' . . . such as you?"

"Yes, and others. Moonrisers."

"Moonrisers . . ."

"As *you* are a Sunriser." Becoming impatient. "You true-blood humans are called Sunrisers, everywhere." She'd lisped *Sunrisers*.

"Not on the River," Bajazet said.

She stared at him. Yellow eyes and odd pupils . . . "In this country, there are *many* Persons like us. And named Moonrisers," she reached out and tapped his knee with a narrow black-nailed hand, "because Sunrisers are plain as day—and we are not."

"I see . . ." Bajazet said. "And also saw three of your 'Persons' killing a tribesman. Eating him."

"You did not."

"I said, I *did*. Three of the big riding things—gone feral, I suppose."

"Mampies," Richard said.

"Oh . . . Mamps." The girl made a face. "They're not *Persons*."

"They are," Richard said.

"Well, they're very stupid, and have no souls."

"They're stupid, Nancy," Richard said. "But they have souls."

. . . Listening to more on the question of Mampies and their possible souls—a subject that appeared not to interest the boy, Errol—Baj was content to sit quiet at the fire. He stretched gingerly, testing his aching ribs.

* * *

Through the day, and into evening—having polished his sword and dagger blades, then rubbed them against rusting with a tallow-piece from his pack—Bajazet drowsed by the Odd-three's fire. The past days' weariness seemed to have settled into his bones . . . and he was very hungry.

At nightfall, a battle-injured tribesman came limping, and tossed thick chunks of horse meat to them. —Tossed, it seemed to Bajazet, as one might toss meat to hounds, after a hunt. No other tribesman came near.

. . . While he ate horse steak, cooked surprisingly well-done, considering his company—chewing, swallowing slowly as he could to keep such richness down a starved belly—Bajazet found himself calm as if he had a future certain, as if all *un*certainty had been worn out of him while he'd fled with death trotting at his heels.

Now, there was the strangeness of his met companions—a man, with some part bear; a girl, some part coyote or fox; a silent boy, part . . . something. Their strangeness, and the suddeness of the traitor king's death, amounting to life for him—at least life enough for a meal of horse meat.

Later, the four of them rested, fire-watching without talk, listening—at least Bajazet listening—to the tribesmen singing down the valley. Sparrows, Thrushes . . . His Second-father had once mentioned that some western, and all the eastern tribes, had years before quit their tribal names for the names of birds, though no one knew why.

"Perhaps," King Sam had said, "—since Middle-Kingdom and Boston have sometimes harried and broken them, East from the river, South from the ice, perhaps the tribes renamed to leave their defeats, their losses behind to start again, feathered for a different future."

The Sparrows, at their many fires along the valley stream, were singing all together a slow, measured anthem, with no har-monies attempted. The music echoed in soft strophes from the hill-sides, as if their ancestors sang with them. . . . Listening, Bajazet thought he recognized an ancient Warm-time hymn. "The Glory In Mine Eyes, is the Coming of the Lord . . ."

The Boston-woman returned in the dark with a scabbarded sword in her hand, as well as the other at her belt. She put back her coat-tails, and sat cross-legged at their fire without asking. —Making, to Bajazet, a fourth oddity present. It felt . . . unsettling to be in this company, while the only true-blood humans paraded the night naked, with filed teeth, singing.

"Woods-hatchets are handy," the Boston-woman said, "—and knives necessary, but they never become the friends swords do. Though they say great Warm-time Bowie was loved by such a belt-blade." Smiling, she lifted the slim, sheathed scimitar from her lap, leaned through the fire's smoke, and handed it to the Made-girl, Nancy.

"—Tom MacAffee was a lazy man, and weak-wristed for being so bulky; this weapon is no heavier than mine. I think, with fox's muscle aiding, you'll find it very comfortable to swing."

The Made-girl said, "Thank you, Lady Patience-Lodge. Thank you *dearly*," drew some inches of fine steel free of tooled red leather, then bent to kiss it.

So, it was some small portion of fox's blood that Nancy had. Now, Bajazet could see it in her clearly. . . . The yellow slit-pupiled eyes, and russet hair soft as fur. The sharp-featured face and long jaw, its white eyeteeth still making his bitten forearm ache.

"Patience *Riley*," the Boston-woman said. "—Only nearly Lodge. . . . Unkind-Harry, the Sparrows' war chief, wanted that sword for his own, but I persuaded him; he's too tall for it, anyway. And you needn't thank me, Nancy. The blade is small payment for your seeing that our Judas goat, here," she smiled at Bajazet, "—was kept safe to draw the treacherous Cooper on and on."

A "Judas goat," the creature that led spotted cattle to the slaughterhouse. Bajazet felt his face heated by more than the fire's warmth.

"I've offended you." The Boston-woman smiled at Bajazet through dying flames. She seemed to smile often, find many matters amusing. "—But only with the truth. Do you think it wise to be offended by the truth?"

"The truth, Lady," Bajazet said, "—is usually offensive, or it would be called something else."

"Ah . . ." She stared at him, and Bajazet could see in the fire's warm light how beautiful she must have been before the years and some grave care had touched her face, and whitened the length of her hair.

"No thank-you gift for me?" Richard's voice was low as a warship's drum. "—Or Errol?" He rose to his feet with an odd rocking motion, and stretched, yawning.

"As for you, Richard," the woman said, "—your great double-ax needs no improvement. And Errol has no notion of gifts, and never will have, as his partial-father weasel had no notion of them. They are as lost on him as conversation."

The boy had looked up at his name being mentioned, and Bajazet saw no sign of that animal's blood in his body, which might have been any wiry human boy's. . . . The sign was in his eyes, empty of all but the fire's reflection.

"So this *conversational* creature is better?" The big Made-man hulked over to her.

"Moonrisers are the best of beast *and* man." The Boston-woman rose to stand the size of a child beside him, and reached up to stroke his cheek. "—And what was meant to be, before Sunriser-humans imagined themselves better than they were." She smiled at Bajazet. ". . . Now, come walk with me, Who-was-a-prince."

Bajazet stayed sitting where he was, not interested in obeying this Boston smiler.

". . . And if I asked, *please?*"

The court's lessons of courtesy were likely the cause of his rising, then, to follow her into the dark. As he went, he heard behind him, at the fire, the soft whisper of steel drawn from scabbard. Then the swift *ruffle . . . ruffle*, of a curved blade testing the air.

"Can you use that lean, straight sword of yours?" the Boston-woman's voice before him in the dark.

"Yes," Bajazet said. "And very well."

"Then, Who-was-a-prince, you might teach Nancy what you

can." Bajazet could see, by starlight, by the faint glow of tribal fires down the valley stream, the woman's white hair leading through thicket. "—Not that her hatchet has been bad practice for learning the crisscross strokes of a slicing blade. But wards, parries, the use of the point . . ."

"I don't see what opportunity I'd have to teach her anything."

They'd walked a fair distance along the valley's brushy slope—Bajazet able to follow more by sound than sight—when a small hand came from shadow to rest on his chest. "Here, is private enough. We will be voices in the dark, you and I—as the tribesmen believe all we Persons to be children of the dark, and made under a rising moon."

Then she was silent for a while. Bajazet heard nothing but the wind down the valley's hills, stirring the tangle of scrub around them. The tribesmen were no longer singing. . . . He hadn't noticed when they'd stopped.

"What do you imagine, boy? Do you imagine returning to Island?"

"No," Bajazet said—and realized he'd decided before knowing he'd decided.

"And why not? The Cooper is dead. His only son is dead."

"Then some *other* river lord will likely be waiting to cut my throat." Bajazet spoke into the night and night's breezes, where only a small, outline woman stood. "—And now I believe it's my turn for a question."

"Then . . . ask."

"You're a New Englander, yet I hear you've said to those others that Boston has helped—I think now, *more* than helped—to murder my brother, and our friends." Bajazet touched his left-hand dagger's hilt, to be sure of drawing. "The Coopers are gone, but Boston remains, and I intend to damage those people and their town, if I can. —Why should I not begin with you?"

"*Why* not?" She grunted, seemed amused. "First, I wonder if you're good enough with those straight blades to take punishment to me—even once you're rested from the chase.... Second, and only for acting as a mother should, I've been declared Beyond-town-limits.... And third, I've just killed Boston's ambassador to Middle Kingdom, *after* seeing to the tribes' slaughter of the Township's chosen River King." A distant night bird called in the sedge, two faint sighing notes. "You will find it difficult, boy, to injure Cambridge more severely."

"Still . . . you are what you are." There was a green scent of bracken on the air, from stems broken, crushed by the savages' battle charge.

"Ah, I hear your cruel First-father speaking there; sad that we never met.... Yes, I am what I am, and Boston made and bred—but the Faculty Selectmen, meeting on Cambridge Common, voted to take my son away. They hold him, though he's a baby, and *certainly* the One Expected."

"The One Expected . . ."

"Yes. They bred better than they knew. My Maxwell swims dreaming down lines of blood, through recalled history of its little bits. He follows those into the pasts of people gone, and looks out through their eyes, though understanding little."

"And this is true?"

"True, even though only a baby's dreams—a baby, it seems, who will always *be* a baby, though wiser and wiser. Wise enough already to frighten those fools who have labored—as other Talents have labored for hundreds of years—to bring him to us."

"And they took him for that?"

"That, and his dreaming into the future, more and more—I suppose by some arithmetic of possibilities the little bits tell him—so he sometimes sees what *will* be seen, though imperfectly." She stood silent before Bajazet a little while, starlight barely salting her white hair. "They intend to cripple him for their comfort. And *I* intend to have my Maxwell back . . . and have their heads, besides."

She'd stood so perfectly still, that Bajazet was startled when she suddenly turned. "*Errol!* Back to camp!" There was, perhaps, a rustling through the scrub, though nothing to see by starlight.

"A turned back," she said, "—after seeing so much killing here, is a temptation for his knives. Any helpless person. And a girl—or boy, for that matter—also a temptation, of another kind. Though young, he's very true to his part-sire, with rutting and murder being close to the same for him."

"More of New England's doing."

"Live on the ice, Who-was-a-prince. Live *in* the ice for the near six hundred years since Jupiter betrayed us, and the cold came down . . . then comment on what talents keep us warm and safely guarded."

Bajazet thought of answers . . . then decided not to speak them. A sharp shoulder of the quarter moon had just edged above a hilltop, and by that light his accustomed eyes saw the Boston-woman—Patience—watching him with eyes darker than the night. She stood close, but there was no odor from her; she might have been the shrub-scented air itself.

"—Now, *my* questions, boy."

"You've called me 'boy,' enough."

The Boston-woman turned to break off a stem of brush, twirl it idly. The little leaves flashed silver in moonlight. "Then what am I to call you? You're no longer Prince Bajazet—he died when you ran *instead* of dying. That 'boy' is dead as mutton. . . . Wonderful Warm-time phrase, by the way."

"I keep my name."

"No, you should not. If the name lies, the man lies. What did your family—when you had one—what did they call you?"

". . . Baj."

"Then 'Baj' is who you are—and should call yourself even inside your head, to keep their love with you. It is your *best* name, as 'Patience' is mine—though not the best description of me."

Bajazet said nothing, though he tried "Baj" to himself . . . and it did seem to bring some comfort. Also, it would likely spare him more of her *Who-was-a-prince*'s. Words so sadly true, revived pain enough to twist any name to a different one. . . . With "Prince Bajazet" lost, then better *be* only "Baj" to himself and everyone, as the broken tribes had named themselves for song-birds.

"So, New-named . . ." The woman turned and walked away— seen quite clearly now the moon was risen—so he had not much choice but to follow, warding brush aside. "As to your returning to Island . . . In all your running away, your scrambling through these hills as a Judas goat—very well, *my* Judas goat—did you ever pause to listen to the drums?"

"I heard cavalry trumpets chasing. Not drums." He shoved thistle and sedge crackling aside.

"Well, the drums were there. Almost always, if you're still, and listen. I've heard them thumping . . . thumping up the Map-Mississippi all the way from drowned Old Orleans, like very distant thunder. The Sparrows say so, too."

"They say what?"

She stopped, turned to face him. The moonlight seemed bright as morning before dawn; it shone on the rolling scrub as if on surf suddenly frozen still. "—They say, *Baj*, that old One-eye Howell Voss has left the governing of North Map-Mexico, and comes up from the Gulf on a galley—he and his dangerous wife— with Middle Kingdom's fleet already at his service, and officers of the Army-United pacing his ship's deck." She tossed the switch of leaves away.

"—The drums echo the fishermen's cheers as that galley passes. Apparently they were happy enough with your brother, young Newton, and mourn his murder. . . . Now, I suppose, Howell Voss will be their king, and Charmian the queen. Isn't it odd? I would never have thought it when I knew them, those years ago . . . and I'm very clever."

"I'm glad to hear it. It makes a difference."

"Difference enough?—say he succeeds."

"Say he succeeds . . . I think there'll be *vengeance* enough, at least at Island. He and his wife and old Master Lauder will see to it."

"Yes." She nodded. "I well remember unpleasant Master Lauder. And that being done—what of you?"

"Nothing of me." Bajazet—"Baj," he supposed he would become—was tired of talking about it. Talking seemed to bring treachery and its tragedies back like swallowed vomit. "I suppose I'd be welcomed. Welcomed for my Second-father's sake. I would have a home."

"But not your home, anymore?"

". . . Perhaps not."

"Perhaps . . ." Patience shook her head. "I wonder how comfortable a man might be, living his life with 'perhaps' as his home. Living with a family not his family—seeing all futures go to others."

"If they fight Boston, I would do it."

"Oh, Howell Voss will have a kingdom to rule—the Great Rule, from Map-Mississippi to the Ocean Pacific. For several years, he'll only hold New England at arm's length. You would be 'excess baggage,'—another fine copybook phrase—though treated however kindly."

"Excess baggage . . ."

"Yes. Isn't it sad, Baj, how unfair the world is? I've often thought so."

"So, only dreary truths from you, Lady—who seem to know so much."

"If you'd prefer lies, you still *are* a boy." She reached out to a shrub, tore free another leafy switch.

"I'd 'prefer' to have my brother back."

"Your brother is where he and endless others have gone, and no returning."

"If not that then, I'd prefer an end to talking." Bajazet—"Baj" would do well enough—turned and walked back the way they'd come, to let the Boston-woman follow or not. He could see the slight track they'd made, the disturbed foliage all silver and shadows.

She came behind him. "It is a pleasure to be dirt-walking, after weeks of going weary in the air. Though the reverse also becomes true. . . . It is more difficult to push the ground away beneath and behind you as one grows older—and I've grown older quickly. Was made to do so, I believe. . . . Boston-talents are cautious makers."

A tribesman—very tall, naked, densely tattooed—rose out of the brush before them like a partridge, but silently. He stared, his short spear's leaf-blade gleaming in moonlight . . . then turned away, down toward the valley's stream.

"No need, Baj." Patience had seen him put his hand on his sword-hilt. "He was sleeping away from their camp. He has an enemy, perhaps a Thrush whose village he's raided, who might come to him as he slept. . . . The tribes will sometimes fight in alliance—except for Shrikes—but not at ease."

They went in silence for a while, until the Made-persons' campfire glowed a bowshot away.

"So," Patience said, coming up beside him. "—where does a young man go, then, to find justice for his injury?"

"I may go nowhere, if these tribesmen choose to kill me."

She laughed out loud—a richer laugh than he expected. "Baj, if the Sparrows had wanted you dead, you'd be dead already. And there aren't enough Thrushes here to decide it one way or the other. . . . The hill-tribes respected your Second-father, the Achieving King—and what an . . . *engaging* man he was—though they did not love him. And fortunately for you, your *First*-father died before he could bring his Kipchaks campaigning to the East, and raise blood debts that only you could satisfy."

"Good news."

"Yes . . . Though except for the great pleasure of this victory—and their killing of the River's King (an unheard of, unimagined thing; Unkind-Harry now strutting under the Helmet of Joy)—the tribesmen might have decided to cut your throat, after all, and the throats of the three Persons that full-humans call Made-things, Moonrisers. . . . And cut my throat, as well, if they could have caught me, though Harry has had notions, as used to be said, 'above his station.' The hill-men hate all Persons, though born of their own captive daughters."

"Perhaps," Bajazet—Baj—said, "perhaps *because* those are born to their lost daughters."

"Ah," Patience touched his arm, "—there I heard the voice of Small-Sam Monroe. . . . How lucky you have been in your fathers." The night wind came stirring her long coat . . . his cloak.

"There seem to be tribesmen enough, in these hills and the hills north, to go up to Boston Town and demand their daughters back."

"Yes," Patience said, "—and they'd be tempted, Baj, but for the Guard. Boston is guarded by two—well, almost three thousand. The same who raid south of the ice, to *take* certain of the tribesmen's young women."

"Three thousand is not such a number. There looked to be almost a thousand hill-men come here to fight."

"No, not such a number, but they are all *Persons*. Our Richard—over there by the fire?—he was a Captain of One-hundred before he deserted Matthew-Curlew's Company. . . . Would you care to fight Richard, Baj? Would you be hopeful if he faced *you* with his ax?"

"I see . . ."

"Yes—and so the Sparrows and Thrushes and Robins have seen, and confirmed in battles Middle-Kingdom and its Rule knew nothing of, deep in the Smoking Mountains. And that is why Unkind-Harry and his people here, would—but for the great favor we've done them—cut our throats."

"You're saying I can have no revenge on Boston-town for the murder of those I loved?"

Patience Reilly smiled; her teeth—small, even as a child's—shone white in moonlight. "I say no such thing. Come with us that long way north and east, Baj-that-was-Bajazet, and what you wish may be satisfied."

"How?"

"That," still smiling, "—is for me to know, and you to find out." Which was certainly a copybook saying, and from Warm-times.

. . . At the fire, the Made-people—"Persons"—lay asleep, the Fox-girl curled on Baj's wool blanket, hugging her scabbarded new sword to her. Richard, a great heap, snored softly on the fire's other side, the boy lying alongside his broad back for warmth.

Patience murmured. "Companions suitable for such a way . . . such difficulties?"

Murmured, but not softly enough. Richard opened his eyes, and lay watching them as the night wind came stronger, seething through the valley's brush on errands of its own.

6

Bajazet woke to dawn's damp cool, and distant voices down the valley. His back, beneath his cloak, was still warm from the fire's coals. His front was colder. . . . Where had he read or heard of people sleeping between *two* fires? Had he read that, or been told of the old Trappers? Winter hunters . . .

He turned, stretched yawning—and saw the Made-boy, Errol, sitting close beside, legs crossed. The boy was staring at him.

"He's only looking." Richard's rich voice. "He's never seen a princely deep-sleeper before—a snorer used to safety, stoves, goose-feather beds, and guarded chambers."

The boy seemed too close. Bajazet—ah, "Baj," now—sat up . . . then stood up. Two days' rest (and horse meat) had left his ribs still sore, but the other bruises and scrapes much better. . . . The bitten arm hardly hurt at all—itched, more than hurt. And his legs felt ready again for traveling; he stamped the sleep out of them. The boy, Errol, watched as Baj belted on his sword and dagger.

"He's interested in new things." Big Richard was hunched, shaggy, by the fire's last coals, holding chunks of horse meat over them, speared on a stick. "Breakfast," he said, his fang-toothed smile disturbing as a frown. . . . Once a Captain of One-hundred, the Boston woman had said.

Baj stepped past the boy, and walked well out into the scrub to piss.

Paging brush aside, he found a place, unlaced his buckskins— very worn and grimy buckskins, now—and began to pee a pleasant stream . . . playing it this way and that, like a child.

"Lucky."

Baj jumped a little—and peed on his left boot, tucking himself away. "For Christ's *sake*." A phrase that would have gotten him burned, decades before.

The girl, Nancy, stood just behind him. "You men, Persons *or* human, are so lucky." The slight lisp there with *Persons* and *so*.

"Yes," Baj did up his buckskins' laces, "—very lucky."

"Well, you are," the Made-girl said, walking beside him back to camp. "Do you know what a task, a *chore* it is to always pull up our clothes, or take off our clothes, to do what men do simply as pouring from a cup?" She kicked some bramble aside. ". . . Not fair."

Nancy was wearing her new scimitar—wearing it on the left side and a little too low, so it might catch her leg and trip her.

"Yes," Baj said. "I can see it would be a nuisance."

"Only one of many we suffer," Nancy said, reached out and struck Baj lightly on the shoulder, as if they were friends, and complaints not serious.

"Your sword should wear higher, Nancy." First time he'd used her name. "Hilt at your waist, not your hip—so the blade doesn't trip you."

The Made-girl—Person—stepped into their clearing, and began a little dance, apparently to see if that was so. The scimitar's curve did catch her leg, if only for a moment.

"Very well, I'll do as you say," she said, and took her belt up a notch with narrow hands, narrow fingers tipped with nails pointed and black.

"Breakfast." Big Richard stood from beside the fire, and held out a long scorched stick, with chunks of smoking horse meat stuck along it. The boy, Errol, came suddenly scurrying, reached up, snatched the first steak off, then went away hunched to protect his meal.

Baj took the second—burned his fingers on it so he waved it a little cooler—and handed it to Nancy, who seemed uncertain at the courtesy.

"Court manners." Richard held the stick out to Baj again . . . then took his own steak from it. "We will be civilized as Selectmen." The big Person sat again in his odd way, took a slow savage bite of meat. "If, that is, you accompany us, Prince."

"Baj, not 'Prince.' And since I have nowhere else to *go* to harm Boston—and no one else to go *with*—I'll travel with you."

"Good." Richard finished his breakfast in two bites.

The horse meat hadn't improved overnight; it took Baj considerable chewing to get it down. He noticed Nancy, sitting cross-legged, gnawing away as a puppy might at a piece of gristle, her lip lifted, using her side teeth. . . . Still, coarse feeding or not, he felt the surge of strength from it. When he finished, he went to rummage in his back-pack for his canteen—found it empty—circled the fire's ashes to pick up their three sewn water-skins, and started down to the stream.

Nancy swallowed a bite, and said, "Not alone."

"No." Richard shook his heavy head. "Not alone."

"Errol . . . !" Nancy looked around for him. *"Errol!"*

The boy peered out of brush across the clearing, a small piece of meat gripped in his hand.

She pointed at Baj. "You go with him. . . . Prince, the Sparrows are afraid of Errol. They think his Moonriser-blood has made him mad."

"Baj. Not 'Prince.' " He gestured the boy to him, then walked down the valley's slope, shoving through thicket, supposing Errol would follow.

He passed tribesmen as he went . . . then more of them down near the stream. As to Sparrows and Thrushes, the only difference seemed to be in decoration. . . . Sparrows wearing feathered necklaces and bracelets. Thrushes—probable Thrushes, and fewer—wearing strung withered fingers around their necks, or wooden beads painted gray or blue. . . . Each of these men glanced at him . . . glanced behind him—at the boy, he supposed—then turned away. They seemed not so much unfriendly as ignoring. He and the boy, Errol—whom Baj could barely hear working down through the tangle behind him—were not "there" for the hill-men. Would likely only *be* there if hatchets and spears were called for.

And there was that possibility in the air. Baj had felt it, a time or two, boarding river-boats where many sweat-slaves hauled and carried, and while riding wide estate fields for hunting reasons or picnic reasons, when long lines of bond-serfs labored there, preparing onion fields, squash and cabbage fields, for Daughter-Summer's eight weeks.

On those occasions—at least a time or two—he'd felt how frail was a boss's whip against so many with picks and hoes ready in their hands, who had glanced at him . . . then glanced away just as these free savages did. Leaving the possibility in the air.

The small stream's water ran clear and cold—and Baj, kneeling, had his canteen and two of the water-skins filled when he noticed an odd rill in the shallow current a few feet down. He finished filling, palmed a wood stopper firmly in—and as he stood, saw a dead man was lying there under only a few inches of rapid shallow water, the morning sun flashing on the stream's surface. . . . A tall tribesman lay there, naked—but with all his feathered decorations, with his spear lying close to hand, his hatchet strung on its rawhide cord at his side.

The warrior's chest had been opened by a trooper's saber stroke from left shoulder down, so white cut tips of ribs—and the folds and lumps of darker things beneath—were seen in bright water as if sunk into a magic mirror.

Standing, looking for them, Baj saw two . . . three more dead men lying one after the other just downstream, buried in that odd way along the creek's shallow flow—so, he supposed, their essence might be carried by the current to whatever hunting paradise these people anticipated. . . . The king's troopers had taken their toll.

He knelt again—careful not to look upstream, so the drinking water might, after all, have no blood of tribesmen threaded through it—filled the last water-skin, stoppered it . . . then tucked the canteen's strap, the skins' rawhide thongs over his shoulder, and started back up the slope to camp. The boy, Errol, ambled behind him, clicking his tongue to a sort of simple rhythm.

Baj took up the rhythm with him, produced tongue-clicking variations—apparently to the boy's amusement—so they climbed past tribesmen up the slope, making cricket music as they went.

* * *

"But do we want him?"

"Nancy . . ." Richard was gathering oddments, sorting them into his big leather possibles-bag. A small buckskin sack of salt; linen folds of herbs that might (or might not) be healthy; a thick roll of fine tanned leather; his horn tinderbox, filled with flossy punk and rattling pieces of flint; steel needles and spools of tendon thread; a chip of obsidian sharper than any edge of steel; a little folding peg chess-set and its tiny pieces, and a small fat copybook of *The Common Prayers of Warm-time Oxford, England.* "—Nancy, he carries steel points like a soldier, sword and dagger." Richard put the last of his goods away, tucked the bag into his wolf-hide pack along with slabs of smoked horse meat, then buckled it closed, leaving a cooking pot and heavy coil of braided leather line strapped to the back.

"I have a sword, now!"

"He has points *and* a bow and arrows. I'd say he's been trained in weapons. He would have made me a good young infantry-man—and an officer soon enough."

"He's a boy. He barely has hair on his face."

Richard sighed a patient sigh. "He's full-human—and if we're told correctly, of Kipchak blood, men who have little hair on their faces. . . . *We* are the hairy ones."

"You are. I'm not."

". . . I've seen you bathing naked, little Person."

"—And you mean by that? What do you *mean* by that?" Nancy hackling like a chicken-bird rooster.

Richard hefted his pack. "I meant nothing but observation of the narrow line of fur running down your spine at the small of your back—in a charming way, to be sure. Now, get your things together. I would rather we didn't wait in this valley until the Sparrows forget the favor we've done them."

"You want him with us, so you'll have a Sunriser to obey."

"You are not big enough, comb-honey, to make me angry. . . . Now, get your things together. And unless you have a better reason than fear he will dislike what your Also-father left in you— then Baj-who-was-a-prince marches north with us."

"You are all beast," Nancy said, "—a bear who talks, as other bears dance at festivals." She bent to roll a blanket, then tie the rolled ends with leather thongs. ". . . If I didn't love you, I would not call you a *Person* at all."

"So, I'm chastised." Richard cocked his head. "They're back."

". . . The hill-men have put their dead into the water," Baj said, stepping into the clearing. Errol ambled in behind him. "And it seems to me to be time to go . . . if I'm going with you."

"Pack," Big Richard said. "And carry your bow strung, while we have daylight."

* * *

Baj thanked Floating Jesus—Mountain Jesus, now—for his two days and nights of rest in Battle-valley, otherwise there'd have been no keeping up with the three Persons. He saw now how they'd managed to parallel pace him up into the hills. . . . The three of them—Richard and Nancy each burdened by a considerable pack—traveled the days from dawn to dark (and its hasty small–fire camp) with only pauses for swallows of water, for smoked scraps of leftover horse meat. They moved—not terribly fast, not running—but steadily *almost* running. And neither up-hills nor down-hills, nor brush, woods, nor clearings seemed to change that pace.

It was a wearying way to go—that oddly became almost exhil-arating as the early-summer sun rose each morning to half-circle over, so Baj kept up in a sort of daily dream where effort became effortlessness. . . . It helped of course, that they were not pur-sued; there wasn't the exhaustion of fear. And helped as well that his sore ribs grew less sore each day's hiking. The girl's bite was almost healed.

But into this dreaming, one after-noon when hard going had became easier going, came visitors almost real—so Baj heard them very clearly, sensed them watching as he labored through budding green, the always sloping country. . . . Once, Baj passed King Sam Monroe—saw him clearly, standing in shadow under a bending willow where a pollen-dusted rivulet ran.

Stocky and strong, his cropped hair gone almost gray, the hilt of his long-sword jutting behind his right shoulder, the king spared only a preoccupied smile as Baj struggled by, splashing shallow water while he followed massive Richard, who smelled like untanned fur. . . . The king was seen more clearly than any other, though Queen Rachel sang an idle song—heard down a corridor, perhaps, or from her solar window while she and Old Lord Peter copied copies, and read them to each other.

Later, going to all fours—as his companions had already—to climb a slope of weathered stone with only hand-holds here and there, cracks to jam his fingers in, Baj heard Ralph-sergeant's hobnailed boots come clopping, then the knock at his door. "Your brother," Ralph-sergeant said, "—is fishing at Silver Gate (though why in the rain, I couldn't tell you) and wishes you to come and bring him luck."

And that was something that *had* been said, years before—and being true, drove the dream away. Prince Bajazet went with the dream, perhaps to join the others, perhaps to fish at the jetty with Newton, on a rainy day. Going, he closed his chambers' door behind him. . . .

As the sunny shadows shifted, Big Richard and Small Nancy led on, changing place every now and then—and, Baj noticed, going easily to all fours on the steepest slopes and rises. They halted for nothing . . . sometimes sucked water from their leather pouches as they went.

Baj labored along just behind—but kept up . . . kept up, while the boy, Errol, seemed to weave past and circle them all like a summer snake . . . disappearing, reappearing. He dropped back from time to time, apparently to scout behind them—then came wending forward to take a long lead, also apparently to scout. The boy's restless comings and goings, all the while Baj and the others were traveling fast, were unsettling in a way, reassuring in another. They were not pursued.

The Daughter's short summer had come upon the hills; they were dappled, as the Mississippi's banks and coastal woods had begun to be, with the warm weeks' hurried dark greens and light greens that rested the eyes, though the trees' blossoms, the thickets' blooms still waited. So, though there was no easy going, there was beautiful going.

"What are you *looking* at, looking around all the time?" Nancy had glanced over her shoulder, apparently an annoyed vixen, though with no brushy tail, no big ears to twitch. "—And what are you *smiling* at now?"

"It's a pretty day," Baj said, slightly breathless, since they were almost-running up a considerable slope with laurel saplings always in the way. "—And why I was smiling, is my business." The saplings did make hand-holds.

"You are slowing us," the Made-girl said, and had lisped the *us*, though not the *slowing*.

"I am not."

As if she were angry with him, though Baj couldn't recall being impolite—and she'd been kind to him before—the girl immediately went faster. She whisked up the rise to leave all of them behind, her dark leather pack bobbing, the sheathed scimitar snug at her waist . . . and disappeared over an outcrop of weather-splintered stone.

Baj climbed faster, though it cost him, and managed to catch Richard and labor along beside him. The big Person, his double-ax strapped to his heavy, furred pack, seemed to flow over the stone . . . flow between the slender young trees where it seemed he was too large to go. He apparently was trying to whistle as he traveled along—his lips, black as a dog's, were pursed—though, perhaps because the mouth was odd, only breathy near notes came out.

At the ridge, Baj was greatly relieved when Richard stopped to look out over rolling hilltops, the deepening valleys to the north and east. Shrugging his shoulders to settle his pack, quiver, and strung bow, Baj tried to take deep breaths quietly. A breeze, almost warm, drifted with new-summer odors across the ridge. Little insects, mayflies, ghosted with it, translucent wings glinting in the sun.

Errol came sidling up behind them. A small strangled cony was tucked dangling at his belt.

"When it becomes later," Richard said—and though no whistler, pronounced book-English as well as Baj had ever heard, and in a fine deep voice. "—When it becomes later, we'll find water in one of those hollows. As we do, so will animals."

"Yes . . . ?"

"You have a bow. Then get us fresh meat to travel on. Horse meat's gone."

"All right," Baj said, "—I can do that," and hoped he'd be able to. He was fair with the bow, a little better than fair, but so much of his hunting had been on horseback, and behind hounds. . . . It seemed the comfort of company brought responsibility with it.

The boy, Errol, made a clicking sound with tongue—and as

if that had been a signal, Richard was off again in a hulking bound down the wooded reverse. Baj galloped after him through whipping branches—running full out to keep from falling on his face and rolling down the mountain.

In the hollow below, Nancy was nowhere in sight, and Baj— exhilaration fading as he scrambled to keep the Persons' pace— began to yearn for the end of this day, as he'd yearned for the ends of the previous two.

But the after-noon seemed to stretch and stretch, as if the sun had slowed its run to match his weariness. There was only trotting through dark leaf mold and tangling vine, then climbing outcrops of rock to haul himself up through brush and saplings— bruised ribs still troubling him a little—then, over a crest, skidding down through more undergrowth, more saplings. His pack, sword and dagger, the quiver and bow all began to seem unfair, unnecessary, only foolish burdens.

. . . When it appeared there would come no evening, no night, but only day eternal, with sweat running into his eyes, and bleeding fingers—where the fuck were his gloves? He'd left them at the lodge more than a Warm-time week ago. . . . When effort seemed forever, unless he called to beg Richard for a halt, then at last the first of sunset's long shadows came sliding across the slopes, promising him twilight at last, and rest.

Deep into the next hollow, Nancy stepped from such a shadow, startling Baj so he shied away and put his hand to his sword-hilt like a festival fool. In woods and under woods, by softening light, her sharp face seemed suited and less strange. "Water," she said, "—and winter-broken branches for a fire."

"Meat?" Richard.

"No animals, no sign now—though coyotes have come through."

"*Shit,*" Richard said, a perfect use of the copybook word. "We were spoiled, coming south as the deer and all animals were coming south with Lord Winter at their backs."

"A thrown hatchet," Nancy said, "—would find a deer."

Richard sighed. "Not in summer season. Unstring your bow, Who-was-a-prince, and let it rest."

. . . The bow, its limbs eased, soon leaned against a maple tree. The same tree where Baj also sat resting, his limbs eased in evening air.

The boy, Errol, lay dozing beside him, while the cony, skinned—and looking very small, a blistered lump—rode a slender peeled branch over a little fire of fallen hardwood, chosen for thorough burning and little smoke.

"We're between Sparrow country and Thrush country." Richard fed the fire a light ration, huge dark fingers deft with twigs and splinters. "—almost up into Map-Kentucky. And if the Sparrows owe us something, the Thrushes owe us less. The Robins, farther north, will owe us nothing."

"Why stay in these tribesmen's hills at all?" Baj said. "Why not go east, into lower country and easier traveling, where there are farms—then north to the ice?"

"One of us makes too much noise traveling, anyway." Nancy, sitting across the fire, smiled at Baj as she said it, apparently no longer angered by whatever had angered her.—Proof, it seemed to him, that no mixture of fox's blood, or any blood, could dilute a woman's to anything but a woman's.

"I know I'm noisy through the woods—and I'm slow, and get tired. But I'll become quieter, and quicker, and soon I won't tire so easily."

"You do well enough." Richard leaned forward to prod the roasting cony with a huge forefinger. "We stay in the hills, at least for a Warm-time week or two, for good reason. Boston finds information in the villages, and from farmers . . . ranchers in the lowlands, east and farther east to the Ocean Atlantic." He leaned forward, sniffed at the cooking meat. "Boston finds friends there, too, since the Guard is their only protection when the tribes come raiding down. . . . Though there are villages that the tribesmen leave alone. That all leave alone."

"We'd prefer no pigeons flew to Cambridge to mention where we are," Nancy said. "Sylvia Wolf-General already knows where to meet us."

"Wolf-General?"

"She commands the First Regiment of the Guard," Richard said. "—Or did, when I served in it."

"And has some wolf mixed in her? No offense. . . ."

Richard smiled his disturbing smile. "Better say she has some human mixed in her."

"It's the Guard we seek," Nancy said. "But only those—so, carefully."

"Boston-Patience to deal with the Shrikes," Richard said, "—and we, the Guard."

"To bring harm to Boston."

"Oh, yes, Baj. A final harm."

"And if neither is persuaded to be with us—not those tribesmen, not the Guard?"

Richard shook his head. "Then, Baj, the Shrikes will do to us . . . much the same as the Guard will do to us."

"But if they agree—then to harm Boston how?"

"How," Richard said, "is secret, and will be as sailing Patience advised us. She sews all together." He leaned to poke the cooking cony again, and Baj saw he was drooling—clear saliva running down a half-furred jaw in glistening strands, making an odd contrast with the rich voice, its excellent book-English. . . . Considering that contrast, it occurred to Baj that traveling with fanged companions had its dubious side, best dealt with by frequent feedings.

"There must be deer in these mountains. I'll try for one, tommorow."

Richard rumbled an "Ummm . . ." of appetite.

"If not a deer," Baj said, "—*something*." And looked up to see a look of gleeful amusement on the Made-girl's face.

"He thinks—" Nancy giggled like a child.

"I think what?" Baj said.

"Nothing . . ." More giggles.

"What?" Richard stopped poking the meager meat, sucked his finger for the juices.

Baj gave the girl a let-it-go look—but she instantly betrayed him. "He thinks we'll *eat* him." Giggles grew to laughing, her sharp white teeth reflecting firelight.

Beside Baj, Errol woke smiling at the sound of her laughter, and Richard's booming "Certainly a possibility . . ."

Later, the big Person dug into his pack, set a small book aside, and brought out a little folding peg-chess set. "Do you play, boy?"

"I play," Baj said, "and am not a boy."

"Forgive me."

. . . But it seemed Baj *was* a boy, at least regarding employment of bishops, and ended the evening humiliated, after a desperate battle in which those nasty slanting pieces ruined him.

"Oh, dear," Richard had said. "Bad luck . . ."

So strange, it seemed to Baj, as he turned beneath his blanket, the ground's roots and stones soft enough for exhausted sleep. So strange to find this odd occasion, this odd company—frightening company in its way, and all of them journeying to no-doubt worse, to more knots in an already knotted cord of trouble. Strange to have some knots untied by nothing but laughter around a small camp-fire, then a lost game of chess.

Still . . . a deer tomorrow.

But the summer deer still winter-hid in deep forest, deep hollows between the hills. Lady Weather's daughter, tragic Summer, had not yet sung to lure them out into meadows.

"I smell them," Richard said, at the perfect middle of the next day, lifting his head to test the breeze when they stopped to drink water, chew strips of the jelly underbark of birches. "—But not close."

Baj supposed Nancy had smelled them also, but preferred not to say so. "If not a deer," he said, "then something else." They'd seen two black bears at dawn—but those at a distance, going south and away. And Baj, stalking around a beaver pond later, had approached in time for an animal to slap its tail on the water, and dive out of sight and out of reach of an arrow.

Richard nodded. "Oh, in time, something else."

Something else already gathered—five small song-birds— Errol had killed with thrown sticks. They hung at his belt like feathered decorations.

. . . The day was beautiful, with cloud-shadows mottling the mountains' soft green. Soft green, soft mountains—though becoming greater. They humped up high along the northern horizon, so low clouds lay draped at their shoulders, spinning out on the wind in misty sunshine.

That beauty made better traveling for Baj, as if the country cupped him in green hands, drifting the warming perfume of growing things as he labored to keep up with the others—keeping up made easier, as he needed to mind only that, while his past and future napped like tired children, and were quiet.

In after-noon, they wended down steep slopes where water-falls came drumming, splashing over stone. These were some-thing Baj had never seen—clear water churned to white water as it fell from heights, and fell heavily. He saw even Richard stagger as he went shouldering beneath the only one with passage after—and was instantly drenched so his furred pack, his own fur crest and the tufts down his long arms turned soaked and stringy as the big Person lunged out from under the fall, and found dry stone beyond it. He checked his pack and possibles—then shook himself like a wet hunting dog.

Nancy went next, snaking under the bright, rumbling weight of water. She struggled through in spray . . . then climbed the rock beyond to find a lie of sunshine, and sit stripping wet from her scimitar's bright blade for fear of rust.

Baj—his quiver's leather cover tied over—went through, and enjoyed it despite the icy battering the falling water gave him as he managed his footing beneath it. . . . In sodden buckskins, sloshing half-boots, he climbed across slippery stone to Nancy's boulder, and stood beside her, whiping water from his bowstave . . . whipping rapier and knife blades thrumming through the air to dry them.

"You greased that sword, Nancy?"

"With horse-meat fat a while ago."

"Not enough; you need to coat the steel." Baj dug in his pack, found his little cake of tallow only damp. "Use this—but be careful along the edge."

She gave him the slantwise yellow glance he should have expected. "I don't cut myself, Who-*was*-a-prince."

"Neither do I—never—but somehow I bleed, every now and then, handling sharp steel."

Nancy said nothing to that, but bent over the scimitar's beautiful blade—an interesting pattern of descending dark bands marking the metal—and began to tallow it . . . but carefully along the gently curving edge.

Baj sat, feeling muscles ease down his back and along his thighs and calves with a mild aching of relief. The Made-girl beside him smelled of soaked cloth and leather, of camp-fire smoke, and the faint sour odor of a fox's wet fur.

Richard—looking only a little smaller, damp—lumbered swiftly past them, and continued along a stony slope, great ax swinging in his hand.

"Go on," Nancy said, bent over her blade, and Baj had grunted to his feet when she said, "He's afraid of the water."

Baj looked where she looked, and saw Errol dancing at the waterfall's other side. The boy ran forward to the toppling wall of water—stopped, and ran back as if it might chase him.

"He won't do it," Nancy said, and stood. "He swims wonderfully, but fears falling water. I'll get Richard to come and make him cross."

"No need. I'll get him." Baj trotted back down the stone, already wondering how to do it.

"Careful!" she called after him. "*Careful!*"

Baj, cautious on wet rock, dropped his pack, unbuckled his sword-belt, and ducked back under the fall's torrential weight. The water hadn't yet heard the last of winter; it was wonderfully cold.

He came out the other side in a shower of spray, and saw Errol backing away as if he were bringing the waterfall with him.

"Won't hurt you," Baj said, meaning he wouldn't and the fall wouldn't, but Errol—thin face pale beneath dirt and freckles—seemed not to trust that. He took more steps back, and drew a knife with his left hand. A broad-bladed knife, its steel flecked with rust . . . but the fine edge bright as silver. There were tongue-clicks; the boy seemed frozen, staring at glassy water toppling to foam and thunder.

Nancy was calling . . . something. Baj could barely hear her through the noise of falling water.

"There are moments," the Master had said once, in the *salle*, "—moments that must not be allowed to become more than moments. They're to be dealt with directly."

Good advice, and though the Master had been instructing on booze-house quarrels and useful ball-kicking, it seemed to apply here.

Baj unknotted his bandanna from his throat, shook water from it, then strolled up to the boy—ignoring the knife, careful not to notice it—stepped around behind him casually as if that had already been agreed to, then gently draped the cloth over Errol's eyes. The boy, blinded, stood still.

Baj, standing close, felt wiry muscle ease . . . and exactly as he would have with a colt caught in a stable fire, began to murmur soothing nonsense, and gently urged Errol along. Urged him along . . . And though the boy stiffened in fright again as the wall of water poured before them, Baj kept his eyes covered, said, "Shhh . . . shhhh," and led him in, holding him close with one arm. They moved together, ducking, buffeted with freezing cold. . . . Then walked out from under.

Errol—standing sodden, his knife still in his hand—tossed his head exactly as a colt might have done, drops flying as Baj took the bandanna away, knotted it back at his throat, and went to pick up his pack and sword-belt, his heart still a little hurried.

Nancy, her scimitar sheathed, pack shouldered, stared at him, said, "Careful along the edge," and walked away.

* * *

Harder traveling then, over rocky outcrops reared surprisingly high past narrow gorges carved from north and north-east by centuries of the short-summers' snow-melt.

Errol had gone on his way, skittering off into stands of hemlock, fir, and stunted spruce grown leaning over granite ledges. Neither Richard nor Nancy waited for Baj, though he could see them from time to time—objects neither green nor granite-gray, and in purposeful motion. And not so far ahead, only a continual stone's throw or bow-shot across some shaded defile. When not seen, their traveling was told by warblers lifting from evergreens, or birdsong gone silent.

For a time, annoyed, Baj tried to catch up with them . . . then, tiring of that, he paid attention to his own hiking instead. The rough touch and grip of fir saplings used for hand-holds, the damp sweet smell and stroke of foliage as he paged hemlock branches out of his way. The soft fern beds giving way to unforgiving stone beneath his boots. He paid attention to the pleasures of moving . . . breathing to move well, and after a while was surprised, on a long downhill, to find Nancy almost beside him, stepping down . . . stepping down, bent a little under the weight of her pack.

He climbed down beside her—going sideways in steeper places for better footing with his boot-soles' edges. In those places, she went sideways, also, but on all fours, one or both narrow hands lightly touching the mat of pine needles, her comb of widow-peaked hair a darker red under the trees.

Nancy's odor didn't seem so strong, now she wasn't wet. Perhaps some rankness had washed away—like his sweat—in the fall's cold water.

"Your boots are stupid. Clumsy."

"They are what I have," Baj said, and climbed beside her down a stand of fir to a run of yellow birches, just in bud, along a narrow mountain meadow striped by late after-noon's shadows. Big Richard was standing by a tree, waiting for them.

"Deer," he said, lifted his head and sniffed the air.

Nancy, beside Baj, snuffled. "Old smell," she said.

"Old today—not old from tomorrow." Richard pointed across the meadow. "They bed down there."

"Not anymore."

Richard sighed. "May I say something without a *no* from you?"

"I won't argue with you," Nancy said. "It's like arguing with a stump."

"I could take my bow across," Baj said. ". . . Wait for them to come in the evening."

"No deer," Nancy said. "Other things come through."

Richard didn't seem to hear. "Yes, do it. There's a creek running there." He glanced down at Nancy. "I *smell* it."

"Creek, yes. Deer, no."

Richard paid no attention to that. "The buck will come in, leading. If he's young—take him. If he's an old antler, try for a follower."

"Okay." One of the most useful Warm-time words of agreement. . . . And it was odd, but Baj now found Richard more human than before—men together beneath birches, planning a hunt, ignoring a woman's carping. "—Okay." He took his bow off his shoulder, knelt to brace and string it, then stooped for a wisp of weed, and tossed it for the wind. "You two stay here—and keep Errol on this side."

Richard grunted agreement, then swung his heavy, furred pack off, set his great ax against a tree, and lay down with the same odd rocking motion he used to stand up.

As Baj selected three broadheads from his quiver, Nancy—leaning against a narrow birch with her hand on the hilt of her scimitar, stood staring yellow-eyed, as if at a festival fool lacking only the little bells in a little hat.

* * *

Baj crossed the meadow in sinking sunlight, his bow in his hand, pleased with walking on the flat after so much climbing of ups and downs. It seemed to be a beaver-dam fill, growing only summer weeds and the first blue stars, with another wildflower—yellow—he didn't know the name of. No saplings had rooted in the open yet.

At the meadow's other side, a steep bank fell away to a rivulet bog with skunk cabbage starting here and there among dwarf willows . . . a stand of alder. Mottled shadows moved across the green as an early breeze of evening began to blow. Tiny insects—gnat flies—danced in the air, almost invisible.

Baj crossed the little run . . . found fairly firm ground past it where a greening tangle of berry vine grew along the bog's edge. He settled there, unbuckled his sword-belt, set it out of his way, and sat with his back to a young alder's trunk. It would be a clear shot, from there, at any deer come to drink—though a long shot if it came downstream, where the willows thickened.

Baj selected an arrow, set it to his bowstring. The fine broadhead's steel had been engraved with the outline of a miniature scorpion, the sigil of the royal armory. . . . Old Howell Voss had fought under that banner. If the Boston-woman, Patience, had been telling the truth, then soon—as king—he would be choosing his own, and new banners would unfurl over the Great Rule from the Mississippi to the Ocean Pacific. . . . Though now, no business of Baj's. No business of his at all.

He sat, the alder trunk still day-warm at his back, closed his eyes, and tried to imagine a Warm-time summer—a *twelve*-week summer—and that after a warm spring, with a warm fall still to come! Lady Weather's daughter lying smiling, sighing, her long soft legs spread for their pleasure. . . . No wonder, as ancient Lord Peter had said, there was no way of knowing such lucky people completely, no matter how many ancient books were found, copied, and read.

Baj sat straighter, watching past budding bramble as shadows grew slowly longer, the last brightness of the day began to fade. . . . A summer so long there was no hurry, when flowers, when all plants, from onion and cabbage to far-southern corn stretched themselves leisurely up toward the sun in months of warm, warm green.

In that climate, any fool might have written poetry without the word *ice* appearing ever. Though it was true that his own River-epic had used the various transparencies of ice to some effect. Perhaps to too much effect. . . . What was *not* written was also poetry, of a silent kind, the mute sister to what was written and spoken. The unseen reverse, as of a silver coin. And if that were true, then all men—all Made-men also, of course—spoke a sort of silent poetry to themselves quite often, even if unmetered and inelegant.

Movement. . . . Movement down in the willows? Baj rose to one knee and began—only began—to draw the string back a little. No gloves; he felt the beginning bite at his draw-fingers. Movement . . . but no deer, only early evening breezes through willow branches.

He relaxed, and relaxed the bow—having a vision of himself triumphant, striding into camp with a gutted buck across his shoulders. Letting it slide to the grass as simply the casual getting-of-meat by a formidable hunter. —Which imagined playlet made it sadly likely he'd occasionally acted the theatrical jackass at Island.

. . . More comfortable to consider the poetry of silence, the poetry of speech. A thing was what it was called, after all, and often silently—as he called himself an archer, in carrying a bow and intending to feed those three Persons. Call them his friends, since he had no others in a situation so startling, so bizarre (*there* was a wonderful WT word) that no poet or romancer could have suggested it.

Baj shifted against the alder's slender trunk—shifted slowly so as not to startle any observant animal. Nothing moved along the boggy run but occasional warblers flighting, and interlaced branches swinging barely budded in the mountain breeze.

Recollection came with that breeze. Of wind at his last archery. When? Not hunting—it hadn't been a hunting occasion. . . . It was a memory of river wind across the north-lawn butts at Island. Prince Bajazet and his friends: Martin Clay, Ernie Parker, Pat DeVane, and Pedro Darry—Commander of Island's Guard *and* middle-aged Master of the Revels. Wonderful swordsman, too, though desperately bad with a bow. Pat DeVane had been their wizard there, though he hadn't shot well that morning. Too much wind—gusty wind, hard to judge.

That memory came to Baj, but not quite freshly, as if those friends' voices, the strumming bowstrings and hissing arrows, sounded only for Prince Bajazet, who no longer lived at Island, or anywhere. . . .

The evening slowly darkened. Bird-flights less frequent, bird-song softer as shadows became shade everywhere.

A bare shrub shook down the way. Then shook again.

Baj, alert, drew his bow a little just as a beast—no deer— shoved through foliage and out into the patch of bog.

A wild pig, then two more came grunting, bristle-fur dark and thick as bears'. A sow and her shoats—shoats grown at least a year. It was the skunk cabbage they came for, the sow already rooting at one, her trotters sunk deep in wet ground.

Baj rose slowly to his feet for the nicest shooting, slowly drew full, and held his shot to be sure of the nearest shoat, the arrow's fletching touching his cheek.

He was easing his fingers for the release, when berry vines exploded to his left and a razorback boar came at him black as night, squealing, champing yellow tusks so foam ran along its great head.

Baj spun that way, released the arrow—then ran.

He ran, as the boar turned to come after him, in a sort of leaping way, as if he might in a moment learn to fly—sail the air as Boston-talents did—and leave the beast behind. He ran kicking through scrub and splashing past skunk cabbage, the sow and shoats standing still, staring as he went past with squealing death coming after.

While his legs thrashed in desperate running, while he fumbled to set a second arrow to his bow, Baj's mind was oddly calm and clear. *If he tears me—if he tears me, I'll die. No physicians, no old Portia-doctor here . . .*

His second arrow, as if helpful, seemed to nock itself to the string—and Baj half-turned as he ran, drew and shot and struck the boar in its shoulder as it came bounding. Then, no more squeals. Only speed and purpose.

Baj angled hard away, knew it was no use, hesitated as the boar came to him, shaking its head, foam flying—then dove up into the air and over the animal, dove high as if into a summer swimming pond as the boar reared and struck at him. Baj hit the ground, rolled to his feet, and ran back the way he'd come, back toward his sword and dagger as the boar spun and was after him, still silent.

Galloping, imagining the figure he made fleeing an angry pig, Baj began to laugh with what breath he could spare. Pursued again. . . . He saw his weapons by the narrow alder, and knew he wouldn't reach them.

Something came down just behind him like a falling tree, very dark and swift. There was a heavy smacking sound. Baj looked back, still in a stumbling run, and saw the boar thrashing in the damp . . . bright blood spouting, spattering where its head had been.

Richard hulked beside, puffing a little from effort, swinging his double-bitted ax to clear blood running at its edge. "She was right," he said. "No deer."

Baj stood bent over to catch his breath. He felt his heartbeats in his throat. "Thank you . . . very much."

"Come to call you in—getting dark. Heard him squealing." Richard picked a handful of weeds and wiped his ax-blade clean. "I do have a question. Why were you laughing?"

" . . . Why not?" Baj said, and the Person smiled his toothy smile.

* * *

There had never been better meat.

Baj had truly never tasted better, though Island's cooks were as near the arts of Warm-time "chefs" as it was possible to be. He supposed it was the sum of circumstances: the fine rich roast itself after hungry days—with danger past, with a snapping fire warming against the night's chill mountain air, and good and interesting company.

To be alive and untorn was pleasure enough; to have searched in near darkness and found his valuable vagrant arrow, and now to chew the hot pork—running fat clear and fine—of what had tried to kill him, made for pleasures additional.

In eating, his companions' odd blood was shown. The boy, Errol, ate alone—had taken his portion, steaming guts and lights mainly, and gone into the dark with it. Big Richard and Small Nancy ate alike, with swift and serious ripping bites—white teeth, dark meat—as if the portion needed further killing. Then followed slightly awkward chewing, as if gulping would be their natural thing.

Baj supposed he ate not much differently, being so hungry, so pleased.

. . . He woke chilled under his blanket into a damp dawn—stretched, yawned, and rolled out ready for cold pork and mountain climbing. Both hams, already roasted, had been propped over the banked fire through the night, for deeper smoking. Charred dark, they would last for long traveling. . . . The rest of the meat would be gone in two or three days, with only tiny wild spring onions found to cut its thick sweet-saltiness. The head had been buried in the ashes, slow cooking, and as the others roused,

Richard—yawning, still sleepy—dug into the fire's gray bed to the last still-red coals, lifted the boar's head free, its curled tusks cracked by heat, then split the heavy skull with a stroke of his ax, and served brains out steaming on widths of bark. . . . Baj let those go by, and took a chop. Brains—and testicles, and the palms of the hands—had been the ceremonial delicacies of cannibal Middle Kingdom, and only two or three generations before.

The three of them—Errol gobbling off to the side, behind a spruce—sat wreathed in the fire's last wisps of smoke, and ate seriously, for strength as much as satisfaction.

. . . By sun-overhead—the old WT noon—they were up and over the round peak of the next mountain north, and though Richard still led with Nancy, Baj kept close behind them even in the steepest places—where they occasionally went on all fours.

Then they were onto long ridges, misty with low cloud and stretching away north and east, so no end of them could be seen. Only wind-bent spruce grew along these crests, seemed to grow from gray stone weathered bald and broken. Eagles—dark eagles, not the bright-headed fishing ones that tree-nested along Kingdom River—swung just above or just beneath them as they traveled. Errol threw stones to strike the birds, but they paid him no mind . . . drifted with the wind along the heights, hardly flapping their wings.

From these high ridges, Baj saw for the first time that the earth was truly round. Slowly turning in one place he found the horizon very slightly curved—difficult to make out amid distant misty mountains, but certain just the same. So, the copybooks' casual claim was proved again as Gulf and Ocean sailors proved it, watching departing ships seem to slowly sink into the sea, so that finally only their raven's nests and banners could be seen . . . then not even those.

. . . As the day grew old, the wind grew young, and blew hard enough to be leaned into—a danger, with damp rock to climb along, and vacant air often close on either side. His first time so high, those long, long falls through sunstruck fog to stone slopes so far below—and, in places, to distant forest browns and greens still farther down—kept Baj's attention on his boots, so he marked every step to make sure of it, and fell behind.

"Keep up!" Nancy, looking back, waved him on.

"I *am* fucking keeping up. But I'm not going to fall, either!"

She stared at him for a moment—that yellow-eyed stare—then went on along the ridge after Richard, and soon out of sight among sloping, broad, bare shelves of granite.

"Jesus-damned things . . ." It seemed unfair the two—Errol also—had animals' endurance and fine footing. Baj thought of taking his boots off, but then his wool stockings would be worn to holes within a quarter-mile over this country.

The girl, so kind and careful when he'd been hurt, now was an annoyance, always with something to say about what he might do better. *Keep up.* And if he hurried and fell off these heights—what then? Fox's tears for his memory?

Baj went a little faster, but carefully.

* * *

"Don't tell him."

"Don't tell him what?" Richard stood idly swinging his ax, surveying the green peaks to the east as they waited for Baj-who-was-a-prince. "—We'll be in Map-Kentucky by dark, tomorrow."

"Just don't tell him."

Richard turned to stare at her. "And what makes you suppose, Little One, that I would—or that the boy would care?"

"I know what men think, humans or Persons."

"You know what *some* think."

"*All*, Richard."

They heard Baj's boots on the ridge's rock.

"Mmm. And did you notice the eagle that was not an eagle?"

"No, I didn't."

"It flew miles east of us, just the same."

Baj tramped up to them. "I'm here," he said to Nancy. "—Satisfied?"

As Richard had seen her—so Patience had seen him and his companions as she sailed past, then on for hours more over country steep enough to take them days of travel. She'd seen the tiny three of them (the Weasel-boy certainly roaming near) filing along the top of the ridge. A dangerous way to go, outlined for anyone to see from miles away, and likely not what Captain Richard would have done if the crest cliffs had allowed him passage a little lower.

Still dangerous going, through Thrush country soon becoming Robin country. The Robins took heads.

Dangerous for her, too, to walk so tired through the air. And so high. The Patience Nearly-Lodge Riley who, at seventeen, had thought her way so easily over the ice from Boston, and down from the Wall—Walking-in-air all the lowlands south, crossing the Gulf Entire, and then into the *Sierra Occidental*—had ended fresh as a summer flower.

The flower was withered weaker now, as flowers failed with Lord Winter's first breath.

If there were such Great Spirits of climate and the rest—and people who were not fools believed it—if there were, then why was the gift of youth-forever, forever withheld? Why were interesting men and women—and interesting Persons, Boston made—why all left doomed to rot, and know it? . . . Violent passing, of course, quite another thing. Poor MacAffee; he'd fenced his four taught strokes, his five taught guards . . . really helpless as a child against invention. Still, a pleasure to have felt fine steel, so keen, strike and catch and draw a man's life out with it. The look on his face . . . on all their faces before . . .

Wind, harder wind came buffeting through the mountain pass. Difficult . . . difficult to Walk-in-air against, it took such concentration. Patience welcomed forest in her mind, and sank a little lower toward it, her coat ruffling, flapping about her. A short-summer wind, at least, and not cruelly cold.

She welcomed forest more warmly, welcomed what ground, what stone lay beneath the trees, so she sailed lower, beneath the worst of the gusts . . . low enough to kick at the tallest spruce-tops with her boots as she went past.

Perhaps her weariness allowed Maxwell to come dreaming in. A dream of baby odors of pee, stains of his wet-nurses' breast milk, and a cloth tit of southern cane sugar—so she felt him resting warm against *her* breast, crooning, nudging to suckle. Patience caught the hem of his dream like a sliding border of silk, and wished herself into it, her left breast's nipple into his wet, soft, baby mouth—urgent, then painfully sweet as he worked his hungry mouth to take dream milk from her. Her breast ached, both breasts ached with the pleasure of it. *Soon. Soon, my baby. My darling boy . . .*

She seemed to bend to him, sharing a vision—Maxwell no longer suckling strongly, restless, disinterested—as they viewed, from some drifting vantage, a great wind-humming space she recognized as Island's Bronze Gate . . . the river surging past, its currents swirling in the stone harbor. There were colors, banners, welcoming music as two people—a man and woman—stepped down a ship's gangway hand-in-hand. Both older . . . so it took a moment to recognize them. . . .

The dream spun back to its beginning, Maxwell tugging gently, nudging, as he lightly suckled like a lover, so the sweetness of it ran like honey to her groin.

No such unlooked-for pleasure, without price. Blind with longing, so deep in her son's dream, Patience struck a tree-top; a limber spruce-branch whipped across her face—and shocked from concentration, she fell through the air, awkward and clutching, until a greater branch snagged her, and wrenched her left arm from its shoulder socket.

From there, she fell and struck the ground.

. . . Patience tried to set tearing agony aside, and lay still for a moment. Then moved her head, moved her fingers and toes, carefully waggled her left hand to find if any nerves had been torn in the dislocation.

All moved. And she could breathe, and see, though suffering several hurts—none severe as the left shoulder's.

Patience took deep breaths, thought mindful warmth to keep herself from further shock . . . then carefully stood up out of a confusion of broken branches, her greatcoat, and sheathed scimitar akimbo. Her hat . . . her hat was nowhere to be seen beneath tall spruces. A Boston hat, broad-brimmed, blue-dyed, and made of beaver felt. An irreplaceable hat . . .

She wandered, stumbling a little, looking for a strong low branch forking into a narrow V. Surprising how difficult that was to find, where there were nothing but trees. . . . She searched, hissing-in deep breaths against the pain, found two almost good enough—and then a third that was.

The left hand would move; its arm—hanging so oddly, almost behind her back—would not move, so Patience had to reach across with her right to grip its wrist. She lifted the left arm with only a single short yelp of agony, hauled it high, and jammed and wedged the wrist into the branch's rough fork. She began to faint . . . but wouldn't let that happen.

Another very deep breath.

Then she bent her knees, and jumped up and away, lunging hard to the right. She screamed, felt a grating almost-click, and landed with a grunt, things tearing in her shoulder, the world swaying almost away from her.

. . . A pause while she stood sick, vomiting a little down her front. The pain was so great that it drove her out of herself, took all of Patience Nearly-Lodge Riley, and left only a stranger standing.

. . . It was this stranger who rearranged the awkward arm, no matter how the woman screamed and wept. The stranger set the left wrist back into the branch's fork, forced it firmly . . . then paused to consider the angle necessary, the turn and twist necessary, the force necessary to leave the left arm's shoulder-joint no place to go but together.

That decided, the stranger allowed Patience back in—crouched stunned for a moment by her agony—then leaped again.

Grinding, and a surprisingly loud *clack* as what fit, fit.

Calling *"Ohhh . . . ohhhh,"* Patience turned slow circles away from pain, then sat hunched on thick spruce needles, rocking back and forth to comfort herself as she would a child. A ferret seemed to cling to her left shoulder, chewing its way to the bone. Chewing at the bone, tearing tendons with its teeth. As if that. As if that . . .

With hours passed, it became only a deep drumbeat of pain, rhythmed with her heartbeat. Patience had sliced a wide strip of her greatcoat's hem free with her scimitar's edge, knotted the cloth into a sling one-handed . . . and carefully tucked her left arm angled in to rest.

Then, there was only the long night left to get through, until less pain might allow the concentration for Walking-in-air. If that proved not possible, then ground-walking the mountains' forest and stone would have to be the way north and east, and pain beside the point.

* * *

It was surprising, how familiarity dealt with fear. Just as he'd become weary of being frightened as the king had pursued him, so Baj became weary, after another day, of fearing falling.

Soon enough, he clambered along the mountain ridges fairly fast, and kept up—or almost up—with the Persons. Not that all these heights were airy, uncertain footing along granite cliffs. These mountains were so soft—anciently worn, according to Richard—that often their ridge peaks were rounded, rich with evergreens and even drifts of berry bushes here and there, though only tiny buds showed on those, and spring leaves hardly bigger, but a dark and bitter green.

Nancy no longer had to call, "Keep up!" and seemed to Baj to be relaxing from whatever annoyance she'd appeared to nurse the days past. She traveled on in her swift pacing way—more lightly than lumbering Richard—paying no attention that he could see to even dangerous passages, where only solitary sailing birds circled alongside possible slipping . . . to certain falling, and death.

When—on scree slopes—Baj went to all fours for a WT yard or two, as Richard and Nancy went more often, he could still feel a tenderness in his bitten forearm, as if a tip of one of the girl's fangs had touched the bone. . . . An odd sensation—and, for what reason he couldn't have told, Baj had the most sudden yearning for Pedro Darry's company. How Pedro—still handsome, still a rake at forty years and more in his leather, lace, and satins—how he would have laughed, standing balanced on a precarious boulder. Thrown back his head and roared with laughter at Baj scuttling along behind small portions of bear's blood and fox's blood, with a measure of weasel circling somewhere behind.

"What in the Lady's name have you been *up* to?" Then, more laughter, observing Who'd-been-Bajazet—grimy, sweat-stained, sparse stubble unshaved—climbing the cliff-faces like a nervous squirrel, his rapier's scabbard-tip tapping the stone behind him.

How sweet that laughter would sound, if it brought Pedro to life again, to stand beside him. No better company in desperate circumstance than that merry swordsman. . . . What had Mark Cooper said at the lodge, those moments before the dagger went in? "Darry killed three of our people. . . ."

And Baj—climbing a merely steep stretch at last—could see it. A stone hallway, tapestries lifting a little along the walls as the river wind blew through. Then steel's bright sounds, bright glances of light along sword-blades flashing. Sad the Cooper man who first met that smiling face over sharp edges, bitter points. Sad the second man . . . and the third. They would have tried to turn him, get past him in the corridor to strike his back.

The fourth man must have managed.

Charm and laughter, all gone to spoiling dirt. And their complicity in that theft of life, only the least of Boston's robberies.

Baj climbed faster, until he saw Nancy's worn leather pack bobbing just ahead. Loss, it seemed, made strength.

He caught up and went beside her for a while—made the mistake of trying to help her over a great fracture in the stone, and received a satirical grin for it, and no thanks as she bounded up and over. It was in that sort of motion her mixed heritage was plain, that and her vulpine odor, as if an elegant vixen had been changed by some Warm-time wizard to a girl.

She climbed without his help, but Baj still kept up with her, so they traveled side by side for a while. At the next fracture—quite severe, as if a side of the great crest had broken—she stepped behind him, put a narrow hand on the seat of his buckskins, and with startling strength shoved him up.

When he got to his feet, she climbed past with that same grin. The long jaw, its sharp white teeth, seemed made for it, as foxes smiled at lost hounds casting.

"Thank you," Baj said, and kept on. It was surprising how even the early-summer sun burned down at these heights, so he wished he had a hat. Hats not common on the River, where the wind made fun and blew them away . . . though ladies sometimes secured them under their chins with bands of far-southern silk. It came to Baj as he threaded through a stand of stunted spruce, that he might not—almost certainly would not—see the Kingdom River again. Not feel the rainy winds that drove down its current in the short-summers . . . not feel the savage sleet that blew as Lord Winter came down from the Wall.

No care by Floating Jesus any longer, uncertain as that had proved to be. No songs of the fishermen sounding on lamp-lit evenings on the River, as they lured the salmon to their nets. No girls chased laughing through Island's glass-roofed gardens. No comfort of the grand company of civilization close around him. Now—and likely forever—wilderness, risk . . . and loneliness, save for odd companions.

Richard led them down-slope at last, down from their third long wearying ridge. "Off the crest," he rumbled, "and safer." Downhill, Richard went as any human, any "Sunriser" man might have gone, standing upright, but with heavy swaying to his gait, the double-bitted ax held casual over his right shoulder, its edges gleaming above his bulky backpack's fur.

They found Errol a considerable way down the mountain's side, squatting waiting by a small rock spring in evergreens. The boy had built a neat stack fire of twigs and weathered fallen wood, and seemed to be waiting for a starter spark.

Baj and the Persons came down to it, unloaded packs, cloaks and rolled blankets. Baj set down bow and quiver, dug out his tinderbox—struck flint sparks into its fine floss, blew those bright, then took a burning tuft and tucked it into the tinder.

. . . Supper was smoked boar; the first cuts off the last ham—though dry, edges fire-charred—still very fine. Richard and Nancy sat at the fire, ripping, chewing from their chunks; Baj slicing from his, with Errol gnawing a distance away. It was surprising how quickly one great ham had gone already. . . .

Finished, Baj left the fire to pee—and downhill, off to the side of that cover, found a small pond a spring had made in a cup of stone and weedy turf. The setting sun shone off the still water in reflected red and gold, that then rippled slightly as the first of evening breezes came cool through the mountains. . . . From this pond, Baj could see over pine and hemlock to more mountains marching north and east, their immense sunset shadows leaning one against the other. The air came into his lungs clear as iced vodka . . . so they ached a little, but nicely.

He bent over the water's edge, looked down, and saw amid

sunset colors a very young man with a grimy older man's face, thin, lightly beard-stubbled, windburned and weary. He would have known himself—but only after an instant's puzzlement.

Grimy . . . And as if with the sight, the stink of old sweat, worn stockings, and dirty buckskins came quite strongly.

He stood back, unbuckled his sword-belt, and balanced heron-wise on one leg, then the other, to pull off his boots. Then he walked down into the water. Its chill, halfway up his buckskins, shocked him to stillness, so he stood only wriggling stockinged toes in frigid fine sand until he grew used enough to go on—and finally, with a gasp, submerged himself in a dark-green world so bitterly cold it seemed to bite him.

Baj stood up in soaked cloth and buckskin—the water to his waist, the evening air now seeming wonderfully warm—and stomped in place, raising dark clouds of sand and green stuff around him. Then he stooped for handfuls of that fine sand and began to scrub his clothes with it as if it were ash-lye soap.

When he'd done what he could for deerskin, far-south cotton, and wool, he stripped the soaked stuff off, threw it up onto a shelf of rock, and scrubbed himself—a painful process with sand and cold water. His scalp and long hair particularly painful to rub hard and rinse, rub hard and rinse . . .

Finished, his skin sore and stinging, Baj rung out his hair as best he could, and marched splashing up out of the water—the air feeling so much warmer. He bent to slide his dagger from its sheath, then knelt naked at the pond's edge to stare down at his reflection, and shave.

Another painful process. Anyone doubting that hot water, fine soaps and lotions were markers of civilization, could be quickly convinced by shaving with a slim-bladed weapon in ice water on a mountaintop.

Considering, watching his face reflected in fading evening light as the dagger whispered coarsely down his cheek . . . considering, Baj decided to let his mustache—admittedly not yet much of a mustache—to let that grow. He would certainly look older with it.

. . . Finished, now blade-sore as well as sand-sore, he dragged his sodden clothes on (all but the stockings), laced the buckskin trousers, buttoned the shirt and leather jerkin, then picked up his sword-belt and boots and went barefoot back up the slope, a wet stocking over each shoulder, the dagger in his free hand.

He shoved through the stand of evergreens—darkening with the first of night—and stepped, dripping, up to the fire.

His odd companions seemed pleased by what they saw. The boy, Errol, smiled. Nancy covered her mouth.

"Not cold?" Richard said. The night wind rising was a north wind. The fire bent and bannered to it.

"A little."

While the three of them watched, entertained, Baj bent to dry his dagger on a blanket corner—sheathed it, and set his weapons-belt aside. Then he stood close before the fire, stretched his arms wide, and turned slowly around and around while drenched buckskin and dripping cloth began to steam.

The Persons seemed very pleased by that, and Errol stood up across the fire, stretched his arms out, and began to turn in imitation, as if joining a tribal dance.

The fire burned close enough, and hot enough, that Baj began to feel less chill—and reminded himself not to dry the buckskins completely, so they'd stiffen and shrink. Same with the cotton shirt, as far as shrinking. . . . Laundry matters, and who would have dreamed they'd ever be a concern of his?

He slowly turned and turned—Errol, expressionless, turning precisely with him across the fire—and felt the cloth drying on his back, felt a warning tightness in his buckskin trousers . . . so stepped a little away from the flames.

As he did, Nancy tossed a pork rind aside, stood—hesitated to find the unison—then joined so the three of them spun together.

Richard clapped heavy hands to keep the beat, heaved to

standing in his odd way, and began massively revolving with them, half-humming, "Boom . . . boom . . . boom." So they all turned and turned, arms outstretched, sending long fire-shadows whirling across the mountain slope.

. . . So primitive a dance seemed to have been dance enough when morning came. Baj—smelling, he thought, at least a little better than before—noticed an easing of difference. Perhaps only an easing of his perception of difference, so Nancy seemed less changeable; Richard less remote. Errol remained as he had, a step aside.

It seemed to Baj, as breakfast pork was finished, and private morning shits were taken in the evergreens, that he appeared to be *living* a sort of epic poem, though with a farcical element. Perhaps too much of a farcical element—thoughtless arrogance turned to terrified flight—for serious poetry.

But good stories, perhaps to be told later. If there *was* a later.

. . . Down one wooded mountain . . . then up the next. By sun-overhead, Baj found he'd developed a permanent prejudice against up-and-down country. The River had flowed level, its banks had been level—even in flood—and it seemed that style of country was in his bones. Perhaps from his First-father's prairies as well. Level seemed . . . more sensible.

They chewed sliced ham as they climbed, drank from canteen and water-skins along the ridge, then stoppered them descending. Baj found the beauty of these steep places, a beauty greener with short summer's every day, their only compensation—at least at the pace Richard and Nancy set. But he kept up, buckskins a little stiff, a little tight.

"And we hurry," he said to the Made-girl—they were managing along a rough fracture-ledge with nothing beautiful about it, "—we hurry to get where?"

"To meet the Guard, campaigning in Shrike country," slightly lisping the word's beginning. *Thrike*.

"Ah . . . I see," Baj said, and was sorry he'd asked and been reminded. That tribe had been heard of even far west on the River—as ferocious, with a custom of impaling living men and women on tall, shaped spikes of ice (or sharpened wooden stakes in warmer weather) in imitation of their unpleasant totem bird. "Wonderful . . ."

Nancy grinned, reached over and patted his arm. His bitten arm—which now only itched.

There were odors—once they'd gotten off the cliff ledge— odors of wildflowers, of woods herbs just springing, sweeter than any Baj remembered. The River had smelled only of meltwater, and the traces men left in its currents. The coast woods also had had something of that dankness to them . . . which these mountain forests did not, their meadows certainly not, since they were carpeted with coming flowers. Pink lady's-shoe, Baj had seen before, and blossoming clover. But the others—yellows, tiny foliate azures—he wasn't sure of, perhaps had never noticed, if they grew in lowlands.

The perfume of those, when he crossed a clearing behind Richard's tireless padding, was delicate at first as if it were the sunlight's own odor, then grew stronger on a breeze.

In one such meadow—deeply slanting off a mountain's crest—Baj stopped with the others as if the grand view commanded their attention. Through the clear air of late afternoon, without even a sailing hawk or raven to mark the sky's cloud-tumbled blue, rank on rank of mountains—their slopes dark with spruce and hemlock forest—marched away for endless Warm-time miles.

"All those to be climbed, I suppose."

Richard looked back, smiling. "Not all, Baj."

"Only most," Nancy said, hitched her pack higher, and made what Baj had found to be her usual slight springing bound, that settled to swift walking. She led down off the meadow, where shaded worn stone hollows still held fragile traceries of snow, and Baj and Richard followed along. . . . Errol, traveling unusually close, skipped and hopped beside then behind them, sometimes stooping for pebbles to throw sidearm at nothing in particular.

* * *

Camped in early evening on a wide jutting shelf of stone almost halfway down a mountainside, Baj found his face and forehead hot with sun-burn—that light certainly striking harder at such heights. . . . He'd read of sun-burn, of course, knew that sailors on the Gulf Entire—and even more so farther south—might suffer it in the short summer.

He'd had windburn and weather-burn, of course, ice-boating on the river. But this sun-redness was new. . . . Another new thing.

Nearly the last of the wild boar's meat was supper, with spring onions and small dug roots, roasted at the fire's edge. . . . Then, sitting back from the green-wood flames, since they stung his sun-burned face, Baj watched as Nancy—humming a three-note tune—polished the blade of her scimitar with a scrap of leather.

He got up, tugged her long-handled hatchet free of a piece of cut firewood, and walked across the clearing to a stand of wind-bent spruce. . . . It took a while of choosing and chopping, then trimming to rough size, shape, and weight.

The light, though, was still fine enough when he came back to the fire. Fine enough, though tinted warm red as the sun sank.

"Here." Baj tossed Nancy a trimmed spruce branch—gluey with sap, sturdy, and curved—a coarse imitation of her sword. The branch he kept was straight, and almost limber.

He stepped away from the fire. "Now," he said to her, using the phrase the Master had used in the *salle*, "—come and kill me."

Alacrity was the perfect Warm-time word. Nancy sheathed her sword with alacrity, came to her feet with alacrity, and leaped over the fire and at him with alacrity, the curved stick in her hand.

She struck at him across and backhanded and across again almost too quickly to follow—whack whack *whack*—and she struck as hard as a wiry man might have. It was startling, and only endless practice over many years of shouted lessons, insults, and bruises allowed Baj to parry in *sixte*, *quarte*, and *septime*, while thinking how fast she was.

Even so, on her seventh or eighth blow, the curved stick glissaded up Baj's length of spruce to hit his fingers for lack of a guard. He riposted then, lunged extended, and struck her hard at the center of her chest as she came in swinging.

"You're dead," he said.

But apparently she was not, since she leaped at him snarling, sharp teeth bared, beating his "blade" aside, hacking with blurring speed, little splinters of spruce flying. It was an assault almost frightening. —Amusing, too, of course, the ferocity in a fairly delicate fox-girl face, its rooster comb of widow-peaked red hair.

Baj went back and back, giving before that furious rush—then suddenly dropped low to his right knee and left hand before her, so the girl lunged almost over him as he struck up hard, driving the end of his fencing stick just beneath her ribs.

"Dead a second time," he said, spinning up and away as she struck at him. "*Passata soto*. Never lose your temper when you fight."

He heard Richard say, "My, my . . ."

Her sharp face still a mask of rage, Nancy turned to come at him again—came quickly a few steps . . . then more slowly as she found she couldn't breathe.

Baj stepped back and back as she followed . . . and began to stumble. He saw her try again to catch her breath, then stand still, a hand at her throat, narrow face pale under that comb of bright hair.

Baj felt a first thread of worry that he'd struck too hard—struck too hard at a girl, and one whose body was not perfectly human. He felt that thread of worry, but while he felt it, a thousand practice afternoons had their way, and he stepped in with no hesitation, lunged, and drove his stick's tip hard where he supposed her heart must be.

"Dead a third time," he said. "Never, *never* lose your temper when you fight—and if you're hurt, don't just stand there. Back away . . . back away on guard to give yourself time to recover."

"*Fuck you* . . ." Even bent and wheezing-in little breaths, the girl had wind enough for that ancient WT phrase.

"We'll fight every evening," Baj said, surprised to be giving an order, "until you can do to me what I just did to you." Then, after receiving a savage yellow-eyed glance, added, "You're very fast—and strong. You're going to be dangerous with the sword."

That seemed to help. Did not, however, help his sore fingers, where her branch had slid up to strike them. —Discomfort continuing when Richard insisted on chess, took Baj's queen unfairly swiftly by firelight, then destroyed him and left his poor people slaughtered.

". . . I noticed," Richard said, tucking the little pieces back into their folding box, "I noticed your boots slowed you a little as you stepped. Once those are mountain-ruined, I'll sew moccasins for you."

"My boots do, so far."

Richard smiled, and tucked the chess set into his pack. " 'So far' is not far at all."

9

Patience was starving. Her sore belly's only relief was attention taken by the savage ache in her shoulder as she traveled the slope of a mountain in late after-noon.

She'd ground-walked east now for three days . . . going carefully over stone and scree, carefully past wooded heights so as not to stumble, fall on her slung left arm. She'd had to use her sheathed scimitar for a walking stick—and was wearing the scabbard's brass tip doing it.

So hungry—her gift of Walking-in-air having come at the cost of great appetite—she'd munched fresh pine-needles, chewed unfolding leaves from sapling beeches discovered in mountain draws and ravines . . . and looking for white grubs under fallen timber, had found a few handfuls of mushrooms instead. There'd been occasional run-off down the slopes she'd traveled, so her stomach, full of limestone water, had sloshed and rumbled.

It had been difficult to avoid bad dreams that might have frightened the baby, so her sleep had stayed fitful, full of intentional calm and simple stories, though she'd had no further visits from him. . . .

There'd been a wolverine that watched her from a rock-fall the evening before—no threat unless it lost its temper. And a mother black bear with two cubs the first morning—but digging for marmots so far upwind as not to notice her. Patience had seen no deer, had no way to take one if she had. . . . How easy it had been, how sure and easy to survey the country from the air. Then, seeing any squirrel, any rabbit, any grazing deer . . . to stoop down silent with a silent scimitar—though mindful of air-walking's necessary concentration—with only butchering and the cook-fire to accomplish afterward.

Passing time, attempting distraction from the agony of her shoulder's dislocation, she tormented herself by imagining meals—recalling them, happy to remember even mess-hall grub (wonderful old word) served by North Map-Mexico's army decades ago. . . . Those tin platters heaped with boiled pork and turnips. Turnips poorly peeled, but wonderful. And the army's rich barley loaves. Rich dark barley loaves . . . soaked in pork-fat gravy.

Patience wondered—so perfect was the recollection—whether some sustenance might not come from memories perfectly complete. If only so, she might reconstruct Boston's slow-cooked beans—simmered, with wild southern honey, in iron pots on bake-shops' great stoves with West Map-Virginia coal bright as sunshine in their bellies. Slow . . . slow cooking, while the stove's shimmering heat funneled up tall pipes into Boston's streaming icy air, its vaulted frozen heavens of blue ice and shining lamps. So, beans of course, and served with seal, lobster, or chard cakes. . . . She also remembered—to feed her spirit at least—venison sword-sliced from the air, butchered out still kicking, then its loin-chops and ribs roasted sputtering over southern hardwood, sprinkled with rough salt from the Ocean Atlantic.

Wonderful in recall—if so much simpler than the wedding feast at Island when she was a girl, where victory had lain smoking with bloody beef-steaks on silver platters, glass-grown vegetables of almost every kind, and cane-and-honey sweetened cakes, pastries, and pies of Kingdom apples and far-southern fruit from over the Gulf Entire. . . .

Her mouth filled with the saliva of imagination, Patience labored along, sometimes a little dizzy. If memories could serve, she would starve never. —But ground-walking in the present-now, and through tribal country, she didn't dare to linger even for the hope of a sometime rabbit, possibly snared with dark-blue thread from her clothes, twisted and set looped beneath a springing branch.

A throwing-stick was a perhaps for squirrel—would have been an almost certain, except she was left-handed. "Bad Goddamned luck," she said aloud, omitting even Mountain Jesus. The continual slope she walked along the mountain had her hobbling, with occasional awkward climbs over storm-blown trees and stony outcrops, as well as burrowing through vine tangles, berry bushes not yet bearing.

She had tried twice that day—as she'd tried the days before—to push the rocky ground away beneath and behind her. Tried and failed to clear her mind of grinding pain, so that rising in the air would be simple as taking a breath. . . . It was almost certain that she would have been able to do it, younger. Then, two—and even three concentrations had been possible for her, at least for short periods. Now, the pain upset all.

She'd failed both times—was frightened after the second attempt, as if to try and fail too often might spoil the talent-piece in her brain forever, and leave her walking the earth as long as she lived.

So she traveled as humans and most Persons did—as she'd done for casual Warm-time miles herself, years before—trudging on the ground, long coat-tails catching in thorn and thicket. Ground-walking really an awkward business, after all—seeming, each step, to lean to a fall . . . then catch oneself to step again. Clumsy as an only means, and stupid as starving to death, which she seemed likely to do.

Being down-wind had spared her the mother bear's attention two days before—and light-headed, weary, her shoulder burning as if a bright coal were buried in it, Patience found being down-wind useful again as, along an uneven slope, she smelled the faintest odor of wood smoke . . . then its companion odor of men.

She sniffed the air as an animal might—as any Person would—and sifted out three men, perhaps four. Men's pleasant, slightly bitter odor, but no woman's sweet and gluey scent. They were above her on the mountainside, just past its massive turning.

. . . There were considerations. First, the immediate of staying alive—she was left-handed, but her left arm was slung and useless.

She'd have to fight with her right, so not as well. Second, there being at least three of them, there was no chance of killing one and settling in peace to roast and eat him—sad though that disgusting meal would be for her purity, and upsetting to the baby if he sensed it. Third, their odor was steadily stronger; they were coming down-slope. And though they were Sunriser-humans, and could hardly scent at all, they could and would see any trail marked clearly as hers.

She might run along the mountain's scrub and rubble—or down into the thick stands of hemlock, to be hunted through the coming dark, hunted again in the morning. Or she could stand and talk—then fight if that must be. . . . Best, of course, would be to spurn this difficult earth, and Walk-in-air, with only curious ravens for company.

Patience stood still, closed her eyes—which she shouldn't have had to do—and tilted her head a little to one side . . . to pour and pour all thought, all consideration out of it, leaving only room for pushing the ground from beneath her.

She felt . . . she certainly felt the beginning of that wonderful vacancy . . . emptiness enough to fill with a single purpose. But still an edge of Patience Nearly-Lodge Riley stayed anchored, fastened to the fact of an agonized shoulder. No matter what trying—mind-dodging this way and that—there was not the singleness and simplicity of setting her mind against the ground, to refuse it, shove it down and away so she rose into the air. . . . It would have been done, but the damaged shoulder ached to stay.

Patience felt the mountain stone still firm beneath her boots, and opened her eyes to evening light and trouble.

. . . Four men, and closer. Tribesmen, by their weather-washed, smoke-stained scent. If they'd been speaking, not hunting, she would already be hearing their voices.

* * *

The Robins' Thoughtful-man, Paul French, occasionally said, "Surprise."

Meaning, of course, that the world, packed with things unknown, was often startling—even discounting the secrets women knew.

The Robins' War-leader, Chad Budnarik, always added, "Response," meaning a man—who was a man—met surprises with speed, force, and modest good sense.

These sayings were not in Pete Aiken's mind on Wild-plum Mountain, but *came* to mind on seeing the lady—of Boston unmistakably by her coat, her style, her curved sword and everything.

No one could say that a Pete-led posse didn't swiftly respond. The notion of hunting immediately thrown away, the notion of killing-or-capturing immediately in its place.

So down the mountainside went Pete Aiken; down the mountainside went Lou and Gerald and Gerald's brother, Patrick. The Boston-woman—a sort of Person for sure, who for sure had not walked far in these Robin mountains—did not rise up into the air, but limped and scuttled like a wounded bobcat down to the hemlocks.

"Ours!" Pete called, and led them down—then ducked since Gerald's brother, running behind, had thrown a javelin . . . sent it hissing barely over everyone's head.

The javelin went nowhere near the Boston-woman, but she ducked away as if it had . . . and was gone, tucked into the stands of evergreens.

"Never again," Pete said, which was taken to mean he wouldn't go hunting with Gerald's brother, anymore. Pete had his hatchet out—better for tangled fighting—so everyone else gripped theirs, and followed him into the hemlocks, calling, *"Yoiks . . . yoiks!,"* an habitual humorous thing that was called after something seen, then treed or dug into a den—the Robins being usually a light-hearted people.

* * *

Deep in the trees, dark under tree-shadow, Patience stood waiting, wishing for sooner night, her greatcoat's blue blending into shade. She'd drawn her sword, *Merriment*, whose slim curved blade—forged so raindrops seemed to dance and run along it—had killed for her for more than twenty years. It had been a gift from her mother, presented perhaps as apology. Perhaps as anger, also, at Boston's womb-shaping of her daughter.

With the next birth, her mother had died.

... The Robins seemed a noisy four, young, cheerful, and confident in their mountain country at the corner of old Map-Kentucky. Patience smelled them, heard them coming in, and caught a distant glimpse of one—then another—between shaggy hemlocks. Presentable young men, lean-muscled, with cropped curly beards and mustaches, and already becoming summer-tanned, possessing the gloss and glow that well-fed savages sported while young. They'd be thickly scarred up and down their bare chests and bellies in sinuous feather-and-plumage patterns, to honor their totem. . . . None would go naked as Sparrows and Thrushes often went. These all would be wearing—as those she'd glimpsed were wearing—the mid-east tribes' leather kilts and strap sandals. The hunt leader likely sporting a headdress of feathers dyed robin's-egg blue.

"*Lou! Try in there.*" That called in fair book-English. Better, at least, than what the tribesmen chattered a Map-State to the south.

One—"Lou"?—was coming ducking through evergreen branches directly toward her . . . perhaps following a faint trail of disturbed foliage.

Regretting her slung left arm, Patience tightened her right-hand's grip on the scimitar's hilt . . . and slowly raised the blade high, cocked it slightly over her shoulder. The odor of evergreens seemed to grow almost overpowering. . . .

The Robin came on, making more woods-noise than he would

have if a deer or armed man were waiting. Or if he were older, and wise.

One of his friends called, a distance through the trees.

The young man, almost certainly "Lou," stepped stooping through the thicket . . . was close enough to almost touch—and saw her standing nearly beside him as he started to straighten.

As always, in her experience of those moments, Patience felt time's sudden winter, a moment's freezing, slow, and difficult to strike through. The young man—blue eyes startled as a frightened child's—crouched for some purpose, perhaps to leap away, then raise his hatchet or javelin for fighting.

Patience saw, as he saw in their shared instant, that would not be possible. *Merriment* seized her arm's strength, and the sword whipped down before either of them was quite ready, sliced the young man across his eyes—it seemed to Patience he died to his world then, died blind even before the second . . . and third thrumming strokes left him spouting, shaking in place without his head, before he toppled.

"Farewell, Lou," Patience said—and almost hidden beneath green hemlock fronds on the forest's floor, the head's mouth trembled as if to answer.

Death, though not noisy, had somehow echoed through the woods, and the other Robins were silent as Patience was silent. Then—as if killing had given them its direction—they came booming, leaping through greenwood toward their dead friend, while Patience fled.

. . . Boston had never preached to praise the night; though perhaps the Productive Mothers, in their pens, welcomed darkness to shroud the remembered sight of their odd or ruined children. Still, Patience composed her own prayers for nightfall while she ran, insistent as if she had every right to demand the whole world go rolling faster. She begged the Mountains' Jesus and Kingdom River's Floating One; she offered what she didn't have to Lady Weather—intending to pay that debt later—while every stride, every leap over winter-fallen timber was a knife-thrust into her shoulder.

The three men came after her, tracking fast, bird-calling back and forth to keep their interval. They hadn't paused at Headless Lou.

Only the mountainside's broken country in dimming light, the tangled rough here-and-there of the thick hemlock grove, gave Patience chances to pause . . . scent the men's quarterings on errant breezes, then scramble in the other direction. Once or twice, she doubled back to almost meet them—so they passed her by WT yards as she crouched panting quietly as she could, mouth open, her eyes closed as if to see was to be seen.

After a while, exhausted—by hunger even more than pain— she become a dreaming girl again, full of wishes. She imagined Sam Monroe had come to stand beside her in the dusk, amused, liking her as he always had through every exasperation. If he were alive, he would come to help her in just that way. Not as a king, but as the war-worn young man she'd met in the Sierra those many years ago. His hard face, kind eyes, the long-sword strapped down his back.

He—and others, if they were alive—would have come to aid her. It seemed unfair that mere death should keep her from her friends.

Night was falling with the last of sunset's shadows, their darker shade amid the hemlocks, but would not come quite soon enough. Patience was running her last run along the top of an embankment choked with toppled great trees—dredged out and thrown down by the mountain's spring flooding years before. The bark was rotting from huge logs piled confused as if the Lady and Lord Winter played there at pickup sticks.

The men were close behind her; Patience could hear their swift steps through the trash.

Soon to be caught. Then a fight—and perhaps another Robin killed before they hacked her down.

She slowed . . . slowed to turn to meet them—and saw amid the splintered tumble of ruined trees below, a possible spoiled hollow. She thought it was a shadow, then thought not—and leaped out into the air to fall thudding into timber . . . rolled off some rough round and fell again through jumbled stacks of trunks and branches, her shoulder a lance of agony flashing in her mind white as washed wool.

When she lay still, bark-burned and bleeding, her scabbarded sword's belt twisted and turned beneath her, Patience took time for only one difficult breath . . . then crawled deeper into the wreckage, crawled beaten and bruised as if her back were broken, to where she'd seen the hollow. She sought through descending night . . . and heard the Robins' chirps and whistles above, as they trotted searching along the embankment's edge.

She crawled and clambered—then saw the dark hollow, its massive log-end angled between two smaller broken trees. Gritting her teeth against groans, Patience struggled over the lowest log—and found the hollow just above her. She reached up, right-handed, into its dark crumbling space . . . hauled herself half into it . . . and had to shake her left arm out of its sling to aid.

Then, with pain past pain filling her mind like an icy ocean, Patience used both arms—left shoulder twisting in and out of joint with soft crunching, brilliant blazes of agony—used both arms to drag herself up and into a rough, narrow space, rotted deep. Cramped so each breath was half-measure, she wriggled deeper into the great log, scabbarded sword scraping, snagging to haul at its belt, then jolting free. She inched farther into darkness, into shredding damp and spoil. Blood ran in her mouth from lips bitten for silence . . . and she finally lay satisfied to die there, if promised never to be found.

. . . Through Warm-time hours poorly counted, Patience lay rough-shrouded in the dark, drifting and dreaming around a core of molten metal searing in her shoulder. She dreamed of her first sight of Max—then tiny, fat, red and slippery with juice and blood. . . . And she'd known in that instant. Though so small, he'd still lain heavy as a man on her breast, crushing the air from her lungs. His eyes had been closed, but he'd watched her through the lids.

"He sees me," she'd said.

"But makes no sound." Woodrow Cabot-Lodge, slender and handsome, had leaned over as if he loved her, though no member of Cambridge Council was permitted that, even one appointed to sire a result upon her. . . . Still, Patience had been certain he *liked* her—as who would not, and she so pretty? So clever.

"He will never speak, Woody," Patience had said, and knew it, though she didn't know why.

". . . *Never speak,*" Patience said, waking in her hollowed log. She took the fullest breath she could, and decided to live at least another day.

Morning would be surely . . . surely near. Time to begin to wriggle carefully back and back through rotting punk, paying the price in pain . . . then finally out into dawn's light and air. Another day or two would pass before the shoulder and starvation left her only lying down to do, to wait for death.

The Robin boys, having hunted through the dark and missed her, might be gone from the hemlocks—but not likely. They'd almost certainly be waiting along the forest's lower edge for vengeance, having lost poor Lou.

* * *

Pete Aiken woke first—had had no fire—rolled from a bed of hemlock boughs in his place at the bottom of the stand of trees, skin goose-pimpled in dawn's chill.

He trilled a territory warble. Heard no reply to east or west, and called again. . . . Then, Gerald answered from the east. But only silence from Gerald's brother—an idiot, and certainly sleeping through sunrise.

Pete stretched till his joints cracked, eased his muscles from a cold night's sleep, then picked up javelin and hatchet, and paced deeper into the hemlocks to shit. . . . The Boston-woman would have to come their way—or climb Wild-plum Mountain to its crest and over, deeper into Robin country.

She would have to come their way soon, come down through the bottom of the stand—or stay among the trees to lick mist from hemlock fronds for water, chew hemlock bark for food. She wouldn't even have sad Lou to eat. Gerald had brought out body and head last evening, both now safe under stacked stone.

Pete found a place, set his legs apart, tucked his kilt well up, and squatted. Paused, peed a little, then the first of healthy poop—a must, according to Charlotte-doctor. "Bad poop, bad health." She claimed that was Copybook, though what copybook she wouldn't say.

Pete took a breath, strained for the rest—and felt the lightest thread of coolness lie across the back of his neck. He thought it some dawn spider-web strand . . . then the coolness cut him, just a little.

Squatting, Pete turned his head, and saw a curving length of steel shining along his nape. . . . Above it, a small, trembling, white-haired woman stood in a dirty blue coat.

He tensed to move—dive left to his hatchet, resting so casual on the forest floor. But the sword above him, as if eager on its own, slid deeper across the back of his neck, so he felt blood begin to run.

"Do I hold your life at my sword's edge, or do I not?" Her voice shook as she shook, and Pete didn't answer.

Drawn very slightly across . . . the steel's edge sliced deeper.

"Is your life in my gift, or is it not? . . . I won't ask again."

Pete, who hadn't intended to answer an old woman who'd

taken unfair advantage, surprised himself by saying, "Yes."

"Yes . . .?"

"My life . . . a gift." And having said so, regretted saying it—and wouldn't have, except for being caught like some child, shitting. Squatting for this Boston thing to creep up, lay her sword across his neck. . . . He wouldn't have said it, but for that.

Cold steel lifted from him, left his nape warm with trickling blood.

"Wipe your bottom," the woman said—and Pete Aiken-Robin, tears of rage gathered in his eyes, took a handful of foliage to use, then threw that aside, stood up, stepped away and straightened his kilt's leather.

The woman, her left arm slung across her breast, was pale as cracked quartz, and swayed as she stood. She wiped her sword's curved edge on her coat, and managed at a second try to sheath it. "I've taken the life of one Robin," she said, "and given yours in return, so no debt remains. By that exchange . . . I claim a trader's hospitality."

Pete heard Gerald coming through the trees.

"Now," the woman said, her eyes black as blindness, "—now we will see if honor roosts with the Robins." And she staggered and fell into the hemlocks as if she were struck and dying.

10

After days of hard travel, and chess-and-fencing evenings, their camp was made back of a ridge overlooking a stretch of low country at last—New River's Valley, Richard had called it. Baj was happy enough to lie resting after eating most of a partridge, the birds taken by Errol's thrown sticks one by one, as they strutted a long hollow, furiously drumming for mates.

The successful hunter, pinched face so dirty no freckles showed, lay with his head on Baj's lap, making faint clicking noises. The boy seemed to have grown comfortable with him.

Baj was satisfied with ease, but Nancy apparently was not, came around the fire to poke and prod him with a makeshift wooden scimitar—the third of those, the first two having been beaten to flinders in attempts at murder.

"Nancy, another evening's rest might be a good idea."

"You said, 'When I can do to you.' "

"You can 'do to me' tomorrow."

No answer, then, but poke poke, prod prod.

"For the love of Mountain Jesus . . ." Baj shifted Errol, and got to his feet to get his spruce-stick rapier—worn and splintered, but usable a last time.

Richard, propped on one massive odd elbow, lay by the fire, smiling. "Lessons," he said, and Errol went to sit cross-legged near him, attentive.

Before this audience, Baj eased muscles stiffened by the day's mountainsides—and was attacked in mid-stretch. He brought his stick-sword up so nearly in time it seemed unfair that her whistling cut went over it and across his jaw hard as a whip's lash.

Baj spun away in considerable numbing pain, and supposing he should be thankful she hadn't taken an eye out, set himself to fighting. The girl was . . . truly fast. There was no time—had been no time the last two lessons to wait to parry on the *forte*. The blows of her spruce scimitar—shorter, snappier strokes in direct attack, now, and delivered in series—needed to be caught early, near his stick's limber end, and allowed then in yielding parry to slide down to a firmer ward where the spruce was thicker. . . . It required elegant fencing.

Required easy movement, too. Stance'y *salle* fencing with Person-Nancy was a losing notion; she circled and struck, circled and struck—and was pleased to close in *corp a corp*, where she seemed to want to bite as she slashed, then stepped away, leaving behind her faint vulpine scent.

"Timing," Baj said, as they fought. "Timing, speed," he beat in second, lunged to her outside low line and hit her, "—and distance."

"Shit." She tried to bind his spruce-blade, tried to kick him in the crotch. Baj found it . . . interesting. He was learning about Nancy—learning perhaps about other Persons, too, as he and the girl grunted and fought around the fire. Stop-thrusts no longer worked against her; she would *attack* swinging aside *in quartata*, lunging off the front foot. An absolutely awkward move that cost him bruises until he learned to simply mirror her motion, so her cut passed him.

They were . . . it was very much like dancing together, but with steps swift, harsh, and unexpected. As the Master would have recommended, he watched those quick little moccasined feet shift and shift, watched for balance and rhythm change—and watched her yellow eyes for surprises, often betrayed by anticipatory glee.

They circled and battled in clattering noise and a haze of human sweat—and sweat slightly different—despite the chill of evening. Richard and Errol, an audience of two, sat entertained by thrusts, curses, slashes, bruises and occasional little stippled lines of blood.

Nancy caught Baj very nicely in the shoulder with her point— the scimitar's point apparently beginning to occur to her after previous evenings' furious cuts and slashes. He took the hit, said, "I'm hurt," spun into her, "—and you're dead."

"*How?*"

He prodded her lean belly with a short stick he'd stuck in his belt, awaiting the occasion. "Left-hand dagger. Always remember the left hand. Always remember *knives*. Don't be so fucking sword-proud." The Master would have been pleased to have his quote repeated—advice original with the dead and honored Butter-boy.

"Not *fair!*" Very angry, her crest of widow-peaked red hair risen like a cock's comb.

"All is fair," Baj said, "—in love, and war." It was the perfect Warm-time phrase, and Nancy Some-part-fox had no answer for it.

"How many years," Richard said, "—how many years to learn such nice use of points? My soldiers were rarely so elegant in sticking . . . chopping."

"Eleven . . . twelve years."

"I will not need twelve years." Nancy tossed her frayed stick-sword aside and sat by the fire on a folded blanket.

"No." Baj held his hands to the flames to warm them as the night's chill settled down. Bruised fingers, bruised hands from fencing with no cross-hilts or guards. No gloves, either. "No, you're very quick. But be warned; I haven't taught you nearly all *I* was taught, and there are men—women, too—who would find me easy to kill with a blade."

"Perhaps dear Patience Riley," Richard said, "—who fought the fat man in the air."

Baj recalled the woman's amusement when he'd touched his dagger's hilt by starlight. "I suppose so . . . yes. She perhaps could kill me."

"Soon," Nancy lay down to sleep, "—soon *I* will be able to kill you."

"Not until you remember better that a scimitar has a point to go with its edge." Baj spread his blanket, that smelled so warmly of goat and wood smoke. "Not until you remember that it's the first two or three WT inches of any blade that does most of the work. And not until you remember the left hand's dagger."

. . . Baj, lying down, tugging a fold of blanket over him, couldn't imagine what copybook "imp of perversity," what odd urge to anger her possessed him, that he added, "And likely not even then, since you're a girl."

Silence.

He looked across the failing fire, saw Richard's heavy-muzzled face a mask of comic apprehension.

Still . . . silence. But through eddying smoke, Baj saw burning yellow eyes.

* * *

In the morning, as he stood behind a fractured boulder, pissing, Baj heard the big Made-man's soft heavy step.

"Brave boy," Richard said, came to stand beside, unlaced to produce a dark peculiar cock, and relieved himself. "Brave boy," he said. "She must like you, despite your smell."

"And you know that, how?" Baj shook himself and fastened up.

"I know it, because you woke this morning with no tooth-marks on your throat."

They went back to the camp smiling, though were not met with smiles. "Robin country," Nancy said, "before and behind. No country for traveling fools."

At mid-morning, halfway down a wooded draw, Richard stopped, shrugged his pack off, and squatted in his odd way, waiting for them to catch up. When Errol trotted on to pass him, the big Person reached out, caught his dirty wool shirt, and held him still.

"Now, listen to me." Richard's great double-bitted ax lay

across his knees, and he absently tested its keeness with a thumb. "I was a Captain of Boston's Guard, and know the country we're coming to—still Robin country, high and low, where the Wall's spring melt has run the New River wider. . . . Then mountains east again, and soon along Map The-Valley-Shenandoah."

"I know those places," Nancy said, "from coming south."

"—This east corner of Map-Kentucky is Robin country," Richard said, "and will be their country in lowland and the first few mountains after, in Map West-Virginia, as on the oldest copied Exxons. . . . We've kept our fires reverse of the ridges the last two nights—but from now on, no fires. If their light didn't reveal us, their smoke-smell might."

"Cooking . . . ?" Baj eased his pack off, and sat cross-legged in an alder's delicate summer shade.

"You must learn raw meat, Baj."

"Very well."

Nancy, leaning on a sapling's slender trunk, made a sound in her throat.

"—I'll do what needs to be done."

Another throat sound.

"I don't care what meat I eat," Baj said. "But I do care where we go, and why, and the achievement-how. You've said Shrikes, the Person Guard, and the purpose a secret. . . . The Boston-woman told me that was for her to know, for me to find out. Well, I want to find it out now. I'm tired of climbing mountains on only the *promise* of harm to Boston."

Richard stared at him. "What we intend is not to be talked of, except to Persons—and Sunriser-humans too—who will accomplish it. You know *accomplish*?"

"I know it. I've read more and better than you, Richard. Words are close to me."

"No life," Nancy said, "—not even yours, *Good Reader*, is worth this being talked of so Boston knows it."

"I'm here," Baj said, "—whether you like it or not. I have my brother's blood, our friends' blood to answer to, and not to either of you."

Richard hummed a considering hum, deeper than most. "Baj, if you should in any way endanger this . . . even inadvertently, say by merest mention to any we might chance to meet going north—I'll kill you."

"Fair enough."

". . . Very well. To come at it . . . Robins are the most many, and the most uncertain of the tribes. They claim to be the old Cherokee, though very few Red-bloods still rule them. They are people who can't be trusted, since they hate hard among themselves, though their daughters—chief's daughters, usually, and the daughters of other important men—have also been taken by the Guard campaigning south from time to time, as even down in Map-Tennessee, the Thrushes and Sparrows have lost girls to Boston."

"Took my mother," Nancy said.

Listening, Errol made a soft squealing sound, a noise with nothing human in it.

"Took mine, also," Richard said. "Made me, and kept her."

"The tribes' women taken, used, then some held in Boston?"

"Foolish boy," Nancy said. "*All* held, that live."

"How else?" Richard tapped the steel of his ax's head with a curved horny nail. "How else hold the tribes at bay, and keep Boston's Guard obedient—but by holding dear mothers, dear sisters, dear daughters hostage?"

"But you deserted."

Richard, squatting hunched and massive, stared at Baj with small brown eyes half-buried in a shelf of brow—and seemed no longer friendly Richard. . . . A little time passed that seemed a long time, so Baj regretted forgetting advice from the Master. "If trouble might come, don't let it catch you sleeping or sitting on your ass."

But Richard seemed to ease, and said, "My mother, Shrike Tall-Edna, cut her throat in the Pens with a broken cup to free me."

". . . Then," Baj said, and had to clear his throat, "—then Lady Weather bless that brave woman."

Richard nodded and seemed satisfied.

"—So," Baj said, "the Person Guard serves Boston with no choice *but* serving, since the city holds a number of their mothers hostage."

"All who live once breeding is done." Nancy showed her teeth. "Not so very many. But Boston holds those, and keeps their names and numbers secret so no Guardsman or tribal chief knows if his loved one lives or not. Boston holds them—and frees them never."

"My mother," Richard said, "—sent me word of her promised self-killing by a Faculty Instructor who owed a favor. Else I would never have known it."

"Still, the tribes . . ."

"Our mothers," Nancy said, "—are their daughters, so both Persons *and* tribesmen are knotted to Boston town by loved one's lives."

"And the Persons' own children . . .?"

"Those," Richard said, "—Boston also takes for itself. Though many of us . . . many cannot have children at all."

Baj said, into silence, "But the woman who Walked-in-air—Patience."

"From her, Baj," Richard said, "—they hold her child."

"The fools hoped they'd made a God-baby at last," angry Nancy lisping the *s*'s into *th*'s, "—to push the turning earth closer to the sun, and bring Warm-times back again."

"That is . . . not possible."

"So I think." Richard nodded. "For a few New England Talents to manage through the air is one thing. But greater than that, they don't have in them."

"They have shit in them," Nancy said. "And Patience's baby is only a dreamer—though a great one, dreaming forward and back."

"So . . . Boston rules the East by holding hostages from both fathers *and* sons."

"See how a Once-prince knows the means." Nancy spat into shrubbery.

". . . I'm sure," Baj said, "that my Second-father understood Boston's way. The Chancellor, and my brother also. But knowing those bonds—and breaking them—are two different things."

"But with the mothers dead," Richard said, "—who are also daughters dead—then the bonds are broken for Persons *and* the tribes."

Errol, restless, tried to tug away, but Richard kept hold of him, made soothing *puh puh* sounds as the boy settled.

"Which is why we travel so far north and east, Clever Fencer." Nancy seemed to smile at Baj, but wasn't smiling. "—We go to join Shrikes *and* the Guard, their peace made to march together against Boston. A great revenge for you as well, Sunriser."

Richard sighed as if he were very tired. ". . . While the Guard attacks the city's southern and easiest gate—an attack sure to fail, and only to draw all regiments of the town Constables there— Patience will lead us and a few others down the north gate, then across Boston to the Pens. . . . There, in what time the Constables allow us, we are to break *all* loving bonds."

Baj took a breath. ". . . *Kill* them? Kill the women?"

Silence, but for gentle winds through summer leaves. Silence . . . that most definite of answers.

* * *

After hours of descending—Baj with scrapes and bruises from a nasty fall—after those weary hours into late after-noon, hanging half the time from stunted tree to tree, they'd reached the first long level of young grasses, wild flowers in meadows stretching along the stream. Baj's legs had said, "Thank you," as he strode at last with no climbing up or down. He'd slid his bow off his shoulder, drew a broadhead from the quiver at his back in case of game here, on the valley's plain. . . . But no game came grazing as they walked to the river named New. Only a red-shouldered hawk swung slow circles above, beyond any arrow's reach.

It was surprising how the sight and sound of the stream affected him—a fair-sized *river*, not simply tumbling mountain waterfalls—a river running in roaring rapids from short-summer's melt, roiling, glittering along. It struck Baj's heart. . . . Memories of so much greater a river, of the Mississippi swollen by centuries of summers' melts from half-a-continent of ice, came to him so he stood dreaming.

The others stood beside him, though recollection of no great river could be running through their hearts. This lesser brawling stream, carving through green country—with, of course, more mountains to climb just beyond it—might it support some lesser Jesus, floating with its currents? . . . Baj, breathing deep of air with river-haze risen in it, felt sick with longing for great water's smell and currents, for the sway of the deck of a summer sailing-boat beneath his feet . . . the slide, speed, and rumble of ice-rigged ships before the River's wind.

For the first time since he'd fled before the king, he found a poem forming in his mind, as if a dam of clotted timbers had been shaken loose by rapids. But the better the poem might be—of loss and the River—the more painful to make and remember. . . . Better pass in silence, than examine wounds with a burning-glass.

"How do we cross this?" he said.

"With great care." Richard untied the thick coil of braided-leather line from his pack. Shook the coil open.

"No easier ford?"

"Likely, yes—but two or three days east, and deeper into the Robins' country."

"It was frozen," Nancy said, "—when we came south."

"This can be managed," Richard said, kept an end of his line, and knotted the other around Errol's waist. "It might be otter blood, not weasel, the boy swims so well—seems to mind only water falling."

"I see." But that thundering stream, though not toppling in a fall, appeared to Baj to be very difficult swimming.

Richard climbed down to a leaning birch . . . and tied the line's end off in a double knot while Errol, appearing eager, trot-ted away a distance upstream with the coil, loosing the length as he went. Then, reaching the line's other end, the boy suddenly galloped down the river's bank there, and dove into the roil of water . . . his knives still in his belt, and still wearing his moccasin-boots.

"Not good," Baj said.

Richard came back up the bank. "Watch . . ."

But there was nothing to watch, except once or twice a flash of slender black line looping through foaming white water. . . . Then, almost halfway across, the river there divided by boulders fountaining up sheets of spray, Errol's head appeared—blond hair slicked dark and flat—was shaken so drops flew, then vanished again. This time, Baj could follow him, and saw here and there un-der shallow racing current the boy frog-kicking . . . frog-kicking, but very swiftly, then seeming to writhe along through and under the river, *with* the river, coming downstream with it at an angle toward the opposite bank, the braided line wavering in and out of sight behind him.

"Wonderful," Baj said, thinking that otter blood *was* possible there.

. . . Errol had almost reached the other side. His shadow lay in swift shallows like a weary char at breeding. He seemed to rest, then raised his head, shook water from his hair again, and crawled out onto the pebbles, apparently weary, no longer magically swift and sure.

"I cross next," Richard said, once the boy had tied his line-end to a tree almost directly across from them. "If the rope holds me, it will hold you two." Baj heard the big Person's belly rumble. Hungry, of course—as they all were. Though occasional birds were well enough, it was long past time for the promised deer.

. . . A crossing easier said than done—an ancient phrase, and one of the most useful. Baj and Nancy stood on a trembling bank of mud and stone, and watched Richard in the current.

His pack left behind, he still seemed to wear one, his back humped with muscle, his loose shirt soaked so drifts of dark hair—or fur—showed through as he fought the river in sheets of spray, going on all fours over stone through shallow furious rapids. Held beside him, the slender braided line whipped and looped over and under swift water.

The river's noise was surprising. There seemed to be shouting in it, a mob's raised voices. Only at Break-up had Baj heard the Mississippi speak—then, and in places where it struck Island's stone walls.

Richard had battered his way half-over—more than half-over, when he slipped. Nancy shouted *"No!"*

He slipped at a boulder—lost the line—then just caught himself, gripping a smaller rounded stone, the river striking him in a wide bright fan of fast water then streaming around and over him like silvered glass. He'd caught himself, but did not get his feet back under him.

Then it was the river against Richard. And while Richard stayed and wasn't swept away, he did no more. Crouched, clinging, he held on—and it seemed to Baj, couldn't shift his grip without losing it.

Baj said, "Absolutely foolish," speaking to himself as he

dropped his pack and pulled off his boots—poor boots, too, soles worn almost through by damned mountains. "... Absolutely foolish." He unbuckled his sword-belt, let it fall, and ran down the bank to the leaning birch the line was knotted to. He heard a *"Don't!"* from Nancy—gripped the wet leather, braided no thicker than a man's thumb, and stumbled, slid, and half-dove into the river.

"Floating Jesus!" The cold gripped him, and the smashing weight of water.

Baj-who-was-Bajazet, a son of great men, will be swept away to die with a thoughtful part-bear—and only two other oddities will live to know it.

He would have been gone in an instant and swiftly drowned but for the rawhide line. It sawed his hands, sawed his side when it looped that way in rapids, but he loved it dearly and wouldn't let it go.

The odd thing was how shallow the river ran over these boulders and shelves of stone—no deeper than his waist, if he could have stood. Wonderfully clear water where it wasn't foam—every pebble beneath perfectly seen. Clear water, the great glacier's milk not yet descended.

It picked up Baj's feet—stockings stripped away at once—and took them out from under him, bannered them away downstream so he clung to the bowing line, and that only. There was no getting to his feet again. The river—New River, as Richard had called it—would not let him.

"Move, or die." It was a voice he knew, and only after hand-over-handing sideways along the rawhide ... slowly out into deeper rolling currents ... did he recognize it as his own.

No getting to his feet. No looking either way. Only his left hand slid left ... his right hand slid to follow it. Cold hands that grew colder as he moved along so slowly, fast water hammering his face and beating his breath away.

After a while that seemed a long while, Baj was no longer

certain he could feel his hands. Thrashed and spun this way and that in the rapids, afraid his numb grip might loosen and let him go—he slowly drew himself up against the current, the most difficult thing . . . most difficult thing. Felt the wet line against his face for a moment. Felt it snap against his face again, opened his mouth to pouring water and braided leather, and bit down hard.

So by hands and teeth he held on. And was able to slowly work one hand's fingers at a time—or thought he worked them—clenching, unclenching in a dream of noise and cold and motion.

Then he opened his mouth to let the line snap free, but still gripped it in his hands—better hands, now—and began again that slow sliding to the left. One hand, then another. . . . Began that, and dreamed he would do it to the other bank, and grow warmer all the time, though the river furled and unfurled him like a banner.

He woke to a shout like a big dog's bark, turned his buffeted head to the left, and saw, amid fountaining sheets becoming rainbows, Richard's soaked heavy-browed face, the thick shoulders awash.

Then, it was the simplest of things. Hook a right elbow over the whipping line . . . let go with the left hand . . . and give the hand into Richard's almost-paw like a gift, so the Person—with that slight additional purchase—made one great heaving motion, caught a rock's definite edge, and hauled himself up to the rawhide to grip it and begin to crawl to the left again, forging a way to the riverside, Baj laboring behind him.

. . . When they stood, sodden and exhausted, on the north bank of New River—Errol already gone to sleep in thick grass beside them—Nancy, on the south bank, a loop of the braided leather knotted around her waist, was busy gathering the three packs and their weapons—the sheathed blades, Richard's ax, and Baj's bow and quiver—into a single very large and ungainly bundle, and lashing it four-square with doubled knots at the rope's end.

"Mistake. The current," Baj said, and cupped his hands to shout. " . . . *It's too big! Tie the packs . . . tie those separately along the line!*" A call quite useless against the river's noise.

"Too fucking big!" Baj and Richard scrambled down the bank to take hold of the rope to haul her across.

Nancy, prepared, seemed to still hesitate.

"Afraid of noisy water," Richard said.

"She went through the waterfall."

"Not the dangerous same."

The girl stood on the opposite bank, the awkward bundle—big as she was—lying at the line's end a few feet behind her.

"It's going to—that load's going to swing downstream as she comes over!"

"Yes, it is." Richard wrapped both hands around the line. Baj stood a little behind him.

Across the river, Nancy appeared to make up her mind . . . stepped carefully down the bank as if the river might rise up to seize her . . . then in a rush ran into the current.

She struck the water, went under, turned and seemed to tug at the tied bundle, so it came heavily toppling down after her and into the river.

Then the girl was swimming, and Baj saw she swam as a frightened puppy might, straining, her head up, paddling in roiling crashing waters.

"*Now . . . !*" Richard heaved back on the line, Baj with him, and the braided leather rose whipping out of the rapids, dipped under again . . . then up, dripping, water squeezed spraying out of it along its length.

Baj saw Nancy's white face amid white water—saw the heavy bundle behind her bob free of some obstruction and begin to drift faster and faster downstream.

Nancy was drawn under.

"No good," Baj said. "No good."

"*Pull . . .*"

"*No good!*"

Halfway across, Nancy seemed to come no closer . . . then began to drift a little downstream with the rapids, downstream after the tumbling bundle at the line's end. Her hands splashed in that desperate paddle.

"The rope's tied off! It'll hold!" Richard heaved on the line, grunting with effort.

"Hold to pull her in drowned!" The river noise seemed louder. "The *packs* . . ." Baj let go of the rope and ran back up the bank. Errol, awake, was sitting cross-legged, watching Nancy in the river.

"Knife!" Baj reached down and drew a blade from Errol's belt, then turned and ran down and into the river, reaching up left-handed to hold the line.

The current—snaking around and past him with such pouring weighty strength and bitter cold—now seemed familiar, a dangerous discomfort, but not dreadful.

He couldn't see Nancy through battering spray and foam, and trusted to the slender slippery line—stretching under strain, and sooner or later bound to snag on sharp rock and part—trusted that to bring him to her. He dragged himself along, half swimming, half kicking over rounded rock and scattering pebbles in the flow, and shouted to her—but couldn't hear himself.

Water smashed into his left ear as if a man had struck him with a fist of ice. The pain lanced through, and Baj ducked his head away as the line yanked at him . . . yanked again, streaming away with the river's flow.

Then Baj went faster, skidded down along the line, glimpsed trees—on which bank he didn't know—and struck large stones with elbows and knees. The river tried to turn him, roll him over and away and off the braided leather. His left hand was burning where he gripped it—burning with the only heat there was in a world of cold.

He heaved up, gasping for a breath in sheets of spray—slid down the line with the river, and struck a softer thing than stone.

A narrow hand . . . wiry arms came round to grapple, and Baj felt the girl's lean smallness buckle to him—saw as they both rose riding a spume of water, her face contorted with terror, and called "*I have you, sweetheart. . . .*" By which he meant nothing personal.

They spun and rode together, and Baj kicked to try to turn them so she struck no rocks. He saw a flashing in the surf, and was surprised to see the knife still in his right hand. It reminded him what it was for, and as they whirled along, Baj steadied with that motion, didn't fight against it—and in the spinning through foam and noise, reached quite easily behind the girl, found the whip end of the line tugging . . . tugging them along, and sliced the bundle free.

. . . Then, much easier, the taut leather stretching from distant Richard by a distant tree, they slowly struggled swinging nearer and nearer to that bank, until Baj got to his feet—bare feet with no feeling—stood battered by crashing water . . . and step by step, the girl clinging, aiding, marched through shallower clear streaming water to pebbles and the sand.

. . . They found the pack-bundle by nearly night, stranded on a stony bar two miles downstream, only a fairly dangerous swim from the north bank. Errol went and roped it for hauling over.

All was there, Nancy'd knotted it together so tight and well. All there—though soaked as the arrows' fletching—and needing a drying fire, the steel blades wiped and tallowed.

* * *

That night, aching and bruised in exhausted sleep, Baj dreamed not of water, but of his First-mother, though he'd never known her, though she'd been murdered when he was a baby—murdered as it was now intended for other mothers to be murdered. The details, in his dream, were vaporous as smoke, but the sorrow hard as iron.

The Lady Ladu . . . He'd seen no portrait of her, had—as he grew—met no older Kipchak merchant or mercenary officer who'd been so privileged at Caravanserai as to have met the wife of the Khan Toghrul. Only the old librarian, Lord Peter, had been able to describe her to him, and that when he was already a young man . . . So, for all his childhood in the court of the Achieving King, Baj had imagined his First-mother as lithe and beautiful, a black-haired slant-eyed queen, ferocious . . . but tender toward him, and loving.

He had still been a little boy, when he was first shown a man's severed head—its pigtailed hair floating, its ruined eyes half-open, bobbing in the vodka filling a large blown-glass jar. It had been his first sight of such a thing, and the only time King Sam had burdened a child with such.

"It was necessary, Bajazet, that this was brought for you to see. It is what is left of the man Manu Ek-Tam, who betrayed your First-father's memory, murdered your mother and your father's friends, then threatened the peace of the Rule."

The king had tossed a cloth over the thing.

"—Now, you need not waste an hour of your days on vengeance . . . but only reflect on your First-father's intelligence, courage, and competence in command . . . and the love your mother and your father's friends certainly felt for you." The king had gripped Baj's shoulder so hard it hurt. "The love we, your Second-family, also feel."

The child Baj had dreamed that night—though instead of his imagined superb First-mother, only a plump, plain woman, seeming to him a nanny or nurse, appeared hovering over, smiling, in the faintest of baby memories.

The old librarian, in description so many years later, had confirmed that dear one as his mother, at last.

Someone was gently tapping the tip of her nose, and Patience slowly woke to it. Woke to hear someone calling, in the distance . . . chicken-birds clucking nearer . . .

"So *fortunate*, at least for the now." A high, chuckling woman's voice.

Patience opened her eyes to see a low ceiling of clay and wattle-stick . . . then a hugely fat woman sitting half-naked beside her in a heap of marbled flesh, great bare breasts, and the tufted red plumage of a feathered kilt. The woman had pleasant brown eyes, a button nose . . . a small pursed mouth with a drift of down across her upper lip.

"How . . . am I fortunate?" Patience wouldn't have recognized her voice; it sounded thin as string.

"Fortunate that handsome Pete Aiken, spared by you, is Chad's sister's only son." The woman's small mouth hardly moved as she spoke.

"All right," Patience said, though she knew none of them. "My . . . shoulder."

"I fitted it more perfectly into place while you slept, then souped, and slept again." Fat hands and huge, white, bare arms mimed the adjustment, then bandaging. "—I strapped it tight, though not too tight. Gave it its best chance . . . but . . ."

"But?" It seemed to Patience her voice now began to sound like hers.

"But damage done. In-and-out of joint, tears matters."

Patience lay still on what felt like stacked sheepskins. The hut held very little light. "Damage . . ."

"The arm is breathing blood, but is a little cool; its message-strings are hurt."

"How hurt?" Certainly now her voice.

"Unlikely hurt to withering. *Perhaps* hurt to a little weakness forever."

Patience stopped breathing, as if that might stop time for a moment. A left-handed woman—with a weak left hand. A crippled woman, crippled Person, with work still to do. "How certain are you?" The Shrikes killed their cripples . . .

"Certain as I can be," the fat woman said. "And I am a Catanianite, a scientific doctor." She leaned forward, lifted Patience like a child, and presented a clay bowl to her lips.

"I knew her son."

"Whose?"

"Catania Olsen's son. She was his Second-mother."

The fat woman set the bowl carefully down, leaned forward, and hit Patience hard on her left shoulder.

. . . When she'd come fully conscious again, and could listen, the woman said to her, "Fatuous lies that claim acquaintance with Greats-from-God are unwise lies to tell."

"That," Patience managed, "—is certainly true."

"You know copybook *fatuous*?"

". . . I know the word very well."

"Here," the woman lifted the bowl again. "Broth from an unfortunate sheep."

Patience drank fat-thick saltiness—wondered for a moment where these tribespeople traded for their salt—and felt hot strength flowing down into her. When she'd swallowed several times, she said, "How long?"

"Two days—now three," the fat woman said. "And surprised me it wasn't more. You have Moonriser blood in you."

"Yes."

"I smelled it on your breath, but of what part–fathering beast I'm not sure. An animal, or perhaps selected men—certainly more than one—groaned seed for the Talents to mix in your mother." The fat woman took the bowl away. "My name is Charlotte. Called Charlotte-doctor."

"Thank you for your care," Patience said, and tried to ease her aching shoulder.

The fat woman chuckled again, apparently very good-natured. "My care *would* have been to peg you to the ground, then slice you into pieces before the children—little pieces, one by one—and kept you shouting all the while. That would have been my care, except that Chad Budnarik fears his sister's tongue, if nothing else. And spared Pete Aiken is her son."

"Isn't it remarkable," Patience said, "—remarkable that a woman's scolding may confound a brute?"

"Said," Charlotte-doctor smiled, "as if you'd *met* War-leader Chad Budnarik. No better word for him than *brute*, though I love him dearly, and have since I was a child."

Patience waited for another blow to her shoulder, but none came while she decided to guard her mouth. "Apologies," she said. That seemed safe enough.

"Oh, it's lies that trouble me," the fat woman said, "—not truths." She held the broth-bowl for Patience's last swallow, then set it down . . . and with great effort, burdened by massive breasts, a huge sagging belly—slowly got to her feet and waddled away to a curtained entrance, her thick, white, dimpled thighs trembling beneath the hem of her red-feathered kilt.

"The shoulder," Patience called after her—amused by the distancing of the question as she called it, "the" shoulder, not "my" shoulder. "When will I know how it does?"

The woman turned ponderously back to face her. "Within one WT week, unbandage and sling it, exercise it gently. If you leave it longer, it may grow to the joint, to move never. —Then, after two weeks slung and lightly exercised, you will know what that arm will be forever."

". . . Thank you, Doctor."

The woman left, billowing the entrance sheepskin so sunlight flashed in for a moment.

Sliced, while she shouted. Patience lay thanking whatever

Jesus or Weather Great for a so-far rescue. Content with lucky minutes, she drifted to sleep . . . and dreamed her Maxwell become a man grown, marvelous and fierce—though lacking humor—the son, truly, of six-hundred years of ice and sacrifice.

. . . When she woke, Patience knew it was night—the small hut now quite dark—and found she needed to shit. But find a possible pot how? She tried to sit up . . . and did, though that made her dizzy. She sat in cool darkness, taking deep breaths. A poop-pot—and her sword. What else could a lady require? These savages would keep her *Merriment* . . . let its wonderful blade rust in their trophy hut.

Really . . . really have to have that pot. Prompted, Patience rolled carefully off her pile of sheepskins, favoring the bound left shoulder absolutely, and began—not crawling—but hitching along naked over a rammed-dirt floor. Would have grimy buttocks and no choice about it. She scooted slowly along, then reached out with her right arm, feeling at the near corner for the thing—there must be one, though clean since there was no smell of it. She found that corner empty, then went along a wattled wall for the next. . . . Soon, would be just in time.

Then, as if in a staged comedy, the hut's entrance hide was paged aside, and rich yellow lamplight came pouring in, with the silhouettes of two big men behind it.

Patience saw herself as those warriors must see her—naked, pale, white-haired and scrawny . . . droop-breasted, bandaged, and crouched in the dirt like a caught cat. In that moment, came to her—not the immediately sensible thing of startled embarrassment and fear—but overwhelming bitterness at age and its changes, unfair to a degree that guaranteed cruel gods. . . . It was rage enough to leave her frozen where she was, instead of scuttling back to the sheepskins to try to draw one over.

"Don't be uncomfortable. We'll close our eyes." A very pleasant voice, speaking quite good book-English—almost a Boston gentleman's voice for tone, though not for accent. Sounding from a shadow shape behind the golden glare of light, it seemed to Patience the careful speech of a man who'd taught himself improvement. "I am Paul French-Robin."

"Our eyes are closed." Second voice—from the other shadow-man—*not* pleasant, sounding like a breaking branch, and speaking very poor book-English.

"Can you get back to your bed?" First voice. "Shall I carry you?"

"Our eyes still closed." Second voice.

A situation gone from enraging back to comic. What on cold earth did not go that way? ". . . I appreciate 'eyes closed.' But I find I need a piss-pot."

Silence. Warrior Paul French-Robin apparently confounded. Then Breaking-branch said, "Over there," and one of them—the lamp-bearer—stepped out into his lamp's light (glance averted from Patience), picked a fat clay pot from a corner by the entrance, sidled over and handed it to her.

Then both men, kilted and feather cloaked, turned their backs—sight apparently the important modesty—and stood while Patience, shoulder aching, awkwardly perched, emptied herself fairly noisily while desperate not to laugh. That once started, there'd be no stopping it.

Done, though with no wipe-leaf available, she scooted slowly back to her sheepskins—her ungainly shadow following along—and wrestled to pull the top fleece over her.

The incident apparently dismissed, both men turned, came to her pallet and sat side by side, cross-legged, lamplight shadowing their faces and the raised feather-scarring decorating their bare chests and bellies.

"Comfortable?" Paul French-Robin (the pleasant voice) smiled. This was a handsome man who knew it, tall, muscled, with a neat beard and long brown hair, glossy as oiled wood, lightly brushed with gray above his ears. Fine eyes, as deep a blue as blue could be. —And, as he'd spoken, every filed tooth still in place, a rarity among tribespeople.

"I'm Patience Nearly-Lodge," Patience said. "—And grateful for your hospitality."

"Yes," the handsome man still smiled, "—and cleverly put, from stupid young Pete Aiken to now. But I'm not yet convinced. I might still prefer you dead, Boston. And since it's a politic question, not a war one, it is under my hand."

"Not so. A matter of war as much as anything." The second man, whose voice sounded splintered—ruined apparently by a blow across his throat—looked very nearly a Person of Boston's Guard, though Patience had smelled nothing but Sunriser-human from them both, with perhaps a faint scent of flowers from Paul French-Robin. . . . This second man might have been a dwarf, with a huge shaggy head, massive arms and legs so short in proportion—but a dwarf more than six WT-feet tall, with eyes an unpleasant light green, and a face, front, and forearms carved white by healed battle slashes. He wore two heavy hatchets, their long handles thrust through his kilt's wide belt.

"Chad Budnarik?" It seemed a good guess, though the dwarf-giant didn't respond. Both Robins sat silent, staring at her.

Patience scented from them all the complexities of men. The held juice of perhaps-soon-fucking, the sweat of mild effort, the harsh breath of meat eaters . . . and the far more delicate and difficult-to-be-sure-of odor of consideration, decision-choosing. All odors had been clearer to her when she was young, gift of the Talents. That gift now fading, with others. "—Perhaps," she said from her sheepskins, heart going *thump thump thump*, "—perhaps I can offer a suggestion that prevents what appears to be discord between you important Robins, which might injure the tribe."

Silence.

"I'm speaking," Patience said, "of a fortuitous escape." She tried a smile. "—In which case, no decision would have to be made, no disagreement caused among leaders. Also no anger *from* Boston if I die the city's friend, no strengthening *of* Boston if I die their enemy—which it happens, I am."

"*Fortuitous.*" Paul French returned her smile, but unpleasantly. "See?" he nudged the dwarf-giant, "—how richly Cambridge educates? Such learning in the Yard. See what a considerable thing she is, to show tribal fools and savages a way past their difficulties. . . . Perhaps she is considerable enough to lie staked before the children, and scream out life's lessons under the knife. Much to teach . . . much to teach, who could doubt it?"

"Boston's enemy—how?" Certainly-Budnarik had no expression on his face, no expression in his eyes. The question might have come from a tree. A tree with filed teeth.

"They've taken something from me," Patience said, "—something that was mine alone. And voted me exiled for protesting, though I was the Township's daughter, *and* Nearly-Lodge."

"What thing?"

"That is my business, Chad Budnarik-Robin—not yours." Patience's stomach turned in fear with that defiance, and she saw herself—after already toileting before these men—now vomiting mutton broth into their laps.

Was that a smile from Budnarik? Perhaps almost . . .

"A liar from a nest of lies," Paul French said. "Though there is charm here, bravery." He had an orator's, a singer's voice. "Might teach our children much of courage, while she dies."

Budnarik cleared his throat. "And you roam our mountains—why?"

"Going north and east, nothing to do with Robins."

"But *had* something to do with killing River's King down in Map-Tennessee? And managed with Sparrows! . . . You understand that pigeons fly for tribes, as well as towns."

"Yes, Commander," Patience said, sure of who he was.

"But why? That fight—what business was it of yours?" A second blow to his throat would have left Budnarik unable to speak at all.

"That king was Boston-crowned. His loss, their great injury."

"And all that," Paul French said, "—which, by the way, left room on the Mississippi for a king we understand to be much more formidable—all that for some *personal* reason?"

"All reasons are personal," Patience said, "—and mine more important than most."

"You don't yet persuade me." Paul French smiled, apparently a habit of charming with him. "You don't persuade me that you bring the Robins anything but difficulty. You claim against your own Boston, but north to Boston I suspect you were flying. Flying until, apparently, you fell and took your injury. . . . I don't yet see the benefit in keeping you alive—and less than that in letting you wander."

"Then if not for politic," Patience said—and noticed that arguing for one's life was excellent medicine; the shoulder hardly hurt at all, "—if not for that, then why not for your tribe's honor and given word? I've traded with your people, and been provided hospitality and food—salted food at that."

"Traded, my ass," Paul French said, not smiling now, and using a very old copybook phrase. It seemed to Patience he'd read well, been very studious in whatever hut he'd grown sharing with newborn lambs, chicken-birds, and the skulls of Robin enemies. "To kill a boy—"

"Young *man*," Patience said, "and hunting me, who had done no harm."

"To kill Lou Pollano, then hold your hand from a second murder, and call that *even?* That is no fucking trading!"

"But the second young man—Pete . . . Pete Aiken. He agreed to the trade, and that it was fair."

"Agreed," Budnarik croaked, "with a saber at his neck."

"But *agreed*—Pete's reasons his own, though it seems to me

that a whole life left to be lived is considerable payment for a single Lou. Certainly seemed fair and square to him. . . . Do Robins now call one of their warriors Dishonorable-Pete, a welcher and exile and no Robin at all?"

" 'Welcher,' " Budnarik said, and shook his head, almost smiling.

"You know the word, Commander?"

"He knows the word, and we know the word," Paul French said. "I wonder how many fine old Warm-time words would be spouted if you're staked."

"I'm becoming curious," Patience said to him, "why you're so willing to consider my death, an injured woman and your guest. . . . Is it possible a Boston pigeon flies to you, and to no one else among the Robins? You seem so to be their friend."

"Nonsense—and desperate nonsense."

"Also, I notice no scars on you but decoration. No sign you've fought the Guard when they've come this way to choose among your tribe's daughters. No sign you've ever fought at all. . . . Perhaps you're too clever a man to fight. Perhaps—so handsome—you have other interests."

"Oh, I have only one interest now."

"Still," Patience said, " 'handsome is as handsome does,' such a perfect old phrase. And you do little boys, I would say, for preference. Do I smell a flowery scent? . . . Lilac?"

Silence. The tribes, losing children to every winter, had little sympathy for those who made none.

"—Of course, if I've offended (and though being a trade-guest), I will happily meet you with a sword, even weary, wrong-handed, and a woman."

An unhandsome look. ". . . There would be no honor to me in that."

"What you do not have," Patience said, "—you cannot lose, 'Lilac.' May I call you Lilac?"

French raised his fist to hit her, but Budnarik reached to grip his arm—gifting Patience with hope even after both men rose, silent, took their lamp, and left her to darkness.

. . . Charlotte-doctor came lumbering with first light, found Patience lying awake, listening to village noises, and knelt ponderously to examine the shoulder's strapping, and scold her. "Sleep," she said. Then, "Raveled sleeve—raveled sleeve!" apparently an incantation, so not so scientific a physician after all.

"I would rather be awake while I can."

The doctor chuckled at that, chins wobbling. "Oh, I doubt I'll be carving you—and too bad; I'm wonderful with the little knives. But," a sigh, "likely not to be. A hostage held *from* Boston, if Boston loves you—or as a gift *for* Boston, if they don't. That's how you'll be kept."

". . . Not the best news."

"Not the worst, either." Fat fingers fairly gentle. "There, that shoulder will do the best it can."

"I believe I have Paul French to thank for holding me."

"To thank for keeping you from my knives, yes. Sweet Chad would have killed you; believes you too dangerous to save—his grateful sister notwithstanding." Charlotte-doctor heaved to stand up. "Now, I'll bring you food. Then, sleep."

When she was gone—allowing a glimpse of a sentry's shadow when the sheepskin swung aside—Patience lay considering bad judgment. Bad judgment such as deliberately angering Paul French, a man of politic—who likely had threatened only to discover what threats might produce—angering him in order to impress Budnarik, a man of action, with her cleverness and courage. And impressed him sufficiently that he decided her execution was advisable.

A serious misjudgement, and barely survived. Which left the question whether it was a blunder from weakness and agonizing injury, or simply the deterioration of a Person *bred* to deteriorate early, so as not to become a threat to the Township. As, of course, she had become already—disobedient, prideful, and grasping of her child.

Now, to be kept. Grim news, since tribesmen were experienced in holding those they wished held. She'd be fortunate not to be blinded . . . or kept cramped in a little wooden box with only room for huddled crouching, until, after months and years, she became a shrunken knotted thing—screaming with pain, occasionally—that whined when children poked sticks through the slit where gruel was poured in, and water.

After only a few weeks in that close-box, she'd be pleased to have Boston people come for her, would weep with relief to be traveling north to the Common for burning in Justice's iron stove.

Ruined. All ruined by a moment of suckle-dreaming in the air . . . and no one to forgive her for it.

* * *

"That's one of seventeen villages—at least there were seventeen, when I served with the Guard." Richard, seeming comfortable with the vacancy beneath them, sat to Baj's left, Nancy's right—his large moccasin-boots kicking idly over the edge of a granite slip overhanging a small stream's valley perhaps a thousand Warm-time feet below. Errol would not come near the drop.

The mountains' haze was laced over the village with drifting smoke from a dozen fires along its creek. All revealed beneath them in miniature—as if a river lord had ordered a savages' set-tlement made to table-top scale for his small son's festival day.

"Robins," Nancy said, "claim to be near civilized."

"Take heads." Richard brushed a fly away.

"Yes. They take heads."

"To steal wisdom?" Baj imagined he was a Boston Talent, and might push off the cliff's edge and float out into the air. A won-derful thing . . .

"Yes." Nancy stared down at tiny huts, where people small

as summer ants wended busily. "Such fools they are. Were Cherokees, once, and smarter."

"We go past?"

"Baj," Richard reached up with an easy motion, captured the returned fly and crushed it, "—we go well past. It's Shrikes we go to meet, not these."

"Why not these? They have no cause to love the Township. Aren't their girls taken?"

"Taken," Nancy said, "—and they have cause. But village Robins hate other village Robins even more, though they prey on Thrushes, and take Finches' heads if they raid farther east. They'll take their own people's heads, sometimes, trying to become chiefs. . . . Boston burrows among them like maggots in rot."

"Then why not bring the Sparrows north, and Thrushes?"

Richard shifted at the brink to be more comfortable. "Bringing those savages anywhere, is like carrying hot water in cupped hands. It burns and runs out through your fingers."

"More honor to the Boston-woman then," Baj said, "—for persuading them to gather and fight Cooper-the-King. . . . Though I suppose my days of scurrying gave her time enough."

"No small potatoes, still," Richard said, using an ancient phrase, "—to have gotten it done."

"I think Unkind-Harry liked her." Nancy leaned over to spit into space. "Thought he might fuck her . . . learn to Walk-in-air. Which shows what a fool he is; which shows what fools the Sparrows are, that he's their wisest and chief."

"Brave, though," Baj said, and heard, as if he were there again, the surf-sound of Sparrows shouting as they came down against Kingdom cavalry.

"Between courage and foolishness," Richard said, and held up an odd thumb and blunt forefinger, almost touching, "—is the narrowest measure."

"I have stood with foolishness, mainly," Baj said, smiling.

"Not true, but you are a fool to say so." Nancy scrambled up from the granite edge—then stood still, staring.

Baj turned to look. Errol was standing a rock-throw back, by wind-beaten scrub pines. The boy was pointing. . . . And Baj saw, down where the slope fell away to the north, four deer grazing amid larger pines and dwarf rhododendra. Two bowshots distant.

He got up, and crouching, went to his pack, unbuckled his sword-belt and let it lie . . . then took up his bow and knelt to string it. The breeze was in his face . . . the deer up-wind. Who would have expected the animals to feed this high? A young buck—looked at a distance to be a six-pointer—and likely three does.

Baj selected two arrows—wouldn't have time for more—and still crouching low, moved slowly down the slope. Difficult traveling over stone . . . through scrub. And made no easier by blisters from the scrap-cloth wrappings on his feet, instead of his lost wool stockings; even with holes worn, they'd been more comfortable in boots.

He wended down the mountainside, his belly—griped and empty—commanding him to make no stupid mistake, no foolish noise or commotion to frighten the deer away. The breeze still blew to him . . . though shifting, shifting a little to his left, so he shifted to face it more squarely as he moved, keeping low.

There would have been no chance to approach them but for the mountain pines. Baj stole along, watching his footing over roots, rubble, and scree, careful to keep at least one wind-bent tree between him and the herd.

After a while more of careful approaching, a blister sore in his right boot, Baj came to a space there was no crossing in cover, a long ledge of light-gray stone with no pine growing—and still high, high above them as the deer drifted, grazing.

Crouched to almost kneeling, he set a broadhead to the bowstring, took a deep breath . . . and waited a moment, the summer sun warm against his face. The mountain's air, the scent of deeper forest far below, and himself as himself all seemed to combine to one, a happiness. He slowly rose, drew his bow—and knew he was about to miss, already saw the arrow's path out and down, just over the young buck's back.

Shooting downhill . . . shooting downhill! Baj relaxed the bow and sank back. Through the last sheltering branches, he saw the deer drifting.

Then he stood, drew the bow, saw his point as beneath the back of the buck's shoulder, and released.

The bow thumped hard in his hand, and he and the young buck below both stood to attention as the arrow introduced them. The buck was gathered to jump when the broadhead went in at an angle behind its shoulder, so it made its leap and leaped again—the does bounding after down the slope . . . then, at a distance, running past as the buck stumbled, recovered, tripped and fell kicking.

Baj unstrung and eased his bow as Nancy, Richard, and Errol came past him, scrambling down, bounding as the fleeing deer had done, sounding—except for the silent boy—odd cheers . . . mixed roars and yelps.

The buck was dead when Baj reached them. Errol had cut its throat.

Then, Richard reached down, gathered the animal's back hooves in a one-handed grip, and by that, easily lifted the buck up into the air and held it high—for lack of any tree tall enough to hang it on—held it swinging, its blood draining, spattering onto stone.

It was an astonishing demonstration of strength. Baj couldn't imagine any festival strongman who could have done it.

And not only that, but Richard held it so—one-handed—all the while Nancy and the boy gralloched, gutted, carved, and butchered out the meat . . . bundled it into the hide for carrying.

"With no fire, Richard," Baj said, "—most will be wasted."

"We should *have* no fire."

"But one last fire, carefully set with weathered wood?"

"Baj doesn't want to eat raw." Nancy, wet red to her elbows, was slicing out a rack of ribs.

"If not roasted, most will rot."

Richard, standing like a statue—the ruined buck, now almost skeletal, still hanging from his hand—began his deep uneven humming of consideration.

"Here." Nancy handed Baj a bleeding slice of liver, sprinkled with gall . . . watched him munch and chew at it, bent to keep blood from running down his front.

"Good?"

Baj swallowed and said, "No. —But that's not my reason. We have days of traveling out of this buck, if the meat is cut thin and cooked in smoke. . . . There may not be another deer."

"The Robins keep sheep," Nancy said. "There will be sheep wandering."

"And missed when we take one," Richard bent and laid the buck's remnant on stone scree. "So the tribesmen come looking."

"A last fire. An evening fire of seasoned wood," Baj said. "High on the slope, and in a hollow, so not seen from below, and no one on the mountaintop to smell it."

"And if seen?" Nancy said. "If smelled? We are in their *country*."

"I killed the fucking deer. It should be cooked!"

Errol drifted closer, apparently drawn by raised voices.

"Now, children," Richard said, "—no quarreling," and loomed over them as might some monstrous mother out of fable-tales. "It's unwise, but we'll have our fire—and hope that lasting meat proves worth it."

Nancy bared her teeth. "I blame you," she said to Baj, "if we suffer for it."

. . . But it seemed they wouldn't, since by nightfall—and a cool wind blowing from the north, Lord Winter's reminder, summer or not—they'd found a narrow space between two boulders in a field of fallen rock, collected only years-dried storm-broken branches, and set their fire so the north wind picked smoke up and shredded it away over the mountain's crest.

Over this careful fire, on greener branches to keep the spits from catching, long strips of thin-sliced venison were draped and turned, portion after portion, slow cooking in smoke through half the night for keeping-meat.

The steaks and fat-ribs were roasted otherwise—quickly, on green-wood forks deep among the brightest coals, roasted sputtering, fat just charred along the edges—and by the Persons, not roasted long.

Richard and Nancy, hunched by the fire with boulders at their backs—and days of hunger also behind them—barely singed their meat before lifting it away, dripping, spitting burned blood—and bit into it, ripping pieces from it as if the deer were still alive, and might escape them. . . . Errol, apart at his usual distance, stuffed as furiously.

Baj found him less disturbing. Any hungry boy, poorly raised and rarely fed, might have done the same. But Richard and Nancy fed as any hounds might have, fangs flashing into meat, heads shaken to tear bites loose to swallow. And all quickly, quickly as if Baj or someone else might reach across the fire and snatch meat from them. There were no growls . . . no snarling, but those seemed ready.

Baj ate, and tried to avoid watching them eat. Those two—who had come to seem so richly human—now displayed again whatever portion of animal had been twisted into their breeding.

There was for him . . . a distaste. And some fear of them, that shamed him.

"What's the matter?" Nancy stared at him, her narrow face dappled with blood and juices.

"Nothing."

"*Not* nothing. You looked at us!"

"I didn't—"

"You looked at us." She elbowed Richard as he chewed. "He looked at us badly!"

"I did not."

"You *lie.* I saw your face, watching." Nancy threw her piece of meat into the fire with a small fountain of bright sparks. "Being disgusted was in your look, you nasty blood-human. And because of our eating!" Her face contorted with rage. "It's our mouths—our teeth. It's the animal that was stuck in us, you fuck-your-mother thing!"

"I wasn't doing that."

"Lie, lie, and lie again like all Sunriser shits who think they're better!" She stood, tears in the yellow eyes. "He waits," she said to Richard, "—to see you lift your leg against a tree. He waits for me to sniff someone's bottom like a dog! To bend and lick myself."

"I don't."

"It's your doing! It is all your *doing!*" And she was gone out of the fire's light.

After a silence in which only Errol ate, Richard lowered a chewed venison rib, and said, "She didn't mean you, as you."

". . . I know what she meant," Baj said. He looked into the fire's coals so as not to meet the big Person's eyes. "I know the only differences between Boston and the River Kingdom are place and custom and arms. The dangerous come-at-you's of both are blood-human . . . as are the Talents' cruel studies, also."

"Trouble," Richard said, "is made by all, Baj, who wish and want." He raised his rib-bone and took a tearing bite. "—And by Persons as much as any."

"I'm back," Nancy said from the dark. "I am back to eat—and if the Sunriser doesn't like it, he can kiss my part-fox ass!" She stepped into golden firelight—red gold on her widow's peak of hair—sat in her place, snatched a chop sizzling from its spit-stick and bit into it, shook her head to tear a chunk loose. Brutish, but for tears still streaking her face.

"It's true," Baj said. "It . . . disturbed me a little, to watch you both eat. I suppose it always has, because it shows the blood in you." He cleared his throat. "Bears have always frightened human people. A wise old man, our librarian, told us once that men used to worship bears. . . . And foxes and men have played hunting games forever—the foxes winning more times than not."

"I'm not listening." Nancy gnawed her bone.

"Those things are true, just the same."

"Talk talk talk," Nancy tossed the bone away, "—talk does not equal one bad look."

"Then forgive me," Baj said. "I apologize."

"You're forgiven," Richard said, "—and now, I suppose I can mention your smell without offense." He smiled a toothy smile.

"You stink," Nancy said. "You smell like an owl."

"I didn't know owls smelled."

Richard handed him a fatty portion, still sputtering. "They smell like humans," he said.

. . . That night, drifting in and out of sleep in his wrapped blanket, Baj, roused by a cold wind come south into the mountains, regretted the fire's warmth and warm ashes. Richard had insisted on moving their camp more than a bow-shot across the slope, in case the fire had given the Robins notice.

Sleeping and almost sleeping, Baj considered the difference between traveling from—as running from a furious king—and traveling *to*, as now he ventured toward the Shrikes and Boston's Guard, for vengeance, and perhaps the cold earth's good. . . . It seemed to him, that direction made surprisingly little difference in journeys.

12

A smith, with spark-scarred hands and singed leather apron, roused Patience in early after-noon, gestured her up and off her pallet, and led her outside past a guard—a short tribesman bearing hide-shield and heavy hatchet, and looking almost strong as the smith.

A short thick iron-bound section of log was waiting, with a yard's length of rusty chain to what seemed a leg shackle.

Patience, having dressed that morning—with the help of Charlotte-doctor—in her boots, dirty blouse, trousers, and worn blue coat—stood a little stunned by sunlight and the busy murmurs of a village of wattle huts ranked steeply down to the left along a mountain stream. A considerable village, seen in daylight— more than forty small dwellings, and three larger ones. One, certainly bachelor quarters. . . . All she could see were handsomely plastered light mud-brown beneath brighter painted scenes of hunting, and perhaps of war, the colors (berry colors, oak-leaf colors, under-bark colors) all oranges, dark reds. . . . The village looked better than it smelled; sheep grazed between the huts, and Patience saw an open shit-pit seething with summer flies beside the nearest beaten path.

The smith, who appeared to speak no book-English, or very little, directed Patience with grunts and gestures, brought her beside the log-round, sat her on it, then tugged her right boot and stocking roughly off . . . set the shackle's hinged limbs just above her ankle, closed them—and tested the fit, turning the iron a little this way and that. It was painful enough that Patience noticed her bound shoulder now only ached, and not so severely.

It seemed the smith judged very well—shook the iron, checked for tightness to the bone—then, like an impatient lover, shoved Patience down along the log, and placed her leg where he wanted it across the round's iron band.

A rivet fitted to key the shackle closed, the smith produced a heavy hammer Patience hadn't seen, and—without pause for care—drew back and hit the rivet's head five clanging savage blows so swiftly she only had time to be frightened by the third.

Done, the smith took his hammer and walked away past two admiring naked little boys, and a small girl who needed to blow her nose. More children were gathering, but the adults—perhaps two hundred men and women, all kilted, feather-scarred, and bare to the waist—paid Patience no attention, but worked among the hutments, choring, tending small gardens.

She stood, found one boot awkward, and tugged it and the stocking off so she stood by the log-round barefoot. She tried a step, found the shackle griping, abrading her skin, and bent to tuck the stocking in around it for a cushion.

A second step proved that hauling the log-round would be constant labor. Even with two good arms, she would not be able to hoist the thing more than a few inches off the ground. And nothing that was not quite light could be carried while Walking-in-air. Chained, her traveling would be by dragging over earth, and no other way.

The tribe would keep her—for themselves or Boston—keep her from Maxwell forever.

Patience had wept only a few times in her life; easy weeping was simply not in her, but she would have wept in sunshine by the Robins' stream, except for being interrupted of the notion by a scatter of dung—sheep dung, she hoped—that was thrown and hit her in the face.

She turned, chain jingling, and saw a naked young boy, summer-tanned, grinning at her. The dung pieces were of no use, so Patience stooped for a small stone and slung it sidearm—sadly, right-handed—so it only whizzed past the boy's head, instead of striking with a satisfactory *tock*. Still, it backed him up, startled. . . . Backed him farther when she searched and stooped for a second rock.

"Two teeth!" Patience called—meaning two to be taken in payment for one—Boston's improvement of the most ancient rule of all.

If the Robin boy didn't understand the reference, he understood the stones, and turned, bent to slap his scrawny ass to her, then trotted away and out of range to join a circling crowd of dogs and children, boys and girls all naked in summer's warmth, all grimy with dirt and their home hearths' smoke and soot.

"No fucking helpless Person ever!" Patience noticed she'd already adopted a prisoner's muttered self-conversation. She gripped her rock, an only friend, tossed it . . . caught it again, and bent to look for another likely one, perhaps a little heavier, to crack a man's skull. The log-round was difficult . . . difficult to drag. She put the rock in her coat pocket. Then—her bound shoulder complaining, though she used her right hand—she gripped to haul on the chain and spare her ankle. The round grunted like a stupid animal, and scraped reluctantly over weedy dirt, while she searched for her second good stone.

The children stood a fair way off, watching. And, Patience supposed, must see a little woman, worn, white-haired, and wounded, hobbling with her weight of log in a blue coat too big for her. ". . .Once," she wished to call to them, "Once I was young and beautiful and fierce, and flew fighting over a great battle. This—this you see, is not who I really am."

Some children were bending, looking for stones.

* * *

Richard came to rouse Baj at dark before dawn—startling him so he rolled out of his blanket, the rapier half-drawn before he woke.

A massive shape in the night, Richard made a reassuring *puh puh puh* sound. "We're up, and we go. We had our fire-place; now we run away from it." He stood waiting while Baj rolled the blanket, settled his sword-belt and dew-damp pack, bow, and quiver, then he lumbered softly away.

Baj yawned and followed, tramping through pine scrub. His battered boots were already uncomfortable—the sole of the left was separating a little on the side.

. . . By sun-well-up, they were off the mountain, and trailing along a draw where little waterfalls ran musical as if the mountain wept to see them go. It seemed to Baj a promising notion for a pretty poem, when he had leisure to write it . . . had pulp-paper, quill pen, and squid ink. And happened still to be breathing.

Nancy had had nothing to say to him all morning. A relief, and an annoyance. Whether it was her part-father fox—whose supposedly minor contribution seemed to have had considerable effect—or one of the parent humans involved, the result had been a girl (a *Person*) very slow to forgive. . . . It seemed to Baj he'd been too easy, too courteous with her. She was not, after all, an Island lady. Not even some girl-Ordinary of a river town. An oddity, was what she was. A pain in the ass . . .

Here, in the folds of the mountain's skirt, breezes blew warm enough for stands of rhododendron just blossoming in thick unfurling purples . . . ragged whites. Baj found it difficult to imagine the Warm-time world, when these must have been cool-weather plants and blooms, not constrained to so short a summer. Those people would have enjoyed flowers for half the year. . . .

Richard leading, then Nancy, then Baj—Errol, as usual, pacing somewhere beside or behind—they trailed wending through flowering shrubs, the green heights of their last mountain close above and behind them . . . the heights of the next rising before.

Birds flew sifting through the foliage, a flock of little birds as bright gold as any Kingdom coin. They whirled, chirping, then spun away into the trees.

Baj followed the others through this wild garden, overarched in places by great oaks and what he thought might be tulip trees.

Then out onto a level sunny enough for drifts of small blue-berry bushes and bilberry, already started fruiting—forced, as all growing things were forced, to hurry before Lord Winter came again.

Poems everywhere, it seemed to Baj—and if not for his boot, and difficult Nancy, he would have been . . . content. He bent to comb a little cluster of blueberries from a short bush as he passed, found them still sour-tart but very nice.

A startled yelp up ahead. —Then a scream.

Baj thought of Nancy, drew and ran, flicking shrubbery aside with the rapier's blade. Damned *boot* . . .

He came running out into a wider glade, and four figures turned to watch him. The three Persons—and a woman. She was short and almost fat, with considerable gray streaked through brown hair plastered flat with grease, and decorated with a tuft of blue feath-ers. Barefoot in a sheepskin kilt, she stood with veteran breasts bare on a torso scarred with intricate feather patterns from her belly to her throat.

A woven berry-basket lay upturned beside her, picked blue-berries spilled like little semiprecious stones.

There were no other tribespeople in the glade.

Baj sheathed his sword, paused to catch his breath. ". . . Is any-one with you? Anyone near?"

The tribeswoman only stared at him, mouth tight shut. Richard and Nancy stood as silent.

Baj walked closer to the Robin—certainly a Robin woman by the feathers in her hair. He held his hands out to show no weapons. "We are travelers, and mean you no harm."

Silent staring.

"Your village . . . how near?"

Then the woman answered in swift clattering pidgin, through which only *fuck* and *you* came in clear book-English. Recovered from startlement, she seemed a little tough.

"Mind your manners, savage!" Baj said, and was instantly

amused at such haughty nonsense—by a Once-was-a-prince with broken boots and partial beasts for friends.

A long silence, then. Only buzzing insects, only a few bird-calls sounding.

Errol came trotting into sunlight, shook his head.

"She came alone," Richard said.

The woman stared at him, surprised apparently to hear him speaking.

"Her village," Nancy said, "can't be far, for her to come out by herself."

"I apologize," Baj said to the woman, "—for my rudeness. This is your country, not mine." He made a passing and going way gesture. "We only travel through."

She stood staring at him. She was more than old enough to have been his mother—certainly was someone's mother . . . grandmother. The picked berries, likely baked in wild-oat flour with sheeps' cheese, would be meant for childrens' pleasure.

"*Baj*," Nancy called as if to wake him. "Baj . . . we cannot let her loose."

"Her village," Richard said, "—must be an easy walk. So, an easy run for the warriors who would chase us down."

A silence, then, of different quality than woods noises left when still. Baj felt a cool shadow, as if a cloud had come over, though the sky was sweet blue, with no cloud in it. "If we left her, and she understood—don't they honor promises they give? Oaths?"

Richard cleared his throat. "Their women cannot swear honor."

Baj saw in the woman's eyes that she understood enough. Intelligent eyes, a very light blue . . . . He saw she must have been pretty, in a stocky, sturdy way, when she was a girl.

She seemed tensed to run a hopeless running. A tiny vessel pulsed at the side of her throat.

I don't have the right, Baj said to himself, then said aloud, "We don't have the right."

"No," Richard said, "—we don't. But must do it anyway."

"Her children," Baj said, and knew it was a stupid thing to say. More of that clouded silence.

Baj felt something in him leaning . . . leaning, and he leaned against it. "We tie her hard to a tree, and leave. It will be a while before they come searching, and find her. Time enough for us to be well gone."

"Unless they come searching soon," Nancy said. "Unless other women come after her to pick blueberries."

"Chance enough to take," Baj said.

"No, Baj," Richard shook his head. "A chance too much to take."

"We tie her," Baj said, "—and leave her."

"No." Richard, looking sorrowful, weary as a festival's dancing bear, took his ax from his shoulder.

As if he were dreaming, Baj recalled his sword's engraving— *With Good Cause*—and drew it. He faced Richard, stepped out a little for room.

Richard said, "Oh, dear," looked even sadder, and held his ax now with both hands.

"We tie her, and leave her." Baj was surprised how steady his voice sounded . . . and how, as he spoke, he was considering what best chance he might have against this so formidable Person— formidable and, of course, a friend. A poor chance. A poor chance no matter what, though perhaps time and space, if he was fast enough, for one thrust only before the great ax caught him. . . . There was the oddest feeling of freedom.

"*No no no!*" Nancy came bounding, shifting in between them as if she were dancing. Baj was pleased to see she hadn't drawn the scimitar. There was not enough of him to kill the girl . . . to save the woman.

He stood still and on guard in the sunshine, as if to let his decent sword decide. The left-hand dagger wouldn't care.

Nancy stood panting before him. He smelled her sweet vulpine odor in the sunshine warmth. "*No . . .*" she said.

"Stand away, dear." Richard took a step.

Baj, though he felt like weeping, also thought he'd been correct to leave matters to the steel, since the rapier turned a little with his wrist for flatter thrusting through massive ribs, its hilt settling into his hand, unafraid, with a slight flourish of the needle tip.

Nancy, standing between them, turned to Richard as he came pacing on. "Worse! Worse than the chance of tying her! This is *certain* badness!"

Baj barely heard. Past her—almost, it seemed, through her— he saw Richard quite clearly . . . noticed every motion of the ax. "Remember an ax has a heavy handle, that may also strike." Some previous Master's saying . . .

"I know why you stand there," Richard said to her. There was a summer insect, perhaps a bee, buzzing through the air—a precious bee, it seemed to Baj, through precious air.

"Still," Richard said, after a moment, "—a chance of badness, *is* better than badness certain." The double-edged ax swung left . . . then right and back up onto his heavy shoulder.

And Baj's sword sheathed itself with no regrets.

* * *

They camped in early evening, lower again, along a rivulet running a wide, lightly treed valley, with birches in wandering stands where the narrow water turned.

An early, cold camp, with cold venison and a handful of blueberries each. Baj, Nancy, and Richard sat eating as if around a fire—Errol still wandering. . . . Finished with his second chop, the big Person turned to manage the thick roll of tanned leather from his pack.

"Baj," he said, "—give me your boots."

"Why?"

"For measure to make you moccasins," Nancy said, "—is *why*. Unless you want your toes out in the weather; we'll be north and out of summer soon enough, and your boots are no boots anymore."

"Moccasins . . ." Baj pulled his boots off. "Thank you, Richard."

Richard grunted, distracted—stretched leather out across his lap, then set the left boot sole to it . . . marked a close outline with a horny thumbnail.

Errol, with a rustle through tall grass, caught up to the camp ahead of his long, fading shadow—stared at them a moment— then dug in Nancy's pack, found a venison rib, and squatted a way away to gnaw it. He seemed to find a tough tendon along the bone, and drew a knife to slice it free.

Baj noticed the blade was marooned with drying blood. —And knew at once, knew himself a fool, and started to his feet. Nancy caught his arm to hold him.

"Baj, we gave him no order. Richard told him nothing, gave him no sign, either."

"But you knew."

"Yes. We knew . . . maybe."

"*More* than maybe. You knew, once she was tied to that fucking tree with a rag of cloth in her mouth—you knew he'd circle back to kill her. It's what the Boston-woman said he likes to do to anyone helpless."

"Yes . . . sometimes."

"I forgot that, forgot him—but you and Richard didn't forget." Baj felt sick with anger, as if this particular killing stood for all foolish murders. "You acted a lie. And still the Robins will find her!"

"But not soon, Baj. Errol hides what he does, tucks it under logs . . . under tree roots. They'll find their dead lady late—and by then, not know who or how many or where they went."

Baj thought of killing the boy, saw the sword-thrust very

clearly . . . then decided not. "It was his knife—but your acting a lie allowed it. I'll remember, when trust-time comes again."

Richard drew a bright little curved blade from his belt . . . began to trace his marking deeper into the leather, deeper, then slowly sliced through along his pattern. "My responsibility, Prince. My fault . . . . We had no more time for the truth, and argument."

"Our responsibility," Nancy said.

"Don't tell me," Baj said. "Go back and tell the woman's people how—when she'd been gathering berries for children's pleasure—you left her tied and gagged-silent, so a beast-boy could go back to cut her throat."

"We are not bad!" Nancy said.

". . . So, Richard," Baj sat beside him again, "—how are moccasin-boots made?" And listened with every sign of interest to relieved rumbled explanations of double-soling, of working inside-out for interior stitching, of uppers to be cross-laced to just below the knee, all while Richard finished leather-cutting, then threaded fine tendon sinew to a strong curved needle.

"We are *not* bad," Nancy said. But Baj paid no attention, and after a while she got up and walked away from camp.

"The toes," Richard said, "—I turn up a little at the tip; to ward mud and puddle-water away. But the secret to moccasins is regular mending, and greasing along the stitching, particularly. Not heavy greasing."

"Regular mending," Baj said, "—and light greasing."

"Yes, and you'll find the foot wraps do better in moccasin-boots than stockings do."

"They'll have to, since my stockings went in the river."

"These will be warmer too, in the north, stuffed with pounded wool. . . . Baj, we are not bad Persons."

"So, greasing—and, I suppose, drying them slowly when they're soaked."

". . . Yes." Richard bent his great head to bite through a strand of sinew.

They sat quiet then for a long while, more than a Warm-time hour as the big Person worked, though Baj heard Nancy stomping under birches by the creek while he watched Richard's huge hands set deft stitches, driven as easily through double thicknesses of leather as single. He used a leather square—what Baj had heard called a "palm"—to back the needle.

Darkness was coming slowly down, a cool cloak draped over them. Odd how missed a fire was; without it, they seemed to fall away into the night, where anything might stand waiting. . . . Soon, a sliced moon began to rise as a wind rose, as if flown into the sky like a celebration kite from Island's battlements. Moonrise, appropriate in company with Moonriser Persons, that gave a clear soft silver light—enough light that Richard seemed to have no difficulty setting his stitches by it, which likely no full-human could have done.

After a while, Richard said, "Try this on." He tied off a last sinew knot, bit it free, and held out what seemed a thick folded something—with long rawhide laces—but no boot. "Left foot."

Baj bent to adjust the cloth wrappings on that foot, then fitted the soft leather on, laced it, and stood. It seemed little more than a thick stocking against the ground.

Richard leaned to feel the fit. "Your feet will be sore in them for a day or two. Stepping on pebbles . . . rocks."

"No doubt."

"But after, very comfortable, light, and easy to move in. You tie the lacing crossways tighter or looser. Tie them all the way up—or fold the top down."

Baj took a few uneven steps through weedy grass. "It seems to fit. . . ." He came back and sat. "Thank you, Richard. They'll do very well—and I won't complain about rocks or pebbles."

The wind—as all night winds—seemed to have a touch of

winter to it. Baj reached back for his cloak as Richard unfolded a second wide strip of leather, set Baj's worn right boot on it for pattern. . . . It seemed the only allowance he made for moonlight, was to peer at his work a little closer.

The night wind seethed softly through the birches, promising that soon they would be north and nearer Lord Winter's wall, and the short summer left behind them like a dream. North to the Shrikes and Boston's Guard—their alliance, it seemed to Baj, likely to turn to war.

"Little chance," he said aloud.

Richard, silvered by the riding moon, raised his head from his work. "What?"

"To win against New England."

"No, not a good chance." Richard looked down at his work, peered closer, and sewed again. "Not a good chance—but better than no chance." He broke a tendon thread, said "Shit," and knotted off the end . . . then rethreaded his needle, an impressive thing to accomplish in such soft light. "Though perhaps Frozen Jesus may help us."

"Frozen, Floating, or Mountain Jesus—they've spent a long time helping only armed men, and rich men, and clever men . . . and no one else at all."

"Yes." Richard raised his head from his work, his great crest of hair . . . of fur . . . powdered with moonlight as with snow. "But that is only surface knowing; an old man with coyote in him, told me that truth-fishes swim beneath all surfaces."

"Gulf sharks, perhaps," Baj said. "Except for the Coopers, I've known only decent people murdered." Saying so, he hadn't meant the Robin woman as well, but saw that Richard took it so.

"Still, wrongs may be made right."

"It seems to me, Richard—and not speaking of the Robin woman—that to go against Boston as is planned, is to win on a carpet of captive women's corpses. In what way is that not true?"

Richard set his needle down. "It is true—true, and the only

way the tribes and Person Guards will be freed to see to it that other daughters and granddaughters and *great*-granddaughters will not someday also be taken for hostage breeders. . . . How can Frozen Jesus object?"

"How not?"

Richard bent to his slicing and sewing. "Baj, you were a prince. What are high Sunrisers taught of Greats and Gods? Is there only Lady Weather, her sad daughter, Summer, and the Winter Lord? . . . Do the Jesuses speak together, or quarrel among themselves, so that many matters go badly? Or is there no Great at all, but only chance?"

". . . I'm not the one to ask."

"You must have considered those questions." Richard bit his thread, knotted the end, and plucked at the stitching to test it.

"Mmm . . . Listen, Richard, I'm twenty years old, and was nothing but a whore-house, booze-house fool many of those years . . . though I did hope to become a competent poet. So, deep questions are still too deep for me, though at least I have the sense to know it."

"But you were taught by wise people."

"Yes. Yes, I was well taught—and paid no attention to any of it, though my brother did. Newton, or old Peter Wilson, would have been the ones you needed for serious questions. They both . . . both would have had good answers for you."

"No thoughts, then, yourself?" Richard turned the moccasin in his huge hands, flexed the double sole.

"No. I've been . . . I've been too busy to worry about it." The night wind was rising; Baj felt its chill through his cloak's thick wool. "—But if you want a *child's* thoughts, Richard, as to Gods and various Jesuses . . . well, when I was ten years old, I imagined that all Greats existed in a . . . a sort of swirling substance, like tumultuous water, like the river we crossed. I thought they all existed there, spinning and sailing this way and that—and if you called (if I, as a boy, called), I might catch one's attention while he or she whirled past. And if I caught them in an eddy, if they were still enough to hear such a minor voice, then they might command something done—or might not, if they thought that more humorous—before the currents of all things spun them away either to pleasures or more important duties—I wasn't sure which."

"That's a picture." Richard set cross-stitches, thick fingers deft, the curved needle sauntering in and out under moonlight barely bright enough for shadows.

"Only a boy's picture, imagining some explanation for the confusions of the world."

"Yes, an unreliable place."

"As I, so young, discovered at every festival, when perfect looked-for gifts—a champion racing stallion, a ten-crew iceboat built by the Edgars—could rarely be depended on. . . . And I've found, recently, that a child's imagined currents may be only a single great whirl-pool, by which we, and every Jesus also, might be taken under."

Richard sighed a deep sigh. "You see, wisdom at ten years old. And grimmer wisdom at twenty."

"Not wisdom. Only wishes and words, Richard—and either of my fathers would have been bored (one politely, the other likely not) to hear me. These aren't the sorts of questions that even Used-to-be-princes are meant to bother their heads with—which was one of the pleasures of *being* a prince."

"Try the right." Richard handed the moccasin over, and Baj stood to tug it on, cross-tie the lacings.

". . . That's really . . . that's comfortable. Thank you very much, Richard."

"I require a payment," Richard said.

"Name it." Baj paced back and forth through moonlight in his new moccasin-boots. They were very light on his feet, and so simply made—sized, sliced, folded and sewn. It was oddly pleasant, wearing them, to feel the details of earth—as he would, of course, also feel the details of sharp stones.

"You are to pay me . . . the beginning of forgiveness for the murder of the Robin lady."

Baj stood still, and noticed that Richard, seated for his sewing, yet nearly met him eye-to-eye. That massive boulder-size seemed to hold sadness to match its muscle.

"Payment given, Richard."

"And in your imagined rapids, your whirling pools," the big Person shifted and heaved to his feet, "—in them, no ship of mercy sails?"

"Only, I suppose, as a Warm-time poet put it: 'in the narrow currents of our faltering hearts.'"

Then a long, deep, considering hum. Baj supposed it was Richard's method for keeping the sounds of the world from troubling his thoughts.

"—I'd be more interested," Baj said, "in what you, and Nancy also, make of the world."

Richard, looming over, smiled his grizzle-bear grimace. "We make . . . do."

When Nancy returned—still silent to Baj, as he to her—the three of them wrapped themselves in their cloaks and blankets under sheltering birches, Errol, innocent as any puppy, curled against Baj's side. And after a time, all—even a wakeful Once-a-prince, remembering a Robin woman's eyes—slept to the conversation of wind and trees.

Until, just before dawn, the rattle and thud of drums came to wake them.

13

Patience thought the drumming was dreamed, aching echoes of her bruises and broken nose.

She woke still savage from the stone-fight the day before, shamed that she'd been driven like a badger into the hut, dragging the log-round's weight and hunched warding thrown rocks. Though she'd left injured children behind her—and would have killed some if she could, despite loving her own . . . her ungrateful son who hadn't visited since she fell.

The drums were rolling, grumbling away like a great departing wagon—already distant, joining others deeper into the hills.

The village seemed to stir and boil in the last of night around her, but no one disturbed the sheepskin at the hut's door.

Her strapped shoulder now only slightly sore, Patience got up from her pallet—with necessary courtesy to her chain-tether and log—and dragged that load to the entrance hide. Supposing she was being unwise, she paged the sheepskin aside to a brightening dawn, the sounds of men running, and women's click-clacking calls and scolding.

"Get back inside." The sentry stared down at her over the shaped wooden beak of a war-helmet. No face to be seen there . . . but the voice familiar.

". . . Peter Aiken?"

"Get *inside*." The leaf-bladed javelin turned slightly in his grip.

Patience stepped back into the hut, let the sheepskin fall, and stood by her log-anchor, waiting.

And as sure as if commanded, Pete Aiken-Robin stooped to enter . . . then stood tall, bare-chested and armed, his carved helmet's blue plume touching the rough wattle ceiling. She saw he belted a heavy hatchet, and a sword. The sword was a scimitar, and hers.

"You look very fine, Peter," Patience said. "You look as a warrior should. —But why are you standing my guard?"

"Three sheep," Aiken said, in fair book-English. "—Given to John Little to take his place."

". . . Ah. Is it possible that honor still lies with the Robins?"

"It still lies with me," Aiken said, sounding to Patience very young. "My word was given—and my word stands." He set his javelin into the near corner. "I took your sword from the trophy lodge."

"And your word stands . . . at what cost?"

Aiken shrugged. "Fuck 'em."—So perfect a use of the ancient WT phrase that Patience couldn't help smiling, and saw beneath the helmet's beak, the young man grinning with her.

"If you live, Pete Aiken," she said, "—if you live, you will be a chief."

Aiken reached up, loosened a strap, and lifted his plumed helmet off. Without it, hair tousled, he seemed only a boy. "Then I'll have to run faster than Chad Budnarik; he wanted your head for the garden."

"Peter," Patience said—and knew as she spoke that she was no longer what she'd been. "Peter, if it's your death, don't do it."

"You're not my mother," he said. "And honor is men's business." He stooped to examine the ankle-shackle and chain. "This would ruin my hatchet to try to break."

There were shouts outside, and they both stayed still, waiting as the noise went past.

"What's happening?"

"We were drummed. . . . Some people, passing by, killed Ed Marble's wife. He's a war-chief just north, and they're a friendly village to us."

"So, your men are going out."

"Yes, they are." He shook the chain. "Hatchet wouldn't break it."

Patience picked up her greatcoat from the pallet, draped it over her shoulders, and buttoned it—one-handed—at her throat. Then, silent, she settled herself into the quietness of anything-might-happen.

Aiken picked up his helmet and put it on. Then he bent to the log-round, gathered it in both arms—and heaved it up with a grunt. ". . . Come on!" He shouldered the sheepskin aside and marched out the entrance, with Patience, barefoot, hopping awkwardly close beside him.

An odd-looking pair—and were looked at, stared at, by several leather-kilted women filling clay jars of water at the steep streamside below. Others, women, children, and old people, were standing far down the settlement, watching a file of armed men trotting away to the north on the far side of the creek, spear-heads bright in first light, their long hide shields at their shoulders. Others, gone before, were only dawn shadows in among distant birches, going away, the drumming going with them.

Pete Aiken, heavy-burdened, yanking Patience stumbling along, strode upslope onto a beaten path above a row of huts—outpits stinking from one to the next as they went. Three children and a small brown dog came to follow them—but at a distance that grew more distant when Patience, hobbling, picked up a rock and bared her teeth at them.

Puffing out effort-breaths, hugging the log-round tight, Aiken staggered on as Patience managed to stay with him, the shackle scoring her ankle each quick awkward step, as if the little brown dog had come to bite her.

They passed a wide garden to their right, and Patience, struggling to keep up, bruising her toes to kick tangling chain ahead with every step, saw cauliflowers growing in it . . . then saw they weren't, but rows of skulls—all full-human, none shaped oddly as Persons' skulls might be. There were some heads still fleshed, but all stuck rotting in the ground for birds and summer

insects to polish to decoration. Brown-feather quills bristle
from eye-holes where broken shreds of white still spoiled. . .
Thrushes.

Aiken stopped at last, and set the log-round down with a
grunt of relief beside the only hut built above the path—a small
open-sided shed, with a neat true-garden laid out just past it
Patience smelled charcoal and hot iron, saw instruments and
steel tools pegged to the shed's back wall. Blacksmith's—and no
blacksmith.

"Willard's gone fighting. That's what he likes to do. . . ." Aiken
ducked in, searching among tools, tongs, and hammers.

It occurred to Patience, standing tethered and sore ankled
long-shadowed now by morning, that the blacksmith's hut pre
sented a future certain—however distant—a future in which
Boston's hostage women, its fierce Person Guard, would have
proved insufficient. The village forges, their tools and shaped
metal, the fine steel beaten out on their anvils—but above the
notion they presented of planning, making, and completing—
would end at last more formidable than any plots, any savage
armies.

Pete Aiken came out into the sunshine with a heavy hammer
and cold chisel. . . . Patience found the chisel particularly impressive. To make a hammer was nothing much. To forge and temper
a chisel, was.

"I don't . . . I don't see how to take the shackle off, and not hit
you." Aiken knelt in sunlight to examine the problem. "But I can
do the chain."

A young woman in a yellow wool skirt, her scarred breasts
bare, had come up to the high path, was standing watching them.
Patience stared at her, and the woman turned and went away . . .
but with purpose.

"Trouble," Patience said.

"My sister—and always trouble. I'm going to . . . I need the anvil." He gripped the shackle's chain and dragged the log-round into the shed, Patience floundering with it, then went outside again for the hammer and chisel.

Time . . . time. Patience felt her heart beating the moments away. Moments for Aiken's sister to come to save a foolish brother from himself, bring other women and some older men, armed, to help her.

"Here." Aiken took her ankle, yanked it so she suddenly sat down on dirt and ashes, then laid her leg across the anvil's iron, and pushed her worn trouser-cuff up out of the way.

Now very brisk and certain, he set the chisel-blade at a chain-link near the shackle, swung the hammer high—then whipped it down while Patience, no longer impatient, sat frozen.

She felt the blow up into her hip—heard the ringing clang an instant later. Pete Aiken bent to stare at the cut, then with no hesitation raised the hammer and struck again, then again . . . Patience, eyes closed, resigned to losing her foot.

"Done." Though he hit it a fourth time, not so hard.

Patience looked and saw the link gleaming where it parted. There were voices down the path.

Aiken shook the chain, worked the link free, then stood, picked up his helmet, and put it on. "Honor satisfied," he said, slid her scabbarded sword from his belt, and handed it to her. "I'll stand to hold them while you run."

A woman—two women—were calling in their clicking pidgin, using no understandable book-English at all.

Patience got to her feet with the severed chain-length jingling, stretched up and kissed Pete Aiken's mouth beneath the helmet's beak. "Brave man," she said, and left him silent— apparently not used to kisses from aging Persons with broken noses. Outside, several tribeswomen, two with hatchets in their hands, were standing back along the path. There were children behind them—and coming trotting the same way, four older men with spears kicked their way through a flock of chicken-birds.

Patience—doubt and fear bundled together and set aside—called out, "Good-bye." Meaning good-bye to honorable Pete Aiken, good-bye to her jailor-log, good-bye to the village of Robins-by-the-Creek. . . . Certainly able now (thank every Jesus) to set aside a shoulder only tender, an ankle only bruised—as she set aside the shouts coming chasing, uproar and argument with Aiken in their way—Patience welcomed restful concentration.

She trotted up the path in sunshine (chain-links musical at her ankle), and said a convinced good-bye to the earth beneath her feet. She emptied her mind of all but thrusting the world down and away, thrusting it behind—and her bare feet going lighter and lighter, till paddling in the air, she sailed gently swaying up . . . and up, with only a futile hatchet whirring its farewell.

* * *

Though Nancy and Richard seemed disturbed at such swift discovery and vengeance chase, even Errol nervous as they packed their packs and ran—Baj felt oddly at ease; he'd been pursued before, and by closer-coming and more formidable hunters.

"I apologize," Nancy said, a little out of breath. She'd bounded up beside while they ran full out past birches and north along the mountain's shrubby slope. Surprisingly fast Richard lumbering slightly ahead, as always.

"Apologize to those behind us." Baj was thankful he was running in new moccasins, not old boots. "Apologize to them," he said, and leaped a tangle of summer vine vine, "—not to me."

Nancy didn't answer, though she gave him the yellow-eyed glance he'd expected. She kept with him for a while, then strayed to the left and up-slope, more comfortable with rougher going.

The drums kept up. No longer deep, rolling growls, they sounded in nervous chasing taps and rattles, as if persuading their prey's hearts to beat to that unsustaining rhythm.

Stones and pebbles bruised Baj's feet through flexible conforming leather, but light swift running was consolation enough. He ordered his legs, and they obeyed. . . . No matter how fast the Robins came, they'd started well behind. "And may catch up, never," Baj said aloud, high-stepping through windfall branches down a draw—dead branches, bare and black from Lord Winter's last several seasons, come down with run-off and rotting to punk. He ran through, breaking some in crumbling wet, and smelled the dank odor of spoiling wood as he went on.

Tap . . . tap tap. The drums coming behind them.

Legs aching but working well, Baj ran up beside Richard—the massive Person pacing along so swiftly, steadily, his heavy, furred pack like a clinging gray wolf on his back.

"How far . . . will they chase?"

Richard plunged into a stand of young evergreens as if they were an ocean's surf, and vanished but for green turmoil as he went. Baj ran downslope through more scattered trees, then upslope again to join as Richard burst into the clear.

"How . . . *far*?"

"To their territory's edge," Richard said, his breath coming short. "—And stop there. They won't . . . want a war."

Richard had an odd way of running—looking odder the closer Baj ran with him. It was a two-legged gallop, and would have seemed more comfortable on four. An odd way, but groundeating, steady and fast.

Baj ran, saw Nancy bounding across the slope above, and heard a wailing cry behind them. He thought some swift tribesmen had caught up—looked back, and saw Errol among evergreens, the boy staggering with his face in his hands.

"Hurt!" Nancy called. "Hurt!" And reversed her run remarkably—in one instant, fleeing north on a saplinged slope . . . in the next, back the other way, so an imagined brushy tail seemed to flirt behind her.

"For God's sake . . ." An ancient oath, and considered indecent in the Kingdom. Baj slowed, stopped, and saw Nancy trotting back to the boy.

Ahead, Richard stood still, looking back. He called out . . . something. The chasing drums seemed to answer with a rainfall patter of beats and pauses—and Baj realized that of course it was drum *talking* they were hearing. Drummed threats, drummed promises being made.

The morning sunshine seemed to pulse with Baj's heartbeat as he ran back the way he'd come, lifting his bow off his shoulder.

Behind him, Richard called again.

Nancy, this side of evergreens, had Errol gripped by the arm, was helping the boy along. "His eyes," she said, "—a branch whipped his eyes, running." Baj saw the line scored across the boy's face, a spot of blood in the boy's right eye, tears in both.

"He'll see again in a moment or two. Lead him away!" Baj knelt to bend the recurved bow and string it, then reached over his shoulder for an arrow. Saw the girl and sniveling boy just standing there. "Go on! *Go!*"

And away she went, half-dragging Errol along.

There was a soft rubbing sound amid the drumming. Some tribesman stroking his drum's taut hide—and heard too clearly, now.

Weasel enough to work back to cut that poor woman's throat—and now, runs into a fucking tree! It seemed to Baj it would have been best to let the Robins have the boy—no use but for murdering, and killing birds. . . . He nocked the broadhead arrow, and scrambled sideways up the mountainside, thinking to wound a man, slow them just a little to make up this lost time.

Though, once he was set and had a clear shot where the ever-greens broke below—the three Persons running north, Richard and Nancy holding the boy half-suspended between them—the drums still seemed a distance behind.

Baj had a little while to wonder if his was a foolish ambush after all—but had wondered it only once when two men came out of the pines with bright spear-points questing. They wore plumed bird-beak helmets, were naked to kilted waists, and wore hatchets, but carried no shields.

Expected, they were still surprising to see, so close behind. Baj supposed these were light scouts and the fastest runners . . . the others farther back, coming with the drums.

He'd expected the likes of Sparrows, shifting savages—but the two trotting across the slope below seemed more soldiers than that. There was a steady deliberation in their tracking. . . .

Baj rose slowly, drawing as he did. The arrow's fletching touched his cheek and he released, mindful to hold a little low.

He should have nocked a second arrow as the first one flew—but instead stared like a raw hunter to see the shaft flick away, at first arching fast, flashing down the mountainside . . . then oddly seeming to sail slower, as if to be certain of its strike. Baj saw the gray fletching dot the near man's side, and he dropped his spear, staggered downslope like a drunk, stumbling, his mouth wide open. Then he tripped and sat down.

Stupidly late, Baj nocked his second arrow—and found no one to shoot. The other Robin was gone racing back into the pines, and would be running to the others with word. It might make them careful enough to slow a little as they came.

"Better," Baj said aloud, and stood, the second arrow still on his string. "Better this way." The man sitting wounded down the mountainside seemed to be looking up at him. Certainly, he should start running after the others. Run—leave the man; leave the arrow. Who would say he should do otherwise?

Baj slid his second arrow over his shoulder into the quiver, then trotted, skidded, down the slope. The Robin sat as if patiently waiting for him—looking, with his beaked helmet, like the get of some unlikely Boston mating of woman and bird.

When Baj reached him, he saw the Robin sat the slope awkwardly, and smelled of shit. A boy, perhaps sixteen, seventeen years old, he stared up at Baj under the brow of his plumed helmet, and hissed-in rapid breaths of agony.

"I'm sorry," Baj said to him—a stupidity. The arrow had gone through from side to side. The fletching nestled against the boy's left ribs; the razor-edged head and inches of shaft stuck out lower, at his other side.

Time tapped Baj on the shoulder, and he—or perhaps a slightly different Baj—stepped behind the Robin, hauled his head sharply back, drew the left-hand dagger and cut the boy's throat. There was . . . a sort of wet sneeze and convulsion, and Baj—head averted so as not to see too much—bent, yanked the irreplaceable arrow on through the boy's body and free . . . then ran away north, strung bow on his shoulder, bloody dagger in one hand, bloody arrow in the other.

Galloping the slope through low shrubbery, over rubble scree, he ducked past a pine, paused, and managed to wipe the knife on his buckskins and sheath it. He ran on, still holding the arrow in a hand gloved with dirt and drying blood. . . . It seemed to him impossible to stay clean in this wilderness.

Behind him, keeping irregular time to his flight, sounded the conversation of drums.

. . . He caught up in a little while. Staggering tired, and with a WT "stitch" in his right side, Baj saw the three Persons in miniature ahead and a little below him, trotting north into brush and rougher country. Richard was forging in the lead, leaving a wake of shrubbery forced aside, with Nancy and Errol following—the boy apparently now seeing well enough.

Baj, still hearing pursuing drums, saw they'd slowed a little to wait for him. —And as if she'd heard his thought, Nancy turned to look behind her. She looked, went on, then turned to look again and saw him. He knew it, even at the distance.

She stopped, let Errol scurry on, and stood waiting . . . watching him come down to them, his bow, still strung, bouncing at his shoulder. Richard stood waiting farther on—standing amid flowering bushes like a bear risen from a berry patch.

"What?" Nancy called to him as he came. "*What?*"

Meaning, Baj supposed, everything. "I . . . killed one. A scout. The other ran back. I think it slowed them a little."

Nancy shook her head as if she'd meant none of that, and stepped through a tangle to stare at him, poke and pat his arms and chest, then stand back. "Ease your bow," she said. "Do Sunrisers have to be told to do everything?" And she was away, running.

* * *

"How far?" Baj, gone to one knee under a young alder, tried to take a breath that didn't catch at his side. "How far does these people's territory run?"

Richard, seeming weary at last, sat panting in rough grass. "Certainly not much farther. . . . Not much farther."

"You say," Nancy said. Errol curled beside her, she lay dappled by early evening shadows in a sapling's shade, her head resting on her pack. "Those villages could own another hundred Warm-time miles."

"Surely not," Baj said.

Drums ticked and tapped as if to contradict him—and sounded a little nearer. He drew in the deepest breath he could, and felt the catch in his side fading. "We need to move."

Richard nodded, heaved up to his feet, shrugged his big pack to settle it, and lumbered away through the trees.

"Where," Nancy said, "—is these mountains' Jesus and His mercy?" She rolled to her feet, took up her pack, and trotted out. Errol, coming awake, scrambled beside Baj to follow.

As they ran through the alder grove and out along a grassy lead—no true creek—Baj, glancing aside at Errol's face, saw only the usual alert and vacant abstraction. The same expression, surely, he'd worn as he came out of the woods, returning to where the woman waited, tied to her tree.

. . . They ran, rested again, and ran—but slower and slower as evening shadows lengthened. Baj no longer felt his legs; they moved beneath him, but separate as wagon wheels or a horse's hooves might be. He had more and more difficulty avoiding large stones and fallen branches, or the hook and hold of thornbushes in his way—and no longer stepped quite straight, but shambled a little to one side, then the other.

The Persons' blood was failing them as well. Richard's tongue, revealed a surprising purple, lolled a little as he padded on. Nancy, panting just behind, stumbled now and then, no longer sure-footed, with Errol pacing slower beside her. They had little run left in them.

"Night." Nancy used a breath to say it—and the four of them labored on as if sheltering darkness waited just ahead, past this water lead, past more alders. Past whatever lay along their way.

". . . Night," Nancy had said, but there was still light enough to see they'd left a mountain behind, still light enough for the next mountain's long shadow to show against its green, when they noticed—Baj first—that only the wind and the day's last bird-calls sounded.

There was no sound of drumming.

They went on, regardless—flight seeming an end in itself—stumbled along for a little way, then slowed, walked . . . and stopped to stand stupid as spotted cattle.

"I suppose," Richard said, "—they might be coming on, silent."

But the Robins weren't. The continuous pressure of chase at their backs was gone. No one hunted them anymore.

Baj and the others dropped as if melting to the grass, tugged blankets around them, and lay cramped with aching muscles until sleep came to keep them company into nightfall. . . . Errol, huddled close at Baj's back, whimpered in a dream.

"Is there no breakfast?"

Baj jerked awake to a chilly dawn, fumbled for his rapier's hilt—and found it as he blinked sleep from his eyes.

There was an old woman sitting on the summer grass, staring at him . . . at the others as they woke. Someone had beaten her, broken her nose and left blood on her face.

"*Breakfast.*"

Then Baj saw it was Boston-Patience, sitting cross-legged and barefoot in a dirty blue coat, grimy white blouse, and worn blue trousers. She held her scimitar across her lap—but now looked too frail, too damaged to use it. Her left arm was strapped in a sling.

"Lady," Richard heaved himself up to stand, "—what happened to your boots?"

"My boots? What of my *nose*, Richard?" She sounded as if she had a snow-season cold.

"Who hurt you?" Nancy left her blanket, went to touch the woman's face—but Patience pushed her hand away.

"I hurt myself first, by dreaming in the air. Later, children threw rocks while I was a guest in a Robin's nest." She leaned a little to her right as she sat, used her sheathed scimitar for support. Her left arm and shoulder seemed strapped firm. "I asked about breakfast—and by the way, the tribesmen no longer follow . . . which is just as well, since they would have caught the four of you snoring."

"We have cold venison," Baj said.

"I'll take some. . . . And how do you do, Baj-who-was-Bajazet? You certainly do *quickly*. I don't think I've ever seen such scurrying away below me, as you four fleeing. The Robins couldn't keep up, and I couldn't keep up—still unsteady Walking-in-air."

"We have no more salt," Nancy said, and handed the woman a strip of smoked deer.

"I will do without," Patience said, then crammed, chewed, and swallowed. "I do need a bath of water to get the stink and dried blood off me—and you, girl, need the same. You smell like a wet dog and worse; do you have your bloodies?" She bit into the meat, tore more free.

"No, I *don't*," Nancy said. But Patience paid no attention, only chewed, swallowed, and bit off more.

"This is still Robin country," Richard said, "and will be, well past the Map Gap-Cumberland."

"Yes," Patience swallowed venison, "—but belonging to a different village than the two that chased you, and unlikely to obey their drums." She took another bite, spoke with meat in her mouth. "Did those chase wrongly? Some chief's wife was killed. . . ."

"They didn't chase wrongly," Baj said.

Patience looked at him, the last bit of deer dangling from her fingers. "So—are we speaking of stupidity? Or of something that couldn't be avoided."

". . . It might have been avoided," Richard said.

"Mmm." She ate the last bite, munching it slowly, savoring. "Our weasel boy?"

Errol was peeing against a small spruce, and paid no attention.

"My fault," Richard said.

Nancy said it almost with him. "*My* fault—and we thought . . . we thought if so, it might save trouble."

"*Save* trouble?" Patience looked at Baj. "Nòt your fault, too?"

"We were all careless."

" 'Careless . . . ' Is there more meat?" Patience took a smaller piece from Nancy, sniffed it for soundness. "Well, none of you have been the fool I've acted." She reached up to tap her bandaged shoulder. "—And I must tell you, if we continue this stupid in the north, we'll die of it." She ate the meat . . . then looked odd, bruised face draining of color so its dried blood seemed black. She suddenly slumped back to lie stretched out in the grass amid delicate dawn ladies-slippers, beneath a sheltering chestnut oak.

Nancy went to kneel beside her, but Patience shook her head, warded her away . . . and lay silent for a while, taking slow careful breaths.

"You ate too fast," Nancy said, and received a hard look, though Patience lay where she was, took more deep breaths. . . . After a while, she said, "I saw glitter nearly in our way." She lifted her right hand, pointed north. "Water. I think a beaver pond. I need to wash myself." . . . And she slowly sat up, looking a little better.

"We'll both go," Nancy said, "—you sailing, I striding; we'll wash ourselves clean."

"I've had few dreams from my son," Patience said, as if someone had asked her. "They'll be interfering with him, trying to force him older . . ." Then, in a sudden lurching motion, she swung up off the grass as if beginning to stand. But instead, she slid, skidded strangely away just above the ground . . . faltered, then rose suddenly as if shoved from beneath and sat cross-legged in the air, rocking unsteadily and no higher than a man could reach.

That beginning-to-fly disturbed Baj as if sea-sickness had come upon him with motions his eyes rejected. She hovered there a moment, a small white-haired lady come to mischief . . . then sailed away, slow swooping off to the north, barefoot, beaten, and bandaged, clutching her curved sword.

Nancy bounded after the fleeting morning shadow, trailing her own. And Errol, attracted to the chase, trotted after them.

Richard dug into his big pack, found his diminished roll of leather, the small kit of needles and spooled sinew. "Little feet," he said, "—so I should have enough, once I measure her." He unrolled the hide. "It's rare for the Robins—any tribesmen—to let captives go. Almost always, they find some use for them. Decoration . . . something." He sighed. "They skin Persons, sometimes, for what pelt they have."

Baj searched his own pack, found a last slice of venison, smoked black, and sat beside Richard to chew it. "She's hurt, and not what she was."

A honeybee wandered between them, humming to itself. Other bees, their motion amid wildflowers sensed as much as seen, drifted back and forth across the glade, their faint constant buzzing a sort of foundation for other summer-morning sounds, small birds singing in the evergreens, a hawk's thin distant cry, the varying ruffle of the mountain winds.

"No," Richard said, "—she isn't what she was. As we, none of us, will be what we were."

"And us not many, set against Boston."

Richard turned to look at him, brown bear's eyes peering from under the shelf of brow. "No, we are not. The Township's constables could step on us five, crush us, and not even know it was done."

"Encouraging . . ." Baj finished his venison, reached over, stretching, for his "canteen," pulled the wood stopper and drank long swallows of night-chilled water.

"That we're so few, gives us our best chance." Richard stretched leather across his lap. "—That and the quality of what we intend to do. . . . Look at this hide, tanned so fine and soft. Oil this leather and respect it, and it won't fail until it's old as a Person—or human—grows old."

"Good workmanship."

"Yes," Richard said, "—and something that had to be discovered again, once the cold came down. I know of no copybook found that explains how leather was treated in Warm-times. Not even the Red-blood tribesmen—Mohawk or Abenaki—not even their people remembered how."

"I suppose that's true." A bird was singing in the firs—two sharp-stepped notes.

"Then someone realized anew that, of all things, piss and dung were required for tanning—though perhaps in Warm-times they'd found sweeter-smelling ways." Richard selected a curved needle from his kit, and threaded sinew through its tiny eye in one easy motion. "What's true of leather, is true of free being. The rawhide of hostage-taking and ruling battles must be worked—even if unpleasantly—worked at last to suppleness, and decent understanding." He set down his needle and thread. "We, who have the forms of beasts bred into us, see very clearly the beast that Sunrisers conceal."

Listening to Richard, as often, slightly altered the previous "Richard" in Baj's mind. "That is craft philosophics," he said, "and sounds more sensible than most to me. But as to that 'even if unpleasantly,' how many women are held in Boston's ice?"

"At least—Patience says—at least hundreds still kept alive."

"Mountain *Jesus* . . ."

Richard measured a length of rawhide lacing in half, then in half again, and snapped the strands in his great hands. "Yes, young Who-was-a-prince, that number of girls and women and old women—all once daughters of important tribesmen . . . and now, mothers of important officers and soldiers of the Person Guard."

"And will the Guard and the tribesmen be grateful to us, Richard—once we slaughter those mothers and daughters, to set their sons and fathers free?"

Richard shook his head. "I thought you realized, Baj. We'll surely be killed for what we do. The Shrikes—some at least—we hope will understand the necessity, and a few come with us. The Guard will have other tasks."

"But 'understanding' will make no difference."

"You see," Richard smiled a sad and toothy smile, "you have a prince's wisdom of costs. Of course understanding will make no difference." He measured and snapped more lacing. "Many tribesmen—and some of the Guard—will never accept such killings, however necessary, without revenge. We are talking about women loved and lost and dreamed of for many years."

"Yes . . . of course. Too loved, too dreamed of, to allow their murderers—in whatever good cause—to stroll smiling through the country, afterward. I see that."

Richard nodded. "If we succeed in killing the hostage women—'a large if,' I believe the copybooks say—*if* we succeed, there will be no place between the Oceans Atlantic and Pacific where we may rest for long with throats un-cut." He set his rawhide laces aside. "Hard news, I know, for Sunriser-Baj."

"Hard news," Baj said, "—for Sunriser or Moonriser."

"Yes."

"And there is no way . . . *no way* we can free those women, instead?"

Richard sighed. "We may not be given time even for murder—and since the Guard, outnumbered, will surely fail at Boston's gate, we'd only 'free' the women into the hands that already hold them captive."

" 'Not given time . . .' But I'm too young to die." Baj had intended that as casually humorous, but found it sounded with a plaintive air, after all—which on reflection made it funnier.

"I am, too," Richard said, very seriously.

Baj began to giggle, couldn't help it—and such was hysteria (he supposed it was the old WT hysteria happening) that he couldn't stop, and soon was lying flat on the grass as sick-Patience had, but roaring with laughter.

Richard, a monument of dark skin and fur-tufted muscle, sat staring at him. Then, slowly the broad-muzzled face widened to its fearsome grin, fangs were bared, and a deep-thumping laugh developed, sounding very like belly-rumbles.

Baj, who'd been beginning to recover, was set off again by that, so both ended laughing in the sunny grass, laughing till their aching sides sobered them. . . . It was, for Baj, the most exquisite relief. It brought tears to his eyes—and visions with them, memories of the ones he'd loved, each laughing at whatever small

circumstance had prompted it, so Baj saw them very clearly . . .
saw behind them the bannered battlement or cut-stone office, the
glassed garden or tower chamber where each stood.

. . . Laughter over, Baj lay resting in the grass, those memories a gift as sweet as if these mountains' Jesus had drifted by
with the humming bees. Feeling older in one way, younger in another, he lay considering the fact of almost certain—no, of certain death, sooner or later—and decided to leave that fact beneath
and behind him for the while, as Boston-Patience dismissed the
solid earth for flights above it.

. . . The women—Errol trailing behind—came back late and
merry, Boston-Patience flying low and badly, Nancy running beneath her, bounding along, leaping once to catch the hem of the
long blue coat, so Patience almost fell, then recovered, swatting
gently down at the girl with her sheathed scimitar.

"My nose," Patience said, landing in camp with a stumble, so
she almost went to her knees. "Difficult to breathe through.
—But I'm clean!" And she was, though her clothes and coat still
hung drying on her.

Nancy's damp homespun still clung as well, and Baj noticed—
couldn't help it—the print-through of two rows of small nipples
down her chest.

She saw him see.

"Handy," Nancy said, through breeze sounds and bee sounds
in their glade. "Handy," looking at him golden-eyed, "—if I have
pups."

It was a relief for Baj to turn away to the Boston-woman,
whose eyes were dark as dug anthracite. "Lady, shall I try to do
what our festival wrestlers do?"

"That depends on which of their doings." Patience sat, legs
crossed. Her bare feet were almost small as a child's.

"The nose," Baj said.

"Ah—well, I suppose you can't do worse to it. . . ."

"Take a breath." Baj went to kneel before her.

Patience took her breath—her broken nose whistling slightly, like a flute. Baj reached out and pinched it hard, felt a little bone or cartilage shift under his fingers . . . then yanked it straight to a soft click.

"*Christ!*" A curse, or prayer, Baj had only heard a few times before. Patience rocked back and forth—almost put her hand up to nurse the nose, then kept it away. "Felt better breaking!" Drops of blood ran down to her mouth.

"Then they use two flat little strips of wood," Baj said, "one along each side to keep the nose straight. Those little strips are tied together at the ends, and both held firm in place with string looped tight around the man's head."

"And must appear charming," Patience said, honking like a goose.

"I can do that," Richard said, and got up to go fashion it.

"If," Patience sniffed at blood-drops, "if I don't come out of this beautiful, Prince, you will need to run faster than from Robins."

"I think," Baj said, ignoring the 'Prince,' "—you will look even more elegant, once the little wood pieces are off. 'Spints,' is what they call them."

"I'm still bleeding." Patience gave Baj a hard look, and spit bright red off her upper lip.

"That will soon stop," Baj said. ". . . At least, it did with the wrestlers." He received another look, so was relieved when Richard came back with two short little splinters of thin-whittled alder, and a length of sewing sinew—moved Baj aside, and sat before Patience to set them.

"We're told those are 'spints,' Richard."

"Really? Bone-holds, we called them in the Guard. Hold still, dear . . ."

* * *

Supper that night—and, after argument, with a small fire hidden deep in a cleared pit—was the last scraps of venison, and a bird: a grouse, taken by Errol with a thrown stick.

"We'll need more food than this," Patience said, though she'd been given the largest small share, and was finishing it fast. "We can't go tottering on our way. I can't Walk-in-air on nothing. . . . Though now, thanks to our Richard—" she stuck out a small foot, demonstrated her new moccasin-boot, "—thanks to him, I go nicely on the ground."

"Last of my leather," Richard said. "So all be careful of rocks and sharp edges."

"I'll take the bow out ahead, tommorow," Baj said. "I'll find something."

"Watch out for boar." Richard grinned at the Boston-woman. "We had . . . an adventure, with a boar."

Errol made his tongue-clicking sound, perhaps recalling the taste of wild pig.

"Whatever," Patience said. "Get us something more than this." She finished a little drumstick and chewed the bones. . . . Bent over the fire's changeable yellow light, she appeared to Baj the very type of Warm-time witch he'd seen drawn in a copybook—perhaps originally meant for children; perhaps not. Her small face, once elegant and fine, now puffed, bruised, and beaten, bracketed with spint-sticks and sinew string as with some half-helmet, ceremonial for a sacrifice.

"You'll look much better soon," he said, then thought perhaps he shouldn't have.

Patience glanced at him—then slantwise at Nancy, sitting silent beside her. "Still young, isn't he? . . . Baj-boy," she said, "never mention possible future improvement in a woman's looks, Person or all human-blood. They will not thank you for the reminder that presently, they look ugly."

"You don't look ugly. You look . . . interesting."

Richard made an *Um-mm* sound.

"Boy," Patience said, "leave the subject."

"I will. Yes."

"Thank you." She smiled. "And I also thank you for the wrestlers' cure. An attempt, at least."

Baj nodded, but said no more. Paid attention to the fire's modest flames.

"Still Robins," Richard said, "further along the mountains."

"Yes." Patience nodded. "At least another nest of them . . . then Pass I-Seven, wide as the Gap-Cumberland. Farmers there."

"Farmers," Richard said, "though too far north, too near the Wall for best growing."

"Farmers to be *avoided*," Patience said, "is what they are. And well-avoided, since they're insane, with children raised to be insane, and they murder those few who are not."

Richard nodded. "Even the Guard stays clear of those. —Or did, when I served in it, for fear madness might be catching."

"What madness?" Baj said.

Patience made a face that looked even odder with her spinted nose. "The madness . . . of longing."

"We'll travel that pass at night," Richard said. "And the lady, Walking-in-air."

A distant chorus commenced . . . WT miles away.

"Wolves." Baj had heard them closer on the Map-Ohio riverbank, as the royal boat—the small one, *Rapid*—had skated hissing past by moonlight.

"True wolves," Nancy said, and Richard listened to the high-pitched wailing rise and fall, then nodded.

"We used to hunt them," Baj said, "—on horseback over snow when Lord Winter came down."

"And caught them?" Patience said.

"The dogs caught them, sometimes—often were sorry they had. Some archers on snow-foots could trail and kill wolves, if the drifts were deep enough. . . . And a snow-tiger came to the river, once, though I didn't see him. Said to have bred in Map-Oklahoma."

"They came," Patience said, "—as your First-father's father came. Over the bridge of land from Map-Siberia."

"I believe that's so," Baj said. "It's what we were taught."

"I've heard of those tigers." Nancy'd spoken rarely through the evening. "Still lesser creatures than the great white bears that come down from the Wall."

"You insult my some-part daddy," Richard said, smiling the smile Baj had grown used to, "—who apparently was only a grizzled."

"I have never known," Patience said, "—what portions were placed and Talent-shifted in my mother's womb to make me."

"I know mine," Nancy said, then was quiet, looking into the fire.

"Well," Richard dug into his great pack. "I, and all *my* portions, are going to wreck our Baj at chess!"

. . . From then, through the game—a rare triumph for Baj—and till time to sleep, only the little fire spoke.

* * *

The next days traveling the mountains north—mountains running above the long valley Map-Shenandoah—they called "turkey time," since wild turkey-birds fed strutting under oaks growing in groves down the steep valleys. Errol took some with thrown sticks, and Baj took many with his bow—requiring an occasional tedious search to recover a stray arrow. . . . They had wild mushrooms to eat—cautious of death-angels—and dug roots, berries, and rabbits. But turkey was the main.

"Is there nothing else, no red meat, living in these hills?" Claiming it a reminder of the penalty for pride and inattention, Patience had walked the ground with them most of that day, climbed as they'd climbed, and clambered with them through tangled underbrush. . . . Now, she sat cross-legged in their clearing amid a stand of balsam fir, complaining while yet another big bird leaned on its peeled stick, smoking, skin popping in the heat of another cautious-laid pit fire. "—No red meat, and of course no salt."

"These foolish fires." Richard shook his head.

"Listen, Goodness," Patience said, "*some* of us have guts too elegant for raw bird. And anyone close enough to see the buried little fires *we* set, is close enough for any—but Baj—to have scented already."

"No salt," Nancy said, "—but we still have berries."

"Won't have them much longer." Richard poked the roasting bird with a finger. "Traveling north out of summer. Colder nights, already."

"Berries," Patience said, "—are poor fuel for rising in the air." It seemed to Baj that she was becoming again the self he'd seen sailing to kill Master MacAffee. Though her nose-spints were still tied in place, her left arm now was only slung. She moved with ease and no wincing, and her small face, that had been drawn, was rounded, relaxed as if she'd lost a year or two of age.

"I hope," she said, having noticed his attention, "—that I'm not about to receive another princely compliment."

"Wouldn't venture it," Baj said.

"Well," Patience leaned forward, sniffed at the roasting bird. "Well, I am feeling better."

"Time before supper," Nancy said, stood up and went off into the trees with her hatchet.

"Time for what?"

"I suppose," Baj said, "for lessons again."

In a while, Nancy came back with two strong green stick-swords cut and whittled. One gently curved, the other straight.

"Good boy," Patience said. "You've done what I asked for her."

"Get up," Nancy said, staring at Baj through firelight. "Get up and fight." It was the first she'd spoken to him in a while.

Baj stood, and stepped aside for room.

"Poor light for fencing," Patience said, "—but all the better."

A distance from the fire, Errol, always interested in fighting, sat up to see.

"They're good at points," Richard said.

"At 'points', dear one," Patience said, "there is no good or bad, but only strike and not be stricken. I thought all old soldiers knew that."

The fire's glow was in Baj's eyes; he looked aside to spare his seeing, and Nancy tossed his stick-sword to him.

Baj expected an attack, but didn't get it. Instead, the girl watched and waited, cautious and cold as a stranger, so they stood with their whittled branches, still as ice-people carved for a funeral.

"Well," Patience said, "—fight, or fuck!" And to Richard, "See how coarse I've grown in exile? I would never have said such a thing on the Common."

"It's the company you keep," Richard said, and they laughed (soprano and bass) as Nancy—now looking furious—bounded at Baj as if to kill him.

He could have hit her once . . . then another time. But only gave room and backed away over high grass, shadowed by fire-light and cooler light as the moon rose over the mountains.

When the girl paused, panting, eyes gold as Kingdom coins, Patience, at the fire, set her scimitar aside and stood. "Well, girl," she said, "you've learned something. But *never* lose calm when you fight!"

She walked over to Nancy, and took the stick-sword from her. "Stand away, now, and watch how it should be done . . . and done weak-handed at that."

And saying so—not quite finished talking—she was at Baj in an odd strutting striding attack, much like a fighting rooster's for posture . . . then sudden flurries of speed, in which her slung left arm seemed little impediment.

She came at him, white hair shining in moonlight, dark eyes shadowed darker, and struck short snapping blows at odd angles, and quickly—pecking, is what it seemed—delivered so unevenly in succession that they were difficult to parry. She had a . . . a style of striking then hooking his reposte away, using her branch-blade's scimitar curve.

It was very elegant, very determined attacking, and Baj found himself fencing as he'd fought only once before, when the Achieving King had come to the *salle* to teach him his lesson.

The fir branches whipped and thrust and whickered together in swift counters, and Baj felt the cool exhilaration of accomplished great effort—felt that for several moments back and forth across the moonlit grass, came close twice to hitting her, and was considering drawing a pretend left-hand dagger when Patience stepped a little strangely, kicked him in the right knee—and as he staggered, hacked him hard to the side of his neck. Then there was a delicate little motion, barely a thrust at all, that would have picked his left eye out if she'd wished, and her splintered branch had been sharp steel.

Lame, Baj still recovered and stood on guard, though he would have been a dead man. Beyond the fire's light, Errol clicked his tongue.

"Well, my Baj," Patience smiled, "you're almost as good as you thought you were. Though . . . a little too *attentive* to your greenwood sword. After all, it's only an instrument of your will. Your *will* directs it, not your wrist. And, of course, fighting includes kicks and other things."

Baj saluted her with his branch, standing a little awkwardly, since his knee hurt. "Thank you for the reminding lesson, Lady. And all the more, weak-handed."

Patience tossed her branch aside. "Oh, well-enough with something so light, fencing a few passes. . . . But you are dangerously good, fighting straight-bladed—those nasty thrusts and lunges—and even better, I suppose, with your familiar steel in your hand." She reached across to nurse her left shoulder. "When you're less concerned with artful parries, Baj, and recall your fighting dagger *and* that moccasin-boots are useful kickers, you'll be an unlucky young man for almost anyone to cross. I don't doubt you'd have a fair chance of killing me, then."

"He did tell me those sorts of things," Nancy said. "He tried to teach me all of them."

"I'm sure he has," Patience said, "though was slow to remember a few himself, when he faced me. . . . And poorly you've learned, Nancy. I've seen women cleaning fish with more skill than you show, girl, and much more sensible temper." She started toward the fire, then turned back. "What stands across from you when you fight, is life or death—and no person at all to be loved *or* hated. Learn that, or bite the dirt with your guts spilled out."

. . . Later, when Baj and Nancy both slept—Errol as usual curled against Baj's back—the moon had risen to its cloudy height, and a cold wind sighed from the north, mentioning distant thunder. Richard and Patience, wrapped in cloak and coat by the fire-pit's ashes, conversed quietly about Boston-town, which Richard had seen only once, years before—allowed the visit as aide to a colonel of the Guard. They recalled its gates, its many streets and passageways . . . and the so-slow changes in its buildings, its cathedrals and courtyards, as the weight of their ice deformed them—to then be re-carved, rounded or angled, and new wall-blocks with altered key-blocks added, so each generation discovered a slightly different gleaming Boston, sculpted as their city.

They discussed that—and the Guard's Wolf-General, Sylvia, who'd once been Richard's commander, before his transfer and desertion. . . . Then, tired of talking, they sat silent beneath a cloud-streaked jewelry of stars glittering the cold night across, and kept to their own thoughts until Patience said, "They're both still so young. Too young to suffer what must be done."

"Sad," Richard said, "—but true." A phrase legacy from Warm-times, and almost always appropriate.

15

Dawn greeted with a rumbling crash and roar.

Baj sat up from his blanket's folds, was struck with the first of hard slanting rain, and drenched.

They all stood from coat, cloaks, or blankets, and trotted with their possibles and packs to the poor shelter of the evergreens, which whipped and bowed to the storm's wet winds, stroking them with soaking branches.

Errol, burrowing at Baj's side, was making shrill piping noises—shriller when lightning cracked past overhead, and another great door of thunder slammed shut.

Richard, fur-tufts sopped and drooping, ducked as lightning flared all a brilliant white—and thunder came smashing after it. Baj saw, in an echo of the eye, Nancy crouched wincing at her pack, teeth bared in fear as lightning came sizzling near, flashed down past the camp and *cracked* among the trees. . . . He saw that, and as the glare faded, noticed Patience standing back, white hair plastered as the rain came down, watching him.

As though, in that moment, he'd seen his Second-mother looking through those black eyes, Baj, keeping Errol with him, went to the girl as wind came whistling . . . knelt beside and put his arm and a fold of cloak around her. She turned as if to bite him . . . but didn't, and the three of them huddled close.

The storm grew more savage, striking near them with bolts that blazed into the mountain, thunder peals that shook it. Then sweeps and sweeps of blowing rain . . . that as dawn lightened slightly to morning, could be seen marching as a shouting army in dark rank on rank across the mountains.

Nancy, fine red rooster-comb of hair soaked black, trembled at Baj's side. "Too loud," she said. . . . The wind brought the white smell of water with it, and the smell of stone and grass from the mountain balds. Brought also an odd hint of burning—perhaps from fires the lightning set, too fierce for the rain to drown.

. . . The storm slowly eased to gusts and spattering dashes, the thunder gone trundling south, then eased again to puddled calm under cool and watery light. They all stood, shook water from drenched clothes, and Patience, stripping rain from her white hair, said, "Lord Winter wakes in the north, and clears his throat."

Dripping in the chill of damp breezes, they shouldered wet packs, and Baj his bow and quiver, the arrow-fletching too wet for use. Errol, recovered, scuttled away ahead, and Patience and Baj drew steel as they went, to whip the weapons through drying air, flicking wet from shining blades. Nancy watched, unsheathed her own, and the three of them squelched over soaked summer grass and rain-slick rock, duelling the wind while Richard marched behind, not troubling to swing raindrops from his ax.

Above, a gray sky slowly became streaky blue, with the clouds called horsetails bannering away south.

The breeze that dried their swords brought more and more the stink of damp burning with it . . . so by sun-straight-up, as they clambered down a steep defile thick with yellow birch—Patience grumbling as she managed, ground-walking beside them—Nancy said, "Serious burning."

"Stop, then," Patience said, blowing out a tired breath. "Stop a moment." And they rested leaning against slender birches.

Richard raised his head and sniffed the air. "Forest is too wet to burn."

Patience sighed. "Then something burned before the rain. I'm weary of stomping and stepping, anyway." She bent her head as if she prayed to these mountains' Jesus . . . then slowly tilted forward as if about to fall. But the fall never came. Instead, she eased out that way, leaning in the air as if on the air, and Baj saw her small moccasin-boots just off the ground.

It had seemed to him before, that the Boston-woman rose in a single almost swinging way to Walk-in-air, but now, watching closely, he saw that wasn't so. It was a rising in gradual bounds, each—timed perhaps to a breath—higher than the one before . . . until she was no longer what they were, or she had been—but a different creature, white-haired and blue-coated, sailing up through sun-struck birch leaves into the sky.

They all—except for Errol, who was on all fours, sniffing at something at the base of a tree—they all stood watching Patience rise, sitting cross-legged, her scimitar held on her lap. Rise . . . then drift away to the north.

It still seemed to Baj an amazement, the gift of a Great, and something past the sensible of life. . . . But not quite the miracle it had been. The so-tedious mind, becoming used to it, had turned it almost usual with the curse of accustom, so it might have been that a familiar hunting hawk had flown from his gauntlet with jess-bells ringing. . . . Well, perhaps an eagle.

Nancy raised her red-crested head, sniffed the air. "Meat," she said. "Meat burning with the other burning."

Errol left his interesting tree and pranced a circle around them, making his tongue-click sounds, then trotted away down the mountainside.

Richard shouldered his ax, said, "Now, we go carefully," and strode off along the slope. . . . The mountains' air, after its storm, was fine and clear, so what seemed almost a Warm-time sunshine spangled through the leaves to decorate Baj and Nancy with flowing gold medallions as they hiked down the birches after him.

It appeared the perfect friendly air of a perfect summer afternoon, but its breeze still brought burning with it as they reached the mountain's wide green apron of water meadow refreshed by rain, and Baj took his bow from his shoulder, paused and knelt in high grass to brace it—making an odd shadow—then drew an arrow from his quiver, blew through its feathers to dry them further, and set it to the string as they went on. Damp fletchings . . . damp string—but fair enough for a short shot.

Nancy had said nothing to him since the storm, but she walked alongside.

There was a low ridge lying across their way, as if a small mountain had begun to wake and rise, then slumped to sleep again. Baj supposed this was the beginning of true lower country—at least for a time—since no succession of green rounded peaks loomed above its pine-furred spine. Lower country . . . "Thank you," he said aloud, imagining these mountains' Jesus listening from his tree.

"Thank me?" Nancy said.

"Well, I was thanking Mountain Jesus for level ground at last. . . . But also, I thank you and Richard. In your company, I've become a . . . more human human."

"That," she said, and was smiling, "—is to go from bad to worse."

They laughed loud enough for Richard to turn and frown at them, so they became serious, and looked right and left across the meadows as they went to the sleeping ridge. It was so like a great creature lying down, that Baj began a poem . . . that turned instead, as he paced along, into a tale for children—of a gentle monster, immense, named Pepperada-Dodo, who befriended all young creatures, animal, human, or Person, and guarded them—though, too shy to be seen as himself, appearing always as a modest mountain, carefully cloaked in evergreens.

A disguise successful, as Baj found—bow now eased, and arrow quivered—climbing the ridge's steep slope, hauling himself up it from sapling to sapling, his pack weighing heavier and heavier, his moccasin-boots slipping in rain-soaked soil or scrabbling up shelves of stone. Less soil, more stone as he climbed higher, Nancy stepping up more lightly beside him.

When they stopped climbing to catch their breath—Richard above them, massive, still moving quietly up the hill—Baj scanned the sky for Boston-Patience, but saw above the evergreens no tiny flag of blue coat drifting across blue sky.

They gathered at the crest—Errol squatting, drawing white lines on a round of surfaced stone with a sharp-edged rock—and met the strongest stink of burning yet, rising up the reverse slope. To the north, where the country sank away to a deep, wide valley, a smudge of light-brown smoke towered, broken by breezes.

"Past that burning," Richard said, "—is the Pass I-Seventy."

"Can we avoid the burning?" Baj was amused to hear himself ask a question that wouldn't have occurred to him only weeks before. Caution and care had come to stay.

"No," Richard said, "—though we can try, by one or two WT miles, going by."

"That's a Robin village," Nancy said. "We passed it, coming south."

"They built too low." Richard shook his head. "Hill tribes live longer in the hills."

Errol began hitting the stone with his rock. *Tock tock tock*, until his rock powdered and broke.

* * *

From the bottom of the ridge, they walked north, keeping to the trees where they could, and hold direction. Filing through birch groves and tangled brush along a narrow glittering run, they saw the smoke still rising, a little to their right.

Baj came last, pressed a little to keep up through dense growths of thorn and bird berry. Nancy trotted in front of him, her light-footed shadow, hunchbacked by her pack, slanting beside her. They stirred whirring grass-hoppers up and around them as they went.

Baj heard that sort of whirring whisper behind him—then cold steel touched the back of his neck. He yelped, wheeling, drawing his sword as Patience hung in the air just above him, smiling, her head haloed by the sun. "It might be wise to watch behind you, Baj Who-was-et cetera. Behind and above. I am not the only Talent out of Boston."

Baj took a breath, put up his rapier, and said, "Good advice."

"You know Warm-time's 'et cetera'?" She sheathed her scimitar, and swung slightly in the air, her face, despite the little spints along her nose, now looking only lightly bruised.

"I know it, Lady."

Patience thrust a small moccasin down. "Pull me to the ground. It feels good in the back of my head . . . something rubs inside there."

Baj reached up to hold her foot, then gently drew her from the air. There was an odd . . . resistance.

"Feels good," she said, sliding down to him and along his chest and belly to stand in the grass. "Feels good . . ." She rested there against him, smiling up into his face, black eyes so close he saw nothing else, so she might have been a girl, and beautiful.

"*Is she hurt?*" Nancy, coming back to them.

"No," Patience said, and stepped away. "I was teasing your prince as if I were still young, and perfect."

"He's not my prince," Nancy said, lisping the *prince* a little, and turned away as Richard came lumbering back to them.

"What have you seen?" he said.

"I've seen what you should see," Patience said. "That is a small Robin village, burning, and the Robins still stand in it."

"I doubt they'd welcome us," Richard said.

"Oh, but they will," Patience said, "—and smiling."

. . . And so it proved. The Robin village, its houses once ranked down along a stream—the water tumultuous after the storm—was burned, burned to nothing but sticks of char and furnaced wattle-clay. The villagers smiled in welcome, some with ravens perched on their heads.

A forest of perhaps fifty or sixty of them grinned, propped upright in the ruins of their homes, blistered black and impaled on fire-scorched stakes. Several curl-tailed brown dogs shied and muttered a distance away, and a little flock of brown chicken-birds pecked and strutted by the stream.

Baj bent and vomited, sickened by smell more than sight. The drifting odor was of overcooked pig, charred, sweet, and delicious.

"No children." Patience cleared her throat, spit, and kicked a cinder aside. "So whoever it was, once the killing was over, had the children herded for serfs. . . . Too far south for this to have been done by Shrikes, though the method is theirs."

"Method?"

"Baj, the Shrikes are *named* for sticking people up on sharp stakes or, over the Wall, on tall made-icicles."

"And not the Guard's doing," Richard said.

Nancy suddenly sprinted through smoking remnants, took Errol by the back of his neck and dragged him, kicking, from what he'd been doing. ". . . No," she said, cuffing Errol still, "this was not the Guard."

Baj wiped his mouth with his bandanna. "Because none were eaten?"

Richard turned on Baj in a surprisingly sudden way. "Eating true-humans is a *true-human* do, as you should remember, since your own river-people are known for it!"

"*Were* known for it." Baj said.

"Oh," Patience said, "—I imagine some backcountry river lords still hold festival lunch. . . . But not the Guard's doing here, Baj. They wouldn't have troubled with burning, and they wouldn't have taken the children. They'd have asked for the chief's daughter, taken her if she seemed useful—but not killed anyone, unless opposed."

"And if opposed?"

"Then," Richard said, and seemed even angrier, "—then, everyone and everything, even singing basket-birds and puppies."

Baj knelt by the village stream to wash his bandanna. "Let's get the fuck away from here." Probably quoting from some copy-book he'd read; it had Warm-times' harsh impatient ring.

"Get away, yes," Nancy said. "But which way to do it?"

"We're almost to the Pass I-Seventy," Patience said, "—and have no choice but keep north to cross it into Map-Pennsylvania."

"Well enough," Baj stood and wrung his bandanna out. "—If soon enough." He breathed lightly and through his mouth, but the odor still came in.

"Away from here, first," Richard said, and strode off down the stream, his shaggy head lowered, apparently so as not to see too much of what he passed.

They all filed after him, Nancy holding Errol by the arm. Patience came last, ground-walking. "What is in the air, is seen in the air," she said.

Richard led them down the Robins' stream—then over it, across cleverly set stepping-stones, big enough that they were only splashed, crossing. Once over, they traveled through scattered forest—of mainly evergreens, with only a few tamarack, aspen, and balsam poplar. The Wall's breath, over this lowland, was now close enough to be too chill for many hardwoods, summer or not.

The trees in these groves bore birds like bright fruit. Baj had seen the red-crossbills and siskens north on the River, but not the little purple finches—very like the pets, though different colors, that ladies kept in their chambers at Island. . . . He supposed Patience, meeting these feathered creatures in the air, must puzzle them.

After perhaps two glass-hours, Richard ducked into a hemlock thicket, stopped in its small ragged clearing—cool and deep-green as underwater—and shrugged off his pack.

"And we stop, why?" Patience brushed an evergreen frond away from her face.

"We're coming near to Map I-Seventy." Richard bent his odd knees, sat, then rocked back to lean against his pack. "So I thought we'd rest the day out here—then go on to cross the open at night."

"And be up into the Map-Tuscaroras by dawn." Patience nodded. "Seems sensible." She sat cross-legged, her scimitar across her knees, as the others shed their packs and settled. Settled as well as memory of the burned Robins allowed.

Baj, drowsing, found paintings of those people in his mind, roasted mouths open, as if they spoke and screamed. He tried to recall the little birds instead. . . .

They lay at ease, or slept through the rest of the day, lulled by the hemlocks' shade and rich perfume—which reminded Baj, when he roused, of the exhalations of court ladies at Island, who'd taken to chewing sugared pine-gum to sweeten their breath. It could be scented sometimes, passing a group of them laughing in long paneled gowns, belted with daggers, and necklaced with ropes of freshwater pearls or Map-Arizona turquoise. Ladies guarded by dangerous lovers, brothers, and fathers, and grown delicate and sometimes cruel as the pretty insect-eating flowers raised in corners of the glass gardens. . . .

Baj woke in early evening—as all the other sleepers woke together, like children in a nursery, and rummaged for the last of smoked turkey-bird.

"A good rest," Patience said. They sat in a fire-circle, eating, though there was no fire in the glade. "I was tired. These mountains . . . I once Walked-in-air, *and* occasionally on the ground, from Boston to North Map-Mexico. And thought little of it."

"How many WT miles?" Nancy was examining Errol's hair for nits, the boy stretched out with his head in her lap like a fireside dog, drowsing.

"I suppose . . . more than two thousand. Though I came down to the east of here, where there is at least some civilization, if you count shepherds and cattle-herders and small farmers. And I did have an occa carrying my baggage—fool that I was not to steal one from the penthouse this last time I left. I would have had to kill sentries to do it . . . had no permission, no Faculty note. *And* the thing would have been complaining all the way. They are . . . sad company."

"MacAffee brought one down to Island," Baj said. "And are they . . . are they Persons, too?"

Nancy took her hand from Errol's hair. "What business is that of yours?"

"It is his business," Richard said to her. "Are all Persons wise? Are all of us gifted with sense? —No, no more than Sunriser-humans are, who have their own fools and witless unfortunates."

"I didn't mean to cause pain," Baj said.

"No." Patience leaned to one side, brought a handful of blue-berries out of her coat pocket, mouthed a few from her palm, then held the rest out to Baj to sample and pass on. "No, it was a fair question. . . . Are occas Persons? Yes, though so sad and stupid. They are Persons as I am, as Richard and Nancy and Errol are— as many in Boston, who do not realize it, *also* are to some degree, since those Talents who believe they make useful improvements will not stop their making, though of worse and worse."

"May be stopped, though." Richard tossed the last blueberries down his throat.

"Yes," Patience said. "If we manage, we will stop them— though their making has allowed many men and women to warm themselves through the worst of Lord Winter's exercise, and gifted a few to Walk-in-air." She sat silent a few moments, star-ing into the hemlocks' deep green. ". . . My Maxwell is by blood-bits the greatest of Talents, made to someday—if it pleases him—made to press our earth a little nearer the sun, to bring Warm-times back again."

Another silence. And though she'd seemed serious, Patience smiled at Baj. "—Or do you suppose that only Wish-fools would think it possible?"

". . . I'm not one to judge impossibility, Lady—for here I sit, alive, and with friends. But our world is large, and we are small."

"Me excepted," Richard said.

"But Baj," Patience said, "—nothing exists, not form or motion, unless first determined, shaped in a mind."

"Rocks," Baj said. "Trees."

"Ah, but those are Second-rocks, Second-trees—and then thirds of them and fourths and infinite numbers of them. But the first, imagined—how else come to be?"

"I think . . . our librarian, Lord Peter Wilson, would have said yours is an argument of prior givens—those creations by thought—and poorly logical."

"Your 'Lord Peter Wilson,' Baj, was first my dear old Neckless Peter of many years ago. And you're right; that is exactly what he would have said. . . . But then, if not in logic, how do I come to Walk-in-air, so eagles sail beside me?"

". . . That, Lady, I do not know," Baj said, and noticed Nancy watching him, staring as if to see beneath his skin.

16

They set out by a rising moon and jeweling stars, traveling down through evergreens and out onto the widest plain Baj had seen since the River's coast, though more soft-summit mountains, the Map-Tuscaroras, could be seen rising to the north.

This was a valley—Map-Exxoned an ancient great roadway once—worn now WT-miles broad by centuries of end-of-summer flooding, come down yearly the distance from the Wall. The last of moon-light revealed streaked shallow banks of mud and gravel braided down the pass, and a wind—likely also from the Wall—came whispering cold.

"Lord Winter begins to wake," Nancy said.

"Hold here," Patience said behind her, and they all crunched to a stop on the valley's gravel, except for Errol, who skittered on into darkness. . . . There was a pause, and Baj supposed the lady had stopped for necessity, though no one looked back to see. . . . But after a few moments, there was a flap and flutter of cloth, and a faint moon-shadow swept slowly over them, though only her white hair could be seen against the sky.

"Safe now," she said above them, voice conversational from a ceiling of stars. "Safe to be Walking-in-air in darkness, unseen. Though once, in a glacier-lead where the Long Island lies, a horned owl came and struck me, almost took my ear. Cruel birds . . ." Baj could just follow—by her hair, by the stars she shaded—as she sailed away.

"That would be pleasant," Nancy said, "—to learn to do."

"For that," Richard shifted his pack more comfortable, "—for that, neither of us have the piece in the brain required."

"And I believe," Baj said, feeling rough gravel beneath his moccasins' soles, "—I believe there must be a cost."

Nancy, stepping up beside, poked him with her elbow—the

first time in a while that she'd touched him. "And what cost is that?"

". . . Beside her always-hunger, I don't know."

"If you knew how old she was in WT years," Richard said, trudging in the lead, "—you'd know the cost."

"Fifty years? . . . More?"

"Thirty-nine," Nancy said, and stepped out so Baj had to trot to catch up.

"Is that true?"

"Yes. And how old do you think I am?"

Baj remembered wise men's lessons. "Young," he said.

. . . They worked their way by star-light, more than the slender crescent moon's, across the Map I-Seventy—the pass certainly much wider than it had been in Warm-times—and, though easier than mountainsides, still difficult traveling over one-after-another low ridge or shelf of mud and flood-trash rafted down, with only coarse grass growing.

They marched hungry, and cold in a north wind—the short-summer seeming left behind on their last mountain to the south. Baj pictured some beast roasting over a hidden fire's careful coals, once they were in the new northern hills.

He managed to imagine the taste of the wild meat fairly well as he marched along. Hot, oily, rank, and wonderful.

Mud and gravel gritted under their moccasin-boots. The stars—brilliant now as sunlit powder snow—shone not quite enough for shadows. Baj heard Errol strolling out to the left, watched Nancy's bobbing pack just before him—then almost walked into her as she suddenly stopped. Richard, bulk barely seen, stood still in front of her.

"What is it?" Baj climbed a low shelf of grassy drift . . . came up beside him.

There was a shallow run-off creek lying across their way, frosted by star-light.

"How deep?" Baj said—then saw the creek was no creek at all, but a narrow roadway running east and west, straight as a taut rope, its crushed limestone-gravel shining white.

"The *Warm-time* road?"

"The WT pathway," Richard said, keeping his voice low, "—if it was here—lies buried deep."

"Yes . . . of course." Baj stepped down to the road, knelt and touched the surface. "Fine-broken, tamped hard, and ditched. This is a Kingdom road, a *best* road—but our people never came so far!"

"Best," Richard said, "—but new, and no Kingdom road. We traveled our way south to the west of here, and saw nothing like it."

And as if his words had called a demon-Great, the softest *chuff chuff chuff* sounded on the wind, as though a giant's boots were scuffing down the pass.

They stood still, listening, as the sound, steady as the beat of blood, first faded as the wind swung away . . . then grew louder.

Light—a dazzle of yellow light flashed suddenly from the west down the limestone road—and as they stood watching, grew brighter while the giant boots seemed to scuff and kick their way along.

"An engine of machinery." Baj's heart was thumping, thumping. "It's a Warm-time *engine*, pushed by cramped steam!"

"No," Richard said, "—it isn't."

"Back!" Nancy clutched their packs, yanked them so hard that Baj stumbled. "*Back* . . .!"

They retreated over mud and flood-trash.

"Down," Richard said. "Lie *down*."

"Errol." Nancy called softly as she could. "Errol . . . !"

Now the yellow light and *chuff chuff chuffing* had come nearly to them, was just down the moonlit limestone way—and looking over the mud shelf, Baj saw Errol suddenly come into the glare like a moth due for dying—come onto the limestone road and go dancing down it, glowing gold as the boot-sound, *stomp* and *scuff*, grew loud as right-beside, with the rolling grind of big wheels turning.

"*Errol!*" Nancy was up and would have run to him, but Baj caught her ankle, tripped her, and wrestled to hold her down. He put his hand over her mouth, and was bitten—then Richard was beside him, and together they held her still.

"Shhh . . ." Baj whispered in her ear. "Shhh, sweetheart." The second time he'd said that foolish thing.

An easy stone's-toss away, Errol stood still, blinking into blazing yellow. There was sudden silence on the limestone road—no heavy rhythmic noises, no motion. Glancing to the left, Baj saw behind the light's shimmering halo, a shape huge as forty Richards.

Time seemed to beat and pulse with the yellow light—from a great mirrored lamp, certainly. Errol stood staring, mouth open, apparently amazed.

Then, barely, by what the lamp allowed of star-light, Baj saw silhouettes of many men—certainly men—climbing down from the big thing. One of them called out, "Do you question?"

Errol stood staring into the light, and Baj saw a weasel's silver circles of reflection in his eyes.

"Do you *question?*"

Richard said, as if to himself, "Jesus-the-Christ," then heaved to his feet and called, "*He doesn't question—doesn't speak!*"

Silence. Then the man said, "Come out. And explain why you were hiding from Manifestation."

Richard muttered, "Be careful," as Baj and Nancy stood to join him. ". . . and ask *no* questions."

"The burning . . ." Nancy whispered, and once she had, Baj smelled—from the huge thing on the road, the men standing by it—the faintest drift, almost a smoky memory of fire.

Baj considered for an instant taking Nancy and fading back into the dark—then thought of Richard left alone with those people, and decided not. Doubted Nancy would go, in any case. His hand hurt; she'd bitten deep into the meat of his thumb . . . second time biting him . . .

He stood and followed Richard over the mud shelf, then stepped down, Nancy right behind, into golden light where a man stood in almost silhouette, other men in the darkness behind him. He held a long, dark, heavy stick—part wood, perhaps part iron.

"Why," the man said, "—do Persons and a human appear to travel the Demonstration Road?"

Baj saw the man's white beard as he spoke. An old man, holding a weighty, polished stick.

"We didn't know it was your road," Baj said. "We intend only to cross it . . . and mean no harm."

"To appear to cross it, is to appear to travel it," the old man said, "—and damage the demonstration."

"Then," Nancy said, "—we'll go around." One of the men behind the lamp's dazzle laughed.

"But this boy—" the old man pointed with his heavy stick, "—this . . . what is he, a sort of Person? He already appears to stand on it."

"An offense may be put right," Richard said.

"It's best put right, apparent Made-man, by ripping up our road and paving again—at least where he seems to stand. And where you three seem to stand."

"I wish," Richard said, "—we had time enough to help do that."

Several of the lamp-shadowed men laughed. "Your help would not be acceptable," the old man said, and turned fully into the light to murmur something to a man behind him.

"*Floating Jesus* . . ." Baj had said it before he'd thought. The old man was wearing dark long-leg cloth trousers and a buttoned dark jacket to match. His shirt was white cloth, with a turned-down collar—and under it, a narrow red neckerchief was knotted, that hung below his beard. His shoes were laced low, and made of black, waxed leather. . . . He might have been a copybook sketch from Warm-times, torn from an ancient page to walk and talk again.

The old man stared at Baj. "Do you have a question, apparent boy?"

"I'm no boy," Baj said—then remembered Richard's murmur: "*No questions.*" "And I have no questions."

The old man stared at him a few moments more, then said, "All of you will seem to come and follow us for discussion—but not appearing to walk on our road."

"And if we prefer to go on our way?" Nancy gripped Errol's arm to hold him still.

"That rudeness," the old man said, "—so close to real, would call for actual demonstrations by Winchesters, Springfields, and Remingtons."

Baj supposed those named were the families of the men with him. Fighting men, apparently, and with kinsmen to back them in trouble. . . . The odor of burning was in the night air with the Shadow-men. Their huge road-traveler shifted behind them, gravel ground beneath it.

"Seem to follow," the old man said. "But walk to the side of our road. To touch it again, would be the same as a question." He walked back out of the lamp's harsh yellow light, the others with him, and Baj saw their dark shapes climbing up onto the big thing, which, after no apparent signal, began again that stomping shuffle, *chuff . . . chuff . . .* and moved, its great wheels crunching over gravel, east down the Pass I-Seventy.

. . . By star-light and lamp-light, Richard led carefully alongside the roadway, walking fast to keep up with the thing and its burden of men. Nancy kept a grip on Errol's arm.

Baj trotted up beside Richard, murmured, "Why no questions?"

"Perfect belief admits no questions."

"Ah . . . And if we fight these people, then run?"

"We could kill some . . . but there are more than 'some' riding their thing. Those sticks are not sticks."

"Then what? Are they the WT *guns?*"

"Shhh . . . They are pretend-those-guns, made to look as the copybooks show them."

"Then what keeps us here?"

"The Guard knows those sticks. They have rows of little steel springs inside them that look like leaves. A notched steel rod is forced down into the stick, that catches those springs and bends them against their will."

Baj found it difficult to keep close with Richard's long striding. ". . . I see. Then whatever grips the rod, if that's released and the springs spring straight—"

"Yes. Then the rod flies out—and will nail a Person to a tree if it strikes him."

"That's a serious weapon."

"Serious, yes—but slow to make work again, and without an arrow's range, or a slung stone's, either. . . . Their spring-sticks aren't the reason the Guard doesn't come this way."

"Then why?"

"Because," Richard said, even more softly, "—madness may be caught, as the pox is caught."

Baj thought of asking more, then decided not to, and dropped back to more comfortable walking.

Nancy poked him, and whispered, "What were you saying?"

"Saying there is no fighting, then running. The sticks are spring-shooters, and dangerous."

"I knew that," Nancy said, not troubling to whisper. "Everyone knows that."

Someone called to them from the road-traveling thing—a different voice from the old man's. "Is there a question?"

"No," Baj called back, "—there is no question. And we are not touching your road."

. . . But there began to be a question as the night wore on, and the road-thing's big wheels turned and turned down the gravel way behind the flare of its yellow lamp. The roadside was graded even, its dirt covered only with rough grasses, but even a level can weary after several dark glass-hours—and tire travelers more, when they are traveling captive. Baj heard Nancy trip and stumble once . . . then, later, again—something she'd rarely done where there was freedom, and unevenness for her bounding pace.

"Give the boy to me." Baj turned, caught Errol by his shirt-sleeve, then stepped aside and stopped to let Nancy by. "Go on . . ."

It seemed that surely the men riding their road-thing would grow tired of riding, but they never did, so it breathed its hoarse boot-step breaths, and its wheels rolled on through hour after hour, until all seemed to Baj—tugging the silent boy along—only a dream as his moccasins marched the night away . . . until at last they brought him into the first of dawn's gray light.

Then, leaving Errol with Nancy, and trotting up past Richard—who made a face and gestured him back—Baj began to see the traveling thing clearly, its lamp's glow fading. It was a huge box—high, wide, and very long—painted the red of rust, and rolling on iron wheels, front and back. *Baltimore & Ohio* was printed along its side in black.

Thirty men sat in three rows, riding the top of it—all dressed in Warm-time ways out of copybooks: jacket-suits and white shirts with colored cloth strips tied under the collars. They all held spring-sticks upright beside them. And none turned their heads to look down at him.

. . . There was a chimney at the front, a black smokestack like those that Ordinary merchants built into their houses on the River. But this was made of painted wood planking, like the rest of the rolling box—and the big light (a cluster of oil-lamps and polished mirrors) was fastened below it.

Though rolling on no iron rails, and perhaps otherwise odd, this was so nearly the chugging "locomotive" copybooks sketched—and now come back after six hundred years—that tears flooded Baj's eyes, and he slowed to wait for the others, touched Nancy's shoulder. "Look . . . *Look!*"

She turned in brightening morning, her narrow face very human with fatigue. "I see it, Baj," she said, and didn't whisper. "I see it, and the faces of the Sunriser-humans riding it—and still smell burning from them."

"Yes. I suppose . . . they destroyed that village."

"There are no children with them. Those must have been sent back with others, and another way."

Baj could smell that faint odor of charring drifted with the red recalled-locomotive. The men riding, sat in their rows along its roof, their faces still as if they slept, though their eyes were open. . . . The old man, beard breezing with their slow steady passage of stomp-chuffing, sat up front behind the chimney-stack, and occasionally tapped one side or the other of the box's roof with the butt of his spring-stick.

With a real—not recalled—locomotive, there would have been weary, relaxed steam coming from somewhere, and smoke from making a boiling heat would be puffing from the chimney-stack. Here, there was neither—only chuff-chuffing.

"What pushes it?—perhaps some great spring-engine mechanical, since these people do metal springs."

"Baj," Nancy said, "are all princes fools?" An exhausted girl. He saw how she would look when old—the part-fox queen of a different country.

"What . . . ?"

"Bend *down*. Bend down and look!"

"Be quiet," Richard said, beside them.

Baj bent . . . had to bend lower as he walked along, and was just able to see, deep under the locomotive's rust-red edge—and behind one of the great turning wheels—ranks of heavy boots stepping all together. Pairs and pairs and pairs of boots—thirty . . .

perhaps as many as forty men working there beneath it, driving the thing along, toes digging in for purchase. Tired men, now. Baj could see some were a little out of step, their stomping almost stumbling.

The sadness of it was surprising—though it shouldn't have been. Had he really thought even remotely possible a true locomotive, with an engine real and panting or unwinding with great power? Who, after all, even in Middle Kingdom, had come close to the tolerances and thousand perfections of the copybooks' engines of cramped steam? . . . Like a child, he'd imagined that so-unlikely thing out of longing, a half-formed wish for the return of an ancient miracle.

Nancy glanced at him. "I'm sorry," she said, an unusual gentleness.

Shortly after, at sunrise—as they trudged past wide fields of carrot, cauliflower, and potato, the rows planted between shielding beds of straw—Errol fell down sound asleep, and wouldn't rouse. Baj had to pick the boy up and carry him—surprisingly light in his arms.

Straight down the narrow road—its crushed limestone brilliant white—the copy-locomotive rolled slowly through a stand of tamaracks shading many long wooden sheds, its hidden booted engines stumbling, exhausted.

"Listen." Nancy cocked her head.

Listening, Baj thought for a moment he heard the River's gulls calling along its shores. Then realized it was children. Children were crying out from the long sheds, calling for mothers . . . fathers, burned and dead.

"Say nothing," he said to Nancy. "Say nothing . . ."

The pretend locomotive rolled slowly, slowly on . . . and on into a place past pretending, a dream to live in. It was a small town of six hundred years before.

The gravel road became a sunny street with scythed green-grass lawns, trimmed evergreen hedges, and rows of perfect little wood houses, painted white, yellow, and pale blue with marvelous pigments—pressed from plants, Baj supposed, or ground from minerals dug in the mountains. Some of these must-be-cottages were shaded by tall paper-birches, tamarack, or black spruce, and each was decorated with neat borders of trimmed fireweed, gold-enrod, and what Baj thought might be columbine—wall-weather plants, this far north, even in the short summer.

Women, some with their hair cut close as their lawns, knelt tending the plants in cloth dresses or very short trousers that showed their bare legs despite a chill morning. Only a few looked up to see the pretend-locomotive roll past, though children dressed in blue-dyed cloth trousers and colored shirts trotted along beside it, waving to the men riding. Baj saw no dogs . . . no strutting chicken-birds.

No one stared at him and the Persons—not even the children—as if he, Nancy, Richard, and Errol were only ghosts of an improbable future, not present in this time at all.

There were wide gravel walkways or drives alongside each small house, and placed on every one was a much smaller box than the false-locomotive—though also of painted wood.

"What are those?" Baj asked the air as he labored along. Errol, sleeping in his arms, had grown heavier.

One of the men riding, leaned down and called, "A question?"

"No question," Richard called back, "—only admiration."

That man, and others, stared down for a moment . . . then seemed satisfied.

These smaller boxes, in many painted colors—and one by every little house—were shaped resting on four fat wooden disks, painted black. Each box on each graveled walk had little square windows cut out of it. . . . The nearest, as they passed, showed curving letters along its side, painted tar-black. *BUICK*.

"Pretend *driving-cars*," Baj said.

Richard, walking ahead, stopped and waited to take Errol from him. "Careful," he murmured, "what words you use. Better not *pretend.*"

Baj decided to be quiet, since these people—mad or not— were so grimly serious. But even in pretense, the town still lay before him as if risen not from copybook sketches and descriptions, but from the reality behind them. . . . The street and tree-shaded houses breathed an ancient perfect warmth, that, as if a great brass cymbal were struck, rang and vibrated from that time to this time and back again, so the laughing children, the plant-tending women in their odd immodest dress, and the silent men wearing button-jackets and trousers, shirts and throat-ties, all seemed to insist that the Age of Ice was false after all, and ancient truth lay here, beneath Lady Weather's apron.

There was a sudden blare of distant music that made Nancy jump and say, "Jesus!" It was music startlingly loud and thumping. There were trumpets in it, and heavy drums, so it crashed and clanged.

Errol jerked awake, and Richard set him down.

As if the music had signaled it, the booted feet beneath their locomotive shuffled to a halt at last. The men riding, climbed down with their heavy spring-sticks. . . . As one was carried by, Baj saw *Winchester* burned into polished wood in small square letters.

The bearded old man, lithe and easy for his age, swung to the street and gestured to Richard and the others. "Drift along, Dream-oddities," he said. "—And see the past and future kiss."

The booted stompers began to crawl from beneath their great rust-red box—crawled out from under, and were kicked into a stumbling line by two of the men with spring-shooters. . . . All finally stood holding hands like children, naked but for their heavy boots. Naked and shaved bare. It appeared that their nuts had been cut away. And their eyes. Their eyes had been taken out, and round little wooden eyes with painted blue pupils put in.

Baj said, "*My God,*" a serious thing to say.

The two spring-shooter men were hitting the naked blind ones—striking them lightly, casually as pig-drovers, to move them, hand in hand, back down the graveled road toward the tamaracks and long wooden buildings there.

"We aren't going to get out of this," Nancy said, and sounded close to weeping. "These Sunrisers do terrible things."

"They cannot keep us," Richard said. "We would spoil their truth. They'll either be easy and let us swiftly go, or turn us into those. And before that happens," Richard made no effort to keep his voice low, "—we fight."

"If they try to take our weapons," Baj said, and had to clear his throat, "—we fight."

The old man called to them again. "Drift along, Apparents!" And they filed after him and the other spring-shooter men, Baj now more frightened than weary. He had a sickening vision of Nancy, ruined and eyeless. Nancy, and all of them.

. . . They were led down that street, and across another. Baj saw more pretty wooden houses down little side streets—noticed each had a chimney-stack, and windows showing cloth drapings inside, but no panes of leaded glass. From these houses, men were coming walking with their friends and families. They carried spring-shooters, and all were dressed in one of four different ways: some in jacket, trousers, throat-tie, and low shiny shoes . . . others in mottled-brown cloth and black lace-up boots (those wore round brown helmets on their heads). Others were dressed either in blue cloth with blue peaked caps, or gray cloth with gray peaked caps (the ones in gray all barefooted). But in whichever color, these peak-cap men wore beards and mustaches. . . . The blue cloth, Baj supposed, dyed with crushed blueberry; the gray by thinned glue and powdered soot; the brown, by nutshells—ground then soaked. In whatever dress or uniform, the men seemed tired, rumpled, unwashed. A number were bandaged. Several limped.

At the far end of the last graveled street they crossed, Baj saw another imitation locomotive standing still, come into the town, apparently, on another of their gravel roads. . . . He supposed they had others as well, and those had brought their men to marching-distance of the Robins.

"Soldiers," Baj kept his voice low. Low-speaking seemed the safest way. "Those are dressed as Warm-time soldiers."

Nancy lifted her head, sniffed the air. "Smoke," she said. "They smell of smoke. More than one village has been burned."

Richard, gripping Errol's arm, looked back. "Shhh . . ."

All those men and their families were walking the same way, the women leaving their plant-tending—and apparently not minding showing their legs—while the children ran here and there, from mothers to fathers, like schools of river fish . . . ran yelling past Baj and the others, so Errol clicked his tongue and tugged to join them.

But none of these people, not even the young, seemed to notice Baj and the others—not even Richard looming among them.

They followed the old man and his neck-clothed Spring-shooters toward the thumping clashing music, surrounded by what might have been veterans of Warm-time wars, many centuries ago.

At what would have been the third cross-street, there was, instead, a very large grassed square with seven or eight wood-built buildings—all painted gray (likely also with hoof-glue and soot)—standing along its eastern edge. Baj could see *National Bank* painted across the front of the biggest. There were letters on the other buildings, but too small to read.

In the middle of the square, there was a garden house—very much like those the river lords built amid their flower gardens along the Mississippi—a raised, open wooden floor, with lattice-work walls and a shingle roof.

The musical band was sitting on benches there, playing very

loud, brass horns and decorated bleached-hide drums bright in morning sunlight. The music players, in odd tall hats, were dressed in red clothes with shiny buttons down the front.

All, Baj supposed, a slightly awkward and innaccurate re-creation of the distant past. . . . On those warm, sunny afternoons of six hundred years before, certainly not all little towns were green, perfect, and pleasant, with musical bands playing in their grassy squares. Though all were certain, at least, of a winter survivable with scientific heating, or, far from their splendid cities, with only a woodstove and warm coat.

Those peoples' lives lived rich in confidence that earth would never turn hot or cold enough to kill them, and destroy the wheat and corn and rice to leave hundreds and hundreds of millions with the choice of freezing or starvation. . . . A confidence proved misplaced by nothing but a slight shift in great Jupiter's orbit.

It seemed to Baj that of all the things this *pretend*, this *nearly*, this *almost* town was not, there was still something it was, though its men maimed and burned. And that something—a re-creation of the past, apparently as instrument of creation-anew—drew Baj to it as the crowd drew him and his friends into the bannered square, into the noisy merry music—sounding old as Island's celebratory "Washington Post," and meant, apparently, to be marched to.

Baj felt that *something*, and saw that Richard, Nancy—and empty Errol—did not. There had been no Persons in Warm-times. That past was not theirs. Before centuries of cold, before the mind-making of Boston Talents, there had been only beasts, and men.

. . . Baj and the others—Errol kept close—were drawn along with the townspeople: the weary soldiers grimy in their odd uniforms, their wives and children, elderly parents . . . sweethearts. Drawn with them as if herded—but always with a distance kept, so the travelers stayed separate in the crowd. Errol was strutting to the music's solid beats, thin legs and moccasined feet pumping up and down.

The biggest flag had been raised on a pole by the garden house, and its cloth, striped and starred, brightly colored as dyed honey candies, rippled out on the north wind—a chill breeze, despite the sunshine—as if in time to the music.

Though to what celebration these people were called—the end of their so-short northern summer, or perhaps only a triumph after killing, burning Robins—had not been spoken of, the festival air lent for Baj an additional magic to this town. A town that might be his in wishes for the past—if he were asked, and lived blind to what it wasn't. If he were willing to maim sweat-slaves, blind them, slice their manhoods so they acted only as engines to power the false-locomotives—power those, and likely other things: a wood mill, a stone mill to crush rock to gravel, a manufactory for spring-shooters. Making all those work, though slowly, poorly, straining in imitation of machinery that once had hummed and roared and whirled in heat and heated oil.

Still, perhaps because of so many boyhood hours reading, perhaps by a would-be poet's imagination that had fleshed the copybooks out, this remembrance-place of a lost time seemed not so strange to him at all.

The soldiers and their families gathered, and gathered Baj and the others with them—though slightly separate—to crowd before the garden house and music band. . . . Then the band stopped playing with a blare and crash, seemed to draw fresh breath, and commenced another, slower melody—to which, here and there, then throughout, the men and women began to sing.

It was a song that began "*Oh, beautiful,*" and continued in such sweet description that Warm-times, even by these sad and crippled ways, seemed to rouse and return to bless them.

* * *

There were rows of rough wooden tables and benches beside the garden house, where people were already seating themselves, and several long serving tables past those, where women dealt with bowls and platters of food, and a cooking pit smoked with roasting meat.

Nancy said, "Uh-oh." One of the oldest exclamations.

A young man in a dark jacket, dark trousers, white shirt and throat-tie, was wending through the tables toward them. He was not carrying a spring-shooter.

When he stood smiling in front of them, Baj saw the young man was weary, unshaven, his white shirt stained and dirty. His face had the drawn look that Baj remembered from when he was a boy, and saw young officers of the Army-United come down the river from the fighting in Map-Illinois. . . . Their faces had been as this man's was. It seemed that burning Robins had a cost.

"Amazing how well I see you all," the young man said. And to Baj. "You, a little more clearly. . . . But all four of you . . . manifestations are invited to eat gift food set out for you. We are . . . perhaps more than usually tender, today, to those drifting out of proper time." He stared at them, shook his head. "—So, what of our food *might* nourish you, you are welcome to eat while fact and falseness touch for this little time." Still smiling, he gestured them to follow him past others, families sitting to their food . . . then indicated the empty benches of a table that must just have been weighted with platters of sizzling mutton—sliced thick, of roast onions, broken potato, steamed cabbage and carrots, a stack of rye flatbread, and a clay pitcher of what seemed barley beer.

"Yours," the young man said, "for what use it is to you. —Any questions?"

"None." Richard shook his head. "But thanks for your generosity to insubstantial guests, only passing through."

The young man nodded, but looked past Richard, not at him. There was a dull brown stain down the front of his white shirt. He had very clear gray eyes . . . an older man's eyes, with an older man's understanding in them. "My father should be thanked for that," he said, "—as we thank him for so much." He smiled again, then wended away through the crowded tables.

Not one other—of the hundreds seating themselves around them, serving out food, joking with their loved ones—not one appeared to see them.

"Does this mean they won't hurt us," Nancy murmured, "—take our eyes?" But neither Baj nor Richard could answer her.

17

Though the town's armed men might still smell of Robins burning, gentler odors came drifting from the cookstoves and kettles as Baj and the others were left as perfectly to themselves as if they still camped high in the Smoking Mountains—though here, with wooden spoons and their belt knives, they dealt with mugs of barley beer and fired-clay plates heavy with roasted mutton and steaming vegetables. They ate, dipped flatbread in gravy, and poured out foaming beer.

"It seems," Baj said between bites, "that terror does not affect appetite."

"Increases mine." Richard folded a slice of meat in flatbread, and ate it.

"You three," Nancy said, apparently including Errol, who had slid under the table with fistfulls of mutton, "—you three are fools." Though she was chewing as she spoke. She tried a carrot, made a face, and looked around, staring at the women. "Light cloth clothes," she said, "—and worn in this never-truly-warm, so close to the Wall. And showing so much, as to say, 'See my bare legs? Come and fuck me.' "

"It's likely," Baj said, refilling his mug, "this is their Last-of-summer festival." Errol slid from under the table, a wad of mutton-fat in his hand, to join boys coursing through the crowd, but Baj reached down and held him. "Stay with us."

"I think," Richard spoke softly, though there was no other table close, "—I think the Robins shouldn't have settled so near these people."

Baj, mashing his potatoes in mutton gravy, turned to look around them. "Yes, and became too much of a contradiction to these believers."

"Believers enough," Nancy said, "—to perch men and women

with sticks up their rear ends as the Shrikes do, then burn them."
An eye-tooth grated on a mutton bone.

Hunger over fear for all of them, Baj supposed, at least for the
moment. ". . . And intend those murders to frighten other tribespeople, keep them from settling near I-Seventy, spoiling this
dream of Warm-times with reminders of now."

"Madness." Richard set his carrots aside with a large horn-
nailed finger. "—And the reason the Guard is kept away. Boston
doesn't want its soldier Persons building their own magical town.
For fear, I suppose, of what they might pretend." He smiled at a
girl-child—the only child who'd come to stare at them, but the
smile proved too toothy, and the child fled. "Oh, dear, and the
only one who'd look at us . . ."

"Maybe pretend it was Sunrise-*humans* the Boston people
made," Nancy said, spearing an onion on her knife, "—and that
Persons were the first on Lady Weather's earth."

"Acting the wish," Baj said, "is the magic they try here, as if
belief must someday make it so." He ate a spoonful of potato. "I
think they give us this food as savages leave meals for the ghosts
of their dead. We're not perfectly real to them, don't belong in
their true time." He ate another spoonful of potato. "—We may
be acceptable, unless we ask questions, or stay too close . . . or too
long."

There was uproar from a long table a pebble's toss away. Two
bearded soldiers, in stained and muddy gray, sat with their wives
and many children, all merry . . . red-faced and laughing at something the taller soldier had said.

". . . But will these Believers let us go?" Nancy ate another
onion from the point of her knife, white teeth nibbling. "You two
philosophicals might consider that, and remember stolen children,
and the ruined things that marched their rolling box. —Every
Jesus. That woman is showing her bare ass! You see her butts
beneath those so-short pants?"

"Could be summer dressing, this far north, to try to hold the warmth a little longer. More wishful magic. . . ." Baj looked around him, leaning on the town's creation to imagine centuries away. "These people make as perfect an *as if* as possible, so reality *must* follow. . . . How Lord Peter would have loved to see this."

Nancy bit into a large piece of mutton, sliced her mouthful free with a close pass of her knife. "And are they too stupid," she said, chewing, "to notice it hasn't *worked*? That Lord Winter still steps down from the Wall?"

"Oh, then," Richard said, "they believe they haven't pretended well enough."

"And so . . ." Baj took another chunk of meat, cut it again, and gave a portion to Errol—who settled with it under the table. The mutton was aged rank, sharp as ripe cheese. "—And so, likely each year these people must try harder, make what they hope are *better* copies of Warm-time things, and live exactly as they suppose those ancient people lived."

"Fools," Nancy said.

"—Until," Richard said, and belched, "it becomes necessary to kill any nearby Robins—who do not copy WT ways, and so spoil everything."

"They're not going to let us leave." Nancy gripped her knife's handle so her narrow knuckles whitened. "And you're talking and talking."

"We're all frightened, dear." Richard glanced at the people eating around them. "But when males are frightened, they must pretend not to be. Still, I do think they'll let us leave."

"Yes," Baj said. "May insist on it. There were no Persons in Warm-times."

Now, only Errol was eating. It seemed that with first hunger over, fear took its place.

"Yes?" Nancy still gripped her knife. "And so they'll let us go? Then answer this, Richard. Do their sweat-slaves act the Warm-times with them?"

"Those destroyed men," Baj said, "I think they've made into only engines."

"Every *Jesus* . . ." Nancy showed sharp teeth. "We should have come north the way we went south last year, and never traveled east to this Pass."

"Then we'd never have seen this—"

"And never seen burned Robins, either, Who-*was*-a-prince!"

". . . There's something else you might see," Richard said, "if you look, without making a show of it, over to the west. Then higher."

Baj did, casually as he could, and saw only a speck, darker than the sky's sunny blue, tracing its slow way above the horizon.

Nancy glanced once, and quickly. "Is she coming here?"

"No," Richard said, "—she won't. That *would* get us killed."

"She's everything they wish were not. . . ." Baj took care to look away, across the grass square, where the row of small wooden buildings stood. Intended, certainly, as Warm-time's store-department, a money bank, and littler shops and offices. Several were painted in tiny rectangles, as if made of baked red brick. . . . The town's physician (scientific as possible) would have his place in that row of buildings. And the marshal-policeman also an office, with a prison cell at the back—and perhaps a false chair-electrical, with a poisoned needle in its frame to cause the correct shaking dying.

There was a small pole, striped red-and-white, set outside the fourth small building along the row. Baj saw one of the serfs, blind, naked but for boots, standing sexless and silent beside it, turning the pole with his hand so it slowly spun, the red-and-white stripes spiraling endlessly up.

Nancy sheathed her knife; her hand was trembling. "*Patience* is what they wish were not?" Hot yellow eyes. "Aren't we three also wished . . . not?"

"We *four*," Baj said. "And if they hadn't just burned the Robins defending this dreaming, then they might be burning us."

"Oh, no. Burning *us*, Baj. But not you, who are as they are—a Sunrise-human and in love with wonderful Warm-times, when there were no Persons." She looked around her. "This, I think, is your dream as much as theirs."

"Perhaps. But I wouldn't burn people for it." Baj had spoken too loudly. A woman at a table nearby raised her head, startled, as if at a sound mysterious.

"Keep your voices down." Richard looked at a last piece of mutton on his platter, but appetite gone, didn't eat it.

"No, Baj," Nancy said, "you wouldn't burn the tribesmen, or cut the sweat-slaves and take their eyes. But still you wish there was no cold, no Ice-wall . . . wish there were no *Persons* made with little bits of this animal or that added in them. Wish there was *nothing* new since everyone (so very long ago) smelled like owls, had ugly hot little houses and women who showed everything, and mechanical wars and were assholes!"

"Talking too *loud*," Richard said.

"Nancy . . . I only understand them."

"It's the same thing!"

"It is not!" And to Errol, who hearing anger, scrambled from under the table. "Stay and be still!"

"You two are attracting these people's attention," Richard said, "—which we do not want."

"—And these Sunrisers, Baj," Nancy said, "these Believers and Burners so dear to you, do you think they have guest-honor? That because we 'apparent' ones have been given food, and eaten food, they won't decide to make engines of *us*?"

"What I think," Baj said, and gripped Errol's arm to keep him sitting still, "—what I *think* is that you need to speak more quietly."

"Ah. A Sunriser commands! The true-human, the *Prince* has spoken, and we're to wag our tails and obey!"

Several people near them now seemed puzzled by some odd disturbance, and turned to look this way and that.

Nancy drew a breath to say more, might have said more—but Richard, humorous as if it were all in play, reached over, took her by the nape like a kitten, and gripped her into silence before he let her go.

Then he stared at Baj. "I'm tired of this conversation," he said, quietly, "—which is dangerous, and not even about what it's about. Do you understand me, Prince?"

Baj said, "Yes, sir," since that seemed wise.

There was only the pleasant noise of others, enjoying themselves around them.

Then Nancy said, "Uh-oh." The second time she'd said it.

The young man who had welcomed them was walking toward their table, pausing to speak with others on his way. . . . He came to stand by Baj, and looked down, but at none directly. "Some have heard what might be questions, here," he said.

"Questions of each other, only," Baj said, "—not of what is real."

The young man seemed to consider that. ". . . Always an interesting experience," he said, "if not lingered on, to stand near temporal error. Innocent error, of course, though still not to be allowed for long." He looked at Baj. "Did you know—by the way, my name is Louis Cohen—but did you know that all things are made of trembling tinies? Both the real, and the only-seeming? Did you know that?"

Baj cleared his throat. "I have heard the . . . idea."

"Have you?" Louis Cohen nodded. "Well, it's a correct idea. All things are made of those vibrations, a sort of music our ears are too dull to hear, but which great men sense . . . and greater men act on."

Baj smiled agreement, very content to keep his mouth shut.

"I have sharp ears," Nancy said, and stared at Baj as if she spoke to him. "Almost all Persons, Moonrisers, hear very well."

"Yes," Louis Cohen said, "and many such Time-lost seem stronger than we, and some"—he smiled just past her—"appear more beautiful. You . . . *apparent* people have a place in this icy, dissolving world, and we do not grudge it. But Warm-time is still to be retrieved, and can be brought back by no lever or engine-motor, by no fiddling of the Boston Talents—but only by *conviction*." He was no longer smiling. "That alone makes the littlest things spin and tremble and fly the way they must to roll time's carpet up again." He stood silent, then, and seemed abstracted.

"We must not interfere?" Baj said, then wished he'd said nothing.

Louis Cohen nodded. "Just so. You've been our transitory guests—barely imagined by the well-taught, though dealt with decently by those wiser, able to see and hear you fairly well. . . . You are, as all creatures out of place in time, interesting in your way." He shook his head. "But you will become more and more . . . *weighty* as you stay near us, and might tear the fabric that marches to perfection and Warm-times again. We cannot allow it."

"Then our thanks to you and your father," Baj said, "for permitting a visit that has hardly happened. And since any . . . occurence here would be even more a disturbance, we are gone as if we'd never been. . . ." He stood up from the bench, and bent for his pack, bow, and quiver, praying to every Jesus that Nancy and Richard would do the same. And, as though he'd drawn them with him, they did—even Errol, drowsy with feeding, stood, ready to go.

Baj didn't look at Louis Cohen again, said nothing more to him, but took hold of Errol and walked away through the crowded tables of people eating, families enjoying their sunny day despite the cold breeze blowing. . . . He walked away, making a spirit of himself that did not see and was not seen—hoping that Richard and Nancy were following.

He crossed the grassy square, and kept on past the row of little buildings, copy-treasures he would dearly have loved to stroll through.

. . . Padding footsteps. Richard came up beside him. "Middle-Kingdom," he murmured, "might have done worse than kept Bajazet-Baj a prince, for swift decision and common sense."

"Don't run." Nancy, behind them. "Don't run . . ."

The buildings left behind, they passed a street of little houses, grass lawns, and shading trees. The copy driving-cars, so brightly painted, rested silent and forever still on gravel drives. . . . A chill wind was gusting over distant harvested fields, breezing down from blue mountains, the Tuscaroras, that rose rank on rank, the northern gates of Pass I-Seventy.

Behind them, the musical band could be heard playing a cheery melody—from the very oldest copybooks of musical notation. An odd and ancient tune, but one Baj had heard before. ". . . Good Vibrations."

* * *

They came over stubbled fields to the northern mountains' foothills in late after-noon, and climbed up into those forested slopes as if into their mothers' laps, for safety. . . . By evening, high in a hemlock clearing, they settled to sleep, curled in cloaks and blankets, to no music but the wind's, sliding though evergreen boughs.

Baj lay awake awhile, saying a good-bye to the Bajazet of only Warm-time weeks ago. That prince uncertain, was now hammered harder in mind and body by mountain traveling, travel's fair meetings and foul. Tempered too late, of course, to aid his brother. . . . He said that good-bye, then turned in his blanket, and slept, dreaming of living in the Copy-town. He knew, within his dream, what the houses were like inside. He was served a breakfast of pork-strips and eggs by a pretty woman in a flowered apron, who spoke odd book-English and called him by another name. . . . Then, still in his dream, he walked down a narrow hall on woven carpet dyed one creamy color, and stepped into a nursery where a baby lay in a huge iron crib. Immense—bigger than Richard—naked, pale, and smelling of pee and perfumed cream, the child turned its great head as Baj came in. It stared at him with eyes a drifting milky blue. —Then Patience stood up at the crib's other side, and said, *"Get out."*

". . . Enjoy your visit?"

Baj, waking after a hunting-dream following the other, roused to dawn's first light and heard Patience ask her question again, and Nancy say, "No."

Lying propped on an elbow under a wind-bent hemlock, with her worn blue greatcoat buttoned to her throat, Patience yawned, glanced at Baj as he threw his blanket aside and sat up. "—And here's a *busier* visitor. One who should learn to knock before he enters others' dreams." She'd taken her nose-spints off, leaving only a fading bruise across the bridge.

"Your pardon," Baj said, startled by the mention—and the cause, though he'd heard of double dreaming, usually by sweethearts.

"Oh . . . not your fault."

Richard came lumbering through brush, doing up his trouser lacing. "All awake, I see." Errol ambled behind him, doing up in imitation.

"Ah," Patience said, "—he has finished his toilet, and finds us awake! As, at moon-down, I settled here to find you all snoring. I could have cut your throats, one by one, and each throat deserving it."

Richard's deep, considering hum as he knotted his laces.

"Before you burst into song, dear one," Patience said, "you might remember that Moonriser ears and noses may have been sentry enough in the south. But we're north, now. It's time and past time we stand night guard, or some other air-walker, for Boston's reason, may sail down silent to kill us."

Richard stopped humming and said, "True. Time to guard against Walkers-in-air. We'll set night watch and watch."

Patience nodded. ". . . And none of you enjoyed your visit to *almost* Warm-times? Warm-times in a blown-glass bottle—where, from the smell of you, you ate a great meal of meat."

"I did enjoy the idea of it," Baj said.

"Ah. The 'idea.' "

"Yes. . . . Such an effort to make imagination real."

"As they did to the Robins," Nancy said. She stood, and walked away into the brush.

Patience sat up, eased her left arm from its sling, and gently exercised it. "You wished to stay?"

"No."

"And why not, if you admired their efforts?"

"Because it's only wishing," Baj said. "And they cripple and murder to try to make it otherwise."

Patience got to her feet, swung her arm in careful slow great circles. "Not nearly the first, not nearly the last to do that. Wishing is the winding-key of history, for—as copybooks say—good or ill. . . . I am absolutely starving."

"Baj," Richard said, "travel ahead a little, hunt for us."

"Straight north by the sun?" Baj picked up his bow, knelt to set and string it. He had only seven arrows left—the rest splintered, or lost despite searches.

"North, by the sun. We'll catch up."

"I'll climb with you, Richard." Patience stretched. "Walking either way, in air or on the ground, stiffens me a little, either in mind or muscle—the penalties of age."

Baj fastened the throat of his cloak—it was not a warm morning—shouldered his pack and quiver, and trotted away uphill, brushing through crowding damp hemlocks as he climbed. Not a warm morning. The air, that had been so friendly all the weeks coming north, traveling with the short-summer—now, closer to the Wall, had turned a warning chill, as if Lord Winter spoke through it . . . whispering, as snow in gathering blizzards whispered, "I will arrive. Shelter, or die."

Baj heard no soft scuttling behind him, Errol not coming after as he often did—perhaps for the first bleeding fruits of the hunt. Perhaps for weasel reasons of his own.

. . . The Tuscaroras were not the mountains of the south. Though a little lower, these were cold-country mountains, cloaked with thick evergreens as if for warmth. Which made easier climbing in a way, with frequent handholds in dangerous places along cliff-rims, on rubble-slides. Easier in that way, more difficult in another, where almost every clearing, every slope required ducking through hemlocks' green fronds, so Baj hunted damp as if under rain.

On these tree-thatched heights, open only to the sky above, it was a relief to recall the wide fields the copy-locomotive had rolled through on its way to their celebration—though chugging by slaves' sweat only, and past the cries of children bereft. . . . Wonderful Warm-time word, *bereft*.

Birds were Baj's only company through the morning. Very small gray-brown birds, and very fat, that chirped among the evergreens . . . liking especially, it seemed, to perch high on tender twigs that bowed and swung in the mountain wind.

There were occasional whistles of distant conies or marmots denned in rockfalls. "A fat marmot," Baj said aloud, "—would not be despised." He imagined Mountain-Jesus listening from where he hung impaled, perhaps by Shrikes, on his immortal evergreen. Listening, and commanding a marmot to show itself to be killed, cooked, and eaten.

Baj climbed, went carefully along a crumbling rim—from this, at least, there was a longer view than green branches and little birds. A view east . . . past the humped shoulders of other mountains, to only a suggestion of green levels and lowlands, so distant an horizon it seemed it might edge the very Ocean Atlantic. . . .

Ranchers, Patience had said, ran sheep and spotted cattle down that eastern territory. Farmers grew barley and rye. Civilized country in its way, though certainly bowing to Boston more often than not—and nothing like Middle Kingdom, its Great Rule from Map-California to Map-Missouri, and south to the Mexican Sierras. Still, the east apparently not all wilderness.

. . . Standing on broken stone a little later, with only air and a sailing raven to his right, Baj glanced up as if a finger beneath his chin had tilted his head, and saw an animal looking down at him from a towering stone chimney much more than a bow-shot away. A sheep.

Not a sheep gone wild. He was certain of a close brown coat, as well as curls of heavy horns as it turned away in no hurry, climbed a wall perpendicular, and was gone. Mountain sheep—which Baj had heard described, but never seen—that must have drifted, over the centuries, two thousand Warm-time miles from the Map-Rockies. And found this rare palace of granite amid soft green.

There was no chasing up that cliff. Baj shrugged to settle his pack, and minding his footing—grateful he was wearing moccasins rather than hard-sole boots—began to climb to the left around that chimney's immense base . . . up and over what rock shelves he came to, keeping the granite height to his right as he slowly half-circled it, sweating in a cold breeze.

Even half-circling that monument, was WT's "slow-going," and took him deep into windy after-noon, when the ram and his ewes were probably already gone to other grazing. But Baj kept to it, since it seemed nothing else in the mountains was stepping closer to his bow.

Foolish . . . foolish . . . foolish. A chant other hunters had certainly muttered to themselves, chasing odd animals from first times to these times. The reason, he supposed, that men—women insisting?—had finally settled to growing southern wheat and northern barley.

Baj stopped to breathe, leaning against the great chimney's

sun-warmed stone, and swung his pack off his back, untied his tarred-wood canteen—unplugged it, and took three swallows. . . . A shadow came flitting over, its dark mark sliding across the rock. He thought it might be Patience . . . then saw a hawk, a red-shoulder, swinging away into deeper blue.

Baj supposed he was happy. Certainly felt happy. It seemed that this traveling through mountains was bound to continue forever—or at least a good while longer—and, in justice, shouldn't end with him being killed. With Nancy being killed. Shouldn't end with any of them dying.

It seemed strange enough that his brother was dead, that Newton smiled . . . nowhere. That Newton worked grimly as he'd always worked at any task set for him . . . nowhere. And was breathing—as Baj now breathed the chill mountain air—nowhere. It seemed so unlikely, as if there'd been a simple error in the loom when this year's time was woven.

Baj put his canteen away, shouldered his pack, and moved on, thinking that surely this granite tower must have an end to circling, must meet the rest of the mountain somewhere.

There'd be no use mentioning the mountain sheep to the others, only so they'd know of the shot he'd lost, the mutton they wouldn't have for supper—a second supper of that meat, since Copy-town. And, truth was, he hadn't minded eating turkey through those many days coming past the Gap-Cumberland. Had pretended to, of course. . . . Still, spotted-cow beef was the best of meats, done not too brown. The best but for Talking-meat, old people said—old people, and a few brute barons far upriver, who still filed their teeth sharp as any tribesman's.

Rounded the tower, and up a last pitch of winter-broken stone, Baj paused to rest and look over and down sweeping steep meadows where clusters of pine and hemlock grew stunted, bent south by northern gales. There were, of course, no mountain sheep to be seen under bright sunshine, broken as clouds streamed high over the range.

Reminded by the breeze's bite, Baj stared north, looking for the distant white line of the Wall. Too distant, supposedly running along the top of this Map-Pennsylvania. From here, even this high, he saw only green.

The meadows made a change from rubble-stone, and, of course, easier going downhill. Baj stepped along swiftly, his strung bow over his shoulder—and had passed a stand of pine to his right, when he heard an odd scraping sound, glanced toward it, and saw the mountain-sheep ram standing a long shot away, staring at him.

The ram pawed the ground, tossed his head as if he might come butt Baj off his mountain. Four . . . five other sheep drifted from the pines behind him.

A wasp, or bee, hummed past Baj . . . then went buzzing down the meadow.

The ram stood where he was, his flock shifting, nervous. . . . It was too long a shot, and there seemed no clever way to make it shorter, so Baj began to walk across the meadow to them, walking slowly . . . and bent a little, to seem smaller. As he went, he eased the bow off his shoulder, reached back for an arrow, and nocked it to the string. Not many broadheads left. . . .

The ram took a step or two toward him, tossed his heavy-horned head again. Beautiful animal . . . short light-brown coat. Streaks of lighter color in it. Baj could see the ram's topaz eyes—there was no fear in them—and he imagined himself being butted along the slope. From prince, to festival clown.

As if he'd shared that vision, the ram trotted several fast steps to meet him—and doing so, came into the bow's range. Still a long shot, but one that could be made. . . . Baj stood still, drew, but didn't shoot. The ram stared at him, pawed the rough meadow grass, and took several swift steps closer with an innocent courage that knew nothing of curved glued wood-and-horn, knew nothing of hammered steel, sharpened for an arrow-head, nothing of fletching an arrow's perfect shaft.

It was unfair. Baj looked past the ram to the others—saw what seemed another male, younger and shyer, standing skittish with the ewes—raised his bow and took that long and unlikely shot, knowing it to have been a boy's decision.

The arrow whispered away from the bow-string's twang, flicked across the meadow, and arched down to strike the shy ram at his flank, and too far back.

Baj ran toward them as the old male backed, then stepped snorting aside—set a second arrow to the string, jolted to a stop and shot the other sheep again. Struck behind its shoulder, the animal bucked and collapsed sliding into the grass. The ewes bleated, whirled and ran down-slope, and the old ram, reluctant . . . certain that Baj was guilty of something, backed, turned, and followed them.

18

It was evening, with banners of cloud colors streaming across the sky, before Baj found the others—wending north, tiny with distance, through evergreens below him. . . . They'd passed him by.

He put two fingers to his mouth and whistled, but the slow cold wind was against him, and they didn't hear, didn't look up. So, burdened by sword-belt, bow, quiver and pack—and with a considerable weight of butchered mutton on his back, bundled in the beast's own hide—Baj commenced as good a gallop as he could manage down the mountainside.

He fell once, and rolled a little with tangles and thumps from his load, sheathed rapier akimbo (wonderful word), but there was no one to see.

. . . After at least a WT mile of downhill hurry through thicker and thicker forest, he came out to an almost level—face streaked red by whipping branches—whistled, and saw Nancy and the others hear, and turn to watch him come.

Errol ran back to caper around Baj, sniffing the wrapped meat's blood odor. He reached up and tugged at the hide, until told, "No," and pushed away.

"Where have you *been*?" Nancy apparently angry. "You were to hunt before us—then wait. Where were you?"

Baj pointed up. "High. Found the sheep there."

Nancy made a tongue-click like Errol's, and turned away.

"Thank these mountains' Jesus," Patience said. "Not turkey." Her left arm was free of its sling.

"No, mountain sheep."

"Baj, I believe you may still *be* a prince. Can we camp? Can we eat?"

"If we find a place close and deep enough for one of your dangerous fires." Richard sighed. "Appetite will be our deaths."

"Better than starvation," Patience said. "*I* didn't feast with the madmen. —Do you know that many of their children die in winter? They think it incorrect to bundle them warm."

"Better the Robins," Nancy said, "than those people. If they are what Warm-time humans were, then bless Drunk Jupiter, and the Wall."

Baj started to say something in those cruel dreamers' defense, then decided not. He was too tired from sheep chasing, and it would mean an evening's battle—Nancy's method of discussion.

* * *

Grumbling, shaking his shaggy head, Richard allowed himself to be bullied for a guarded fire of windfall, in a dense stand of balsam poplar damp enough to catch no sparks. "Though I suppose, if we're seen in these hills, it will likely be by those we *come* to see."

Baj, with Errol helping, dragged two weather-seasoned logs to lie side by side with a bed of dry branches between them.

"Meat's going to taste of sap." Patience sat with her coat unbuttoned despite the chill.

"Do you want this fire?" Richard said, "—or don't you?"

"Yes, I do."

"Then stop complaining."

"Well," Patience said, "we're all getting tired."

. . . But all were less tired when the meat was roasted, spitting and running fat, showers of sparks rising into a windy night. Richard carved out smoking slabs with his heavy knife, hung each on a whittled stick, and passed them to the others before hacking out half a haunch for himself. . . . Comparing with the village meat before, Baj found this mutton—wild, fresh, tainted by no notion of Warm-times returning, no cropped slaves, no weeping children—to be the better supper.

They ate sitting close to the fire, except for Errol, who gobbled under a shrub—and Patience, finishing a second thick chop, sitting relaxed against a hemlock trunk. "I have," she said to Baj, when he offered her a blanket, "a Warming-talent, failing a little, but still firm enough to cozy me." She smiled at him, her nose now straight—though with a little bump at the bridge. ". . . Are you settled this evening, Baj? Safe, resting, and full of rich meat?"

"Yes, I am."

"Perfect," Patience said, and drew the scimitar resting across her lap as she leaped and lunged long to slice him lightly just below the knee as he rolled back and away with yelp of startlement, then pain.

He came to his feet, hopping backward into the trees, his rapier drawn as she came to him, saying in a conversational way, "Edge only. Three cuts wins." And demonstrated in shadowing firelight by feinting, then striking him backhand along his left side, slicing his buckskin jerkin over a rib.

Nancy shouted, "Don't!"

Baj parried the next two slashes, but by very little. Patience, fighting sometimes two-handed now, gave him little room to fence. ". . . The time for spruce-branch fighting is over, my dear."

In the midst of surprise, sudden speed, and effort—still careful to deny his rapier's point in the ringing clash of steel—Baj, though already cut twice, found himself satisfied. As clearly as if truly seen, he saw King Sam before him in the *salle*, delivering that lesson of fighting over fencing-in-duels.

He kicked Patience in the belly to force her back for room, struck her swinging blade a fast hard parry to knock its line aside, and drew his left-hand dagger. Feeling her slight difficulty still in using the left hand, even to assist, he cut her lightly at the hip, withdrawing from a lunge. Then parried a cut to his head, held her steel sliding with the rapier, stepped in and struck her tender shoulder with the butt of his dagger. . . . As she received that pain, he drove her back against the fire—Richard rolling aside, Nancy calling again, "Don't!"

Patience, coat smoking, tried to wrench away from the flames. Baj let his rapier-edge meet her in a minor stop-thrust cut across her trousered thigh—and as, too late, she beat that blade aside, he struck lightly through her coat's sleeve with the left-hand dagger's edge . . . felt the give-and-part of cloth and skin beneath the blade. Third cut.

He stepped back to drop his weapons, stepped forward again to haul her free of the fire . . . and pat out flame runners along her coat-tails.

Patience was laughing, breathless. "Oh, very well done! Done *very* well—though, it's true, against only a small older lady, still fighting mainly wrong-handed." She wiped her blade on her coat's cloth, slid it into its sheath. "Your two fathers came to fight with you, isn't that so?"

"Perhaps." The cut beneath his knee was stinging worse than the other. Blood on his buckskins there.

"No 'perhaps' about it. Your Second-father, for workmanlike common sense; your First-father, for no mercy shown. My shoulder hurts . . ."

"You are both fools!" Nancy stood glaring at them.

"Of course," Patience said, shrugged off her greatcoat, and examined it, "—as are we all. Who but fools would be here, and for our reasons? . . . My poor coat."

"Come here." Nancy tugged Baj into firelight. "Where are you hurt?"

"Only little cuts."

"Nothing worth sewing up, I'd say." Richard smiled his toothy smile. "Good fight." Errol, sitting close to him for warmth, a little piece of mutton-fat stuck to his cheek, tongue-clicked in apparent agreement.

"And you're a fool, too," Nancy said, "—with a fool beside you. Can't we wait for Shrikes or the Guard to chop us? So *stupid*." She turned Baj this way and that with calloused narrow hands. "Your side . . ."

"Nothing much, either of them." He wiped a red drop from his dagger's blade, found none spotting the sword, and sheathed both.

"Too bad," Nancy said. "A real wound would have been a lesson." She turned to Patience. "And you—he hurt you three times."

"Hurt me lightly, dear," Patience said. "Kitchen cuts, and will clot—though I know a real wound would have been a lesson."

"*Ha ha,*" Nancy said, a very old Warm-time ironism. Baj had read it in copybooks of course, but couldn't recall hearing it used. "And you," she said to him, "—the next time we practice, I'll use Janice." And she walked off into the evergreens.

"Janice . . . ?"

Richard, who'd been smiling, stopped, and spoke softly. "So you don't ask her, Baj . . . She names her sword in revenge-reminder for her mother. A Thrush, and very young. —After the Faculty had made Nancy in her belly? The next time, they made an occa. Her mind fled away and never came back, and she died."

Baj sat by the fire, his leg stinging where Patience had touched him. His side hardly hurt at all. "What a pleasure it will be—a duty *and* a pleasure to ruin that city."

"Difficult duty," Patience said. "And time for us to sleep." She shrugged her singed coat on, and lay down beneath her hemlock. "Though they say sleep cannot be stored—still, weariness can be."

"No truer words. . . ." Richard lay down, settling by the fire, drawing his blanket over as Errol came to cuddle beside him.

"I take first watch, apparently," Baj said, and went down through the evergreens to pee. . . . Finished, he laced his buckskins, and was wending back up through foliage to the fire, when he saw Nancy standing in a little space, looking out to the north through a break in the trees.

He stepped beside her, looked out . . . out past a mountain's low shoulder, and saw in the distance the faintest fine horizontal line, a spider-web thread, shining white under the moon.

"The Wall. And still must be a hundred WT miles away."

Nancy turned, narrow face moon-shadowed and forbidding. "More. —And why are you always . . . present?" she said. "Isn't it possible for me to be *alone*?"

"Of course. I don't—"

"So fucking stupid," she lisped the s. "Your 'three cuts' non-sense with that crazy woman."

"Nancy, she—it was a lesson."

"You're always glancing little looks at me, too."

"That's not true."

"It is true, and I'm tired of it."

"I don't—"

"Yes, you do, liar. Always little looks . . . staring at someone who's so strange—who's so much an *animal*." She put out a hand and shoved him. "From now on, stay away from me!" She shoved him again, harder, teeth showing in moonlight—Baj took her wrists, and it became a wrestle. Then a fight.

She wrenched a hand free, hit him hard in the face, then came at him biting—a snarling quick snap of white teeth—and Baj, not wanting to hit her, grappled her close, lifted her off her feet, and fell rolling amid evergreen branches as she kicked and struck at him, wiry strong.

Frightened she'd draw her knife or try for her sword, he hugged to pin her arms, saying, "Sorry . . . I'm *sorry*," though for what he wasn't certain. She tried to knee him, and he thought of calling to Patience for help, but that seemed so embarrassing. . . .

Then, though she'd fought so fiercely, suddenly she lay still beneath him, so he thought he'd hurt her.

"Nancy, I didn't mean to . . ."

A cold look from moon-shadowed yellow eyes. "Get off me, Sunriser. —And keep away."

"I can't," Baj said, surprised that was what he couldn't do. . . . And having said it, for no real reason he bent and kissed her. Felt her mouth, the slender bones of her long jaw as she turned her head aside, but he didn't care . . . felt against his lips a canine's needle point, and didn't care. He kissed her as he'd kissed no girl in his life; there was nothing left of him but kissing. . . . She lay still, but it made no difference to him. He hugged and gripped her as if he might squeeze all pleasure, all sweetness, all good news from her. He wrestled her softly and sliding, licked her throat, found her little ear in the thick soft crest of her hair. "Love," he whispered to her. "And has been love. . . ."

Then, after what seemed a wait of years, a slim arm—as if reluctant—rose to circle and hold him.

"Forgive me," Baj whispered, "—for not saying so sooner."

"You are a fool," Nancy said. "A fool . . ." She lay back under moon-shadow, unbuttoned her wool shirt, and drew the cloth aside to show six little tender-nippled breasts in two rows of three down her chest. "Look," she said. "Look."

And he kissed them up and down.

When their clothes were off, strewn in evergreens—all but the moccasins, which were too much trouble—he found other differences. Shorter sturdier thighs than a full-human girl's might be—but smooth and white as Map-Alabama marble. Muscular buttocks, a slender drift of russet fur down the small of her back, and thick brush of the same between her legs, so he had to search for a moment to find a soft pout that parted into oiled warmth and slippery entrance—first for a finger as he bent over her, she clutching his cock with a calloused little hand . . . then for that, when she said, "There," and put him to her.

Then the different smell of their fucking, her slightly harsher odor than a Sunriser girl's . . . and the different angle of it—so she soon eased him out, turned beneath him for comfort as she went to all fours, hollowed her back to present herself, and moaned as he found her again.

Baj drove into her and into her to the rhythmic soft sound of wet, and on through a time that was no time, until Nancy twisted and thrashed beneath him as he came . . . then bit his bracing arm, convulsed, and called out to her mother.

. . . The wind's cold, the forest's discomfort they hadn't felt at all, then slowly returned to them. They found clothes and cloaks to draw over for covers, to tuck under to pad the hemlocks' windfall. Then they lay content, hugging, damp with sweat.

After a while, kissing her, Baj found tears. "What?" he said. "What . . .?"

"Oh, Baj . . . Baj, my dear, I come to you not new." She took a breath. "Not *new*. I have—"

"—Not been with me. But now you are. And I love you."

"Well, you are a fool," Nancy said, and sat up, searching for a bandanna. She found Baj's with his shirt, blew her nose, then lay down again to more kisses.

". . . Richard?" Patience spoke softly from beneath her hemlock.

A deep, rumbled "Umm" by the fire.

"Do you know the phrase, 'Babes in the woods'?"

"I do now."

"What will happen to those children?"

"The same, dear, that will happen to us."

* * *

Three days later of cold mutton and hard traveling—Patience, the third day, sailing slowly only a bow-shot above them—they'd come down from the mountains to foothills, and then onto an endlessly-wide tundra plain, its mosses and sedge grasses, brown and green, streaked with dotted drifts of tiny white flowers and the little colored blossoms that Baj knew, of bilberry and crowberry. Small brown-winged butterflies flew among those.

Along the plain's distant northern horizon lay the glittering line of the Wall. Baj had seen it close, once, from a fast ship rigged for wet, and rowed far up the river to North Map-Illinois. The glacier's frozen ramparts had risen two miles high over distant hills of moraine and milk-white lakes fed by great waterfalls of summer melt. . . . Nameless furred tribesmen (tribeswomen, too) had paced the ship through stunted scrub along bitter riverbanks, shouting, presenting naked buttocks in insult, and hurling futile javelins. "Ah . . ." Pedro had said, standing at the rail beside him, "—the free, the *natural* life."

". . . How far would you say, Baj?" Richard standing beside him, smiling down.

"Thirty . . . forty WT miles. I have seen it, from the River."

Patience laughed. "Over tundra is deceitful viewing. Try almost twice that."

And as she said it, the changeable frigid winds brought from the west—once . . . then again—the faintest reedy fluting of pipes, the faintest rumble and boom of kettle-drums . . . music sounding, then silenced, then sounding again with contrary breezes.

Richard cocked his great head, "The Guard, marching. We are to be met."

". . . But that music," Baj said, "—doesn't it warn that they're coming?"

"They don't care whether it warns or not," Nancy said, and spit to the side.

"Still many miles away," Richard said, listening. "Patrolling to meet us along the plain's border—or perhaps only to strike the Fishhawks . . . what's left of them."

"But marched down from the Shrike campaign, from that fighting." Nancy looking to the western tundra, empty of all but cold wind and distant music. "Come as Patience said they would."

"To meet us as friends?"

"As friends, Baj," Nancy said, "—or not."

"Wolf-General decides," Richard said, shrugged under his big pack, and strode off to the west.

"See . . . ?" Nancy looked up, pointed.

High above—higher than she usually now Walked-in-air—Patience wheeled west in a flutter of blue coat-tails. Baj thought he saw her glance down at them, indicate the way with her sheathed scimitar.

. . . Hiking with Nancy side-by-side, Baj found some reluctance in going with her toward that faint wind-broken music. Holding his hand as they managed awkward tussocks, Nancy seemed changed in the last days, as if a different girl with fox's blood—perhaps a sister—had come to him, golden eyes tart-sweet as honey-lemon candy. . . . And matters seemed to be shifting in Baj, so now-and-never-before ran within him like a summer spring.

. . . Hints of that music had come to them all through the day's difficult traveling—over bog, where clouds of the season's last mosquitoes rose . . . then on smooth mossy stretches and ankle-sprain tussocks. But only the wind's hum and whistle sounded through a bitter night under racing moonlit clouds. There was no cover, no shelter on the tundra plain, no makings for a fire. After diminished scraps of cold mutton, there was only the shelter of sleep. . . . Errol huddled against Richard under his blanket, and Baj and Nancy warmed each other, wrapped in wool and discovery.

Fairly at ease in her worn blue coat only, Patience took first watch, and sat in moonlight on a tussock with her scimitar across her lap, her white hair blowing in the icy wind now steady from the Wall. She listened for her baby's breathing in her mind—heard nothing, but still thought, *"Coming to you, my darling,"* just in case. . . . And he might have listened, for she thought she felt—was almost certain she felt the baby's so-dear, dimpled, pudgy hand seize and enclose her left arm, gripping hard for comfort, so her fingertips tingled.

. . . The morning was still and frosted, the dawn sky just brightening to jeweled blue when Nancy, on last watch, woke them to a definite distant melody, pipes in a cheery wheedling tune.

" 'Yanking-tootle,' " Richard said, rising massive from his blanket, yawning Errol spilled aside, "—a copybook song for morning marching. Now we get up . . . *up!* Eat, and drink water—pee, and poop. The scouts will find us before mid-day."

After meager bites—the last of the mutton—and hasty gulps of icy water, the party divided. Patience and Nancy, with no shrubs, no tree cover but knee-high dwarf willow, went off to one side while Richard and Baj turned their backs—Baj reaching to turn Errol as well. Then the males went out to the other side of tundra to toilet.

Pissing, Errol looked up, made his clicking noises—and Baj, following his gaze, saw a great herd drifting far to the north. Three . . . four Warm-time miles away. Drifting north, apparently grazing on the sedge grasses and lichen as they went.

"Caribou."

"Yes," Ricard stood watching them. "Small herd."

"*Small* herd?"

"Baj, I've seen them take two days and nights up here, to pass. With wolves and grizzled bears following."

Rattling tongue-clicks from Errol. The boy's empty blue eyes filled with attention . . . longing.

"He loves chasing, and the end of chasing." Finished, Richard shook his odd member, tucked it away. "Speaking of which, better if we go to meet the Guard, than have them come for us like hunters."

"Yes." Baj laced his buckskins. There was a little flutter in his chest at this end to traveling only with friends. Accustomed traveling. . . . Now, Nancy would not be as safe, would not be only with friends. He imagined for a moment (childish imagining) that regiments of the Army-United—come a thousand miles north and east—stood in formation at their backs, with the certain new king, old One-eye Howell Voss, sitting his charger at the van and joking with his officers, complaining about the mess-cooks' breakfast.

An imagining that left no comfort behind.

Baj settled his pack and quiver—paused to kneel and brace his bow—then loosened sword and dagger in their sheaths, and held out his hand as Nancy came to him. "Stay close to me."

She gave him a look. "I have my sword."

"I know. I'm depending on your protection." And received a sharp elbow to the ribs.

A rustle in the air above them as they hiked—the morning wind still very cold under a rising sun. "They're coming," Patience said, swung so low that Baj could have jumped to touch her greatcoat's hem. "—And I see no other Talents Walking-in-air above them."

Baj stared ahead . . . but saw nothing but tussock grasses combing in the wind. Heard the distant merry tune piping on.

They walked west—spots in the tundra occasionally coldly wet and soft enough so they sank almost to their knees, and had to haul their moccasins sucking out. "A few WT weeks ago," Richard said, marching a little hunched under his big pack, "—warm as it gets so close to the Wall, the mosquitoes would be coming up in numbers to choke you, breathing them in."

Baj said, "Thanks for small blessings, then." And when Errol suddenly stopped and stood staring, glanced past him and saw something running toward them. Coming at a gallop.

"Another one," Nancy said, and pointed to the right. "They're stupid, barely Persons at all. . . ."

Two. Coming at a run and very fast.

For a moment, Baj thought they were deer, only trained somehow to scout. Certainly they were four-legged hooved things. Then he saw that the front legs bent at elbows, and ended in knot-knuckled hands. . . . Small packs and scabbarded light hatchets rode their backs where saddles might have gone. Their skin, mottled brown, seemed hairless . . . their necks—longer than men's necks—curved up to small heads barely human, with eyes set wide as horses'.

One, galloping up, called, "Whooo?" in tenor very like an owl. The other echoed him. —Her; Baj saw two soft breasts between the long front limbs. Both scouts stood restless, a short bow-shot away.

"Richard from Shrike!" Richard called. "Once, a captain of the Guard!"

"Patience!" Patience called, sweeping down to settle. "Patience Nearly-Lodge Riley. Citizen . . . in exile."

The closer Scout nodded, intelligent enough to take that in, then turned her head to examine Baj . . . Nancy.

"Baj!" he called to her, "—who was Bajazet, of Middle-Kingdom."

The Scout stared, and shook her head slightly, as a horse might have. The other stood silent.

Nancy called, "Nancy . . . from Thrush! And this boy is Errol, once scrubber to H-Company Mess, Second Regiment!"

"I know *youuuu*," the Scout said, lifted her long, inhuman right arm, and pointed with thick-caloused knuckles.

Nancy said nothing.

"All under*stoood*," the Scout hooted—then suddenly wheeled, and galloped away.

The other didn't follow. It turned, prancing a little, bent its head to snatch a bite of tufted sedge, then stood waiting, apparently to accompany them.

"The Wolf-General," Richard called to it, "—Sylvia is with these companies?"

The Scout stared, but didn't answer.

"She'd better be," Patience said. Then, certainly from a copy-book, added, "Or we're screwed."

"Let's go." Richard strode away. Toward silence, now; the distant rise-and-shine music had ended.

They walked the lumpy tussocks, looking west, while the Scout trotted in easy wide circles around them. . . . Errol, after a while, ran out to chase him, and wouldn't come to calls. But the Scout—after an initial shying away—seemed not to mind, left his hatchet scabbarded, and he and the boy commenced a chase and be-chased game over the tundra, though Errol was never fast enough to catch him.

"Two more," Richard said, and Baj saw movement . . . then made out two other Scouts galloping toward them. These did not approach closely, only circled once, then again, and ran away west.

Errol, panting in exhaustion, had just come back to them, when Nancy said, "There." And pointed. . . . What seemed at first animals—from their compactness, their brown fur—gradually became nine . . . ten . . . a WT-dozen men trotting toward them in a long extended line.

Sunshiners, it seemed to Baj. True-human tribesmen, by the look of them. Short men, rounded with smooth fat over muscle, and wearing parkies and trousers of caribou hide trimmed with fisher fur, the parky hoods tucked back and away from their faces. Each carried two or three light javelins, and an atlatl tucked into a wide belt with a sheathed long-bladed knife.

"Shrikes." Richard stood still, and swung his double-bladed ax off his shoulder.

One of the tribesmen—the man on the left of their line— whistled a single shrill note, and the others slowed and drifted, while he come forward.

A round face, smiling. His teeth were filed to points. As he came, he called, "Captain Richard!" his breath smoking in the icy morning air.

"Dolphus . . .!" Richard spoke softly over his shoulder. "I fought against him on Berkshire ice. He's an Under-chief, important."

"And a relative," Patience said. "Isn't he?"

"Was my mother's cousin," Richard said, and the Shrike chief, hearing, nodded as he walked up to them—stepping neatly, Baj saw, always between the grass tussocks. The furs he wore—the parky, and caribou-hide muk-boots and trousers—were beautifully dressed, decorated with the fisher fur, ermine tails, and little fans of porcupine quills dyed orange and blue.

"His mother—my father's brother's eldest daughter," the Shrike said. He spoke in a humming drone, as if on a single alto note. It was, Baj supposed, where Richard had gotten *his* thoughtful hum.

The Shrike chief didn't seem fierce; he seemed pleasant. His hair, the color of southern straw (though with gray mixed in it) was plastered with animal fat . . . drawn into a clubbed pigtail at the back. His green eyes seemed amused.

"Heavens," he said, "—what a bunch." A reader, Baj thought, filed teeth or not, and comfortable with copybook-English.

The Shrike smiled, examining them. "A deserter from the Guard, an ex-Boston air-walker, an army whore, an idiot boy, and . . . someone who *was* someone, but isn't anymore."

Baj felt Nancy standing still and silent beside him, and anger rose hot, seized his mouth, and spoke. "Enough of a someone," he said, "—to run a steel blade up your fat ass!"

The Shrike widened his eyes in a demonstration of surprise, glanced from Baj to Nancy, then smiled his pleasant filed-tooth smile. "It must be love," he said. "If I offended, Prince, I beg your pardon. —And the lady's." Certainly a literate savage, and unimpressed by threats.

Nancy said nothing.

Richard took a side-step to stand between Baj and the Shrike. "What are you doing with the Guard, Dolphus?"

"I'm doing what you intend doing. Persuaded to try it, in any case. Boston is becoming . . . tedious."

"And the Guard?"

"I won't say they'll welcome you, Richard—weren't happy to welcome me and my men. But they've admitted a truce with us . . . for a while. The rest of the Guard companies—fewer—have been sent down to the Coast-Atlantic on dubious, but convenient orders. Orders that might hold just long enough." He shrugged. "It's sad, really, since we were preparing an unpleasant surprise beneath the Wall for your so-clever Sylvia."

"You'd be the first savage to manage it."

"Well," Dolphus-Shrike smiled, "—sooner or later, someone is bound to."

The tribesman spoke the easiest, most authentic book-English that Baj had heard since fleeing Middle-Kingdom. Better, more . . . relaxed, than even the Wishful-believers had managed. It was as if a man had traveled the centuries from Warm-times, wrapped himself in fur, taken up javelins and atlatl, and filed his teeth.

"Sylvia's with you?"

"Oh, with respect still due, I'd say we're with her."

Baj noticed that the other Shrikes had casually moved to circle them. It would be difficult to defend against javelins hissing in from all directions. He reached back to his quiver, slid an arrow out, and nocked it to his bow-string. . . . Dolphus-Shrike, noticing past Richard's bulk, winked at him, and said, "In case of difficulties—me first?"

"Who better?" Baj said.

"Then thank heavens we're all to be friends," the Shrike gestured to follow, and walked away, "—as long as we live."

"What of him, Richard?" Patience seemed at ease, though her hand was on her scimitar's hilt.

"Dolphus? He's a shaman, an educated man among the Shrikes."

"But a fighter."

"Oh, yes. He doesn't have to be—but he is. Got bored with copybooks, apparently."

"And the Robins, south, fear those people?" Baj said.

"Robins," Nancy said, "—and the Thrushes and Fish-hawks. The Shrikes are very clever. And cruel."

"If he hurts you again," Baj said, "—with his well-read WT mouth, I'll kill him."

". . . I should have told you," Nancy said, and Baj saw tears in golden eyes.

"You came near enough telling me, sweetheart. But it would

have made no difference, and makes no difference now." He took her narrow hand as they walked along . . . and tried, as he could see the Shrikes doing, stepping only between tussocks.

"Don't . . . Baj, don't fight him."

"Not if I can help it. He frightens me."

Nancy laughed, and wiped tears away with her sleeve. "Even for a Sunriser," she said, "—you're odd." She hugged him, so they walked awkwardly, then leaned up to nip his earlobe, so Baj imagined happy years of minor injuries. . . . Still, there crossed his mind a shadowed scene of Nancy naked in firelight, drunk, laughing, surrounded by a hulking pack.

The thought, the image shamed him . . . and all the worse since there was no way to beg pardon for that treachery of imagination.

He held her closer, so they stumbled along, awkward as Festival sack-racers. Bent, and kissed her.

. . . Soon, standards heaved up on the plain, and formations could be seen beneath them, mounted and foot—some shining in steel, some uniformed in furs, and others, it seemed, in multicolored woolens. All marching east—without music, but together, so their ranks swayed slightly to one side then the other, as they came.

"Who is Sylvia," the Shrike chief called to them, smiling, "—that all our swains commend her?" It sounded to Baj like a copybook quote, though he didn't remember it. . . . Old Lord Peter would have known.

Ahead of them, riders came galloping from serried ranks bright with polished armor under the morning sun. Five . . . six, coming fast under a green staff-banner rippling to their wind of passage.

Lances. Baj saw lances held socketed easily upright. And, he thought, bows cased beside their saddles. . . . But it was not horses they rode. And not the great pale Made-things some Boston people shipped to Middle-Kingdom for their mounts. He'd seen those . . . *Mampies*. Seen others later, gone wild and murdering.

These mounts coming, were like deer, but black, and much bigger—and had a swift odd ambling pace, fast as a horse, and looking slow to tire.

"What—?"

"Moose," Nancy said. "Only females, and bred big."

"Female moose," Richard said, "have bad tempers, can break a Person's back with a kick."

"I've ridden one," Nancy said. "They won't let Richard near them."

"My grizzled portion," Richard said. "But I was Infantry, anyway. . . . Uh-oh." He swung his ax down to the tundra, left its handle leaning against his leg. "Baj, quiver that arrow, and ease your bow. Do it *quickly*."

"The Wolf-General," Nancy said, reached out for Errol, drew him to her, and held him still as Baj knelt to unstring the bow.

"You know," Patience said, "I've only seen her in Tea-party Parade, with other Guard commanders."

"Be careful," Richard said. "Careful. You're about to meet . . . she who no one cares to meet."

19

There was no sound then but the north wind . . . and the rapid, approaching hoofbeats of the six riders, their dark mounts— big-eared, droop-nosed, humped at the shoulders—galloping with a stilted rocking gait that seemed not troubled by knots of tundra grass.

Baj could make out the rider in front, dressed dark, and sitting knees-high like a racing jockey. . . . The others glinted in steel armor. One of them—with a furred head, and looking wide as two men—bore the green-banner standard.

They came on as if they were charging to kill.

"Stand," Richard said, ". . . stand still."

They stood still. Through the hide soles of his moccasin-boots, Baj felt the tundra trembling to hoofbeats.

The first rider came to them—and pulled up hard in a short slide, so the rearing moose's heavy split hooves ripped tussocks, spattered Richard with cold mud.

"*My General* . . ." Richard started to raise his right hand.

The rider's voice sounded high and harsh as a woodsman's saw. "If you salute me, Deserter, I'll have your hand off."

Richard put his hand down as the five other riders thundered up, and the Wolf-General laughed. It was a grim laugh to see—a snouted muzzle, barely a mouth, wrinkling away from wolf's fangs, a long red tongue. Then she sat her saddle, silent . . . examining them.

Certainly, it seemed to Baj, the General had much human in her, but it showed only enough for a wolf's head swollen larger for sense, for shorter ears—though furred slate gray—for claws become useful almost-hands, for shoulders enough to swing a sword or ax . . . and for slanting eyes a woman's deep and lovely blue. She was white-furred at the throat above a breast-and-back cuirass of some dark metal—bronze, Baj thought—shaped down its front to indicate rows of small breasts. She was lightly furred, thigh to stirruped boot and along her arms. Her dark gray hair rose—much as Nancy's—in a crest from her forehead. A bronze pig-nosed helmet swung from her saddle-bow beside a scabbarded heavy straight saber.

Neither she nor her restless mount bore any decoration at all. There was only muscled bulk, bronze, steel, fur, and fangs.... The Person's eyes, though—so gentle and rich a blue as she sat considering them—seemed to Baj decoration enough.

Of her escort, four—lean riders in steel chain-mail—seemed almost fully human, near-Sunrisers, though with odd bones under scarred and savage faces. The fifth, the banner-bearer, was a Moonriser-certain, short, squat, and wide-shouldered. He was tufted black, with paler undercoat, and had round furred ears. The muzzle was blunt, the small eyes the color of stone.

"General," Patience said, "—I've seen you on parade."

The Wolf-woman stared at her. "You will not Walk-in-air, unless by my orders and *following* my orders." Her voice, harsh with high vibration, was unsettling to listen to. "—Disobey, and I'll send riders to follow until you grow tired. Then they will bring your head to me."

"If I choose the air," Patience said, "and without your orders—you'd better send formidable riders to try to take *my* head."

"I have no others." The Wolf-General sidled her big mount almost into them, then leaned from her saddle and held out a clawed hand. Patience went to take it.

"Sylvia," the General said, shook Patience's hand WT style, then straightened in her saddle and glanced at Nancy, Errol, then Baj. "You, Sunriser-boy, are supposedly son of the Achieving King?"

"He was my Second-father . . . ma'am."

"And your first, the Khan Toghrul?"

"Yes, ma'am."

She stared at him. "It's difficult, just the same, to see any greatness in you."

"Difficult for me to *feel* any greatness."

The General grunted, said, "Hello, Nancy," turned her mount, hacked its huge side with bright spurs, and the moose lunged from among them . . . gathered and paced away into its swift and awkward gallop.

As the five riders reined to follow, the banner-bearing Person said, "Captain, welcome back."

Richard said, "Fuck you, Sergeant." And, as the escort rode away, "Stay clear of that one."

"Might be a good idea," Baj said, "—to stay clear of all of them."

"If we didn't need them . . ." Patience sighed. "I suppose we're to follow?"

"*Go!*" One of the Shrikes gestured with a javelin.

"My question answered," Patience said, as they hiked on. It was, Baj found, almost impossible to step between the grass tussocks—unless, of course, one had been raised to it from childhood. It seemed better to simply stomp along, hoping for no sprained ankle . . . though where the tussocks didn't rise, the mossy tundra was soft and flower-decorated as fine carpet.

The Shrike chief, Dolphus, came to walk with them. "Our general," he said, "is in an amiable mood. She rarely shakes anyone's hand. Rarely has casual conversations. And often is having someone skinned and sprinkled with sea-salt. . . . An expensive hobby."

"And is this fierceness," Baj said, though disliking the Shrike, "—is this fierceness her talent, or beside it?"

The Shrike turned. "Ah . . . a sensible question." He walked along, javelins across his left shoulder—and stepping, Baj saw, neatly between clumps of grass. "Her fierceness, I think *is* beside her talent. She's beaten us in battle three . . . four times, large fights and small. Never as a furious wolf might leap for your throat, but rather as a pack will chase and pace and circle until you stand surrounded, exhausted, and already bleeding from bites."

"True enough," Richard said over his shoulder. "She has a genius for it."

"I would say," Dolphus-Shrike smiled at Baj, "—I would say that she would have given either of your fathers fits. You know that usage?"

"I've read as much as you," Baj said. "And written, besides."

"No!" the Shrike made his face of astonishment. "A truly literate River-prince. Well . . . 'Will wonders—' "

" '—never cease,' " Baj said, and he and Dolphus-Shrike exchanged a fellow look, though guarded.

. . . They came to the marching camp—the Shrikes drifting away—and into noise and broken formations, what seemed, at first, only confusion as the soldiers, infantry and cavalry, were settling in.

A sentry, ax-armed and in steel half-armor with a small bright brass circle riveted to each shoulder pauldron, stood in their way. A Person of Richard's bulky blood, though not quite as large, and with fur-tufts rust red, he said, "What's your business here?" The tone incurious at such an odd party arrived out of wilderness, though the small brown eyes were interested.

"Our business is our business, Corporal," Richard said. "Now, whistle up your officer."

The corporal stared a moment more, then placed two large horn-nailed fingers in his jaw, and whistled a single high trilling note. He wiped the fingers dry on his leather sleeve, and stood watching them . . . waiting.

Soon enough, a Person came trotting to the camp's perimeter— of Richard's blood again, though again not as large—trotting in exactly Richard's swift lumber, though in armor, a double-edged ax balanced in his right hand.

"Won't state their business, sir."

The officer, a gold chain-link at each armored shoulder, examined them with eyes the color of his ax's blade. "Good Lord," he said—an ancient usage, that once, far south, would have been risky. Then, "Captain, you're a fool."

"Who isn't, Terry Fish-hawk?" Richard smiled. "When the link?"

"More than half a year ago."

"Ruined a good sergeant," Richard said. "You're too smart to be an officer."

"Well," Terry Fish-hawk said, "—that might be true." And to the sentry, "Corporal, the Shrikes brought these people in at the General's command. Pass them, but slate the number, and note that it's a daylight pass."

He sketched a one-finger salute to Richard, said, "Captain, I'd stay clear of Infantry Street; people there still mind your running." Then he glanced again at the others, turned and trotted away.

The Corporal surveyed them again, said, "Five," and waved them on their way.

"Formidable," Patience said, as they walked into the ordered turmoil of the camp.

"Terry?" Richard smiled. "These are all formidable. Good soldiers. Better . . . much better than Boston deserves."

"And you miss them," Baj said, "—miss the Guard."

"Of course I miss them." Richard shook his head. "Wouldn't one of your First-father's officers have missed his squadron of Kipchak horsemen? One of your Second-father's commanders miss the regiments of the Army-United?"

"Hear men's nonsense," Nancy said—and though Errol, apparently uneasy being back in a camp, was staying close—she took the boy's arm to hold him closer. "Persons or otherwise," she gave Baj a look, "—they lose their wits when trumpets blow, like children at a parade."

"Sadly true," Patience said, "though sometimes very useful."

Then they were among rows of rising shelters. Oil-blackened leather lean-tos—weather-breaks rather than closed tenting— were being pegged with stands of arms spaced along: long-shaft pikes, short spears, shield and swords, and axes. . . . There were the shouts, the apparent confusion, the colors and equipment and various odors nearly the same as in any marching camp of the Army-United that Baj had visited—but not quite. The trotting columns of moose sweated ranker than horses. The Persons did not smell quite like men. Their voices were more various.

"Do you know?" Patience said, hesitating a step to scrape moose dung from her moccasin-boot, "I've never visited the Guard. Had no idea they were . . . so busy, bustling about."

"Soldiers," Nancy said, "—are always bustling, or asleep."

As they walked through the camp rising around them, hundreds of soldiers were swarming to Under-officers' loud commands—rough book-English being used in odd tones and accents.

A file of Persons lumbered past—many of these big as Richard, and looking very much like him, though fur-tufts varied to black, grizzled, or (for the largest) white. Each of these soldiers wore back-and-breast steel armor, and all, that Baj could see, carried the big double-bitted ax. . . . Two wore the same little silver crescent moon, necklaced, as Nancy, Richard, and Errol.

Only one of the file, a huge white-furred Person, had turned his head to stare at them as he passed. It was an unfriendly, carniverous look from small pitch-black eyes in a massive wedge-shaped head, its humanity precarious.

"Never trust a White, Baj," Nancy said, noticing. "Those have a mind beneath their mind, that changes when they're hungry."

"My mind," Richard held up to let another formation by, "—is changing with hunger right now. That passing Ice-oaf, by the way, was Albert-One. His brother, Albert-Two, is also in the Guard, and was in my company. Neither of them worth much, always complaining. . . . Nancy, hold Errol with us."

"No need. He's afraid someone will take and fuck him," Nancy said. "And I know these companies." A buzzing snarl in her voice, deeper lisping. "—They care only for their nasty dicks, whatever their blood may be."

Baj reached to her, but she pulled away. He reached again and gripped her narrow hand until she settled, so they walked like children hand-in-hand among the soldiers.

They passed riders—Persons of the same breed as those four near-Sunrisers who had ridden with Sylvia Wolf-General. Cavalry, in high boots, hide trousers, and hide jackets with chain-mail over, they wore long fur cloaks, and were armed with heavy straight sabers slung at their belts. Their Under-officer, at the head of the troop, had lost an eye to the same slash that trenched his forehead.

Jingling by, only two of the cavalrymen had spared Richard and the others a glance.

". . . We'll camp on the Lines with those boys," Richard said. "They'll bear me no infantry grudges." And he turned to follow them.

Stepping aside as a four-team of moose came hauling a loaded wagon by, Baj noticed several soldiers of what seemed the third most common bloodline of Boston's Guard. The bear-bloods, near-Sunrisers, and these . . .

A group of them were standing beside a folded stack of shelters dumped there for distribution. They were talking, laughing, with three women—also Persons, but much smaller, wearing red boots, caribou vests, and striped pantaloons decorated with bits of metal and reflecting mirror. These Person women—one richly furred a cloudy gray, her face (great-eyed, soft-muzzled) apparently reflecting some part lynx—wore their vests loosely open, to reveal naked armpits, and hints of breasts.

The soldiers, six . . . seven of them, were less finished versions of the Wolf-General's savage perfection, but still weighted with wolf blood—though one was slighter, possibly from a portion of coyote, and apparently was the jokester. . . . The seven, their laughter white with fangs, red with tongues and gullets, were armored with bronze cuirasses, and cloaked and trousered in thick-woven wool, striped red, yellow, and black. . . . Each of them bore a round hide shield slung at their backs, belted a scabbarded short-sword, and leaned on a leaf-bladed spear.

"Those," Nancy said to Baj, and nodded at the women, "—are what I was, before I stuck a knife in Jesse-Thrush, and ran, because he was cruel, and tried to fuck me wrong and hurt me. That was from Service to Company D, then under Sylvia's command, so I committed Breach-of-contract. . . . A very serious thing."

Baj stopped walking, and took her arm to hold her still, Errol beside her. "Then thank every Jesus," he said, "for Jesse-Thrush, who began your travels to me, my dear one."

Nancy said nothing then, but golden eyes said much.

"Baj," Richard called back, "—keep up, and don't be noticing those you don't want to notice you."

As he and Nancy walked on—Errol clinging close—Baj tried to estimate numbers. "How many soldiers are here?"

"Two thousand," Nancy said. "Twenty companies."

"*Supposed* to be," Richard said over his shoulder, "—but never are. There's no such thing, never has been such a thing as a full-roster on campaign."

"Yes," Baj said. "I understood that was so of the Army-United."

"Ah . . ." Churning after the cavalrymen through tundra becoming mud, Richard lifted his head, sniffing. "Moose-feed and moose-shit, the troopers are leading us home."

To the right, where the camp streets seemed to cross, Baj saw a great pavilion rising, its leather panels painted gray and gold.

"Hers," Nancy said, "—and her relatives'."

"Cousins, brothers, and an aunt," Richard said, turning and walking backward for a moment to talk. "All officers, all *good* officers—and none of them, particularly the aunt, wise to cross."

Wending after the cavalrymen as the camp was completing around them, stepping aside for troopers riding past, and burdened work-parties, it became plain to Baj that what might have seemed confusion, was its opposite.

"These are disciplined people."

Richard turned his head to stare down at him. "What did you

think? That we—that Moonriser Guardsmen would be a mob, or hunting pack?"

"No . . . of course not."

Richard grunted and lumbered on. Nancy stuck a sharp elbow into Baj's ribs. "Runaway tongue," she said.

. . . The Cavalry's Lines lay along the western edge of camp. Past them, soldiers were digging a wide ditch in the tundra's grass and flowers, pickaxes swinging, spades shoveling down to permafrost. "They always circle-ditch a camp," Nancy said, "—to hesitate a rush if tribesmen come."

"A useful thing, particularly at night. . . ." Richard led them along a row of great black buttocks, the moose standing short-tied to a long chain anchored at measured places by heavy stakes driven into the ground.

"Step wide," Richard said. "They kick."

Baj stepped wide.

Midway down the Line—as the file of cavalry was halted, the men dismissed to their duties—Richard went past to a lean-to shelter where two of the near-Sunrisers, officers' gold chain-links fastened to their mailed shoulders, sat on stacked saddle-blankets, scribbling on slates. The older one, tall, and slightly stooped, looked up as Richard came.

"And why, by the Wall," he said, "—aren't you skinned and screeching for desertion?"

Richard didn't try to salute. "Too valuable to lose, Colonel."

The stooped officer *naaa*'d a short laugh, and Baj saw a goat's horizontal pupils in human eyes, a human face. "Best one today," the colonel said, then glanced at Patience, "The Township lady . . . ?"

"Yes."

"Umm-hmm. And you, Richard—and these—are troubling me . . . why?"

"For bedding and rations, sir."

"Ah. Why don't you and your friends—hello, Nancy—why don't you and your friends go bother the infantry?"

"Because it would mean fighting, sir."

"*Fighting,*" the colonel tossed his head. "Can't have that, can we, Burt?"

"No, sir," the other officer, a two-link captain, said. His eyes were gray, and entirely human. "Can't have fighting."

The colonel stared at them a moment. "All right, Richard-Shrike. Bedding and rations—but stay *off* the feed bales—and away from my troopers."

"Yes, sir."

The colonel looked at Errol. "That's an idiot boy."

"Twisted weasel," Nancy said. "Mess-kettle cleaner since he was little, and they beat him." Errol, uneasy at the attention, tongue-clicked.

"Well," the colonel said, "if he gets among my moose and disturbs them, I'll have him nailed to a feed box. Understood?"

"Understood," Richard said.

"No offense meant to you, Lady," the colonel said to Patience, "—by these notices."

"None taken."

The colonel bent to his slate, and said nothing more as Richard led them away and down the Lines to a shelter where a large sergeant of supply—with odd hands and an unpleasant corporal—grumbled in poor book-English, then had thick bracelets of red ration-strings looped around their wrists, and fat rolled pallets tossed to them, each slate-noted.

"Fuckin' be sure you return these," the corporal said. "*I'm* not payin' for 'em."

. . . They spread blankets, unrolled pallets, then settled onto soft tundra turf just beyond the Line, wind-sheltered by canvas feed stores raised close on either side. Soldiers were digging the encampment ditch an easy bowshot away . . . and past them there was only a great level, the plain of sedge and dwarf willow—grass green, moss brown—stretching the Warm-time miles north, to the frost-white horizon of the Wall.

Wind came streaming from that northern ice, weighty, biting with cold that here proved short-summer's date a lie—so Baj, Richard, and Nancy wrapped their cloaks around them, and Errol burrowed under a blanket. Patience, her scimitar in her lap, sat cross-legged, looking north—her worn blue coat apparently warm enough.

It seemed to Baj that he and the others were changed in some subtle fashion. No longer quite what they'd been in the mountains—so few in the freedom of those grand landscapes. Here, in the Guard's marching camp, they appeared diminished, cramped (as they *were* cramped, hemmed in, and at others' mercy). Here, a simple order would see them dead—though after a scrambling fight, to be sure. An order, the necessity of which, Boston might have anticipated.

The icy wind come ruffling, Baj imagined Nancy dead in this place, huddled hacked and ruined on bloody blankets at the feet of panting soldiers. The golden eyes gone dark with death.

That, and his death and all their deaths, required only a few grating wolfish words—and from more a muzzle, than a mouth. So much coarser than Nancy's elegant indications. He needed to write a poem to her . . .

They all lazed, eased from traveling, as the glass-hours passed into after-noon. Nancy lay drowsing beside Baj, and Errol slept, twitching in some weasel dream.

"*What*," Baj said, when the wind, that had been so steady, shifted to westerly, "—what is that *stink?*"

"The bales," Nancy said. "Feed bales. Moose don't care much for grass."

"Under-bark and summer water-plants, bog cabbage," Richard said, "—packed damp, then the bales frozen on the ice in slit hides, so some air comes through when they thaw."

"And stink," Nancy said.

"Mountain-Jesus knows it," Baj said.

Nancy shook her head. "Frozen-Jesus here, Baj, held forever in the ice. Or, of course, we can call to Lady Weather."

"This odor . . ." Patience said. "There are disadvantages to moose, though heroes have ridden them."

"It must," Baj said to her, "be such a gift to travel in the air . . . and not afoot or riding some reluctant beast. But everything clean and clear, with distance meaning so little."

Patience stared at him.

". . . I meant no offense."

"You don't offend me, Baj. I'm only surprised you still think there is some wonderful way, that is not wonderfully dear. . . . I travel in air, Walk-in-air, at the penalty of making myself a sort of idiot, most of my mind empty of everything but keeping the earth away, so only by . . . *leaking* notions past can I think of anything else." She shrugged. "When I was young, there was more room in my head for other considerations—and I could still hold altitude while mulling them."

She paused so long it seemed she'd lost her thoughts' thread . . . then said, "There may be harder work, for one growing so swiftly older. Perhaps rowing an oar in a Kingdom warship. Perhaps hacking fire-coal from the tribal hills of West Map-Virgina. —Perhaps those are harder work, but I doubt it. One week of Walking-in-air, unspools months of most Talents' lives." She smiled. "Though, when I was a girl, and very strong in that piece of brain, I disregarded the cost—as I disregarded everything that was not a wish of mine."

"Then rest on the ground, dear," Richard said. "Sylvia Wolf-General meant what she told you."

"I'm sure she did," Patience said, "and only hope she also still means harm to Boston. I sent a Mailman to her in Lord Winter's season—an expensive young Mailman sacrificed, 'lost to hawks,' since I killed it on its return, for secrecy. . . . Also, on the ice at

Salem, I spoke to her sister, a major, as well. There was—*is*—an agreement, if she hasn't decided for the Township after all."

"Sylvia's mother and an aunt both died in the Pens, birthing." Richard tried his ax's edges, then searched in his possibles for his whetstone. "—Supposed to have been a Sparrow shaman's daughters, captured by Fish-hawks in a raid. Then the Guard came to the coast, and took them. . . . I doubt the General has changed her mind."

"Still," Baj said, "she commands for Boston."

"And doing so," Richard stroked stone along a gleaming crescent, "—hones these companies to use against it."

Nancy sat up and stretched. "Do these near-Sunriser Persons mean to feed us?"

"Soon. Trumpet'll call Mess in about a glass-hour." Richard tested his edges with a thick brown thumb. ". . . It's always an ax-fighter's question, whether to sharpen both edges keen as can be—or leave one very slightly duller, so as not to turn on armor, but drive through it."

"One keen edge," Baj said, "with a spike opposite, is the battle-ax favored on the river."

"Ah . . ." Richard set his weapon down, "—but your spike may become stuck in whomever, have to be levered and wrenched free. And while a Person is busy with that, what's an enemy at liberty to do?"

"Mischief, I suppose." Baj noticed his breath smoking with the cold.

"Mischief absolutely, Baj. Though, with a light ax, and long-handled . . . less of a problem."

"We had a heroine who fought with one."

"I know that story," Nancy said. "Many women know the story of that brave girl and your old queen—a reminder that females are not baby-squirters only, but can fight." She slid a length of her scimitar's steel from the scabbard by emphasis, then slid it back. ". . . I wish," she said to Baj, "sweetheart, I wish we'd practiced more."

"I couldn't have survived more practice." He leaned to kiss her ear, lying so nicely tucked in her soft red mane. "You're too fierce for me."

"I'm not."

"You are." Another kiss.

Errol, curled on a blanket, opened his eyes and tongue-clicked at them.

"Quite right," Richard said, "—ridiculous."

. . . As they waited the mess-call, with Patience and Errol both sitting against a feed-shelter's canvas wall—each looking out over distance past distance, and seeming to dream awake—Nancy sat under a sheltering blanket, and watched while Baj, his fingers stiff with cold, played fast, no-pausing chess with Richard. Fast and losing chess. Soon, his king was desperate, hobbling back and forth from one square to the only possible other.

"Give up," Richard said.

"Never."

"You've lost. Give *up*."

"No. Anything might happen." At which, a saving trumpet soared out three long notes. "See?"

Richard heaved to his feet. "I've won."

"Have not. My king still stands."

"Nonsense."

"My Baj," Nancy set her blanket shelter aside, "—is true-human, and not to be trusted."

"No question." Richard held out a massive hand, helped Patience lightly to her feet. "Nancy, keep the boy close. —We go; we stand in line at the kettles. We get our rations; we leave and come back here. No conversation."

"All right." Patience smoothed tundra grass from her blue coat. A ragged strip of its hem was missing.

"—And if some moose-rider insults you, bear it."

"Any insult, Richard?" Baj moved his king the one square to safety, and stood.

"*Any* insult. If the cavalry foots us out of their Lines, we're in trouble for a peaceful place to sleep."

"Okay," Baj said (a perfect WT usage). "This doesn't seem a good place for argument. But we leave our packs here, our goods?"

"Leave them," Richard said. "No one steals in the General's camp." And he led off toward the trumpet's repeat, as troopers came strolling past.

. . . Having waited their turns in a long line (with no conversation)—then, at the stoves, having one looped red string snapped off their wrists—they each were passed a big tin bowl of stew, and a fat dark round of barley bread.

"Spoons," Richard said, his only conversation at mess, speaking for all of them.

A tall, shambling cook made an exasperated face, rooted in a wicker chest, and handed over spoons. "Issued *once*," he said to them.

. . . Then, with spoons and bowls and bread, they retreated past a number of uninterested or unfriendly glances to their patch of tundra over moose-lines. And sitting on wool pallets, wrapped in cloaks or blankets—except for warmth-talented Patience—they began eating the food before it chilled.

"Dear *Jesus.*" Baj hadn't intended to complain, was prepared for the expected military "chow." Or thought he was.

Nancy reached to pinch his cheek. "What's wrong, dear?— who was a prince, and pampered."

Richard smiled his toothy smile. "It's seal meat in the stew, Baj. Guards' main ration. People take them from the ocean ice . . . butcher out, and let the meat freeze for transporting."

"Better become used to it," Patience was dipping bread into her bowl, "—from here to the Wall, then up onto the ice, it will likely be frozen seal meat or herring."

"Unless an army moose dies," Richard said. "—or one of the Shrikes' caribou. . . . Errol likes it."

And so it seemed, since Errol was crouched with his face in his bowl, making feeding-dog noises.

Baj held his nose with the thumb and forefinger of his left hand, spooned with his right . . . and got some of the stew down. A rank and oily puddle, it lay in his belly restless. The bread, though, was quite decent . . . helped cleanse his palate. "And we have no mutton left at all?"

"No, we don't," Richard lifting a bit of stew meat on his knife. "You may find you grow quite fond of seal. Become a judge of its various qualities."

"I'm sure . . ."

"And my Baj is so *brave*," Nancy said, "holding his nose as he swallowed."

It hadn't occurred to Baj before to test whether a little fox blood made a girl more or less ticklish. And—after some spilled stew, wrestling, muffled shrieks, and attempts at biting—he had his answer.

The answer beyond that answer, of course, was soothing and stroking. Apology, and kisses.

"Prince," Patience said, "try for a little conduct."

And Baj did, straightened, and brushed grass and a spot of stew from his buckskin jerkin. "So, from here—sustained by seal meat—where?"

"To the Wall," Richard said, "if Sylvia Wolf-General keeps her promise."

"To the Wall," Patience said, "—then up onto the ice, and weeks of fast going with Shrikes, north and east to Boston town." She set her mess bowl aside, kept a piece of bread.

"And these companies of the Guard?"

"Will, I hope, follow."

"Too many and too heavy for the Shrike's fast sleighs," Richard said, and tucked his issue spoon down into his moccasin-boot. "The soldiers'll likely march forty miles up Apley Lead—it's called the Crease—then climb the ice from there to freighter-sleds. Shouldn't be more than five, six days behind us, coming to the Township."

"*Shouldn't* be," Nancy said.

"But if they are?" Baj said. "And come late?"

"Then, Baj," Richard sighed, "they will find us executed—and their loved ones still held alive and hostage."

"We need these people." Patience chewed some bread. ". . . First, and most important, we need their *threat*, to hold the Constables' attention to the south, while we go down North Gate and into the city. No units of the Guard have ever been allowed within Township limits, or even close. Senior Person officers, yes, for parades and honors. But their soldiers, their companies, never."

"All right." Baj's heart had certainly been listening. *Thump thump thump*. "First, you said, we need them for threat, and misdirection. And second . . .?"

"Second," Richard said, "we do need these companies for force. They'll have to at *least* skirmish, engage the Constables at South Gate, while we come in at the North. And an attack, an apparently determined attack, would be that much better."

"How many Constables?"

"More than three thousand, Baj." Patience buttoned her blue coat as the wind came stronger.

"More . . . than three thousand."

"Thirty-five hundred," Richard said, "more or less. All Sunrisers—but trained fighters. They wield pole-arms, halberds with heavy heads. Ax-edge, hook, and spear point."

"*Charming*. . . . And a thousand five-hundred more of them than we have here."

Richard nodded. "With the great advantage of standing on the defensive. Worth numbers in itself."

"And all Boston born, Baj," Patience said. "Officered by our best families. None Irish."

Baj took a deep breath. "So—we deal with those . . . then murder perhaps hundreds of women."

"We won't deal with them," Richard said. "We'll wait until their reserves march south to meet the Guard. Then, we go to the Pens—quickly, with the Shrikes."

"And to the Pens . . . how far?"

"Across part of the city, Baj." Patience reached to pat his knee. "Only two . . . three WT miles, but fast as we can. There won't be time for slow and secret going."

Silence . . . And useless to say an only-if, but Baj said it anyway. "If my Second-father, if the Achieving King were alive, the Rule's fleet might have come up the coast of Ocean Atlantic to strike with us."

"Yes . . . but even so, Baj," Richard leaned forward to draw a faint map through tundra lichen with a horny nail. "Even so, the sea is shrunk back from ancient WT Boston by a hard day's march at least. I'm no sea-fighter Marine—the Township has none—but even I can see what time it would take to get an army off the ships there, and organized to move inland over the ice. . . . With that delay, they would find the city's gates carved free of steps, steps they'd need on steep, polished ice—and no other way to enter Boston-town but try to hack out their own, with the Constables waiting."

Baj sighed. "I can't picture well what I haven't seen. But so few of us—Shrikes with us or not—it seems . . . desperate."

"And so it is." Patience smiled at him.

"But you are with us!" Nancy, lisping *us*, gripped his arm.

"Oh, yes, I'm with you, sweetheart. My dead brother, my dead friends would never forgive me, otherwise." He tried a smile of his own. "And, of course, I'd miss the adventure of the thing."

Nancy hit him on the shoulder. The girl had a rough way about her. Biting, elbowing, hitting . . .

* * *

In late after-noon, as if to balance the earlier fortunate interven-
tion by mess call, Baj was interrupted *winning*—with both
knights and a surviving bishop, having made hacked meat of
Richard's pieces, now pursuing his terrified queen—when a
Wolf-blood Person came trotting to order them to the General's
pavilion.

"No!"

"Yes," Richard said, smiling, "—and *I* have not lost."

"Leave the pieces; leave everything the way it is."

"Nooo . . ." Richard pulled the little pegged pieces free, dropped
them into the set's tiny drawer. "Someone—some passing sergeants or saddlers, might try to complete the game."

"Unfair," Baj said.

And Nancy said, "Unfair."

"An echo?" Richard tucked the chess set into his possibles-
sack. "Did I hear an echo on the tundra?"

"My coat's in rags," Patience said, as they went through camp, a bitter wind blowing as if to hurry them along. "Makes a poor impression."

"Nancy," Richard said, "—keep hold of that boy."

Errol was swinging this way and that in her grip on his hide-jacket's collar, tongue-clicking at soldiers as they passed.

Baj saw two or three Persons—Guards-soldiers sized and shaped by bear blood—stare unpleasantly as Richard went by.

Richard had noticed. "They don't care for an officer running—then returned and spared—when they'd be skinned alive and salted."

"To WT hell with them, then," Nancy said, turned and made the oldest gesture.

Baj turned her back. "No *trouble.*"

"*I'm* not starting trouble."

Errol whimpered, yanked to get away, and Nancy hauled him back, thumped him on the head. *"Behave."*

. . . A guard mount—eight of the near-human cavalry, their sabers drawn—were stationed at the Wolf-General's pavilion, posted in twos at each of the four cardinal directions. Their officer, his blade bared, came to meet Richard, looked him up and down, looked each of them up and down, then said, "Your weapons—and the fool boy—stay here."

"Good news, Lieutenant," Nancy said, and pushed Errol to him. "Better hold fast—oh, and beside the knives, he bites."

The officer said, "Wonderful," took hold of Errol by the back of his neck, and gestured one of his men to collect swords, daggers, and an ax. ". . . Now, you others go in to the General, and respectfully."

At the pavilion's entrance, a Person, blunt-muzzled, pelted black—the same wide banner-bearer who'd ridden with the

General to greet them—stood beside a grass-green standard.

He stared at Nancy as they went by, but said nothing.

As the entrance flap closed behind them, Baj saw four . . . five hulking wolf-bloods, their tufted fur gray as their armor, crowded at a long, folding camp table. Great sheets of southern paper lay spread across it.

"Make *room*." With that rip-saw voice—and after a brutal shove that clanked cuirass against cuirass—Sylvia Wolf-General came to stand central, smiling at them over the table. It seemed to Baj only perhaps a smile.

"I assume," she said, "that you are all familiar with our intentions, going north to the city."

"They know what we plan, Sylvia," Patience said. "I've told them."

"Very well, then—details, and review. In pursuit of this . . . correction . . . of Boston, of Cambridge Township, I intend to march north in the morning. You, and the Shrikes in camp, will march with us. *March*," she stared at Patience, slanted eyes blue as cornflowers, "—no sailing away in the air."

"I understand."

The others, her officers, relatives—her pack, Baj supposed—now stood a little back from the table on either side. The pavilion smelled of those Persons, as if their General's harsh voice had taken odor, and there were no pretty blue eyes among them. . . . One, older, fur whitening, and—by the rows of bronze breasts molded down her muscle-cuirass—a woman, had only a single eye, squinting, intelligent, and merciless. The General's aunt? . . . Certainly the General's aunt.

"So, we march to the Wall." The General's sharp black nails tapped maps and papers before her. "And you people up and over it—where, I'm informed, a small tribal levy will meet you. The Shrikes had, I believe, originally planned a greater number, something unpleasant for my companies." She smiled. "But now, all friends."

"*Friends*," the probable-aunt echoed. The voice wavered with age, the single eye did not.

"Yes, dear," the General said, "—and are to be treated as such for this campaign. With, of course, your company always kept in reserve, in case of . . . a misunderstanding."

Her aunt nodded.

"—So, to continue, you people will then sled with the Shrikes the considerable distance north and east to Boston and then the city's north gate, and should arrive, burrow, and hide there until *we*—having gone up a different way to preserve our mounts and supplies—reach South Gate." A fingernail tapped a map. "There, we'll begin assaults likely in the end to achieve nothing—considering the numbers, the reinforcements they can call on—nothing except to distract the Cambridge Constables, draw their regiments away from you and your sad duty." She smiled, showing fangs. "You *will* wait for us before attempting to enter the city. We'll arrive, though we move more slowly than tribesmen. Hurry is not the Guard's business."

"Inevitability," her aunt said, "—is our business."

"Yes." The Wolf-General nodded. "And for this campaign—for this task and this time only—I ally with a rebel Boston Talent, *and* allow a deserter to live, *and* permit a camp whore to serve as soldier . . . as well as a Sunriser supposedly once of importance elsewhere." She stared at them. "But not Lady Weather, not Lord Winter, not Frozen-Jesus will save you, if I am disappointed."

"I trust," Baj said, and was startled to hear what he was saying, "—I trust that we, in turn, will not be disappointed by your command."

He could not remember in his life before, such a silence as fell then. It was a quiet absolute, so even the camp noises seemed muffled around them, while they all stood in a lamp-lit and soundless well.

". . . Forgive him," Patience said. "He's young."

The Wolf-General turned to her. "When I require your

instruction, *Nearly*-Lodge," the rip-saw voice, "—I'll ask for it."

Silence again.

The Wolf-General stared at Baj, and licked her chops absently, apparently considering. Her eyes were remarkable, as if a tragic and beautiful woman looked out from that dreadful mask. "You," she said, "—have spoken up, I suppose, as your great fathers would have done. Meaning as well, fuck me if I didn't care for it." She smiled, or seemed to. ". . . We will see if you're wise enough never to do so again."

Baj bowed, and kept his mouth shut.

". . . We have fodder, food, and supplies," the General said, "—for eight WT weeks, and of course, will not be in the south to requisition additional. Still, sufficient for our purpose, for that . . . attack, that *distraction* that will cost so many of my soldiers' lives."

"Worth it," Patience said.

"Yes, to break Boston's grip at last." Sylvia Wolf-General lowered her fur-crested head. "Break it . . . then mourn the necessary deaths of the mothers."

"There is," a younger relative, apparently part-sired by a quite handsome wolf, "—there is some discontent in the ranks at that."

"I know." The General shoved her maps aside. ". . . Let three things be understood by the soldiers—the sergeants to see to it. First, we *all* bitterly regret this necessity, which will cost many of us those they love, and who gave them birth. Second, it is being done to save all future Persons' mothers—and tribesmens' daughters—the same suffering. And third, any grumbler continuing after today, will be tied to a mess table where camp-streets cross, and his liver taken."

"I'll see that word is heard." The handsome officer—fur tufts, fur-crest granite gray—bowed, and leaving the tent, said, "Nancy," and smiled at her as he went.

"The other companies," the Wolf-General said, "—are too few—and by now too far south and east to trouble us. The nearest force is under Philip-Robin, and would be no trouble in any case."

Her officers smiled.

"—What could Town Council have been thinking in that promotion?" She shook her head.

"Perhaps," her aunt said, and smiled, revealing yellowed fangs, the left broken at the tip, "—perhaps they consider one good general enough."

Sylvia laughed, a woman's laugh with no wolf in it. "*More* than enough." She studied Baj and the others. ". . . And when Persons and a Sunriser take responsibility for action in my presence, I consider that an oath of service. Do you understand?"

There was a small silence, and she picked up a slate, scribbled on it with her thumbnail, and handed it to an officer. "Louis, see this done. I want every mount sound, or slaughtered. If a moose founders going north, the colonel and his officers will carry that load—the trooper or supplies—on their backs."

"Ma'am." The officer left the pavilion.

The general looked across her table. "Well . . . ?"

"For this campaign," Richard said, "—yes, my contract oath."

"I also swear to it," Patience said.

"Yes." Nancy nodded. "I swear."

"And so for me," Baj said, ". . . if the General does the same."

Another run of woman's laughter, the dangerous head thrown back to reveal a sinewy throat, lightly furred in white. ". . . Perhaps you *are* your fathers' son. And certainly fortunate I'm in such a good mood. I think rebellion suits me."

"Suits you very well, Sylvia," her aunt said, "—and earned you many beatings at my hands."

"Don't remind me," the Wolf-General said. Then, to Baj and the others, "As you swore campaign-loyalty to me and my companies, so I swear mine and theirs to you. And will forsake you, in or after battle, living or dead—never. . . . Also, each of you is assigned a private soldier's credit against pay," she smiled, "—pay to be issued when, and if, the paymaster's wagon is encountered. . . . Now, get out."

". . . This is something," the Sentry-officer said, as they came from the pavilion, "—that needs its head taken off." He shook a bruised Errol severely to make his point. "He tried to draw a knife on my men."

"Well done," Nancy said, "—for nine soldiers to bully a brain-sick boy."

"Get the fuck off my post," the officer said, and shoved Errol into them.

"His knives," Nancy said.

"Henry," the officer said, "give these . . . people . . . their weapons. *And* the knives."

"The General," Patience said, as they walked down-camp to Cavalry Street, "—appears to fulfill her reputation."

"She is the best Boston has had commanding the Guard," Richard said, "—since Peter Fish-hawk. He conquered almost all the Coast of the Ocean Atlantic."

"More than a hundred years ago," Patience said. "And didn't he go mad?"

"He was mad to start with." Richard led to the right along Cavalry, toward the Lines. "Wolverine blood—even the usual eighth, and its tiny bits persuaded just so—is an uncertain portion to have."

"The standard-bearer," Baj said, "—the sergeant at the pavilion?"

". . . Badger."

They were passing a number of soldiers lounging at what seemed to Baj a sort of makeshift tavern—the usual leather lean-to, though larger than most, with a long counter of planks resting on six barley barrels. The Persons were drinking from leather jacks. Off-duty, none were armed or armored.

"Beer . . . ?" Baj said.

". . . Yes. The sutler's *is* a notion." Richard turned on his heel, started across the camp street.

"Absolutely not," Patience said. "*Richard . . .*"

"Don't go." Nancy tugged at Baj's sleeve, held Errol's hand with the other. "It will only cause trouble."

"If we're her sworn soldiers, sweetheart—at least for a time— then we'll take soldiers' pleasures, and cause no trouble doing it."

"Well," Patience said, "this is stupidity."

But the Person troopers, though they stared, shifted aside to give them room. And a certainly Sunriser-human—small, withered elderly, and bundled in stained sheepskin against the wind— hobble-stepped up behind the plank counter, apparently lame.

"And for a Boston lady," addressing Patience in a booze-worn voice, "—and memories of old times, I regret to have only barley beer and blueberry pie."

"Do I know you?"

"You knew me once. My colonel had me keep you back with the cooks when the Kipchaks came to Map-Arkansas."

"Nearest Jesus," Patience said. "You're Sergeant—"

"Givens, Lady. Jack Givens. An' General Butler's staff-officer said, 'Keep that little bitch away from the General.' Which I did try, but you'd fly away like a fuckin' bird, and what was I supposed to do, snow drifted up to our assholes?"

The guardsmen, down the plank at either side, were interested.

"It's a pleasure, Sergeant Givens," Patience reached over the plank counter to shake the old man's hand, "—to meet you again. Though I'm surprised you knew me after so many years."

"I'd know them black eyes anywhere," the Sergeant said. "Thought at first you were that girl's mother—then said to myself, 'Don't be an ass, Jack; it's Patience Nearly-Lodge, the creature herself!'"

"And so I am," Patience laughed, "—the creature herself."

"Those were days . . ." The old man stepped to dipper into a barrel—staggered a little, so Baj saw he'd already been drinking beer or better—filled a jack, and passed it over the planking. "Beer for you, darlin'—an' I brew it, an' it's good! Bake the fuckin' pies, too. Here," he filled and handed jacks over to Richard, Baj, and Nancy. "—The kid?"

It was the first time Baj had ever heard that so-common copybook word spoken, and not for a baby goat. *Kid*. Ancient slang for a child.

"Better not," Nancy said, and took a swallow of hers. ". . . Excellent."

"Always," the old man said. "Try pie. Friends of the Nearly-Lodge eat for almost free."

"Good pies," a cavalryman said, looking human except for his ears.

"This beer," Patience smacked her lips, "—is wonderful, Jack."

Richard and Baj hummed agreement.

"My problem," the old man said, "—is fuckin' freezin', so I got to beg a certain Person to be reasonable an' let me keep my beer kegs with the mooses, keep 'em just warm enough. —You know somethin' about pie? Pie can freeze. Don't hurt it. Give me a little fire to thaw 'em, an' I can serve pie the whole Lord Winter's season."

"Is that so?" Patience said.

"It is absolutely so," the old man said, and soldiers up and down the planks agreed.

"An' I got dried apple from down south, an' apple butter, an' vinegar jerk-meat—well, sometimes. That's a short-summer thing, mainly."

"Vodka?" Baj said.

"One cup," a soldier said.

"What he means," the old man made a face, "—is I can sell just one cup to each guardsman. One cup a day. More than that, Sylvia will cut my nuts off . . . not that I'd notice now."

Amusement along the plank.

"An' of course, no such rule for me. I drink what I fuckin' please."

"You were in the Army," Baj said, "—in the Arkansas fighting."

"Yes I was, young man. Army of North Map-Mexico, servin' under Sam Monroe an' Fightin' Phil Butler—while the General lived—until there was a disagreement over a local young lady, that turned to a killin'. Not my fault at all, though I was chased up the river by cruel Provost-men like it *was* my fault . . . an' here I am after how many years wanderin', endin' among *this* bunch."

". . . You saw the Kipchak *tumans?*"

"In that fight—yes indeed I did, came up the hill at 'em with poor fuckin' Oswald-cook an' his messmen, an' me pissin' my pants, you may be sure."

"You saw the *Khan?*"

"No, I did not, thank Jesus-in-the-Wall. An' that was battle enough for me. A fight's one thing, a battle's another—an' a sensible man knows the difference." He took a sip from his cup. ". . . An' speakin' of sensible, I see you're a proper Sunriser, young man, 'stead of havin' beastly portions beyond the traditional."

Good-natured fists drummed along the plank. "Listen to 'em—an' take a look at this." The old man stooped to a shelf and brought up a large pie, its scalloped crust singed along the edge. "Costs me a fortune of money—tradin' up true rendered pig-fat an' wheat flour an' beet sugar from so fuckin' far south, then payin' camp whores to pick them dwarf berries, *then* bribin' the mess-oven cook—so I charge accordin'."

"And that is?"

"One slice—one day's pay. Credit's good."

"Thief!" a Wolf-blood soldier said, and was agreed with down the planks.

"So? —Then fuckin' pick an' bake your own, Larry!" The old

man set the pie down and leaned over his counter. "You an' me, young man—what *is* your slant-eye portion?"

"Kipchak," Baj said.

"Well . . . well, that's true-human, anyway."

Groans down the plank, but pleasant enough. The old man was liked.

"For you an' Lady Nearly-Lodge—an' your friends—a wedge-slice out of this particular pie for one half-day's pay each, collected at the count-out table on count-out day. . . . But not the dummy."

"The boy, too," Baj said, Errol huddling close.

"No."

"All or none."

"Absolutely no."

"Then, none."

The old man smiled; three upper teeth were missing. "Loyalty? Kin'ness? Willin'ness to share? —How old are you?"

"Twenty."

Satirical hums along the planks.

The old man addressed his customers. "A fuckin' baby! . . . Listen, Twenty, you want this pretty girl here to think you're a clutcher what can't part with pay?"

"All of us," Baj said, "—or none." And was encouraged by a chorus along the planks, more thumping of odd fists.

"You're embarrassin' me here, Sunriser, among all these hairy Persons—"

More noise under the lean-to.

". . . All right. All *right*! But jus' this one time, an' out of a generous heart."

Several cheers along the plank, and the pie was cut, the first big slice passed over to Baj to be hand-held, running blue juices.

Then, silence at his first bite through rich crust into sugared sweetness, crowded tart little blueberries crushing to syrup.

Baj swallowed . . . and said, "Wonderful."

Cheers again from the soldiers, pleased at his pleasure—and Sergeant Givens passed four more pieces of pie, then drew more beer.

". . . That could have gone worse," Richard said—as, hands stained blue (and their mouths, even after second jacks drunk)—they walked down Cavalry Street to the Lines. "Could have gone worse, and might have gone worse if some hadn't already heard that Sylvia'd seen us . . . and sworn us. Camp news is faster than falcons."

"That old man," Patience said. "Sergeant Givens . . . As I recall, always busy with some scheme involving Supply. And usually mildly drunk."

"But delicious pie," Baj said. "Unless, after so long, any pie would be delicious."

"No. It was very good." Nancy licked her fingers. "Wasn't that good, Errol?"

A tongue-click and rare smile.

. . . The supply-sergeant's unpleasant corporal was waiting at their place past the Line, standing beside a bulky stack of blankets, woven cloth, hides, furs, muk-boots, mittens, and fur cloaks. "Listen up . . . While you people and so-forth were seen drinkin' beer—nothin' better to do—all this was finished-up an' delivered. Issue ordered for you by the Ma'am this mornin'—*Guards* goods, and you're responsible; they're slated out to you. Lose somethin', *I'm* not fuckin' payin' for it." And he walked away.

Nancy and Patience knelt to go through the clothing, though Patience said, "I won't need any of this."

"This is a good issue." Nancy held up immense caribou trousers, huge muk-overboots—their fur-side in—and a wolf-fur parky and mittens to match.

"Richard . . ." She handed them over.

"If anything fits," Richard said, "—it will be a first for the Guards."

. . . But everything did fit.

"The General's command is why," Richard said, posing even larger in furs. "And ordered this morning, just after she rode back to camp."

"So never a question," Baj said, too warm in a fisher-lined caribou parky, "—that what had been planned would be done, and that we were going with them. A settled thing, apparently."

"Generals," Patience said, "being chosen after all, for decision."

Dressed, they were all richly bundled, except for Patience. For her, after distribution to the rest of them—Errol's issue, cut roughly down for him, as complete as the others'—there was left only a pair of fine woolen mittens, a pair of small, furred muk-boots, and a long, hooded coat, thick-wooled and generous enough to wrap Patience double-breasted, before fastening with fat round horn buttons (apparently moved and reattached), and colored as the Wolf-blood soldiers' cloaks were colored, in pretty bands dyed red and black and yellow.

"That's an Infantry Colonel's change-of-season coat," Richard said, "—but cut shorter for you. Sylvia must have ordered it particularly."

"Took pity on my blue tatters, I suppose."

"No," Nancy said, "—she has no pity. Likely, she thought you weren't able to warm yourself as well as once you could. Wanted to be sure you'd be useful on the ice."

"Then," Patience said, "—the bitch can kiss my ass for being right. I'm *not* quite as capable as I was." She folded her ragged blue coat, stroked the stained cloth. "The best made by Boston. . . ."

"No, dear." Richard touched her shoulder. "You are the best made by Boston."

* * *

That day, and the hard-traveling days that followed—marching farther east to pass miles of bog, then turning north to the

Wall—Baj first tasted the military life, tedious, routined, strenuous and oddly comforting.

Though these soldiers and their officers were all Persons, often odd, many furred and fanged to at least some extent by tiny bits twisted from animal co-sires, and planted in their mothers—still, they were soldiers, veterans of the trade, and allowed Baj to understand both his fathers better.

Kipchaks, North Mexicans, or Middle Kingdom's armored infantry—they still were brothers in arms to these Moonriser guardsmen, and Baj could feel something of what Toghrul Khan, of what Sam Monroe had felt in command of such forces. Forces formidable . . . and oddly innocent. Regiments of dangerous children.

There was a comfort in the surrounding armed and armored troops—though all were Persons, many of whom spoke only poor book-English . . . while some, perhaps incapable, did not speak at all. Still there was a comfort, a fellow feeling, as if all made a greater One. And the notion came—though of course illogical—that these formations were a family indestructable by any enemy.

Pedro Darry, in a rare serious moment, had once mentioned to Baj and Newton that men and women had a natural tendency—natural as short-summer flowers bending toward the sun—to bend, themselves, toward the nearest strength of arms, wealth, or wits. . . . Traveling with the Guard, Baj found that was so, and took some care to maintain a certain easy distance from the pleasures of lean-to fellow feeling, barley beer and pie. Took care to remember that he, Nancy, and his friends, only lived and breathed because a general found them more useful than not.

The companies, still skirting huge stretches of bog, moved as Richard had moved north through the mountains, at a steady pace—never hurrying, never dawdling (wonderful old copybook word)—the infantry just keeping up with the cavalry mounts' ground-eating amble. . . . Except for the wheedling pipes of march, everything, from "Out an' Up" to "Down an' Shut It," was ordered through the day on infantry bugle and cavalry trumpet sounding together, then thumped at the finish with a drum. In a service always professionally tense for assault, these rhythms of habit seemed to Baj a soothing medicine—as if guaranteeing a tomorrow the same as today.

He felt, sometimes—at leisure, usually—when there was a chess game to lose, when he and Nancy . . . murmuring, murmuring in blankets, rested in each other's arms after making love behind stinking bales, Baj felt at those times as if his fathers stood together, watching, exchanging between them an amused glance of hard-won experience observing . . . *in*experience. At those times, so fleeting, it seemed to him their ghosts were at ease, at home with soldiers (of whatever kind) marching toward battle.

And with battle in mind, Baj resumed Nancy's lessons—and took lessons from Patience, whose left arm and shoulder grew swiftly stronger. Lessons in bitter winds—first with lean-to bracing-sticks for swords (costing many bruises), and then with their blades (costing minor cuts, and blood), being cautious to parry with the flat, to save their fine edges.

These bouts—at dawn or sunset, the light always chancy—drew soldiers as summer blossoms drew summer bummer-bees, and Baj grew used to rude comments as they fought Over-the-ditch, since any weapons brandishing—even for training—was forbidden in the camp.

Baj, Nancy, and Patience fought to blood and bruising until their swords seemed to leap out of the scabbards at any place of practice, the blades themselves appearing to become more wicked, as if they learned as their owners did. . . . In those bouts, Patience's skill became more and more evident, despite her white hair—as behind those black eyes, there seemed a second Patience come to fence, young, swift, and merciless.

Baj often thought of poetry as they marched east, then north to pipes and drums, Tail-end Charlies to a strolling squadron of farting moose, but he wrote none—the days of poetry seemed past—except for a lyric shaped for Nancy, and scribbled on brown regimental roll-paper with a lead-point pencil.

> *I've been bitten to madness by a pretty fox,*
> *A vixen in silver light, but a girl in gold.*
> *Now this fortunate fool finds no fear stands*
> *Nor any trouble; they, as if by summer winds*
> *Are blown away through beauty's gentle magic.*
> *A madman's luck—with yet a richer measure:*
> *Her auric eyes to mirror our love's pleasure.*

She'd read it, mouthing the words to herself—something he'd noticed she always did, as if reading needed reminding as it went along. Read it, then raised her elegant head, and looked at him. "I love you, Baj," she'd said, "—but love the man who wrote this, more."

They had became so close there were no longer quite two of them, and Baj thought not of the rest of his life, but resting his life with hers. And was afraid for her.

"I want Nancy out of this."

Patience, sitting cross-legged in her warm new coat of colors— it draped almost ankle-length on her—was finishing a bite of seal-meat jerky with effortful chewing. "Of course you do— even more than *I* want Nancy, and Richard, and you out of this. Weasel-boy as well."

"I mean it."

"So do I," Patience said, and took another bite. When she'd chewed and swallowed, she said, "Do you imagine, Baj, that you're the first to come to me with this?"

"I thought so."

"Nancy, already denied by Richard, came to me the night of our first day with these guardsmen. She wanted you safe and away. . . . I told her what I'll tell you. I've come to care for you all—Errol excepted, and even there, some affection—and, since I've become older and foolish, might even die to save any one of you." She sniffed at the jerky. "Seal meat, even dried, doesn't have to be this bad. . . . Yes, might even die to save you, so silly I've become. But I will never let you go." Her black eyes seemed darker than black.

"—And will certainly do my best to kill you both, if you run. Your life—our lives—balance very poorly against what Boston has done in its hostage taking—crimes I admit perfectly comfortable for me, until they took my son. . . . They fear my darling so, fear the past truths he dreams—fear even more what futures he may find, traveling blood's probable highways. Find, or perhaps someday make come to pass."

She took another bite of jerky, spoke while chewing. "I've seen that for Sunrisers or Moonrisers, love is always lost sooner or later, as the man or woman is always lost, to death if nothing else. . . . Learn to live with loss to come, Baj; prepare to fight as your fathers fought—and never come begging to me again."

21

Relieved of hope, Baj felt oddly content, and as march followed march, now to the north—and the Wall grew from a white ribbon . . . to taller, and taller . . . until it *was* a wall, stretched across the northern horizon—he kept Nancy close for the pleasure of her closeness, so they walked through the camps' habitual temporary streets a couple, with Errol—wandering, circling, having to be called or hauled back—acting their restless child.

The wind, some days, became bitter with deeper cold, notice sent down from the glacier as if a great messenger-pigeon of crystal ice were bringing word of Lord Winter's awakening. Unless in fur mittens, with parky hood up, Baj's hands and face were numbed by these breezes. . . . In their weeks since Battle-valley, he and the others had traveled the summer away.

After chow, the evening of their sixth day marching, Richard—who had a fine gift for it—settled on a blanket by their small dry-dung fire, with his ax and their knives and swords lying beside him to sharpen. He always began with a coarse small stone from Map-Missouri . . . then, after the most delicate strokes—his huge hand light, light along the steel—he went to soft Map-Arkansas, both very expensive stones imported through three tribes, Owls to Blue-birds, then across the river to the Thrushes. Last—Richard's secret—he used palm-sized chunks dug out of permafrost, the ice finely powdered with the ground granite of glaciers advancing and retreating centuries ago, to stroke along edges already shaving sharp.

Finished by stropping on moose-hide leathers, then touched with tallow against the damp, Richard's worked edges were keen past testing. Touched even lightly, they cut.

"And still," he would say, handing over this or that murderous instrument, "—still sharpened at a sensible angle, so no wire-edge, no becoming delicate on armor."

Richard was bent to this chore—Baj and Patience playing pick-up sticks by firelight—when there was the faintest cry out of fallen darkness, from john trench.

It was barely a sound . . . only the trace of one—but Richard was up with his ax in his hands. Other soldiers near the Lines were standing listening—some sergeant already shouting an order—when Baj said, "Nancy," picked his sheathed rapier up from Richard's blanket, and went running.

He jumped fire-shadowed shelter tie-downs as he went out from camp row toward john trench, and heard soldiers coming behind him. The Wall—immense, though still many miles away—gleamed before him under a rising moon.

. . . The cry again—with strangled fury in it.

Running hard—feeling oddly light, as if he could float along—Baj reached the latrine trench, turned down along it, and saw a Person bent and struggling, his broad back touched by moon-light.

Nancy yelled again.

Baj saw her held beneath, kicking, biting. The Person on her turned a broad head, a blunt-muzzled face to Baj as he came. Nancy's shirt was torn away, her small breasts showing.

Baj gripped his rapier's hilt to draw as the soldier stood with a quick hunch and heave to face him—when a breeze and flutter swept above. "*Baj, don't draw!*"Patience swung down through the air beside them. "*Death, to draw steel in camp!*"

The Guardsman smiled, teeth glinting in moonlight, huge hands held up and empty. There was blood on the side of his furred face, where he'd been bitten.

The Master's voice sounded in Baj's ear, clear as if reality. "Never. *Never* lose your temper in a fight."

Baj swung the sheathed rapier back—and whipped its limber length whistling across the soldier's face. It struck with a stock-lash's heavy *crack*, and wiped the smile away.

Baj spun in reverse, brought the blade around, and caught the soldier not quite guarded on that side, so the scabbarded steel struck him across the side of the head, across a small fur-tipped ear.

Either blow would have sent even the strongest human staggering, would have knocked a weaker man down, but the Guardsman still stood, his face now a fanged mask of rage. He came with one swift heavy step—and a Wolf-soldier in half-armor, brass Provost-chain gleaming across the steel breast, stood between them.

"Continue," the officer said, his grating voice harsh as his general's, "—and die."

*　*　*

"I went to piss," Nancy, bruised, spitting like an angry grain-store cat before their fire, "—and he came and took hold of me. He saw I didn't have my sword!"

"Who is that thing?" Baj said, sitting with his arm around her.

Richard sighed. "That 'thing' is a sergeant. The general's banner-bearer."

"*Yes*," Baj said, "it was that one. The Badger-blood. Always staring at her. . . ."

"If you'd drawn on him, Baj," Patience shook her head, "they would have executed you."

"And for attempting a rape?" Baj started to stand, but Nancy tugged him back beside her. "What does the Guard do for that?"

"For a rape—out of camp and after fighting—no penalty," Richard said. "Otherwise, a beating with harness leathers, fifty strokes. Sylvia decides if with the metal buckles, or without."

"They will not beat George Brock-Robin," Nancy struck the turf with a small fist. "That fucked-his-mother will say I was a camp whore and *am* a camp whore, and felt and tempted him—then changed my price unfairly."

"And they will let that go . . .?"

"His word against hers, Baj." Richard shook his head. "He's a shit—but a good soldier, fighting."

"Sad, then, that he'll be missed," Baj said. "Now, tell me how I can bring him to my blade."

"You can't."

"And you shouldn't," Patience, sitting cross-legged by the fire, shook her head. "Nancy was frightened—"

"I was not."

"—but not hurt. And we are with these companies on a razor's edge."

"All the more reason," Baj said, "to see they respect us."

"And your fathers," Patience said, "would have agreed. But they had armies at their back."

"And therefore—since we do not have *tumans*, do not have regiments of the Army-United behind us, the more reason to earn their respect."

"Baj . . . Baj." Patience shook her head. "Whether true or false, that is not the deeper truth of the matter, is it?"

"It is a truth," Baj said, "—but the truth you look for is that I will not have Nancy abused. I'll kill whoever does it."

"Baj . . . don't."

"Sweetheart, this is already decided."

"It is *not*."

Errol, observing upset, began tongue-clicking.

"Baj," Richard said, "it's easy to talk of killing, and honor to you to intend it. But the doing would be . . . difficult. George-Brock is a serious soldier, or he would not be bearing the Wolf-General's banner."

"Bigger than you, Baj," Patience said, "stronger, and swift . . . and has killed, no doubt, many *many* times."

"I said he'd be missed. Unfortunately, he didn't keep his paws to himself."

"He won't fight you," Richard said. "It would have to be a decided duel—and over-the-ditch from camp. He won't fight you; he'll laugh."

"Will he laugh if I call him a liar?"

"Yes, he will. Everyone *knows* he's a liar."

"A coward?"

"Baj—everyone knows he's not a coward."

"Then I'll have to think of something that *won't* make him laugh."

"Oh, this is just so unwise." Patience leaned to touch his cheek. "Baj . . . Prince . . . please let this go. Will you allow your pride to damage us all—damage the cause and reason we came here?"

"I think I've learned something of soldiers, now," Baj said, "though I've never been one. I'll let this pass, if Richard can say to me that two things are *not* so. —First, that justice requires the Banner-bearer to answer to Nancy, and to me. Second, that this camp—including the General and her officers—is waiting, curious to see what we do in answer. And in waiting, are judging whether we are serious in *all* our intentions."

"Richard," Nancy said, "tell him *no*."

". . . I can't," Richard said.

Patience stood, angry. "So unwise!"

"Unwise, perhaps," Baj said, "as any sensible woman would likely say. But necessary, as any man would feel in his bones."

"Listen, foolish . . . foolish boy," Patience tapped her scimitar's hilt. "I can fight two-handed, now, and could cut you crippled, prevent your stupid fight. Better you're crippled than dead."

"Listen to her!"

"Nancy, I would fight you *all* to be free to deal with George Brock-Robin." He smiled. "Though I'd undoubtedly be somewhat whittled, come time to duel him."

"He'll likely kill you," Richard said. "You know that?"

"He'll have an excellent chance, no question. Certainly frightens me."

"He'll kill you," Nancy said. "Please please *please* . . ."

"No, sweetheart . . ." Baj tried to kiss her and was pushed away.

"Listen to her," Patience said. "You think she'll respect the memory of a fool?"

"No," Baj said, "listen to *me*. I'm not a fool, and while I've had no soldier's experience of battle as that Person has, I have considerable experience of duels. . . . And I doubt if he's used to that lonely fighting, with no comrades by him, right and left."

"Bigger," Richard said. "Stronger, and fast."

"Well," Baj smiled, "of course, luck will have to come into it." He got up, walked away into the camp, and didn't turn when they called to him.

. . . There was time enough, searching through the Infantry rows, stopping at camp-fires to curious glances—glances from eyes often reflecting silver circles by firelight—there was more than time enough to consider and reconsider. To say to himself, "*My God*," that ancient and most basic of Warm-time's copybook pleas for attention, salvation. "*My God . . .*" What had seemed both clear and clearly necessary only a while before, now seemed dubious, badly mistaken.

Nancy—how would she do if he were killed? What slashing blow in a storm of fighting would catch her unaware, with him not there to parry it? What injury, even accidental, on the ice and surrounded by Shrike savages? . . . And he lying dead here in permafrost, broken by a brute, and left behind forever.

Certainly, it seemed to Baj—walking through freezing night past fires' warm shadows—certainly the woman in Nancy would forgive him if he decided on caution after all—and after all his speech-making. The woman in Nancy would be relieved, understand, and forgive what there might be to forgive.

But the fox in her—even the small portion contributed—would not. The vixen swimming through Nancy's veins, crested with russet fur, golden eyes slit-pupiled, would never quite trust herself to him again . . . nor wish Baj to sire her kits, who must be brave.

So, foolishness perhaps, and perhaps not—but he was surely, in the copybook phrase, "stuck with it."

At the eleventh fire, he found George Brock-Robin—recognized him by the broad, furred back, the wide flat skull and small, rounded ears. Very little Sunriser-human to be seen—at least from behind.

Brock-Robin was with other Moonrisers—four bear-bloods— so he sat the smallest at the fire.

Baj took a breath, and stepped beside him—watched though the smoke by brown eyes under great shelves of brow.

"You," Baj said, "need a lesson in keeping your hands to yourself."

The badger-blood looked up, his thick neck requiring some shoulder-turn to do it. Brock-Robin's eyes were gray, their pupils very small. "You're not the first to say so," he said, the words sizzling a little liquidly, from the muzzle conformation of his mouth.

"The last, though," Baj said, "that you'll be hearing."

One of the others chuckled.

"Sounds dire," Brock-Robin said, "—but the girl's a whore, and our quarrel about money." He turned back to the fire.

"I've been told it's no use to call you a liar—"

"Been told true, boy." One of the others, his voice as deep and fine as Richard's. "That's only description, not insult."

Chuckles around the fire. They seemed jolly soldiers.

"And to call you coward—I was told everyone knew otherwise."

"True." Brock-Robin turned to look up at Baj again, and seemed to be smiling.

"Then, the rest of what you are must be due to your mother. In Boston's pens, instead of the Talents' tinkering, she must have preferred to go to all fours to be fucked in the ass by the boar-badger itself . . . to produce the shit you are."

Then, no chuckles. The camp-fire's flames seemed to fall and flicker to the beat of Baj's heart.

Brock-Robin slowly stood, close enough so Baj could smell his harsh odor amid the dung-fire's stinging smoke.

"Say that what you just said, Sunriser-boy, is not so."

"I will—after you come to Nancy-Thrush, kneel down before her, and beg her pardon."

Standing, the Person was a little shorter than Baj—and easily twice as wide. In only hide trousers, hide jerkin, and boots—unarmed, unarmored—he still looked able to grip and break Baj's arms at the shoulder-joints, to kick and stave in his ribs . . . and considering fangs, tear out his throat.

"Not in camp!" One of the soldiers at the fire.

"No," Brock-Robin said, "not in camp. Will you fight a decided-duel, boy? Come over the ditch with me?"

"Now and by moonlight, if you like."

"Dawnlight will do." Brock-Robin nodded pleasantly, and gestured to their fire. "Join us? We're discussing this interesting expedition north."

"Thank you, no," Baj said, and bowed to the others. "—I'll need a good night's sleep to kill you clean." And walked away from more fireside chuckles. . . . Jolly soldiers.

* * *

"You are a fool a fool a *fool!*"

"More than possibly, sweetheart. But I offered him a chance to come and apologize."

The four of them—including Errol, who seemed troubled as if he understood—sat staring at him. Then Richard sighed. "Baj . . . " pronouncing the name as if in mourning. "Baj, in a decided-duel—and the Wolf-General may not allow it, would *not* allow it if you were in the Guard, and a higher or lower rank—in a decided-duel, you meet over the camp ditch, with officers presiding. You fight with personal weapons only, and wear no helmet, no armor."

"Fair enough." It was beginning to seem more a dream than not, with a dream's floating, almost sensible conversation.

"We can go," Nancy said. "We can *go!*"

"No," Patience said. "We can't—and wouldn't be allowed to, unless Sylvia permitted."

"I don't mind!" Nancy tugged on Baj's arm. "I don't mind. I forgive him—he was drunk."

"But I *don't* forgive him, sweetheart."

"You'll have your sword and dagger, Baj," Richard said, "there'd be no objection to them. He'll carry short-sword and shield."

"Shield . . ."

"That's what he fights with, Baj. What all Light Infantry fights with."

"But he rides."

"Rides, yes—to carry the standard. But he's still Light Infantry."

"The shield," Patience said, "will make a difficulty."

"Then I'll have to make it *his* difficulty."

Another silence, and staring, as if he'd changed to a great mushroom.

Richard cleared his throat. "Tomorrow? No delay?"

"Tomorrow, as I understand."

"Too bad. Too bad . . . We could have practiced you a little against sword-and-shield. Many, many tricks to that."

"I have practiced that sort of fighting, Richard—though not often. I won't really know his way, and he won't know mine."

"Yes . . . Remember this, Baj: a shield is also a weapon. I've known fierce fighters killed by the edge of a shield, with no blood on a sword at all."

"I will keep that in mind."

"You *have* no mind," Nancy said. "You're a boy and a fool. I should have let him fuck me, and been quiet—and you would have known nothing!"

"I would have known . . . everything," Baj said, and when she began to weep, caught her in his arms.

* * *

Fearful when he lay down with Nancy curled tight against him under their blankets, Baj sank to sleep surprisingly swiftly . . . and was surprised again on waking (after no dreaming at all) to stretch luxuriously under warm wool, against a warm girl, and feel very well in gray end-of-night, with a light snowfall drifting.

Lord Winter had stepped down from the Wall.

He was up, and the others were up—even ignorant Errol—looking worried, weary in the weather.

"The cold will slow you, Baj—and snow on the tundra makes it slippery. . . ."

"Richard, I'll step light and wear no parky; the exercise will warm me."

Nancy, crouched striking sparks into grass starters for their fire, mouthed the word *exercise*, but didn't say it.

As the little dung-heap lit, smoking nastily, its chunks rimmed red, Baj—feeling perfectly calm, really very well—noticed with surprise that his hands were shaking. A fine tremor that seemed to vibrate up his arms. So, if he wasn't frightened, his body seemed to be.

If the others noticed—and they must have noticed—they said nothing.

Patience, wrapped in her new greatcoat of colors, walked away to the mess-tent with their tin bowls.

"A light breakfast, Baj."

"Richard, I *know* a light breakfast."

"And only boiled hot water, no morning beer."

"I know, Richard. Only water . . ." Baj began the stretches and postures he'd been taught as preparation for great effort, for fighting. There hadn't seemed time for those formal attitudes—not through all the weeks of flight and mountain traveling. Now, he wished he'd taught them to Nancy. . . .

Errol seemed intrigued, the poses striking him as dance, perhaps, so he stood and joined in excellent imitation . . . bending, stooping, slowly squatting to leap upright, twisting first one way, then the other . . . all to easy heartbeat rhythm. One deep breath to every six beats. Step, step, and cross-step to the right. Step, step, cross-step to the left. Slide-step forward . . . slide-steps back. Arms slowly swinging up and around . . . down and back around. Wrists flexed, fingers flexed and clenched. Flexed . . . and clenched.

Stepping lightly, and a little higher for the uneven ground—ground already powdered with snow.

A group of troopers paused as they came by from mess, to watch him finish his exercise—Errol mirroring precisely the same easy come-to-rest at finish. By then, Baj's hands were still as stone.

Richard, shaking his head, muttering in some argument with himself, sat by the fire bent over Baj's rapier with a piece of granite-powdered ice, persuading its keenest edge.

. . . After a rye-porridge breakfast almost uneaten except by Errol, who had eaten what he could of everyone's, they walked out of camp into clearing air . . . and the glow of sunrise to the east. The cold was of that variety that Kingdom-River people called "Hello," meaning just sharp enough to alert a person, put them on notice of grimmer freezes to come. It was also called "First breath," meaning Lord Winter's first breath, come down from the ice.

It would be no trouble, fighting.

"Not too cold after all," Richard said. None had worn their furs. "But watch the snow on this sedge grass."

Nancy said nothing, towed Errol along by her accustomed grip on his jerkin.

"Baj," Patience touched him on the shoulder. "If there is a choice to kill or cripple him—kill. Crippling will make enemies that killing won't."

Baj nodded as they walked along, but said nothing. His world was no longer quite their world, as if a sheet of the Wall's ice had slid between them. What was said to him now, seemed sent as if by pigeon, or one of Boston's little Mailmen.

. . . They were walking to a crowd of hundreds of soldiers— all, off-duty, standing silent as ghosts of some ancient tundra battle, and all unarmed, unarmored, except for Provost officers, brass chains glinting on steel breastplates.

George Brock-Robin stood aside and alone in boots and leathers, a round hide shield leaning against his knee. He was swinging a double-edged short-sword in his right hand. . . . Baj was pleased. *Right hand—better than confusing left, with its reverses.*

Brock-Robin waved a greeting as Baj came up, and called, "Good morning," his breath smoking a little in the chilly air. He seemed in good humor.

Baj said, "Good morning."

"I'm going back," Nancy said. "I'm going *back*." And she turned away to the camp, dragging Errol with her.

Brock-Robin watched her go, and glanced at Baj—a look between men, satirical."Women," the look said.

A Wolf-blood officer, the handsome one Baj recalled from the General's pavilion, came between them. "We are not wasting time with this. Get it done—to the death or not—but get it done."

George Brock-Robin nodded, and Baj said, "Yes," unbuckled his sword-belt, drew rapier and left-hand dagger from it, and tossed the belt behind him.

The crowd of soldiers, silent, circled and shifted until they'd made what they must have made many times before—a fighting space generous enough, of tundra carpeted with lichen and snow-streaked sedge.

A few gray thrushes flew past them, as if on more important business. . . . To the north, the Wall loomed two miles high.

The handsome officer drew a cavalry saber, flourished it, then struck it across his cuirass, so steel rang on steel.

George Brock-Robin, shield up, came trotting.

Baj circled away to his right, keeping to the Person's left—his shield side. Brock cut that angle in a bounding rush, caught Baj as he backed away, and as their swords clashed on guard, points aside, hit him a smashing blow with the shield.

Baj thought he felt his right cheekbone crack, a little snap as his head went back. He spun full around to his right again to stay on Brock's shield side, avoid the short-sword. Blood was coming down his face; he could feel it. *Should have guarded left-hand, with the dagger.*

No sound from the watching soldiers.

Made more cautious—not by the injury, which hardly seemed to hurt at all, was only a numbness—but by Brock's moving so fast, striking so surely, Baj, smelling crushed grass in cold air, feinted changing his circling from right to left, and saw Brock's boots shift beneath the round shield to stay with him.

The Person stepped in and struck with his short-sword, thrusting low inside—a to-be-parried blow, it seemed to Baj, so Brock could judge his ward. Baj took the thrust in *quinte* on the left-hand dagger's long blade, gave with the blow's slashing power so it slid whining off his steel . . . then moved to his right again, cautious of the shield as Brock shifted—lightly, swiftly—to follow him.

Shield blow and sword thrust had proved the Person twice, perhaps three times stronger. There'd be no meeting him force to force, but only by indirection. . . . As he circled to his right—careful, careful not to stumble—keeping away, keeping Brock's shield *his* shield as well, Baj saw the soldier had been trained to never leave his sword arm exposed, never be caught wrong footed, with his shield out of line. It was a fine way to fight in ranks—even open ranks.

For that sort of battle fighting, it was perfect—and Brock, immensely strong and very quick, appeared to use that strength with disciplined restraint.

But it seemed to Baj that the soldier's veteran practice might be used against him. . . . And as they circled—he already feeling weary while Brock moved so smoothly, so fast, in a sort of close constant dancing—Baj suddenly stopped and stepped to the left. And as he saw, beneath the shield's rim, Brock's boots shift neatly to follow, he lunged full-length—knee almost to the grass—thrust down into the soldier's right boot, felt the blade-tip slide through leather to the splitting resistance of little bones—then recovered and was again circling to the right as Brock grunted and came after him . . . not limping.

Determined *not* to limp, apparently, Brock stepped out perhaps even more firmly—and Baj, just as he had the moment before, suddenly halted, feinted to the left, lunged and thrust into that booted foot again.

"Nasty," the Master would have said. "Unfair—and the perfect thing to do."

His face no longer numb but in increasing pain where the shield had struck him, Baj circled again to the right, to Brock's shield side—swift blind sideways steps over uneven turf, invitations to trip and be killed, watched by a silent circling wall of soldiers. Blood was running down his cheek . . . his neck.

Brock, shield held a little lower, came after him—with him— his black boot spattering red. Limping now, but limping very swiftly, the Moonriser cut the angle again, drove into Baj with his shield, and thrust up to gut him.

Baj parried a second time with the left-hand dagger—felt his wrist sprained by impact hard as a horse's kick—and lunged turning off-balance to thrust his rapier's point down into Brock's suffering boot again, so firmly planted for that sword stroke. Then spun away, scuttling to his right as before. Fleeing, was what it was.

Brock seemed to take a moment to settle himself, to put pain in its place. Then, gazing annoyed over his shield rim, he came again.

Baj tried to flex his knife wrist, couldn't feel it as Brock struck at him—leading with the short-sword now, his wounded foot a little refused.

Baj tried to ward that fast stroke with the left-hand dagger again—parried it, lost the knife humming away from an agonized wrist—and leaped to thrust the rapier over Brock's shield. The shield came up to block and Baj whipped his blade away to feint at the injured foot now exposed. The shield came down, and Baj thrust high and over again and caught the soldier shallow in the throat—then side-stepped fast to his right from an instant savage rush and quick spearing thrusts of the short-sword, certain soon to catch him in the belly.

It seemed he'd managed only a slight injury, no more than an inch or two of slender steel into a massive throat, fur-tufted, corded with muscle.

Tiring . . . tiring, considering what next he must do, Baj misstepped on tundra turf but recovered, still circling away from that determined short-sword, snap-thrusting with more than human speed, quick as the tongue of some southern snake.

Breathing hard, Baj sidled to the right, circling, legs uncertain with fatigue—and knew that weariness, and having lost the left-hand dagger, were going to get him killed. Now he fled half-turned to his left, bringing the rapier's length across in limber parries of those murderous ringing strokes coming low inside.

He bitterly regretted having been so shy with that single thrust to the throat—an instant more of off-balance risk would have sent the steel another inch deeper. But he'd been afraid of Brock's blade.

Baj stumbled, circling . . . circling to the right, exhausted as if this had been a fight for hours. Brock still came after—the muzzle-face, gray eyes intent over the shield's rim—but perhaps came more slowly, without such driving ferocity.

Baj thought it might be the wounded foot; the soldier left wet red now with every step. The tundra's snow-dusted grass was dappled with bright blood along the circling way they'd fought. Some of that, Baj supposed, was from his face where the shield had struck him.

There was blood, also, at the soldier's mouth, a thread of it down one side into his whiskers as he came, moving more slowly. He was making a sound. Baj, forever side-stepping to his right, away from that short-sword, heard it very clearly . . . a sort of soft snarling, but with liquid in it.

Brock suddenly stopped and stood still. . . . Grateful, Baj stopped also, ceased the circling-away that was making him sick, with his cracked cheekbone hurting so badly. He stood taking deep breaths.

The soldier made that soft liquid sound again. Some blood came spilling from his mouth, as if he'd drunk blood, taken too big a swallow of it—and Baj realized George Brock couldn't breathe, had been strangling on his blood for some time. That inch or two of steel . . .

They looked into each other's eyes.

Then Brock coughed out a great spray of red—turned half-away . . . and whirling suddenly back, hurled his shield sliding off his left arm and scaling sideways so its edge slammed into Baj's shoulder as he tried to dodge, and knocked him down. Then the massive soldier, mouthing crimson foam, came staggering with his short-sword in his hand.

Baj rolled up and caught Brock on the rapier's point as he came. The thrust hesitated at the belly's massive muscle, then slid in. Up on one knee, gripping the hilt hard, Baj lunged to the right, turning full out and away so the rapier's blade—a foot of its length still buried—was left almost behind him, the slim steel deeply curved in desperate guard as the short-sword's edge swung in.

It was a clear sound at the shock, a bell's clanging note. The rapier, hammered, leaped free—and springing straight, numbed Baj's arm, but didn't break. Something, the short-sword's edge, glanced to just touch the right side of his head, above his ear, with a quick kissing sound.

Baj scrambled back . . . and saw George Brock-Robin slowly kneel, slowly go to all fours so the short-sword's bright blade was pressed into snowy grass, his massive head thrown back as he tried to breathe.

Baj then wanted . . . wished to do anything else. But instead, weary, trembling, he climbed to his feet—steadied, placed his sword's point—then drove the blade down through George's ribs . . . searched for the great heart, and found it.

22

"Damn you, Baj." Richard was kneeling before him, grimacing, watching as a near-human Guards physician stitched along the right cheekbone, as he'd already sewn the wound over Baj's right ear. "—I told you to watch his *shield!*"

"I didn't know they threw them. . . ."

"They do *every* fucking thing with them!"

"The cheekbone is cracked, but very slightly." The physician, whose eyes had been contributed by an animal Baj didn't recognize, had gentle hands. "Cracked, but not busted—you know the WT word *busted*?"

"Yes, doctor, I do."

"Well, it isn't. Leave it alone, don't hurt it again, and it will heal quickly." He recommenced his sewing, tugging at Baj's cheek, hooking the small, curved needle in and out. "Good scars," he said.

"Poor Baj." Patience was sitting watching. They all were watching, gathered in their canvas-walled patch of tundra, duplicated exactly, camp to camp. "Our prince will not be so handsome, now."

"And he shouldn't be. He's a *fool*." Nancy was wincing as Baj winced, while the needle went in and out.

"Hold still," the doctor said. "Tender Sunriser skin . . ."

Nancy was recovered after a long while of silence. Richard had found her lying in the tundra, halfway back to camp. She'd been lying with her face in her arms—Errol whining beside her, worried. When Richard turned her over, her eyes were tight shut.

"He's dead," she'd said, having heard only the clash and ring of steel, and no notice from hundreds of silent soldiers.

"No . . . no." Richard had cradled her in his arms. "No, not dead!"

"Dying," Nancy'd said, and wouldn't open her eyes when Errol came scurrying, having retrieved Baj's left-hand dagger.

They hadn't allowed Baj to come to her, since he ran blood—right cheek split open, scalp sliced above his right ear.

Patience had knelt by Nancy in sedge grass. She and Richard both reassuring her.

When Nancy did open her eyes, she'd said, "You don't know how much I hate him."

"Yes, sweetheart," Patience had bent to kiss her. "We know how much you hate him."

". . . Other one just missed the top of the ear," the physician leaning to bite off his suture's excess at Baj's cheek.

"Too bad," Nancy said, watching. "George Brock should have taken that ear, and the other one too."

* * *

Baj, having vomited dinner at sunset, lay alone behind the bales in his blanket pallet—Nancy gone with Patience to rouse Sergeant Givens for soothing vodka—his head hurting as if it rested in hot coals. The left shoulder, where Brock's thrown shield had struck him, was mottled dark blue, and very sore.

Patience had asked the Guard doctor for some herb or far-southern poppy paste, and the physician had stared at her in astonishment. "He's not a *child*."

"Not a Person, either," Patience had said, but the doctor had snorted, gathered his gear, and gone. Still, Baj found the cold a fair comfort, its sunset wind stroking, chilling the wounds to dullness, though he still felt the stitches pulling.

He recalled the duel—but as if it had been only the beginning of pain, and of no other importance. He supposed George Brock-Robin might have killed him, fighting as his nature would have ordered. A terrible leaping rush, fangs bared—a smashing shield and slicing blade—with no practiced ranker's restraint, none of the Guard's trained battle discipline. . . . He would have hacked Baj down like a storm.

Fortunate Baj, a victor, lay with his wounds to the wind, and would have been happy with them frozen solid and senseless. . . . Still, he slept a little while, then woke in darkness, feeling very clearly, in his right hand and wrist, the stumbling throb of George Brock's heart as the rapier's point found and pierced it. . . . *WITH GOOD CAUSE*. Perhaps.

And as if that thought had called her, Nancy came out of the dark, and knelt to him. "Are you awake?"

"Yes."

"We have vodka—do you want some?"

"No, sweetheart; I'm doing well enough."

She arranged the bedding, then unlaced her muk-boots, pulled them off with the foot wraps, undressed, and squirmed under the blankets beside him. She reached to hug him close, so he felt smooth bare belly, the tender proddings of her twin rows of little nipples, the weight of a soft strong thigh.

"I forgive you," she said, lay with him under the combing wind . . . and soon, so lightly, began to lick his wounds.

* * *

Travel was difficult the first day. Though his injuries were not much, a severe headache had come with them, which sunlight made worse, so Baj marched squinting, Nancy wincing with him when he misstepped on mounded tussocks. The guard-troopers, slouching by on their big mounts, glanced down in passing, but said nothing to him concerning the duel.

At evening, and grateful for the day's end, Baj found fading light easier on his eyes, and the headache less severe, so he managed seal stew without upset. He also, encouraged, beat Richard at chess—an almost accident, since both of them had forgotten a knight hidden in plain sight. Which prompted a discussion of accident and oversight as determinants of history.

A discussion acting perfectly as a medicine draft to send Baj to sleep where he sat. The last he recalled was Richard saying, "Well . . . that's rude."

The usual trumpet—then rye-porridge—at dawn's first light, found Baj's headache almost gone, the sewn injuries less uncomfortable, the sore shoulder much better. And the sun, that morning, troubled him only a little.

These improvements lasted half the day, until the goat-eyed cavalry colonel trotted past, cursing an unlucky officer who—riding beside him—said only, "Sorry, sir." The colonel glanced down, saw Baj trudging along—and pleased, perhaps, by the shame that had been visited on the infantry, a tender-ass Sunriser having slaughtered one of their own—called out, "Get this young swordsman a ride!"

For which kindness, ungrateful Baj cursed the colonel through a freezing after-noon, since while horses had a gentle gait, moose did not. The headache returned, as copybooks had it, "with a vengeance."

Still, no trooper, riding beside him or riding past, mentioned the fight. Only Dolphus-Shrike—fur bundled, javelins over his shoulder, his yellow hair knotted at his neck—come jogging along fast as the trotting mount, smiled up at Baj, and said, "I see I'll have to watch my mouth before such a champion, such a Jack Monroe."

"Not today," Baj said, standing a little in the stirrups to ease jolting, and the Shrike laughed.

So, a difficult after-noon, and a day that brought the Companies to the Wall's wide lap of moraine—ten to twenty WT miles of huge rounded drumlin hills, outwash rubble, and milk-water cirques appearing in the tundra . . . then great shallow lakes, ice-skimmed and stretching out of sight with flocks of ducks and geese rising in roars of wing-claps from them, then swirling away over other shallow waters that had to be splashed through or widely skirted, and fast foaming streams to be forded with difficulty and some danger . . . occasionally crossed twice as they wound and wended in the way. It was slow marching.

At necessary halts, some troopers, whirling humming slings, galloped along beneath the sailing clouds of birds—their moose pounding through puddles in spray—and sent stones hissing up to bring down several.

At one such delay, Nancy ran up alongside Baj's mount with his bow and quiver in her hands.

"Oh, for Christ's sake . . ." That ancient exclamation still risky in some places.

"Get one!" said the merciless girl, and reached them up.

The moose had no change of gait beside ambling rolling trot or a dead run, and dead run would be required for duck chasing. There also seemed a question whether the reins had any function—they'd certainly had none for Baj so far.

He gritted his teeth, which hurt the hurt cheek, strung and braced the bow in the saddle—something he'd done before, hunting, though not with a bruised and aching shoulder—then drew an arrow from the quiver—one of his last from the River. He took the rein-ends in his teeth, nocked the arrow to the bowstring . . . and drummed his heels into the moose's massive flanks.

What reins and cluckings did not do, kicks apparently did—and Baj found himself tearing along from a brutally wrenching start, going at a racehorse's speed but with side-swaying and surging up and down like a festival crank-ride.

The velocity, and tossing this way and that as the animal galloped—hammering sedge, smashing through milky runs of melt-water—had all the discomforts of nightmare. Baj's sore head and sore shoulder seemed to snarl at him as he flew across the tundra, out of the saddle as often as in it.

It was so bad, so painful it became funny, and Baj released

himself so he seemed to drift laughing beside that unfortunate rider, reins in his teeth, clutching his bow as he went flying, jouncing, reeling across the country on a great, black, bulge-eyed beast.

"Hattie," the trooper had named her as he'd handed her over, dubious, but giving Baj a leg up.

Baj called "*Hattie! . . .*" muffled by bitten leather as he leaned back, hauling on reins apparently set in stone.

Then he gave up, spit the leather out, and went along—as copybooks often had it—"for the ride."

He even managed to draw with an unhappy shoulder and shoot at seven ducks whirring over (though not going much faster than he was)—missed the flock by a distance, and of course that arrow lost in melt-water.

Hattie gave no sign at all of slowing, but Baj, growing used to windy great speed, jolting pain, and eccentric motion, managed to nock a second arrow—shot it at almost random, and out of a great whistling dark ceiling of geese, killed one.

* * *

The day after, they were under the loom of the Wall. The companies, at sunset, camped two miles from its base in a wilderness of foaming rapids not yet frozen, and fractured fallen mountains of blue ice and white ice. Boulders—seeming, in number, a heaped limitless drift of river-bank pebbles—lay with many big as manor houses, and all ground smooth-sided as planed planks.

The milky river rapids, the threads of short-summer's melt— though many ran several bowshots wide—thundered in waterfall down from massive ice-faces, parapets, ramparts here rising two miles high, to crash in fountaining spray, then surf along great dunes of the glacier's till. . . . That sound, continuous as it had been for centuries—though greater or lesser with freeze and thaw—shook the ground, drum-rolled to echo from the Wall, then rumbled away to the east and west as if the Wall asked and answered questions fundamental, along three thousand miles from ocean to ocean.

Kingdom River, the Mississippi, could have run along the base of that frozen monument, and been no more than moat to a fortress inconceivable.

Somewhat subdued since his ride the previous day—Hattie having been retrieved by her concerned trooper, carefully examined, kissed on the nose, then taken away to the Line to feed—Baj had seen the Wall before, from a headwater branch of the River, though at a much greater distance. . . . But this was the near thing itself, a miles-high, horizon-wide palace, its vaults ice-white, ice-gray, ice-blue, with glittering sheets of melt in sunset light, their roaring waters carving down great crevasses, shaping ice canyons in the air, persuading immense formations—twice, as he stood watching—to slowly lean . . . lean out and away from the mass, and topple dreamily down.

Then the thunder and breaking in huge fountains of white spray, while the soaked soil shook under Baj's muk-boots, vibrated like a drumhead.

Nancy came to stand beside him, looking up as he looked up, and raised her voice to nearly a shout. *"It isn't a get-used-to thing!"*

"No, it isn't." He saw the making of their centuries of cruel weather, the destruction of ancient Warm-times represented by this magnificent thing—that of course proved no Lord Winter, but matters senseless, and much greater than even a God's deciding.

"Come eat," Nancy spoke into his ear, and they walked hand-in-hand over rubble and freezing drift, though air drafty with blowing mist, heavy with the odors of ice and stone.

. . . Though Baj's aches and injuries, already much less painful, wouldn't have troubled him after a second evening's bellyful of goose and its grease, roasted over horded dried dung—the Wall's earth-shaking, its crashing sounds, did not permit a night's sleep in more than snatches. So he rose—as they all, and the companies rose—weary in a bitter morning, to their rye-porridge.

It seemed to Baj, despite the night—and present noise—that the glacier's towering front had become slightly more peaceful.

"Probably," Richard said when he mentioned it, "—summer melt's ending, so it'll be a little quieter every day. Already be starting to freeze hard in places along the rim. Let three, four WT weeks go by, you could camp here in almost quiet. . . . And after that, in very quiet, though rivers run beneath it always. —Lord Winter's piss, the Shrikes say."

Errol stood up with porridge on his chin, and pointed over the outwash plain, its ponds and lakes gleaming with night ice. More than a mile away, past a great mounded drumlin-hill, a herd that must have been thousands of caribou was lacing through frozen cirques and melt-leads. . . . Baj could make out swifter, smaller shapes sifting through the herd's edges. Wolves.

"No better hunting," Nancy said, "—than before the Wall." Her breath steamed in the frigid air.

"For white fox, white weasel, white hare, wolf, white bear, musk-ox and caribou." Patience was packing her possibles. "The white bears also hunt *us*."

Errol, still staring out at the caribou, was jogging in place as if to chase them.

Nancy clapped her hands for his attention. "Come sit!" He turned to her . . . wandered over.

"What when he's grown," Baj said, "—and won't come when called?"

Errol stared at Baj, head cocked.

Baj smiled at him, though his sewn right cheek felt stiff as he did. "Yes, I'm talking about you—but not in a bad way."

"He knows when we talk about him," Nancy said. She tongue-clicked for his attention, patted a space of hide beside her. "Want to come sit?"

Errol stayed where he was, turned his head to watch the caribou.

"And when he's grown?"

"Baj," Richard smiled, rolling his blanket, "none of us are likely to have much more time to grow."

"Why," Baj said, "do I keep forgetting that?"

"Because you wish to." Patience stood, shrugged on her pack.

"Because you're a fool." Nancy came, crouched, and began to tickle him.

"Don't." Baj tried to get up and get away. "—I'm wounded!" But she tickled anyway.

Richard tugged on his furred muk-boots. "We have company."

Four mounted Persons were galloping toward them—their mooses' splayed hooves making rapid dull thump-thump-thumps over drifts of till.

"The General." Richard stood up. Baj and Nancy as well.

Sylvia Wolf-General rode in among them as she had before, as if to use her saber—it seemed to Baj her accustomed approach—and pulled up hard in the same sliding stop as her troopers followed, her big mount tossing strings of clear slobber.

"You," she said, the harsh wood-saw voice. She pointed a long black-nailed finger at him, "—You have had what sword-play I permit, and cost me a Banner-bearer. Never again, in any camp of mine or near it, whatever the future we go to."

"Understood, ma'am." Baj bowed to her.

"Not good enough, Son-of-great-ghosts." She reined her sidling mare-moose still, and stared down at him.

Looking up into that inhuman—*more* than human—face, a carnivorous mask with lady's eyes, Baj felt sudden admiration for her, and for the Boston-Talents whose centuries of merciless mind-making and science of so-tiny bits had resulted at last in such savage perfection. . . . And, of course, in his darling Nancy.

"I understand, ma'am—and will obey."

The Wolf-General nodded. "Now, you four and your idiot-boy listen to me. We part here, we to march east along the Wall—and you, to rest the day. *Rest*, eat your rations, and so be ready to climb with Dolphus-Shrike and his people at first light, tomorrow." Her lip lifted from an eye-tooth. "They are lying Sunshiner barbarians, and certainly treacherous when it suits them. But they are what you have—and you are what *they* have—so make do." She stilled her restless mount. ". . . Remember, once you get to Boston's North Gate—you are to wait 'till we reach the south of the city. Only then, when their Constables reinforce south to meet our assault, go in with your Shrikes and do . . . what must be done."

The Wolf-General sat for a few moments, staring at them. "We will at least divert and keep the Constables busy for you. We will hit them hard, with all our strength. —But I promise, if you fail to free our people's mothers from their lives, I will *not* fail to free you from yours." She spun the mare-moose rearing, spurred it . . . and was gone, her troopers after her, back to their busy preparing camp, where trumpets were announcing preparations to march.

". . . And Dolphus," Richard said, "—comes right after."

Baj turned and saw the Shrike trotting over icy waste toward them, carrying a heavy pack, his javelins tied in a slender bundle over his shoulder. Seven more savages were coming with him, each in caribou parkies, each burdened, each armed.

"Baj," Patience touched his arm, "—and you, Nancy, both of you guard your tongues with these people. Shrikes are clever, and Dolphus-Shrike speaks very well and has read deeply in Warm-time's copybooks. But a savage he remains—forget it, insult his shade of home ice or his uncle, and he and his men will cut your livers out if feeling kind . . . or skin your head and let you wander screaming, if *not* feeling kind."

"Shrikes on the one side," Baj said, "Sylvia Wolf-General on the other."

"—And Boston waiting." Nancy drew her scimitar, and sat with a piece of tallow to tend the blade from icy mist gusting now and then.

"You can joke with the Shrikes," Richard said, "but be sure they know you're joking. . . . We go with them to likely kill a few of their sisters."

"We'll be very courteous." Baj found he was feeling fairly well . . . no longer as sore, head or shoulder, though the cracked cheekbone was tender, and likely would be for a while.

"Good morning!" Dolphus-Shrike trotted to them.

"Good morning, Chieftain," Baj bowed.

"Ah . . ." Dolphus blew out frosting breath. "The Champion has been warned not to upset such a collection of ice-dwelling brutes as we are."

"To a point," Baj said.

"Of course. With everyone, it's only to a point before points come out." He gestured his men forward. "Here's Henry . . . Marcus . . . Christopher . . . Paul, and so forth. These last three are too worthless to name." The last three—all like the others, short stocky men with blond or ginger hair, round-faced, light-eyed, and apparently pleasant—grinned file-toothed, and nodded.

Each Shrike was burdened by a bulky pack, weighty rolled hides, and thick coils of greased, braided leather line. They also belted pairs of light adze-hatchets (hatchets for ice, it seemed to Baj, since each narrow head had a curved back-spike), and carried as well, a row of steel hooks, snap-circles, and grapnels clinking along a rawhide bandoleer.

"And we don't go today?" Patience said.

Dolphus shook his head. "No. A day of rest is in order for ice-virgins such as yourselves—though I know you're familiar, lady. A day of rest, first—and it seemed to me we might as well camp together. Begin to understand each other."

"Fair enough," Baj said.

The Shrike grinned. "I'm so glad you agree. And, Warmtimes' 'by-the-bye,' we'll bring more burden for you. Rope lines, seal-jerky and so forth. We cannot carry your everything."

"Again, fair enough," Baj said.

"Now . . ." Dolphus and his men began to shed their packs and equipment, one tossing chunks of dung on the fire to increase its heat. "—Now, I don't know what Sylvia and her people told you of our timing. I wasn't invited to the General's pavilion, being only a Sunriser *tribesman*. . . . But this is how we'll go. We climb the Wall, which will take," he looked them over, "will take at least six or seven days, with possibly a halt to rest you." He smiled. "—After which, we meet friends, then run the ice certainly more than two WT weeks north and east to Boston Township, killing any unluckies we encounter along the way, to keep our secret."

"*More* than two weeks?" Baj said. It seemed unfair to have come so far, and still have farther to go. Traveling over the ice . . .

Dolphus-Shrike nodded. "Oh, yes. —Then, with luck, and after a time snow-buried by the North Gate, we'll find the Guard come up south of the city to join us, slow as always, and with a longer way to go. . . . They'll have marched up the Crease, where the glacier's split open, to leave their mounts and find easy climbing. Then met our freighter-sleds—twelve teamers—to accommodate all their supplies, their armored numbers, their . . . notions of civilized campaigning."

He turned to look at the Wall, was silent for a moment, then turned back. "In the morning, we will *not* linger. So, at first light, you'll finish furring; see your blankets are rolled tight and tied where you buckle your packs; strap swords—and that ax, Captain—to your packs to be out of the way, climbing. . . . And you will wear the mittens. They'll be corded to your sleeves, so when you need your hands bare to climb, take them off, then mitten-up right after. If a finger or toe turns black, we cut it off. If a hand or foot—the same. And who slows us too much, we also cut off." A smile. "I hope I don't sound cruel."

One of his men—Marcus—said, "No, no, never cruel," and the other Shrikes grinned. They seemed to Baj a merry group.

"A last few matters," Dolphus said, kicked stones away, and sat by the fire. "We will lend you ice hatchets, two to each, and expect their return. We will also lend you strap-spikes for your muk-boots, and expect those to be returned. . . . And lady," to Patience, "if you can Walk-in-air up the Wall, more power to you; you're with us now, not the Guard." It was the first time Baj had heard that copybook phrase actually used. *More power to you . . .*

"And eat," Marcus-Shrike said, settling alongside his chief with the other tribesmen.

"Yes," Dolphus said. "Eat rich while you can; we'll hunt ducks, today."

"Drink water." Marcus.

"Yes, drink a *lot* of water." Dolphus took something—a piece of seal-blubber—from a parky pocket, held it out to the fire for a moment, then began chewing it. "And now, Tender-ones—rest, doze, nap like babies. . . . Oh, is there one among you who considers him or herself useful at pick-up sticks? Would care, perhaps, to wager?"

"I might," Patience said. . . . And that game had just commenced, when trumpets announced from the camp. Then drums. And as Baj, Nancy, Richard and several Shrikes stood to watch, the leading elements of the Guard swung from their pebble-drift camp, and marched out, unit by unit, splashing through milky run-off on their way.

Scouts were trotting south of east, to come to easier marching along the Wall. Banners came behind them—and among them, Baj could see the Wolf-General quite clearly. She seemed to be laughing at something one of her staff-officers had said.

And behind her, in long columns, the companies marched in step, arms and armor gleaming in morning light. The bloods of infantry—bear and wolf—their drums thumping, were spaced between Supply's pack-moose and two-wheel wagons, and the trotting squadrons of near-Sunriser troopers . . . whose trumpeters, loping past the ranks, sounded the first notes of "Yanking Tootle" as they rode.

Watching those formations . . . those solders go—old Sergeant Givens certainly perched on a wagon, with his barrels and baked goods—Baj felt his fathers standing beside him.

* * *

Just-before-dawn was announced by an avalanche thundering off the Wall—to startle all of them, even the Shrikes.

"Wall calls," a sleepy tribesman said, and awake, the Shrikes, with Baj and the others, gathered around a fresh-started dung fire to warm themselves a little in freezing silvery air, and eat frost-coated pieces of yesterday's ducks.

Food finished, and all having scattered into the landscape to do the necessary, equipping began of possibles, extra coiled leather line, rolled blankets, fat leather sacks of seal-jerky and strips of frozen blubber. Ice hatchets, cords looped to their handles, were thrust through belts, weapons all strapped firm to back-packs, and full canteens and water-skins swung on cords beneath parkies to keep their water liquid.

"Here . . ." Dolphus-Shrike distributed leather masks with dangling rawhide ties, each narrowly slit for vision. "Wear them when the sun is out, or the ice will blind the fool who doesn't."

A sad loser of many honor-promises to Patience, playing pick-up sticks the evening before, the Shrike-chief seemed a little out of temper. ". . . *Also*, since our princeling here," he went to Baj's pack, plucked and tugged to test straps and lashings, "—since he was lightly touched in his so-honorable duel, we will make a morning's allowance for that, and haul him up where he must be hauled. But from this after-noon, Champion, you do your own work."

"Understood."

" '*Understood . . .*' " Dolphus and another Shrike, Christopher, walked behind each, including fellow tribesmen, tightening, yanking at pack-straps and whatever load's rawhide ties.

Finished, they all stood thickly furred, slightly bent under bulky burdens—the Shrikes most encumbered with coils of braided line, and their jingling bandoleers of steel hooks, rings, and little grapnels.

Dolphus-Shrike looked the party over, nodded, then turned to Nancy. "Women have difficulty holding their water, then have to bare butt to lose it. Done your pissing?"

"Fuck you," Nancy said. And at a glance from Patience, ". . . Just joking."

Dolphus smiled, his first of the morning. "—And no one has packed what is not needed to live?"

". . . Little chess set," Richard said. "*The Common Prayers of Warm-time Oxford.*"

The Shrikes were amused.

"We're ready," Baj said.

"Then," Dolphus said, "—catch us if you can." The Shrikes all turned together and trotted away north, where the Wall—a flock of sailing geese only infinite specks across its gleaming front—grumbled awake to a rising sun.

. . . It took two glass-hours of fast marching across moraine—much of the time skirting streams and a shimmering lake of milk-white melt—to reach the base of the Wall.

The thunder and volley of toppling ice, the seething rapids they hiked beside—the Shrikes moving steadily—echoed to Baj something of the sounds of Warm-times, at least as he'd always imagined them . . . continuous racket, rushing, roaring, thumping, flushed with color and busy with millions of men and women racing here and there in bright, whining machines—having work adventures and love adventures and crime and war adventures. . . . Of course, there must have been boredom, discontent—those appeared in the copybooks, as well—but surely very little and only among fools, when the whole world was open to them, and warm . . . warm, so winter for them was only an interesting season's passage.

As now, below the Wall, it was not.

The cold there did not settle on them as Baj was used to from the river—as if a great soft coverlet of freezing-invisible had come down through the air. This was a cold that sought them out as if deliberately, with intention. Sought each of them out and gripped them, squeezing warmth away like some great festival wrestler, muscled with ice, and in Lord Winter's pay. . . . Cold the more frightening in air as still as deep water, except when some falling great structure disturbed it.

The cold took Baj's easy breaths away, and allowed only careful breathing between guarding lips to keep his lungs from freezing. He put his arm around Nancy—hooded, richly soft in her plush of furs—and she smiled up at him. "Careful," he said to her—meaning, he supposed, she was to be careful of the cold, and climbing. Careful of everything. . . .

His word, "Careful," dissolved before him in a little cloud of crystals that sifted down like snow. Nancy stuck her tongue out at him, but only for a moment.

. . . The base of the Wall was an enormous confusion of massive fallen cliffs and towers, great gaps and crevasses snow-bridged or open to reveal depths blue-green to black. Through this immense and dangerous labyrinth, the Shrikes led fast—in morning sunshine, now, brilliant light that warmed not at all—crawling, climbing great broken tilted slabs of ice, to descend again. Scrambling over or around gaping pitfalls and many-storied structures of blue ice, white ice, and gray ice caverned by foaming water come rushing, spouting from the glacier's grand foundations.

Baj was surprised how difficult it was to keep up with the tribesmen—each of them so laden. . . . His right cheek still ached slightly, occasional little needles of pain flashing down the stitching there, and along the side of his head. But it was his bruised shoulder that gave him trouble. What he would, it did—but stiffly.

Dolphus-Shrike, though never turning back to look, seemed to have the talent of Who-is-where, so almost always when Baj slowed, climbing some steep, there would be Marcus or Henry or one of the three nameless men suddenly beside him in support. Muttering, the Shrike would boost him up, taking one of his booted feet in hand to place it properly. —And twice, Baj was simply seized and tossed up to better holds. Impressive demonstrations of strength, though still a strength gathered, however swiftly. Sunriser strength, rather than George Brock's instant and terrific impetus.

. . . Baj couldn't have said when not-quite-the-Wall became the thing itself. There was a rise that continued to a steeper rise, with no longer even a slight descent, but only going up.

Here, a Shrike was single-roped to each of their charges, except for Patience, who—sitting cross-legged on a snowy ledge, scimitar strapped to her small pack—slowly drifted sideways with the Wall's wind, seeming not to rise very much at all . . . until she did, with her colored greatcoat ruffling in the wind like the bright plumage of some bird of myth.

The Shrikes—who until then had been clambering as Baj and the others did, though much more easily—unlimbered more of their thick coils of slender braided-leather line, knotted the ends to the steel hooks they carried . . . then buckled and strapped odd little sharp steel points to their heavy-soled muk-boots . . .

and lifting the similar boots Baj and the others had been given by the Guard, fastened the spikes for them as if shoeing horses.

These points were not comfortable, made simple walking difficult. But using them, and the spikes backing their hatchets' heads, the Shrikes began to demonstrate true climbing—staying, Baj saw, on good green or blue ice where they could, avoiding rotten gray. . . . Working in steady cooperation, they often wove running guard-lines of braided leather—threaded through small steel circles, and anchored with hooks and grapnels—to support them and their charges as they climbed.

It was a remarkable skill to see, to try to imitate, and kept Baj's mind, mostly, from their height above the ground. He'd climbed trees, of course, and various granite walls at Island, sometimes perilously high above the river's currents. But the Wall's ramparts—so very much higher—were different in kind, their ice (so various, patches of it rotten) much more treacherous than solid stone.

He wished Nancy had been left behind, left with the Guard, so he didn't have to watch her climbing just above him, hesitant, hacking at ice with her hatchets or, mittens tugged off, clutching with freezing hands to crucial holds made only of frozen water. . . . Concern for her—and concern for himself, since his rolled blanket and pack (rapier, dagger, bow and quiver strapped to it), seemed to conspire to tug him out and away from the ice cliff to fall.

He used the Shrike hatchets at first awkwardly, so their heads' sharp reverses bounced off ice, or skidded to the side. . . . But after a time (and occasionally in terror), he slowly found the short swinging stroke that drove the narrow points picking into the ice as a war hammer pecked skulls. His wrists looped to the hatchet handles, he picked left-handed into sound ice . . . hauled himself up to pick higher with the right . . . then kicked-in standing places with his muk-boots' spikes to swing the hatchets again.

It was brutal work, extraordinarily wearying . . . but the left shoulder loosened under the discipline, its stiffness fading as the Shrikes' attention to him faded. Soon—the sun past straight-up— no Marcus, Henry, or Christopher came to hoist Baj along.

Above him, Nancy (and Richard, higher) climbed laboriously as he did, with careful hand and foot—while Errol, staying with the leading Shrikes and apparently unconscious of height, seemed to scamper up easily as a southern squirrel, leaving wind-blown banners of fine ice-particles behind him.

As Baj, already very tired, worked his slow way, a huge cornice, large as a river lord's hold and detached a mile or more above by the sun's mild melting—fell ponderously moaning past, turning . . . turning as it went. One of many such, large and small, sailing, cascading down throughout the day. Only fortune, only luck unreliable, kept any one of them from wiping all the climbers from the height.

The sun threw a passing shadow across fractured ice beside him, and Baj—minding a slippery stance, a tenuous hold— looked carefully out to see Patience in mid-air, a pebble's toss from the ice-face . . . drifting cross-legged, eddying like a leaf in wind. Her eyes were open, but she didn't seem to see him. She slowly swung away, away from the Wall's sheer . . . and it appeared to Baj that she flew—Walked-in-air—with some awkwardness, as if spurning both a cliff of ice and the icy earth below, made for difficulty.

To hold oneself in the air by only thinking it was now so frightening a notion it made Baj look away from her, not wanting to see anyone hanging on nothing—where truly *was* nothing but empty air . . . and a great distance to fall.

He stared instead at the ice close before him—and saw, in its crazed surface, mirror enough to make out a hollow-cheeked, scant-bearded man, sewn with scars and no longer truly young. Baj closed his eyes and held on, stayed clutching where he was . . . only for a few moment's rest. . . . Then, with a scrape and rattle of ice-chips, someone came clambering swiftly down to him, and Dolphus-Shrike, close as a lover though on ice vertical, whispered in his ear. *"Who won't climb up, will be thrown down."* And was gone, scrambling the cliff, leaving ice powder sifting on the wind.

Baj opened his eyes and climbed.

23

The evening seemed to come after forever. . . . During the climbing day, Baj had imagined falling—worse, imagined Nancy falling—so many dreadful times that terror itself seemed to weary. After that, he'd climbed only for grim effort's sake—trying clumsily to imitate the Shrikes, for whom these towering battlements of untrustworthy ice seemed nearly a home.

Still, ceasing was a pleasure as the sun set—so that west, down the Wall's horizon, its glittering immensity gradually diminished to a distant gleaming thread. . . . Evening shadows grew swiftly in and about spires of ice where the climbers held fast, tiny as twelve specks of dust in a world of vaulted white. The Shrikes—like furred swift far-southern spiders—began to weave a web of braided line and steel ice-hooks between sheer walls, shelves, and notches of blue ice and white ice as the wind hummed through.

Baj and the others—excepting Errol, who seemed at ease playing along their wind-swept ledge—roosted together like exhausted swallow-birds, clinging to their best holds while watching the Shrikes work.

"I was so frightened." Nancy, fur-hooded, gripped Baj's arm as if to prevent a fall. "I was frightened all day. . . ." Her breath smoked out on freezing air.

"I, also." Richard hummed for a moment, deep as a bass banjar. "I'm too big for this. Too heavy." He was clutching an anchored leather line, his crest and fur-tufts spangled with ice. "—We came south last year from the barren grounds, Map-Ohio. Ran from Matthew-Robin's company. Never been on this . . . thing, since I was basketed down as a boy to train to join the Guard."

"I wasn't frightened," Baj said, keeping his breathing shallow to save his lungs from frostbite. "I was fucking terrified." A perfect use of Warm-time's *fucking*, so often misplaced in modern ignorance.

A weary giggle from Nancy. "We're all terrified, except Errol."

"And what," Richard said, "—at least four more days to go?" He had to raise even his voice against the evening wind, which had begun to sing several songs at once, blowing through cathedrals of ice.

"Look at that fool!" Nancy called, "*Errol*—stop . . . stop doing that!" The boy was traversing a slender braided line hand-over-hand above nothing but icy air.

The Shrikes, busy working—hammering in hooks with their hatchets, swinging from here to there—seemed pleased with Errol. Called encouragement.

"Stupid Sunriser assholes. . . ." Nancy gave the Shrikes hard looks. "Savages."

Baj saw one of the tribesmen seem to hear her over the wind. "Shhh . . . Sweetheart, this is absolutely not the time or place for insults."

"*Absolutely* not," Richard clutched his leather line to him, "—though it's likely we'll freeze in the night, anyway."

With a rattling flap of colored coat-tails in the wind, a pinch-faced Patience swung out of the sunset and into the ice just above them . . . scrabbled for a grip, found one—precarious, where the surface had cracked like a fallen pitcher—and hung there.

"I need . . ." She could barely be heard. "I need help."

Baj, shamefully reluctant, took a cold-stiffened hand from its good hold (remember to mitten, remember to mitten) began to climb to her—and was greatly relieved when a Shrike, apparently sensitive to climbing trouble, seemed to stroll across a monstrous vertical, took Patience in a hug, and with only casual managing, brought her down to the others.

"Stay," the Shrike said, and was gone back to web-making.

"My fault," Patience said, her teeth chattering. ". . . My fault for getting too swiftly old. I came off the Wall years ago as if it were a snowbank, and no more. Now, the earth seems a long way down . . . difficult to push against."

Nancy shifted to put an arm around her. "Then don't Walk-in-air, dear. Stay and climb with us."

"Soon, I'll have to—and give the Shrikes another clumsy creature to care for."

Dolphus-Shrike, looking cheerful with a round ice-frosted face, clambered down to them. "Shake a leg!" And to Baj, "—Know that one?"

"No, I don't." Baj imagined the clever chieftain with a dagger-blade in his belly. . . . A refreshing vision.

"Oh, very ancient WT," the Shrike perched smiling, his filed teeth a polished white. "A naval term—means to start a dance, a celebration."

Baj couldn't help himself. "Sounds absolutely wrong—fragment mis-read, and wrong. If truly naval, probably had nothing to do with dancing."

Dolphus stopped smiling.

"If we freeze to death here," Patience said, "—while two fools argue what neither knows, we will make very angry ghosts."

Dolphus smiled again, said, "Princes *should* be ignorant; it's the only advantage of the ruled." He gestured *up* with his thumb. "Climb. It's bed-time."

. . . The "bed" had been woven for them, a long narrow hammock—sling seating—its casual wide-spaced netting, braided-rope. It hung from six lines fastened down its length, and anchored with steel hooks hard into blue ice.

"Sit," said Dolphus-Shrike when they'd climbed very cautiously to it. "Tuck your muk-books up, and wrap your blankets *over* your furs, or you'll freeze in the night. . . . And if pissing or shitting must be done, then push down fur trousers and hide trousers, and do those things through a netting gap—but with care. No dirty ropes in the morning!"

He and Henry-Shrike saw them settled in a row, crowded side by side—Baj, then Nancy, then Patience, then Errol, then Richard. "Birds," Dolphus said, "—on a branch," and Paul-Shrike swung down with a rolled caribou hide, and tucked it around Patience.

"Won't need it," Patience said, but Paul-Shrike only said, "Bring feet *up*," and swaddled her over her coat of colors.

Baj found their perch, hanging from a rough overhang within a great shallow bay of evening-colored ice—a vaulted space perhaps three bow-shots across—found it at first, very comfortable, though two great ice-chunks had fallen whistling past, just in front of them. . . . Henry-Shrike had run a length of the greased, braided line tight across their chests, to keep them sitting back firm in the sling. It seemed . . . pleasant enough, all swaying together slightly in the wind, Baj feeling Nancy close and warm beside him. Comfortable, secure enough to look out and wonder at the landscape hundreds of Warm-time feet beneath them.

From their roost, the glacier's moraine and outwash country made a rough brown-and-white wrinkled map stretching out of sight to east and west . . . and south, far, far to the hint of mountains. Nearer, the Wall's lap lay plated with broad lakes—red-gold as the sunset struck them—and threaded with braiding streams, the swift rivers of melt. . . . A view from the air, and though not from greater height than many mountain peaks, still was different from even the grandest of those vistas. A view, it seemed to Baj, that transformed the earth into something to be observed, something less solid than for those who walked it. —He found he understood Patience better, her . . . removal, remoteness. For her, all others and their landscapes lay essentially below. To be visited only.

The sight of such immense vacancy, the limitless country beneath, seemed almost worth the long day's effort to climb the ice wall to it—as if the effort, the fear, had been coins of payment.

. . . They sat in their row, and passed leather water-bottles and Baj's canteen—the water still liquid from their bodies' heat. Then shared out strips of frozen seal to chew, while, higher and to the side, the Shrikes rigged individual and skimpier woven rests—a few casual loops only—hammering guyline hooks into healthy ice with ringing strokes, using the flat sides of their hatchets' heads.

Night came quite suddenly. There was light, and airy vision, and all the warm colors sunset reflected from glaze ice, frost ice, fractured ice, and the country below—then, in the time a few breaths might be taken, the heights and air and the world beneath were only grays. . . . As the dark came down, the wind came up, and began to whine and warble past pinnacles, pillars, and massive fluted columns of ice—humming there with a vibration so great that Baj felt his teeth and bones sing to it.

He pulled off a mitten, reached over to Nancy's pack, and tugged loose the blanket-roll's ties . . . kept a careful grip as the wind flapped it open, then tucked the thick wool close around her, and under her fur-booted feet. Then he untied his own blanket, wrapped it around him—and saw Richard—already only a shadow—doing the same for himself and Errol.

Pulling his mitten back on, Baj found almost too much warmth in furs now wrapped in wool. . . . Almost too much warmth, but only for a little while, until pitch-blackness absolute came down the Wall, and the wind gradually rose to howling, buffeting so they swung and swung with it, once thudding back against the sheer ice they were fastened to. Then, cold slid in like narrow knives, with slow and searching thrusts, so he put his blanketed arm around Nancy and hugged her, burrowing deep as he could in furs and wool, as if into safety from a monstrous world.

It seemed a storm extraordinary, so endlessly savage—though Baj supposed this was the storm of every night along the Wall. The wind, cold, and terror of the gulf below their frail web of woven leather line, seemed to gape to swallow them as if the night had sense malevolent. . . . Their narrow sling swayed in the blasts of wind, shook—and Baj had visions of small steel hooks wrenched looser and looser from crumbling holds . . . of greased braided leather, frozen to fragile, suddenly snapping so they were spilled to fall endlessly . . . until even screaming faded to silence, and they fell quiet as if already dead.

There was no rest—any exhausted drift to dreaming was driven away by wind-noise screaming and continuous, and the sudden jolting of their seating as greater gusts came booming in, the storm battering at the Wall. . . . That accustomed meeting of wind and ice seemed too important, too mighty a thing to share presence with living creatures.

Baj gave up his life several times as the night roared on . . . gave his up, but refused to part with Nancy's. He made her his jewel in the dark, his place of refuge and silence—too valuable to lose to anything. Though the cold, if it continued so bitter on the wind—furs and blankets become only wishes for warmth against it—would certainly kill all but her.

He held Nancy to him, clutched her blanket about her, made certain her feet were tucked in, her fox-face deep in furs—found an icy little ear, once, and covered it. She became his reason through the night, and he was certain no Jesus in the world would deny him.

* * *

The Shrikes, chewing frozen lumps of seal-blubber, hauled them from their sling at first light—handed out frozen portions of the same—then hurried them to roll their blankets, drink water from flasks their bodies had warmed through the night, piss out into empty air (Nancy and Patience squatting in the webbing). And those accomplished, hustled them onto vertical ice and climbing.

Annoyed at first, still weary, and frightened by what seemed casually dangerous rushing, Baj saw as they began that Dolphus-Shrike and his tribesmen intended them no time to freeze in fear . . . wanted them, as Warm-times had had it, to "hit the road." This road being all ice, and two miles high.

As they had roused them up and out, so the Shrikes harried Baj and the others along, kept each of them usually roped to one tribesman or another, but climbing, always climbing—hauled up, hoisted up, directed up and expected to *do* as directed—with only very short rests on rough ice ledges or clinging with handholds and the muk-boots' steel points to sheer verglas walls. . . . They were not given time for consideration to become terror.

Dolphus-Shrike's orders to them, were all the Shrikes' orders to them. "*Move.*"

Baj found, even so, that fear for Nancy had been growing in him like a crab-tumor despite the hurry, the agonized labor of clawing his weight and his pack's weight up . . . and up. Clinging to inches-deep frost, coating a height of blue-green ice adamant as leaded glass, he heard a Shrike's impatient snarl beneath him, and hastily swung his hatchets—picked the points in, first left, then right—and heaved himself up, muk-boot spikes kicked in for fragile supporting steps.

The Shrike climbing beneath him said something unpleasant in very poor book-English, and struck Baj's left boot. "Move the ass," the Shrike said, pronouncing that perfectly.

. . . Still, there were places—many places—where even the Shrikes took care, and cared for their clumsy companions with double roping, belayed to steel ice-hooks hammered in. There, where the glacier's wall had opened, or some massive block had fallen free, was . . . a space, a place entirely air, over which first one tribesman, then another, had to swing . . . swing back and forth, gathering momentum, swing sailing through gusting wind until he struck and held so tenuously that Baj felt his own gut grip to help the man hold on.

Then the ice-hooks were pounded in, a slender braided line knotted to them—and a second and third Shrike went hand over hand above two thousand feet of nothing . . . and beckoned first

Richard (his weight sagging the thin rope), then Patience, then Errol—who went easily as the Shrikes had gone, unworried—then Nancy (while Baj closed his eyes). Then his turn.

. . . Slowly, through this second day, Baj became almost as interested as afraid. The Shrikes' every move was education in ice climbing. Consideration of the varying quality of the ice above all—rich blue-green to crumbling gray—the use of hatchet picks, roping and belaying, the use of muk-boot spikes to kick tiny steps to stand on . . . and occasionally even their javelins used butt to point as temporary bridging over vacancy. It was interesting even during exhaustion, muscle-wrenching effort, and fear of falling—and all the more interesting since only that education kept them alive.

Baj learned, and saw the others learning—though of course as children, compared to the Shrikes' veteran certainties.

And there were odors of ice—some clear as clear water, others dank as spoiled springs. Those odors, and the bitter cold that struck like willow switches, cutting at any exposed skin while the wind whistled, moaned, hissed past them on vertical pitches, tugging at their heavy packs to pull them out . . . away from their fragile holds into the perfect freedom of falling.

. . . Baj spent considerable effort, through a brutally effortful day, in avoiding looking down—but couldn't help it, sometimes. Then, the sunlit gulf, the sheer down-diminishing face of the Wall—shining in places blinding white, in others flashing reflected blues, greens, and diamond clears from broken battlements infinitely greater than any raised in stone by men or Persons—these all fell away beneath him to a singing emptiness that drew him down.

He avoided looking beneath them, and warned Nancy—climbing just above—against it.

Panting at a place, clinging with her hatchet-points, she'd turned her fur-hooded head and said, "I close my eyes." Then, "Oh, Baj . . . be careful."

And he was—was careful for both of them, constantly considering how he might catch her, reach out and grip her arm if she fell past him. Catch, hold her, and let go never.

... The notion of "catching" did suffer, as evening came after what seemed a week-long day. Baj—hugging a cracked ice-face (kissing it, nearly)—found it very difficult to raise either arm, very difficult to close his fists. His arms burned from fingers to shoulders; his left shoulder ached. The wounded cheek and side of his head felt as if snagged with fish-hooks.

The pain a blessing in a way, since it kept great heights from his thoughts.

Still, Baj missed the day, when the dark came down.

Higher on the Wall, the second night was worse than the first had been, the wind rumbling to crash against the ice cliffs like surf. Twice, almost asleep, Baj lurched alert in terror, sure a flailing anchor-line had worked free . . . and the fall begun.

Nancy had whispered in his ear, her breath the only warmth in an everything savagely cold. "Even if we die here, we're together."

"We won't die here, sweetheart," Baj said, and kissed her, as if saying and kissing must make it so.

... By morning light, it was seen that Henry-Shrike had fallen. Only unraveled webbing and a swaying guyline's end—worn through where it had rubbed and rubbed on an ice edge in the dark—were left behind.

The smiling Shrikes were smiling no more, silent as they hurried their weary charges to climb. . . . And as he began hacking, kicking his way up, just beneath Nancy—no tribesman helping him now—Baj tried to avoid imagining that death, the shocked wakening at the line's parting, then the sickening long fall . . . down and down through darkness so complete there'd be no knowing when the impact would come.

If a Shrike could fall—so could any.

Baj minded his hand-holds (kept mittened when he could), and used his hatchets very carefully, left and right, to pick his way up—all the while watching Nancy climbing above him . . . intending to catch her, or fall with her if that proved impossible.

For whatever reason—perhaps believing Henry-Shrike was sacrifice for all of them—he paid less attention to his own mortality, and found he was climbing better, discovering rhythms to it, an odd affinity for the ice and its different sounds when his steel struck it, ringing or rotten dull. . . . Their height now was such that it no longer seemed a height at all, but a fixed emptiness with only the rule of not-to-fall.

They'd hardly slept, been eaten by exhaustion and fear the day before—fear confirmed by Henry's death—but Baj saw that he and the others were climbing better, learning, as Warm-time copybooks had it, "in a hard school."

. . . By sun-straight-up, Patience, having tried the morning air—and sunk slowly away, down and down—had struggled back up to them, sitting cross-legged, eyes closed in effort—and swung in to stay. From then, her scimitar strapped to her pack, she climbed fairly well, with a Shrike beside her. . . . Errol, of course, still scrambled the ice like a squirrel a tree, as if he'd been born to it.

Sun-warmed, the Wall began shedding its great pieces, and those murmured, whistled, moaned past as they fell. The Shrikes, their brief mourning apparently over, sang along with those missiles' sounds . . . made little songs of them, dying away as the sounds of falling died away. So the long day was passed in great effort and risk, to those cheerful tunes . . . and to a night as dreadful as before.

* * *

. . . But the next morning brought the pleasures of survival, and introduced a good day, climbing—as if deep exhaustion (occasional visions vibrating in colors unnameable), with trembling arms and legs, freezing hands and feet—were just what was required to rise on great ice. Roped occasionally to be hauled up by a snarling tribesman—but still not quite as helpless as before, Baj began to imagine himself a climber, at least becoming competent on high ice, so he swung his pick-hatchets with a will, while chewing a mouthful of frozen blubber.

This imagined competence lasted only until a small cornice broke away under his right-hand point—and he fell several endless soundless feet before striking with his left-hand hatchet into an inch of salvation ice. It was a grateful . . . *grateful* Baj, then, and he said thanks to everything, looked up, and saw Nancy—her face still a mask of horror, staring down.

"*Don't*," she called to him. Meaning "Don't fall, don't die, don't let me see you fall and die. Don't leave me. . . . Don't be such a fool!"

"I *won't*," Baj called up to her, and became careful being careful.

Still, it was a good climbing day—bitterly cold in still air, though dazzlingly sunny, so the Shrikes saw to it they wore their leather eye-slit masks tied round their heads. Still, the light blazed through, reflecting off wind-polished ice in rainbow colors, shimmering bright as the sun and impossible to look at directly. So, in certain places, it became blind climbing . . . spiking steel into pillars of ice by touch and balance . . . listening to the Wall's resonance to hatchet blows, muk-boot spikes kicked in. Listening to others' grunts of effort, and to the murmurs of the Shrikes, conversational.

They climbed, gasping-in freezing breaths, hauling themselves up by wooden aching arms—and once, slowly up through an immense chimney of ice blue as sapphire jewelry, where even the slightest breeze sounded through in a breath-flute's soft uncertain notes. Here, Baj did look down—and was sorry—since the gleaming tunnel, diminishing hundreds of feet below to a tiny circle of sunlight, seemed to call and call to him. *"Decide . . . Loose your hold and fall, to be changed from what you are to something else entirely, imperishable."*

He looked up—saw Nancy's fur-trousered bottom, her scrabbling muk-boots as she struggled for a higher hold—and climbed to set his shoulder beneath her, let her rest on it for a moment.

He took a shallow breath, called out, *"Adventure . . . !"* and heard her laugh. Heard Patience laugh above her.

. . . Though it had been frightening while they were in it, the chimney was the sort of climbing Baj and the others had almost become used to. When, late in after-noon, the Shrikes led over the abyss on a narrow wind-sculpted snow bridge of rotting compact—mealy, pocked, mottled gray—they found their last days' fears of hard ice cracking were great comfort beside depending on surface that was no surface, but only fragile possibility.

Richard, passing over it, nearly stepped clear through that ruined stuff into empty air. . . . And here, with the Shrikes now silent, fear returned redoubled, so Baj and the others moved slowly, uneasily as if in a fever dream . . . and forgot any Jesus, forgot Lady Weather and Lord Winter, and prayed only to the narrow, delicate corruption beneath their cold-numbed feet and red, chapped, wounded hands—unmittened for desperate gripping.

Baj began a prayer for Nancy as she inched across, panting. Then he stopped praying, afraid it would only bring attention, would remind reality that it could let her fall. The prayer unfinished . . . she crossed safe as all the others.

Baj, climbing last, started across crouching as if that made him lighter, less a burden to this span of spoiled snow and frostfeathers. He wished—as he had wished many times, climbing—to reach over his shoulder, loosen the rawhide ties of his awkward bow, his awkward quiver, his dear awkward sword, and let them fall so as not to hinder him. He wished, but didn't do it . . . and went on, crouching, muk-boots sinking deep, so he felt the gulf waiting just beneath them.

He thought the snow bridge trembled. Wasn't sure, but thought he felt it—and out of sympathy, out of a sort of understanding, as if the bridge's difficulty were his, shared by both of them, he went carefully to his knees and lay down, lay full-length on his belly in the worst place—what he was sure must be the worst place, since here the bridge certainly trembled beneath him, eager to let itself go, fall, dissolve into vacancy.

On his belly, he began a sort of slow swimming motion in crumbling snow across the span, gentle as a fish in easy currents. A Shrike had snaked out a line for him to take as the others had taken it to be helped across the last of the bridge . . . hauled up where a great spike of hard ice—blessedly glass-green—was belay.

But something, perhaps a shift in the shallow spoil beneath him, perhaps a faint sound he hadn't known he'd heard . . . something advised him not to kick and lunge to take the braided leather lying only feet away.

Baj accepted that advice while the Shrike—one of the nameless ones—clicked an impatient tongue (exactly like Errol) such a short safe distance above him. A distance greater than to a star.

Baj didn't even shake his head "no." He continued his odd slow swimming—felt absolutely a tremor beneath him—swam on as if *he* were delicate, clotted, and gray, the same sort of stuff exactly. Swam on . . . did not attempt the rope-end when he came near it . . . and was then surprised to come at last where a knife-edged ridge of sound ice rose a little above his left hand.

In sudden panic, he reached out, gripped it—and as he hauled himself up, clinging to that shelf, heard a groan just behind him . . . then a soft *thump* and great hissing, rushing noise as the snow bridge fell away.

Perched to the side on muk-boot spikes while coiling the line, the nameless Shrike shook his head at beginner's luck.

"*Baj* . . .!" Higher, Nancy had looked back and seen the bridge go.

Baj smiled, tried to call back, *"Adventure..."* but found his throat closed to speech.

... That night, hanging suspended in blizzard, they all dozed—to come awake, frightened, when their sleeping sling thrashed hard to the gale... Baj and Nancy clinging close, wrapped in stiff ice-crusted blankets over freezing furs.

* * *

Toward morning—at least what seemed toward morning, the storm slowly eased, rumbled away east, and was replaced by a silence that seemed as loud.

In that frigid stillness, awake, Nancy murmured to Baj the story of her mother's suffering... of the barely remembered breeding-pens of Boston town, when she was a little girl and kept a pet rat named Dandy before they took her away, as they took all children from the mothers.... Then of being assigned to the Companies at her first bleeding-between-the-legs. Of being protected from the worst by Richard, a kind lieutenant... then captain. And, after three years, fleeing with him following the stabbing, and *his* trouble with Major Donald-Fishhawk.... Errol, the mess-cook's bruised chore-boy, trailing along.

Then, WT weeks of wandering... until, one late-winter day, Patience had sailed down to them out of a gray sky, stumbled a little on landing, and said, "I've been watching for two days. And it seems to me, that you foolish lost ones might have something better to do than journey in circles, and cook squirrels for supper."

... Kisses from Baj, then, to comfort her.

Dawn had barely marked the east, when a cheerful Dolphus come sliding down out of darkness on braided leather to kick their swaying nest. "Oh, what a treat we have for you brave climbers!"

"What?" Richard grumbled, hoarse.

" 'What?' " Dolphus reached out to grip the netting and shake them alert. "A day of *rest* is what! You five have nothing to do but loll in your net, chew delicious seal-blubber, sleep, and pee down the Wall. A day of rest—a gift, though it slows us."

"Thank Frozen Jesus," Richard said, as Patience roused, and Errol, yawning, clambered out of the sling to explore.

Baj shoved a stiff-frozen blanket aside, and kissed Nancy good morning. "I think they're concerned they'll lose us."

She peered out of ice-powdered wool and fur to look out where day's first light poured into vacancy. "*I* think they wouldn't mind if we all fell. They've already lost one of their own, and we hinder them."

"Whatever their reason . . ." Baj stood in his parky (balancing carefully on springing netting), breathed-in air as thin and edged as a knife blade, and stretched, feeling muscles easing down his back. "Whatever, I'm grateful."

"And here's more to be grateful *for*." Marcus-Shrike, overhearing, sailed swinging by them, trailing frosting breath, a muk-boot resting in a loop of narrow line. He tossed short sticks of frozen blubber to them as he went.

"Only seal?" Patience sat up in the netting. "Nothing else at all?"

"Those people," Nancy said, as the Shrike climbed his rope like a southern spider, back onto the wall. "—People who don't mourn their dead." She tucked both pieces of blubber beneath her blanket, and sat on them to thaw.

"*Better melt your drinking water as well, Lady . . . under that pretty bottom.*" The Shrike, calling from high above.

"Savages," Nancy said.

"And what's worse," Baj said, "full of very good advice." He found the water flasks among their covers—one chilled to granite, the other only rattling with ice when shaken—grimaced, and tucked them under him.

"Two chicken-birds," Nancy said, "sitting on eggs," and began to giggle.

Richard turned his massive head. "I find no reason, in such a place, for laughter."

"Thaw your water, Captain of the Guard," Baj said, "and become wise."

... Feeling oddly secure in their netting roost, that once had seemed so frail, so insubstantial, Baj and the others—except Errol, who climbed here and there, encouraged by the tribesmen—Baj and the others sat at ease, only standing to stretch, through the day's empty hours.

Patience sang several very old songs for them, her singing voice as light as a girl's. She sang a song about dancing in the dark, and two or three others, while they drifted, dozing, munching half-thawed seal blubber, and drinking ice-melt water. They began conversations that often dissolved into the booming winds of the stupendous landscape they swung above ... above even the trooping clouds that cruised under the early-winter sun over miles and miles of lake and tundra, sending their shadows across the distant mountains far to the south.

The four of them—and sometimes Errol—rested, only occasionally startled as monuments from the heights above, melted free by the sun, came ruffling, strumming past, slowly turning as they fell. . . . The Shrikes did not rest, but chattered among themselves in tribe-talk, clambering over the glacier's face from perch to perch, filing ice-hooks sharp, sewing torn furs and muk-boots, and testing, greasing, rebraiding their slender lines.

... That sweet ease darkened to a wind-whining night—that faded into a next day of sun-blaze off mirror ice, frost ice, ice sea-green, pine-green, gray-green. And ice—the best, the most reliable—a richer blue than any sky.

Climbing, hacking their way up, slowly approaching two miles of height with bone-aching effort in numbing cold became the truth of living—and all else, all memory and expectation, a foolish lie. Breathing, in air so sparse, was additional labor . . . required thought, deliberation, and care not to frost and ruin their lungs.

The fear of falling came and went at odd moments, so that Baj, certain he'd come to terms, would discover—at only the slightest slip—that he had not. And the same, he knew, for Nancy and the others, except for carefree Errol.

The Shrikes, as always, climbed their confident, accomplished way, even having lost a man.

. . . That after-noon, the tilting sun flashing furious reflections off the ice, Richard fell—though only to the stretched and strumming end of his belayed line. Fell, jolted to a savage stop, and spun there, breathless.

Looking down from a rough cornice, Baj saw the great Person's heavy-muzzled face all too perfectly human in terror. The tribesmen saw as well, and Christopher-Shrike, like a copybook angel, descended to Richard, swung him to the ice face—attached an additional slender, braided rope—then persuaded him up.

Toward evening, the wind rising—calling amid immense spires of crystal green and blue—Baj and Richard worked side by side, clinging to a steep and hacking hand-holds. "Now," Richard said, panting at the labor, "—now I know what it is to be *absolutely* fearless. I pissed all that away when I fell. Every drop." . . . And it was true that he'd seemed to climb, since, with greater ease and certainty, as if a pact had been made with gravity.

. . . By the sixth day's morning, Baj and the others, climbing now *with* the Shrikes as well as beside them, found the world beneath and to the south—twenty miles of moraine, then eighty . . . ninety miles of tundra beyond that to the mountains— was now only a feature to them, and meant no more or less than a painting of such things.

Since Henry-Shrike had fallen, no one else had died.

One tribesman had had a little toe turn black after stitching had torn in his left muk-boot and let the cold in. Dolphus-Shrike had cut that toe off with his ice-hatchet's blade—an occasion for laughter among the Shrikes—and the nine-toed tribesman had smiled in good humor, folded cloth to the stump, used sewing-sinew to repair his muk-boot . . . then climbed away.

Baj, by this sixth day, had grown used to exhaustion's visions—found them interesting—but was careful not to be distracted when King Sam Monroe appeared climbing beside him just before sun-straight-up, though dressed in buckskins for hunting. The Achieving King seemed to need no ice hatchets for his holds. . . . Strong fingers, strong wrists. "I like your girl, Baj," he said. "Fox blood does well by her."

"And she'd like you, sir."

The King, climbing quite steadily, had glanced at Baj, smiling. "If I were alive, you mean."

"I . . . suppose I mean that. Yes."

"Look away, son," the King said then. "Look away from me."

Baj did—and there seemed a change of light beside him, a shadow fled, and the King was gone.

That was the best imagining, the richest vision that came to Baj weary on the Wall, since it seemed to him that the King *had* loved him truly as a son—and not only as ward, as responsibility, as an amusing boy. The King's face had been a father's.

And there was something else—an odd thing, but he was certain of it—that if the Khan Toghrul, his First-father, appeared at the Wall, it would be as Baj was falling.

24

Below, in the landscape world, Dolphus-Shrike had said at least six or seven days, and a day of rest, to climb the Wall. And it was late after-noon on the seventh day that they came to the overhang.

Here at its crest, the glacier had thrust out a massive curling wave, like a great sea-roller—but frozen still and hard as granite, though brilliant blue under the sun, and so perfect that many depths were seen in it.

Baj and the others—exhausted veterans now, worn, wind-and-weather burned, bellies aching from days of melt-water and seal-blubber—clung to their pick-perches and examined the thing. The notions of falling, that had to some degree receded as they'd climbed and grown to understand the ice, now came back to them—to Baj at least—with sickening force.

It seemed to him that time for payment might now have arrived under this gleaming great ceiling of gorgeous ice reaching out . . . far out into the air.

And the more disturbing, since the Shrikes were disturbed. Dolphus and the others seemed surprised by this jutting shelf. They hammered ice-hooks in to swing out to left and right . . . surveying to find a way past it.

And found none. Baj, wrists aching, hands stiff claws on the handles of his ice hatchets, saw it in their faces. The overhang ran too far to skirt.

"What are we going to do . . . ?" As she'd grown more tired, Nancy had taken to asking Baj these questions, as if he, who loved her, must know an answer.

"We're going to watch the Shrikes rig lines out beneath it, sweetheart—and probably send one man out, then another, until they're able to climb up and over."

Nancy turned her head, staring up at that immense and shining shelf.

Richard clung close to the ice just past them. "I don't know," he said, and coughed. The freezing air had dried their throats, cracked their lips to bleeding. "—I'm big, maybe too big to hang out there." Though he *was* big, his massive weight of muscle a handicap on vertical places, Richard had shrunk a little in the climb. It had diminished him, brought out the vulnerable human in him very clearly, so he no longer seemed a bear-man—a Moonriser Person—to Baj, but only a big man, and very tired.

"They'll manage, my dear." Patience, annoyed as Errol—above her and restless on a narrow shelf—scattered ice-chips down, had done very well. Slight and strong, though older, and tough with whatever blood her mother had accepted, she stood up against the ice on muk-boot spikes as if part of the Wall. The hem of her colored coat flagged as wind came sweeping past. "Shrikes are good managers. . . ."

As if to prove it, the tribesmen bit off chunks of frozen blubber to chew, clapped mittened hands to warm them, and began to manage . . . muttering among themselves in slurred near book-English.

They gathered almost all line—leaving Baj and the others sharing only two anchored belays and what purchase they'd made for themselves—and handed through the slender braided ropes, checking the greased lines for fray and ice cuts. . . . Jingling bandoleers of steel ice-hooks were examined, and the curved points of ice hatchets, and the spikes strapped to their muk-boots. Careful preparation.

The day was cruelly cold, but clear as the best silvered mirror. Clinging to ice, Baj turned his face from the Wall to see, two miles below, the rest of the earth lying inconsequential. . . . What had been boulders and ice blocks, immense, immeasurable, had now become grains of sand—which, with those infinite lakes reduced to puddles, now made a map of miniatures. What appeared only a patch of tundra, green and brown, seemed to stretch a few feet to little hillocks, whose ranges might be stepped over by a child. . . . And past those, the definite, gentle horizon-curve of the round world itself.

"Worth it," Baj said, his breath frosting.

"What?" Nancy carefully turned from watching the Shrikes' preparations.

"All worth it, to see that."

She followed his gaze . . . clung looking out as Lady Weather might, above and over the earth. "Almost," she said, "—except for losing Henry-Shrike."

There was stirring among the tribesmen . . . a releasing of holds, and changing stances on ice vertical. Then one, Christopher— heavy pack and possibles left hanging from a hammered hook on the Wall's face, his hood thrown back, his mittens off and dangling from sleeve strings—reached out and up to the great ceiling overhead, while two men belayed a line knotted around his waist.

He leaned far out . . . took a small ice-hook from his bandoleer, placed it up against the overhang, and using the flat of his hatchet, hammered it in, listening for the sharp notes of firmly-set. Then he reached back, caught the tossed end of a second line, and fed it through the hook's deep curve, where the steel nearly closed upon itself.

. . . Christopher drew that slender rope through and along, then pulled himself up it to hammer in a second hook, and slipped a loop of his belay line through that. —Then he swung free . . . dangling now farther out with the second line draped over his shoulder. Baj saw the Shrike take a breath, then begin to swing with purpose, back and forth, as the other tribesmen clung to their holds, gripping both lines fixed to anchoring ice-hooks and steel circlets.

Christopher swung out, struck up into the ice ceiling with his hatchet to pick a hold—and failed, the hatchet rebounding as if it struck stone. He swung back, swung forward . . . swung back . . . forward, and struck up for a hold again. The hatchet's pick snagged a place, held, then broke free, and Christopher swung back and away . . . used that momentum to swing forward again, struck up at the ice ceiling a third time, and the pick held.

Dangling in vacancy, he reached up with his free hand to twist a hook shallow into the ice—and hanging from one hatchet, took his second from his belt, hit the ice-hook three hard blows. Then he set and hammered in another.

Tugging for slack, he looped each his lines side by side through this second pair of hooks.

As Christopher swung away, a hook broke—its steel snapping clean with a *crack*—and he fell, seeming slowly . . . almost drifting down, until yanked to a hard halt at his line's end, the belaying Shrikes grunting at the shock.

Christopher spun slowly one way, then the other, his ice hatchets swinging on their cords. Only a worn leather line, slender as a finger, held him above two miles of air.

Nancy said, "No . . . no . . . no."

"The cold," Richard said from his place. "The fucking cold brittles the steel. . . ."

Christopher—Baj saw the Shrike's eyes were closed—swayed back and forth with the wind, the rope knotted tight around his waist so the brown fur of his parky was gathered in.

Then the tribesman opened his eyes, gestured "up" with a thumb, and as the other Shrikes heaved and hauled together from precarious perches, rose in surges up . . . up . . . and up, took another hook from his bandoleer, hammered it in, then gripped and hung from it to gain slack to pass his line through.

Swinging back, then forward from that second set of ice-hooks, he reached out and up, caught a hold with his hatchet's pick . . . then hammered in a third pair, ran the lines through them.

"Brave man," Nancy said. "Brave man . . ."

Laboring, Christopher-Shrike swung to place his fourth pair of hooks. And having traveled that distance along his slender two strands—the free line running through its hooks in parallel with his belay—he swung on above emptiness, to extend his highway.

. . . It seemed to Baj to take a great while for Christopher to reach the edge of the overhang. Once there, out so far, the Shrike hung suspended in air, mirrored beneath its blue ceiling, with both running ropes now knotted to him. He lay there a time to rest.

"Frozen Jesus . . ." Nancy lisping the *Jesus.* "*Not* worth it."

"I don't think," Richard said, "that it will hold me."

"It will hold you," Patience said. "We won't lose you now."

As they watched—even Errol, above them, attentive—Christopher-Shrike, having rested enough, and with both ice hatchets in his hands, crouched precarious at the overhang's edge, a booted foot supported in a rope-loop taut with strain. . . . Then, very quickly, he reached up, drove a hatchet-point into the ice—and hanging from it, lines now sagging—hauled himself up, kicked in boot-spikes, and climbed, swinging his hatchets left and right, onto the overhang's face and out of sight, the ropes feeding after him.

Patience said, "*Marvelous* . . ." The perfect old word—and the more powerful since Patience Walked-in-air (though no longer high as she had) and was familiar with heights.

. . . Then there was only waiting, and the slow periodic paying out of braided lines through six pairs of hooks as Christopher climbed the Wall's crest, unseen.

The sun had slid lower to the west, when both lines drew

taut . . . and there was the faintest shrill whistle, that might have been an eagle's but for its ascending note.

Dolphus-Shrike leaned far out to reach the lines, hauled hard to test them—then swung aside against the Wall, and gestured Paul-Shrike and one of the Nameless to climb out and on them.

Those two unmittened, and swung out hand over hand, swaying from one rope to the other as monkey-animals were said to do in the forests of South Map-America. Hand over hand— and those hands nearly frozen, chapped and cut from cold and climbing.

"I will not be able to do that." Richard shook his head.

Dolphus heard him, and laughed. "We'll haul you over and up like a killed walrus, Captain. You'll wallow, but you'll go."

Another Shrike clambered up to Errol, tapped the boy's nose for attention, then handed him down to the others. Dolphus-Shrike lifted Errol up to the lines—saw him take his grip on each—then let him loose.

Nancy called "*Don't*," but no attention was paid. And none needed, since Errol—apparently enjoying himself—swung along the lines as if the ground lay only just beneath his feet . . . swung out and along the slender ropes to the overhang's edge, then climbed up them as they ran out of sight.

"The rest of you," Dolphus said, "—will be bundles, with short rope-ties hooked to each line. It will be a pleasure trip."

. . . And so it was. Baj and the others became packages, relieved of responsibility. Short lengths of rope were knotted around them, then hooked right and left to the twin lines running out under the ice ceiling, so they had only to draw themselves across, hand over hand, lying on their backs—the blue ice, two feet above their faces, reflecting weariness as they hauled themselves along, supporting the hanging weight of their packs and weapons.

They each trundled across, with a Shrike waiting to transfer their short-rope hooks around the ceiling hooks as they reached them. —Richard first, while a tribesman watched the rig for strain, then Patience, then Nancy . . . and Baj last. It was their easiest time on the Wall.

And remained easy at the overhang's lip. There—still a bundle— each was met by a Shrike on one of two thicker lines lowered from above, ropes hanging down the cresting shelf's great face, a hundred-foot vertical . . . the ice, wind-polished, blazing white in the sun.

Knotted to the free rope, given no chance to climb, they were drawn up to signaling whistles—up in swift surges, scraping . . . spinning off the ice, warding it as best they could.

. . . Baj, having seen Nancy disappear above him, was circled with a heavy line knotted tight enough about his waist to hurt him, then patted on the shoulder by a smiling Paul-Shrike. Paul whistled painfully shrilly, and let Baj go to swing up into the air as hard hauling took his breath away, pained his back as if the line were sawing him in half.

Rising, he struck the ice face several times . . . tried to get his feet up to guard, but spun away.

There was a rounded foam of soft snow above him as he rose . . . the sky above its edge an extraordinary deep blue. The borderline between the snow and that blue seemed another color entirely than either of them, abrupt and perfect.

He was yanked up into the snow—its resistance spilling, clouding around him as he was pulled through it, then dragged a way over gritty surface . . . and left to lie there on his belly.

Lie . . . It was the first time in twelve days that Baj had been able to lie down. The first time his body's weight had stretched out easy on a level, wonderfully pressed down by his pack and what had been the clumsy, maddening impediments of sheathed rapier, dagger, bow, and quiver. The sensation was so wonderful . . . so new and old at once, that he closed his eyes to enjoy it. He heard conversation, people saying something much less important than lying still on a surface that wouldn't let him fall to his death.

"Baj . . ."

"What is it, sweetheart?" Still lying with his eyes closed, feeling muscles easing after days of desperate labor, and the cramps of fear.

"Baj, look."

He opened his eyes . . . and sat up to see they had climbed the Wall.

He and the others—all but Errol—sat or lay in the snow like exhausted children. Most of the climber Shrikes sat also, while their tribesmen—having camped spaced along the crest, waiting—ministered to them, giving them body-warmed water-skins to drink from, laughing and joking with them about what had been, apparently, a near-record slow ascent.

The last of the climbers, Dolphus, came over the rim, stumbled in the snow, but kept his feet. "So far," he said, "—so good." Wonderfully apt, certainly from a copybook.

Baj, reluctant to leave the level even to stand, crawled to Nancy, took hold and hugged her to him, feeling that small strong body deep in plush fur, kissed her and was love-nipped on a chapped lower lip. He squeezed her hard, grappled her to him as if tears of honey might be pressed from golden eyes. . . . His prayer for her, or his avoidance of prayer, had been answered, and she lived.

"Well," Richard said, and coughed, "—we're alive. And thank Frozen-Jesus for it."

"Thank the Shrikes," Baj said.

"Yes," Patience said, "thank the Shrikes." With some effort she got to her feet, and went to those climbers as they sat resting, or stood coiling line, and kissed each on the cheek.

Murmurs from the other tribesmen. Baj counted fourteen, fifteen men. They'd brought no women with them.

A number of long light sleds lay near—with each harnessed team, three pairs of caribou, standing restless, casting the stretched shadows of end-of-day. A small herd of the animals shifted in a rope enclosure, antlers clicking softly as they touched others. . . . Past them, the gently undulating plain of snow, the great glacier's cap, stretched away and away to its own horizon.

The waiting Shrikes, short and sturdy in their caribou parkies and high muk-boots, javelins casual over their shoulders, were taking their friends' heavy packs, rope-coils, and bandoleers of gear from them, to pack on the sleds. . . . Three came to Baj and the others, and shouldered their packs to load. Left them their weapons.

Baj stood, took Nancy's hand, and walked back near the Wall's crest as if to assure himself they'd truly done what they'd done. There, standing safe from that supreme vertical, it seemed to him this snow-prairie was one world, and the land miles below, quite another. So strong a notion was this that he looked up as if a third—a sky-world—might hover still higher over their heads. . . . But there was only depthless blue.

They walked back to Patience and the others; Marcus-Shrike and several tribesmen were standing with them. "You all," Marcus said, "did very well, for strangers. But that witless boy," indicating Errol, who was peeing a pattern on the snow, "—he did best."

"We are very sorry," Patience said—and was certainly going to say "sorry about the loss of Henry-Shrike" when she noticed a change in the tribesmen's faces, so she never finished. And no one else mentioned it, either.

"I know why," Richard spoke low to Baj later, as the Shrikes rocked their sled-runners loose, preparing to travel north. "For them, what is not spoken of is not completely so. They will never want a final good-bye for Henry-Shrike, since that will mean he's truly dead."

Whistles, then. Apparently the Shrikes' equivalent of drums and trumpets. Whistles for the start.

* * *

All the climbers rode for a long while, resting, as the sleds glided behind the caribou over glittering perfect white that undulated slowly up, then slowly down, as if they sailed a calm snow-sea. But after a distance gone toward night and halting, first the Shrikes, then Baj and the others, climbed off to stretch their legs, trotting alongside. Poor trotting, with staggers and tripping at first, even for the tribesmen, the level taking getting used to.

The relief from every instant's threat of death also took getting used to—Baj startling the tribesmen once by diving into the snow to stretch and roll like a hound freed from kennel, in celebration of the gift of safety. Nancy fell to join him, and Richard also lay ponderously down. Then Patience came, and Errol bounded over to flop down beside them. . . . They all mouthed the snow of safety, as the tribesmen turned to watch them, and the sleds slid by.

Then all were on their feet again, trotting unsteadily over the snow in sunset light after the Shrikes' steady-pacing teams, whose harness jingled with steel-and-copper sequins. They hurried along the narrow ruts the sled-runners left behind, Baj holding Nancy's mittened hand to confirm he had her still.

. . . At nightfall in a sled-circled camp—the rising moon blurred by buffeting wind, blowing ice-crystals—Baj and the others, drowsy as tired children after meat and blubber cooked over cold-dried caribou dung, were steered to hide-sheltered fur pallets. Where, nested with Nancy in an odd little leather tent pitched within a larger round one—for additional warmth, apparently—Baj had no reason but fear-remembered to jolt awake, certain a braided climbing-line had parted, and the long fall begun.

. . . Then, what more delicious than safety realized? Safety, warmth, and love, with Boston's North Gate seeming only a Map-place, to be found in some forever future, but never now.

25

The glacier's snowy plain—broken only here and there by stupendous crevasses whose depths, blue vanishing to black, echoed to no tossed chunks of ice—proved otherwise featureless but for its gentle rises, gentle descents.

It became a dream's frozen landscape for Baj as they traveled on, trotting beside the sleds, then riding for a while, then off to trot again. They traveled as if through time, on time's white and frozen road—from day to night, night to day, day to night once more—with only occasional howling storms come over endless ice to fasten them to a present.

The Shrikes ran almost silent over the glacier's broad back, but for impatient whistles, signings of this task or that to be done: lashings to be checked; the restless caribou stung with whipped leather lines to stay hauling each sled in harness together; scouts to go running ahead . . . scouts to drop behind to catch up later. Then, as early evening fell in shrouds of hazing ice-crystals or blowing snow, the caribou unharnessed to wander in a guarded herd, pawing the snow for last season's lichen. The sleds unpacked, the great round hide-tents—"biggies"—set up supported by long fanned struts of precious southern pine. Then "bitties"— little hide tents placed as dens within the great ones—were pitched with tensioned cords tied strut to strut.

And all labor made twice—three times—the labor by cold and wind. At its gentlest, the wind sliced slowly, shallowly as a stroking razor; at its fiercest, it struck like an ax.

When—rarely now, as days went by—the sun came flashing off the ice, it blinded for hours anyone who stared without slit-goggles to take pleasure in it.

The cold days' work wore fingers raw through every glove or mitten. Made numb faces, feet, and hands. So Baj saw, in their world, the forming of the Shrikes by weather with no mercy, no forgiveness in it, where only green lichen and the caribou made life possible at all.

Still, there was an ease. When lying exhausted in a close bitty-tent, with Lord Winter bellowing a gale outside the biggy, Baj rested wonderfully warm by a single tallow candle and the heat of naked Nancy beside him on the furs—her odor mingling fox with weary girl—so his sleep was the richest he'd known, a pleasure anticipated through each traveling day.

. . . More than a Warm-time week had certainly passed when this fine sleep was broken by an animal's bleating scream—and Baj was off the furs and out of the bitty-tent, struggling into his parky, hopping to get fur trousers on, and muk-boots. Then out of the biggy's entrance-flaps into still and absolute cold under rich moonlight, bending to set his bow. Nancy was coming out behind him, scimitar drawn, when the animal screamed again—and Baj saw, an easy stone's throw away, a great mound of snow with dead-black eyes standing upright over a fallen caribou. The mound of snow opened dreadful jaws, bent for a great ripping bite, and the caribou's screams ceased.

Icy arrow nocked to the string, Baj stood clear of a sled's heaped load, drew to his ear—and as he released, was struck hard across the face with a whipping *crack* as the bow exploded in his hand. Its ruins hung by the bow-string as Shrikes came running in shuttling moon-shadow, setting javelins to their atlatles.

The white bear turned toward them. Annoyed, unafraid, one huge paw resting on his prey.

"A relative!" Richard, heavy double-bitted ax in hand, had come up beside Baj.

The javelins began to hum, the Shrikes grunting with effort at each throw, and Baj saw what their atlatles provided—another foot-and-a-half of throwing leverage as they whipped the light spears away. The javelins flicked over the snow, far, and almost quick as arrows. They hummed like short-summer bees, swarming, converging on the bear, impaling him *thump thump thump* so he staggered, snarling, quilled with them. He turned to pace away as if disgusted, leaving spattered blood black in moonlight.

The Shrikes, with shrill celebration whistles, ran him down, thrusting javelins here and there—and as the great bear stumbled, two leaped on its massive snowy back, hacking, stabbing with their knives as it moaned, shuddered, and lay down to die while still the long knives worked away.

It was a sample of Shrikes in battle, and sobering.

Richard set his ax on his shoulder. "Your bow . . ."

"Went to pieces."

"Must have frozen through on the Wall, Prince!" Dolphus-Shrike returning from the killing of the bear. "Too many woods glued together . . ." He tossed a javelin in the air, caught it. "In Lord Winter's country, simplest is best."

"Yourself excepted, I suppose."

"I," Dolphus-Shrike said, "—am the exception that proves the rule." And on that fine copybook quote, strolled past.

The tribesmen retrieved the huge hide only—and squatted around it in the snow, industrious in the moon's uncertain light, scraping it clean of fat and sinew with their knives. They brought no meat to camp.

"Eat black bear or brown bear," Marcus-Shrike, answering Baj's question, "—and you get strong. But eat white bear, and you get sick and sometimes die. There's a badness in the flesh, for certain in the liver."

"No one in Boston," Patience said, "—eats white bear. Same reason. Either tiny worms in the meat, or something unfortunate in the liver."

" 'Unfortunate.' " Marcus-Shrike shook his head. "So much meat left to the ravens and white foxes."

. . . After the encounter with the bear, Baj looked for other interruptions, other events as they traveled. But there were none—except a painful interlude, when Patience plucked out the stitching in his cheek, and the side of his head. . . . Otherwise, nothing to vary the running alongside the sleds to spare the laboring teams, nothing to vary the occasional ride to rest, the sled's runners whispering, sliding through snow behind the pleasant tinkling of decorations on the caribou's harness. . . . Patience, usually running with them, sometimes Walked-in-air—but low, beneath the horizon's line of sight, and watchful of sudden crevasses falling away beneath her. . . . Once, as she trotted beside him, Baj heard her murmuring to her son, as if the child might hear her over a wilderness of ice and snow. *"I'm coming to you, darling. My sweet, sweet boy . . ."*

They traveled through various weathers. As if to a rhythm Lord Winter might be beating out, there came brutal cold in brilliant sunshine days, when the snow plain flashed and sparkled unbearably bright, so even the eye-masks were insufficient. Then, Baj and the others—the tribesmen, too—ran sometimes with eyes shut, depending on the sounds of the rest to stay close, and not stray out and away over the blazing prairie to wander alone and blind in searing light.

There were those days, and—almost alternately—days of blizzard, not quite as cold, but battering by howling wind and driven snow that flayed exposed skin, so Baj imagined the Wolf-General, head thrown back, howling as her condemned were flayed on Headquarters Street.

It came to him, as they ran and sledded, that the affairs of Sunrisers or Moonrisers would always seem of less importance, since Lady Weather had administered her lessons of the Wall, and the glacier's plain of snow. They were all only climbers, only travelers-by, whether Sunriser Kings or Khans, Moonriser Generals or Boston Talents. Even dear Nancy—and himself—were only come . . . to go, while the cold-struck earth, seeming so mighty a traveler, rolled on through even colder, grander emptiness, that noticed it not at all.

. . . As the days passed, then a second WT week, the drinking of snow melted in canteen or water-skin tucked against the belly, the chewing of seal blubber and strips of caribou slow-roasted over dung-fires—became the only way, and thoughts of other drink, other food, other weather, only foolishness. The climbing weariness was long gone, and Baj and the others ran as the Shrikes ran, and rested rarely.

Sometimes, in the evenings, he and Nancy fenced lightly—cautious for their steel's fragility in such cold—and both practiced hurling javelins from atlatles, providing amusement for the Shrikes, who stood out beyond the sleds as targets for them, considering that safer than bystanding.

"I see no reason," Dolphus-Shrike said, watching them one evening as their javelins gadded hissing off to left or right, "—I really see no reason why we Shrikes should not rule the world."

. . . Days later, in a clouded gray dawn following a snowstorm more severe than usual, the Shrikes rose only to squat in circles—as if around ghost fires—chewing the inevitable sealblubber. Waiting, not traveling.

Baj and the others stood together, also chewing.

"Well," Patience said, "—who's going to ask, to be certain?"

They'd learned that the tribesmen, like all primitives—and, of course, many of those not primitive—counted power in momentary increments, so that to *have* to ask indicated weakness, and to *be* asked, strength, no matter how unimportant the question.

Baj sighed, and went to ask.

"Why have we stopped?"

The Shrikes at that circle seemed surprised. *Why?* Why have they *stopped?* Startled at such ignorance.

The Shrike named Paul looked up at him. "We stopped, because we're here."

"Here . . ."

The Shrike pointed with his thumb. "Boston—nine WT miles that way."

"Ah . . ." Baj thought of avoiding the next question, which would cost him respect for at least the day—then remembered he'd been a prince, and asked it. "How do you know?" There was certainly no sign of habitation . . . no buildings to be seen anywhere in that direction.

Satisfied smiles around the circle at that. "We smell it," Paul-Shrike said. "The city breathes, farts, as a man breathes and farts. It smells on the wind."

Baj found that closeness oddly shocking to hear—snow travel, and for nearly three weeks, did not lend itself to arrivals. Even less, to this arrival.

He went back to the others with the news. "I thought so," Patience said, and Richard nodded. They had all thought so—from wind-carried odor apparently—except of course for Errol, who neither knew nor cared.

Nancy took Baj gently by the nose. "Sunrisers are poor smellers."

"The Shrikes knew."

"The Shrikes are savages," she said, and leaned up to kiss the nose she'd pinched.

"But no houses . . . no structures at all."

"Boston, Baj," Patience said, "is in the ice, and of the ice."

"Yes, I knew it was, but . . . *all* of it?"

"*All* of it," Nancy said, and tried to pinch his nose again, so had to be parried, then hugged. . . . And doing so, Baj thought of the women waiting in Boston-town. They, so soon to be slaughtered, would feel much as Nancy felt in his arms, sturdy, small, and soft over slender bones. His heart began a familiar tattoo. It sounded in his chest as if it had concerns of its own, of fear, and preparation for action.

"Baj . . ." Golden eyes, that saw into him as the Shrikes' javelins had entered the bear. "Baj—when we go into the city, I will kill the women for you. Richard and I, and Patience and the Shrikes will kill them. You stand guard for us against the Constables coming."

"Yes," Richard said, his breath smoking in morning cold.

"No. I'll do what must be done."

"And be changed," Patience said, "—from Who-was-a prince?"

"Or not," Baj said. "How many innocents died under the yataghans of my First-father's *tumans*? How many under the sabers of my Second-father's cavalry? Though neither might have wished it so." He tried a smile. "Who am I, to deny my heritage?"

Breezes, that had brought the odors of the city to the camp, slowly began to strengthen as the night's storm wind—reversing its track—now began to sweep back from a dark horizon. Small swirls of snow were spinning across the glacier's frozen prairie.

* * *

The Shrikes, having considered, had risen as one to travel through blowing snow. A semicircular route, a day-long curve at first to the north . . . then, by night, around east to settle at last where blizzards had driven their burdens into great snow-dunes, only three Warm-time miles from Boston's north gate.

Baj, trotting beside laboring caribou, had time enough to think of other things than necessary murders. . . . He imagined one-eyed Howell Voss, certainly now the King—a man in his fifties, thoughtful, merciless—and with a Queen his equal. Many spoiling heads, all those friends of New England, of the Coopers, would be grinning from Island's battlements. That King, that Queen, and the old ferret, Lauder, would have hunted them down.

A lesson, as well, to the whole Rule—Middle-Kingdom, North Map-Mexico, Map-Texas, and the Western Coast. What Small-Sam Monroe had achieved, would stand.

And the Prince Bajazet? The adopted brother hunted and likely lost in the east's savage wilderness—at most a minor legend, and soon forgotten.

There was . . . a comfort in the knowledge of it. A freedom the then Prince Bajazet had never known, even in brothel brawls along the river. What he'd been, had vanished as if swept away on the Mississippi's current. What he became, would be of his own carpentry.

Commencing, of course, with the slaughter of innocents. The hostage womens' blood, girls' blood, would run along the rapier's blade to obscure its legend. *WITH GOOD CAUSE* . . .

Under a setting moon, after the last day and night of traveling from the Wall, they reached the snow-dunes—the only major rises Baj had seen in more than two weeks on the plain—and the Shrikes prepared to shelter in them.

First, they loosed their caribou herd—and all the teams but three pairs—scattered them to wander back into freezing emptiness. Then they killed the last—cut their throats as they stood in harness, so the animals, spattering blood blackened by moonlight, slowly knelt in place as if praying to whatever Beast-Jesus cared for them.

Baj and the others then joined the labor of butchering out— Baj realizing as they did, that the Shrikes, expecting death, had left themselves no way to escape it.

The offal—and the sleds, still loaded with shelters and gear— were snow-buried for concealment against passers-by, under drifts the next snowfall would bury deeper.

. . . It was by the last of moonlight, that the Shrikes began to burrow snow caves deep into the dunes, for shelter and concealment—mining in with knives and ice hatchets and hands to run six to eight-foot tunnels into darkness, then shape and hollow small round buried dens, their snow hard-packed, and with only a javelin's piercing, higher, for through ventilation.

Baj and Richard, having watched, and crawled into one to see how it had been done, began their own—which ended badly when their entrance tunnel collapsed, so Nancy and Patience (Errol tongue-clicking, capering useless) had to dig them out.

Dolphus-Shrike strolled from moonlight, smiling. " 'If at first you don't succeed . . .'" A partial and annoying quote. Then strolled away, still smiling, when Richard snarled and picked up his ax.

An annoying quote—but proved. The "try again" was successful, though the den they scooped out with great effort (and seeming large in the labor) was so small they packed it like barreled salt fish. Errol, restless, uneasy in darkness relieved by a single tallow candle, kicked and bit when crowded, until Nancy lost her temper and hit him on the head.

Oddly, it made for a very comfortable place of sleep through the day—except for condensation dripping—warmer than swaddling furs, and out of the wind. Here, by flickering candlelight, with rich twining odors, the silence interrupted only by Errol's restlessness—and once, Richard's thunderous fart—Baj lay with Nancy squeezed close against him, so close that only a small unlacing of fur and leather was necessary to find her dampness and enter it, so they lay locked . . . hardly moving, happy, and complete.

It was a sweetness so great, so simple, it made Baj weep. Nancy knew it, even in near dark, and licked the tears from his face.

. . . As the vertical terrors of ice-climbing had become a way of life, then the endless snow prairie another—so days of denning became a third, crawling from snow-tunnels at night for the necessaries, for exercise (mad moonlit races through the dunes), and to share portions of raw caribou, caribou heart, and caribou liver with the Shrikes. It became simply how things were done.

Hibernating in the snow-cave's candlelight, Baj once roused from a dream of his birthday, a celebration at Island. His birthday . . . his birthday . . . What was the present date, Warm-time? Not deep enough, yet, into Lord Winter's grip. On the last day of the ancient October, he would be twenty-one.

Time became built of sleep, and waking from sleep, of crawling carefully through the narrow tunnel to eat, then squatting in blowing snow to be rid of what had been eaten . . . though the rhythm was interrupted once, when seven of the Shrikes came trotting in moonlight from a scout south, with no news yet of the Wolf-General's Guard, though with news of a sort. A family of hunters—New Salem trash, out after musk-ox or bear—had been found by the Shrikes, and killed for secrecy. A baby had been considered to be spared, then not.

" 'Can't make an omelette . . .'" Dolphus-Shrike, all silver from the moon, had winked at Baj and Patience, who, out for rations, had heard the scouts' report.

"I'm getting weary of Warm-time quotes," Baj said, as they crawled, dragging a raw rack of caribou ribs into the narrow night-dark tunnel to their den.

"I've been tired of them for years," Patience said, coming behind him. "Those people knew too much—and too little."

. . . Raw ribs in the den, meat stripped and chewed—chewed longest by Baj and Patience and Errol, chewed briefest by Richard and Nancy, as tearers and gulpers. Then the long bones splintered for bloody marrow.

The next two long, warm, close days, ended at dawn of the third, with Paul-Shrike bulky at their den's entrance.

"The Guard has come to the Township's south," he said, then backed out down their tunnel.

It seemed to Baj somehow unfair, and much too soon to have to come out of warm caves a last time, and stand in slate-gray light, a bitter wind blowing. They gathered in groups, unsheltered in daytime at last, the tribesmen testing the steel points of their javelins, the edges of their knives. . . . Patience wielded her scimitar against hissing wind gusts—Nancy the same in imitation— while Richard left his great ax at ease over his shoulder, familiar past any exercise.

Baj drew what seemed a reluctant rapier, and gently tried the narrow blade's flex and spring. He cut his left thumb slightly, touching the edge.

As the wind died to icy-breezing, Nancy came crunching to him over the snow. "You stand guard for us, Prince—once we're in."

Baj shook his head. "I said, *no*. The women, the girls I kill—you won't have to."

"Oh, Baj . . ." She looked away from him, eyes cloudy with tears, "—we should have seen that you ran free, and not have taken and used you for this."

He hugged her, their sword-blades clashing slightly in the embrace, as if jealous. "Then, sweetheart, I would have had no fox-girl . . . and no happiness."

* * *

Baj had imagined a great gate, pillars upholding grand doors of ice as the north entrance to Boston-town. But no such thing.

There was instead an immense mouth—barely visible with the sun just risen—roughly round, and two . . . three bow-shots across, a vast open mouth in the plain of snow. It was a gape of shadows sinking to blackness, where icy flurries blew fountaining up on a deep humming wind that bore the breath of many lives lived far below.

"Home," Patience said. "And my son."

"The Constables . . ." Dolphus-Shrike stood beside them. "We'll do what we come to do—but not be butchered before."

"The Watcher-constables station along Third Tier and lower, now," Patience said, and spit a blown snowflake from her lip. "And only a few. We New Englanders have grown soft with cleverness. . . . They used to stand Watch-sentry up here in Lady Weather's apron, and those without Warming-talent died of it sometimes."

More driven snow came stinging, as if to demonstrate.

"—Start your people down the Steps-forever, Dolphus. The

Watchers will not think to guard themselves against a Boston-Talent." She drew her scimitar. "None on Third Tier will live to meet you, or toss warning whistle-balls below."

"So you promise—" Dolphus said, but didn't trouble to finish, since Patience had side-stepped away . . . side-stepped again, and swept up into the air. She sailed out in a flutter of striped wool greatcoat, to soon be seen tiny in snow-blown emptiness over Boston's great, dark, deep-droning mouth, her sword-blade a last wink of light.

Then she fell away.

. . . It took a time for the Shrikes, seeking around the gate's rim, to find the first wide step—deep chipped from ancient ice in the gateway's wall, and gritty with wind-blown snow.

Then the Shrikes led, with Richard, Errol, Nancy and Baj following behind. The ice steps gradually . . . gradually spiraled down to the left—ice steps hacked into a wall of ice, with Lord Winter above, and darkness below.

One slow . . . slow great-circling down, then another—the humming vacancy to their right, the gate's rough-finished ice wall harsh against their left. The grit of filtering powder snow made stepping down without slipping just possible, though it seemed to Baj that each step he took, each step Nancy took, was dangerous. He'd thought he was done with steep places. . . .

Errol capered easily—stepped up, stepped down—but Richard went ponderous, and cautiously.

. . . After what seemed a very long time, Baj, looking up, saw they had descended deep. High above them, the gate mouth formed a perfect great circle of morning light. He saw—as if he were Patience, and drifting out in empty air—their small party seeming even smaller, tiny figures along the narrow edge of an immense well of darkness.

It struck him that for the last many weeks of flight, he had always found himself in grand landscapes, gigantic features diminishing him to insignificance, so that his true self—so minor, though adamant—was revealed at last, formed on those huge anvils of perception.

. . . Near the end of the second great circling down, Dolphus-Shrike stood waiting, pressed against the gate's ice wall, then stepped out to follow Baj just behind.

His bright javelin-head swept out to the right in demonstration. "This is death *before* dying," he said, apparently uneasy at being so far beneath the snow plain.

" 'After the first death,' Baj said, "—there is no other.' "

It was the perfect ancient quote. So fine, so apt, that Dolphus-Shrike was left with no reply, and they stepped down silent behind the others, as all were silent but for the thump and scrape of muk-boot leather, and weapons' soft clink and rattle. Sounds barely heard under North Gate's deep thrumming breath.

. . . The great circle of gray morning above them had been diminished by their third slow, descending spiral, when the Shrikes stopped and stood still on the steps below. Dolphus eased past and went carefully down to see. A pause, then . . . before the Shrikes moved on.

When they reached the place, Errol stood and stared, tongue-clicking. A man in furs and bronze half-armor lay on frosting scarlet steps beneath a smoking oil-lamp. His head lay beside him, separate, its eyes a little open, its bearded face remote, dreaming.

"Patience," Nancy said.

A weapon leaned against the niche wall—a tall staff halberd, topped with ax, hook, and point. The Watcher-constable, greeting a Boston-Talent come Walking-in-air down the dawn's first light, had not reached for it.

. . . As had hiking the Smoking-mountains, as had climbing the Wall . . . so the endless stepping down became Baj's world, all their worlds. This was what was done, carefully, and nothing else. The shrinking circle of the brightening winter day above, the column of breathing darkness to their right—darkness now relieved a little by filtering beams of sunlight—were of little interest compared to steps of ice, with hundreds and hundreds left behind . . . hundreds and hundreds waiting.

Baj's knees ached, his leg muscles burned as if a fire stood beside them. He looked down, and saw that Richard limped a little. Nancy and Errol, so slim and slight, still went sprightly, untroubled—as Baj *was* slightly troubled—by the yearning tug of that gigantic cylinder of emptiness beside them, as if falling might fill it for a little while.

"Careful," Baj called. "Nancy, careful . . ."

The Shrikes hadn't paused as they came to each of the next four Watchers. One of those—naked but for his armor—had died still smiling a greeting as Patience came sailing down to him. Another, stricken, had huddled in his sentry niche, been struck again, and disemboweled. . . . Which made for careful stepping past.

The fourth constable had fought. Freezing blood twinkled on his halberd's point. He'd then apparently received a cut that hacked his knee. A second to his face.

This last, like the first to die, had lost his head. . . . Patience had given none the time to toss a warning whistle-ball into the Gate's gulf.

. . . The Shrikes, Baj and the others following, went down the Fourth Tier, and Fifth, circling . . . circling always to the right. Then, the Shrikes stood still on the steps.

"Light," Nancy said, her voice hard to hear in the vibrating drone of upwelling air, air now even richer with odors of life and life's doings.

"Light," Patience agreed, from emptiness just above them. "Lamplight below, and Boston-town." She came to settle—the morning's sun a distant brightening disk over her shoulder—came down, stumbled on a step, and recovered in Richard's swift grip. "It is, despite everything foolish, everything cruel, the wonder of the world."

"How bad?" Richard said to her, considering blood on a halberd's point.

"Caught a little skin along my ribs." Patience slid her hand beneath her open coat, brought the hand out stained dark. "I think he knew me, knew I had no business here any longer."

"What of that light?" Dolphus-Shrike, climbing back to them.

A soft rich red-gold glow lit the last tier of steps far below, so the steps' chipped ice glistened.

"Last tier," Patience said, raising her voice a little for the other Shrikes to hear. "Another turn and we will be on North Gallery. . . . And below that gallery is a boulevard-thoroughfare—Adams—and a muster yard."

"Constables . . ."

"Yes, Dolphus. Their Formations, the headquarters for North Gate is held there."

"How many?" Baj said.

"Three Formations. Over seven hundred men, with officers and band."

". . . Then we certainly wait," Baj said, "until the Wolf-General moves against the city, and those people march south."

"Or we're discovered here," Dolphus-Shrike tapped his javelin's butt on an ice step, "and someone throws a fucking whistle-ball down. Then 'those people' will come up and cut us into bait."

"Have a busy time," Richard said, "coming up against us on these steps."

"Not as busy," Baj said, "as we would have, trying to go down against them."

"The Watchers are dead," Patience said, "and no relief till after-noon. No one will climb the steps to meet us. . . . Take your people down, Dolphus, but carefully."

"On your head, lady." Dolphus-Shrike started down to his people. "On all our heads. . . ."

* * *

The last few steps—no longer Steps-Forever—Baj became worried for Nancy, a slip now seeming somehow more likely, so he gripped the hood of her parky as they went, Errol capering below them.

Then he saw Shrikes stumble down the way, saw them stagger at being on a level at last, so they stepped oddly for a distance.

. . . Eleven final steps counted, and he and Nancy and Richard did the same, stepped down and stumbled, their leg-muscles cramped—but cramps easing as they marched along on evenness at last through what seemed an ice-tunnel, a tunnel wide as a royal road. "Thank Frozen-Jesus," Richard said, "for being off those fucking stairs."

Then Patience, running from behind as fast as if she flew, coat flapping, called softly loud, *"Leave them!"*

The Shrikes, ahead, held still as she and the others caught up. Nancy reached to grip Errol's arm, keep him with her.

In warming light, in a steady draft of odorous air, Dolphus and the other Shrikes held javelin points to six brown-furred bulks clinging to the ice of the tunnel's wall. Baj saw great yellow incisors, small black-button eyes looking down at them, observant, apparently unafraid. . . . There were clawed, black, thin-fingered hands, and splayed clawed feet, webbed, clinging to the tunnel's ice. Each strapped a leather sack and small steel adze from a rounded shoulder. . . . There was a sharp and oily odor.

"Leave them!" Patience jostled the Shrikes aside. "They're Carver-Persons—they shape the town's ice, keep it proper."

"I've heard of these, but why let them live?" Dolphus kept his javelin-point at one Person's throat.

"Because . . ." Patience took hold of the javelin shaft, pushed it aside, "Because they are beaver-bred, and not for sense—only for chipping ice and removing what they've chipped. They don't speak . . . and will give no warnings."

"Still, why leave them, perhaps to come behind us?"

"They make and remake Boston, is *why*, Dolphus. Leave them."

Dolphus-Shrike sighed a small cloud of frost, said, "As you say, lady," and raised his javelin's point as the other tribesmen raised theirs.

26

Into growing brightness and richer-scented air—but air still freezing cold—they traveled the tunnel to a glittering blaze of light, then stopped, huddling there.

"North Gallery," Patience said. "Dolphus, move—move your people. There'll be no one. The gallery's for Change-of-Watchers . . . for Carvers."

The Shrikes stayed reluctant, shading their eyes from the light. Baj stepped past them . . . and walked out into openness, glitter, sparkle, so he squinted down the gallery—narrow, and vanishing into distance—and out past its carved-ice railing into a towering vaulted space, a brilliant dream of ice columns ranking away, ice ceilings past any bow-shot's reach, and reach again. And this apparently only the first in a succession of great chambers along a wide avenue of frosted ice—public spaces grand as any he'd seen in Island's stone.

"Lady *Weather* . . . !" Nancy come with Errol to stand beside him. "I never saw this. Only the Pens . . ."

It was impossible at first to look with open eyes into the gleam and glare of hundreds . . . perhaps thousands of great whale-oil lamps, each apparently backed by panels of mirror glass, and hung high in chain-looped chandeliers down those great halls, reflecting and re-reflecting off walls of polished clear ice, columns of ice shaded green or blue, roofs frosted a brilliant silver. . . . The brightness flared, and seemed to chime, as if too much for sight alone. Beneath these clustered lamps, occasional great tethered banners—black and white, red and yellow, rippled out on a steady frigid wind, so a sky of blazing light and shifting color was made for Boston-town.

Baj had imagined the city—but not imagined well enough.

He raised a hand, as all the others except Patience raised their hands, to shade their eyes until they grew accustomed. But still he saw well enough, over a carved-ice balustrade, to make out Sunriser true-humans a bow-shot below—men, women, and children—some calling out in Patience's crisp accent exactly, and all hurrying along the ice-paved boulevard. Hurrying . . . and some, running.

"They know," Richard said. "They know the Guard has come to South Gate."

Many of the Boston people wore only colored-cloth skirts or trousers dyed in bright blues, yellows, and reds, so women's breasts and men's chests were bare; others—and all the children—were wrapped thick in furs, furs also brightly colored, many dyed in stripes to show like snow-tiger pelts. . . . Most men and women seemed to wear their hair combed out long, to their shoulders—except that some young men wore a single thick braid, with colored ribbons knotted in it.

The near-naked were Warming-talented, Baj supposed; the furred, those who were not. And needed furs against the bitter breeze blowing down the gallery . . . blowing through the great high-ceilinged spaces and along the roadway below—the freezing guarantee of Boston's columned halls of ice despite lamp-warmth, and human warmth, beneath the great glacier's overbearing.

It was . . . as if a scene from dreaming, but brilliantly bright. Baj took off a mitten, and gripped the gallery's ice rail, so the shock of cold might wake him.

"Stand back," Patience said, and tugged at Baj's parky. "Back and out of sight from the boulevard. These Constables haven't yet marched south."

"And may *not* march south," Marcus-Shrike squatted by the gallery's ice wall with the other tribesmen, "if the Wolf-General has changed her mind about attacking."

As if to prove the possibility, Baj, crouching low, saw through thick-carved ice balusters a man come from a passageway below, to stand leaning on a halberd's staff. This man—pale, bearded, corded with muscle—was naked but for a bronze cuirass. He wore no boots, stood barefoot on ice in a city of ice.

"An officer, Baj," Patience stooped beside him, "—proving Warming-talent. A Formation commander at least, though I don't remember him. . . . Well, perhaps Franklin Peabody, though he looks too young to be Franklin."

"Whoever," Richard had come on all fours to join them . . . Nancy close behind, gripping Errol's arm. "—he seems to be a *worried* Sunriser. Has heard of trouble coming."

"Which better come soon," Nancy said. "If one of these people Walk-in-air, they'll see us up here, call those Constables."

"No." Patience shook her head. "It isn't done to air-walk in town, unless in emergency or for lamp-tending. We're safe here for a while."

As she spoke, Baj saw her hand was trembling, saw she now seemed weary, older, matching her silver hair at last. . . . Perhaps, he thought, from killing the Watchers down the Gate.

As he noticed, Nancy said, "Your wound, dear one," and opened Patience's colored coat. It was a seeing and knowing together that Baj had found more and more, is if he and Nancy were becoming a wiser, more observant creature than either was, alone.

"Nothing," Patience said, but held still.

"There now. . . ." Nancy lifted clotted torn shirting away. "Runs along the rib."

"Little enough." Patience set Nancy's hand aside, drew her wool coat closed. "I'm alive." . . . Though her eyes, black and gleaming, seemed to Baj more than alive—as if the young Patience, tireless, still lay behind them.

They crawled back to settle against the wall with the Shrikes, who huddled in their furs against the cold flowing with the slow river of wind down the township's vaulted spaces.

The voices of the people passing below seemed to Baj oddly

noisy—beyond their clipped accent—and high-pitched. "Frightened," he said.

Nancy leaned against him, soft beneath fur's softness. "And who is not?"

Dolphus-Shrike, down the way, had heard them. "And time," he said, "—*past* time for these ice-den fuckers to feel fear."

"Still," Richard said, "the Guard will only be demonstrating at South Gate. It's shallower than the North—"

"Much shallower," Patience said. "With double-staircases, and broader passage."

"—And the more easily reinforced by the city, because of that." Richard hummed a moment, thinking. "The Guard will come hard enough to draw them south—but then, three and a half thousand of these city soldiers, defending, will be too many for them. Sylvia Wolf-General will be fortunate to be able to retreat her companies."

"The attempt," Baj said, "should be enough for us."

. . . They waited against the ice gallery's wall, the tide of cold seeming to muffle further talk, so they became silent watchers, silent listeners in a glittering palace of crystal reflections, the precincts of Boston-town.

Beneath them, on the boulevard, New Englanders in rich-colored furs or few clothes at all hurried past on worry's business, sounding uneasy voices. A few towed little white dogs on cords, dogs small as rabbits but very lively.

Then, through and over everything—vibrating in Baj's bones—there was a grand note struck . . . then struck again, that sang and rang up the boulevard. A great bell's tolling.

"That," Patience said, "that is the bell of alarm. —I've never heard it struck, except in Constable-drill. No one now alive has heard it seriously struck." Still crouching, she drew her scimitar. "—There are two dreadful great bells, and it is the first. The Guard *is* attacking at South Gate."

The great instrument tolled again, its voice deep, resonant, and rich as Lord Winter's voice might be. . . . Then again.

"Not too soon," Marcus-Shrike said, and Dolphus gestured the other tribesmen ready.

"The Wolf-General," Nancy said, "has keep her word."

"Yes," Baj said, loosening rapier and dagger in their sheaths, "—and expects us to do the same." It seemed to him now a sad, inevitable tragedy. The Guard, Boston's Made-Person sword and shield, had come home to their gate at last, come concerned no longer for their suffering mothers' lives. Those, already decided lost—and with them, the city's dark and ancient leverage.

. . . The bell's continuing slow-measured notes rang in Baj's ears. There had been bells hung at Island, bells in chapel to sing songs to Floating-Jesus. But no bells as great as this—and hung, no doubt, in a tower of ice that trembled, shining, as the bronze spoke. —Baj found he feared now only for Nancy, and the killing to come. All other concerns, as for himself, were winnowed away. It was an odd sort of freedom to feel.

He crouched with the others, his fur hood up, his breath frosting in the air, and imagined—as if from a great distance—the life he and Nancy might have had together, but for this. He saw them somehow at Island . . . welcomed at Island. Nancy wearing the paneled dress, the gleaming jewels of a Lady Extraordinary, so her narrow lovely face was framed in fisher-cat fur, her slender throat banded in sapphires and silver. . . . They would have had chambers in East tower, and he would have handed her down stairways and along tapestried hallways—their harsh stone so much warmer than Boston's ice. Would have handed her down and along, her far-southern cottons and silks rustling beside him.

King Howell Voss, one-eyed and ferocious as Warm-time's God-Odin, would have made her a favorite. She might have sung her high, harsh notes in quick counterpoint to his strumming banjar. . . . With the years, all at Island would have come to love her, and found her golden fox's eyes a pleasure. . . .

There were shouts of command below—then a crash of many *little* bells.

Those sounds became a swift, rhythmic, pounding jangle over the continuing ponderous, paced thunder of the alarm. . . . Baj, Richard, and several Shrikes, keeping low, went to the gallery's balustrade and peered down at the boulevard now filling with grim men, rank on rank in bronze half-armor, chest and back— many lightly clothed beneath it, others colorfully furred, some naked but for the metal. All carried halberds slanted over their right shoulders.

Bell staffs—Baj had read of them, but never seen one—rose at the front of every long column . . . then were struck down together in a great ringing chorus, and the hundreds of Constables stepped off together, left feet first—booted or bare. They swung away down the boulevard to the rhythm of shaken bells, so their gleaming halberds' heads—each ax, hook, and point—swayed all together, a sparkling awning of bright steel above them as they marched.

"Soldiers," Richard said, "whatever they're called."

Dolphus-Shrike nodded. "Yes, soldiers. . . . Patience, do they go to South Gate?"

"Wait." She stood up to watch. "If they turn on the Street of Flowers . . ."

Baj, Richard, and Dolphus-Shrike also stood to watch the wide formations march away through shimmering light, frosting breaths streaming behind them, their columns cleaving the people to either side as they went.

"A halberd," Richard said, "is a difficult weapon to deal with. A slight soldier—Sunriser *or* Moonriser—strikes with its weight as if strong. A strong soldier is made even stronger."

". . . They're turning," Patience said. "Turning down Flowers— toward South Gate." The great bell still tolled, steady as a giant's heartbeat.

Dolphus gestured his tribesmen to their feet. "And that's how far?"

"From here, more than a WT mile." She stood in her colored coat, still watching. The bell staffs rang in the distance, a song crystalline as their city.

"You must have heard those little bells as a child," Nancy said to her. "Wakened to them in the night."

"Yes," Patience said, and turned away. "Heard it and loved it *and* our Constables, before it became the music of betrayal . . . and these people took my son."

The jangle of marching-bells was muffled to quiet as the last ranks, far down the way, turned out of sight . . . so only townspeople and their children were left hurrying along the frozen boulevard, past its great gleaming columns.

"Now," Patience said, "—and we must go *fast*, or lose our chance. Pass or kill any who interfere . . . but remember what we came to do." She trotted down the gallery with Baj and the others catching up, and the Shrikes after them—some skidding on slick ice as the regular ponderous notes of the great bell rang shivering.

Down the long gallery . . . to wide flights of frost-dusted stairs—Patience, then all of them running, jumping two steps at a time to reach the boulevard.

. . . Hurrying Boston people saw them, saw them but seemed to pay only temporary mind—as if on a day of surprising threat from the south, a certainly-township lady might reasonably lead a party of oddities and ice-tribe hunters. Leading them somewhere . . . perhaps necessary in the emergency.

Still, Baj noticed one or two paying more attention.

"This leaving us alone won't last," he said.

Nancy laughed beside him, breathless. "That's why . . . we're running."

Down the boulevard—even wider than it had looked from the

gallery, its pavement-ice scored with deep cross-hatching for better footing—Baj saw several of the brown-furred Carvers chipping at its curbs as Patience ran and more-than-ran before them. She sailed sometimes just above the ice, white hair streaming, with Baj and Nancy running just behind and to her left, Richard lumbering swiftly by her right side. . . . Errol, very lively, skipped behind with the Shrikes.

The great bell still rang its deep, slow measured notes, that seemed to jar the icy air around them. . . . Under its sound, Baj heard the swift whispers of their boots on frost.

They ran and *out*ran people's occasional shouts, starts, commencements of some sort of action—ran past and were gone. Though at last, just past where the Street of Flowers crossed, ran not quite fast enough.

Baj heard a curse and scramble back among the Shrikes— turned and saw one of the tribesmen wrestling, dragging a young Boston boy along. The Boston boy, furred in dotted colors, had a knife. He took a javelin-thrust through his belly and fell kicking, looking astonished as the Shrike ran on.

Baj drew his rapier, and ran with it in his hand. Beside him, Nancy had her scimitar out. And glancing over, he saw Patience had drawn also. There was a run of bright blood—from her killing down the North Gate—still frozen along the curved blade.

As they ran the streets of ice—smaller ice buildings standing on each side, their doorways seeming to be sheeted iron, painted black—as they ran, Patience leading fast, the great bell of alarm still rang, its vibrations hanging in the air.

. . . They'd left the turn, the Street of Flowers, well behind, and Baj—feeling now tireless, though Boston's frigid wind was numbing his face—wondered as they went, why "Street of Flowers," and supposed snow flowers might have been meant. Or whores, perhaps. . . . He saw—and his boot-soles felt—small lumps and bumps of debris frozen into the street's frosted pavement. Things people had thrown away: scraps of food, broken matters, certainly little frozen turds left by dog-pets. All become a pavement of *garbage*—wonderful WT word. "Garbage" frozen into the streets of the glittering city. A city whose lamps cast constant shadows, constant light—where no sun, no moon, shone for day or night.

"Obvious rhyme there," Baj thought, congratulated himself for some remnant of poetry still kept—and his mind off his feet, tripped on nothing much in the street, skidded on ice trying to recover, and went down hard onto his right knee.

"Baj." Nancy sliding to a stop.

"I'm up—I'm up!" And he was, with a Shrike shoving him along to hobble at a run on an unhappy knee. It seemed to Baj that stopping to fight someone would be a great relief from this forever running the streets of Boston. . . . Streets—their citizens also now rushing here or there—where running boot-steps gave back flat rapid echoes from ice buildings close on either side. Echoes, and different smells than Island's rich scents of river, fish, and granite. Boston's odors were of humans, freezing air, and perhaps a drift of coal smoke lingering before the cavern wind blew it away.

And, as if his prayer for relief had been answered with a fighting pause, a man came out of Warm-time's "nowhere" and struck at Richard with something—an iron something—and was struck back so Richard had to wrench his great ax free . . . then gallop to keep up.

More trouble behind them with the Shrikes as well. Baj heard it, heard a woman screaming, but didn't look back.

They all turned again as Patience turned, to run down a quiet narrower street with no one watching, no Bostons hurrying after with iron in their hands. Only the hard-rain sounds of their boots as they passed staring men and women, and the soft squeaks and clinks of leather and steel. Baj's knee, having complained, was feeling better.

. . . Though panting for breath, still they went swiftly—

trained by weeks of sled-running. They followed Patience to the right around another corner through bright revealing light, under constellations of hanging lamps glowing on their chains above them. Chains depending now from slightly lower ice ceilings, whose vaults still no thrown spear might reach, nor even the most forceful arrow. They ran on ridged and frosted white, pacing beside their active shadows.

The narrow street was fenced each side by walls of ice rising three, four stories, and pierced in regular rows with small square windows where—in many—lamplight glowed. Between those close walls of window lights, Patience half-ran, half-flew with Baj and the others after her like hounds.

People shouted from those windows as they went, and Nancy said, "Apartments . . ." She caught her breath. "They keep everyone together, but still apart."

Apartments of ice, not Island's stone. . . . Baj was sorry to be reminded of what was missed by this charging like cattle-broke-loose, running past bright-lit wonders all the Map-Country had heard of, and almost none had seen. . . . And he here for nothing but murder, so he ran in darkness, despite the light.

Over a building's high roof (tiles of ice shone there), he saw a flight of several Walkers-in-air. Men or women—they were too high, too far away to tell—sitting up, sailing just beneath the gleaming ceilings, sailing past bright lamps and wind-stirred banners. Tiny birds they might have been—bluebirds with their blue coats—passing out of sight in echelon. Going south.

There was shouting from apartment windows. A Shrike, Christopher, sprinted up and called, "Dolphus says chasers!"

Baj skipped steps as he looked back, and saw, where the narrow street began, men, citizens, coming after them.

Patience rose above them in the air and turned back to see, her coat's colored cloth ruffling out around her. "They will slow us, fighting! . . . Dolphus!"

Baj thought he heard the Shrike answer her.

Patience, sailing backward in billowing stripes, shouted again, a war-goddess's trumpet call. "*Leave six . . . to hold them!*"

Baj thought he heard the Shrike answer—skipped again to look back, and saw five . . . six of the tribesmen trot to a halt, left behind.

Then Baj bent himself again to running, though now the cold air poured into his lungs like hot ashes as he wearied. Errol galloped up beside, keeping close, tongue-clicking in excitement.

It was surprising how soon the noise of their passage was sliced with screams sounding the street behind them, as six Shrikes held the narrow way they could not hold for long.

Nancy stumbled and would have gone down, but Baj caught her arm. He called "Slower!" but Patience paid no attention, bounding, flying on as if they could fly after her.

Richard lunged, reached up and caught her coat-tail, hauled her in like a fish. "*Slower . . .*" He caught his breath. "Slower, my dear . . . or you'll lose us."

"Slower, then," she said, but gave them a cold look—then settled to the ice-road and trotted away, her scimitar swinging in her hand.

A little farther on, she went up a flight of wide steps, their ice worn clear blue, and Baj and the others followed then down a long way of mirror-ice colonades, past a confusion of Boston people rushing—likely to their homes or places of duty—with children being hauled along wide-eyed, and two . . . three little dogs tugging on their collar cords. Some adults called out as Patience led past. . . .

Baj and the others went reflected in the columns' gleaming rounds, so they seemed to meet themselves again and again, running figures—though running slower, now—with familiar faces appearing, then smeared, stretched away, and gone.

There were shops along those streets. Shops deep in niches between the pillars, with men and women hurrying to put their various goods away—goods laid out on ice counters or likely rare wooden counters, or counters apparently made from slabs of stone. Wonders in all shapes and colors. Great soft drifts of fur displayed, black, striped, spotted-gray, and white. And a niche of trays of southern fruit, brought somehow—on the frozen sea?— all that long way north. . . . Then stacks of knitted-wool clothes . . . shelves of bright steel tools.

All wonders, for Baj, in a town of wonders—marvels being passed by at a labored run—and all for a purpose of murder. It occurred to him how delighted old Lord Peter Wilson would have been to see it all. . . . A city so magical.

Were there Boston poets for this . . . this frozen city? Perhaps crouching naked, warmed by their minds over desks of ice, and writing of the souls of Persons their Talents had made, souls now grown richer than their own.

Wearied to a near jog-trot, Baj and the others followed Patience past a shop where a woman and her daughter—the girl looking so like her mother, though naked where her mother wore furs—were emptying trays of loaves and biscuits into bins. There was the wonderful odor of baking. . . . Looking back, Baj saw the women glance up as the Shrikes went past, and stand frozen, their hands to their throats.

He tripped again, almost fell—then trotted on beside Nancy, paying better attention. . . . Baking, *baking* in a city of ice. Baking or any cookery—what pots, what pans? Certainly iron or fired clay for their stoves, which must burn black-rock coal, skidded on sledges in deep winter all the long way from West Map-Virginia, then likely hauled up onto the ice from some deep lead. . . . Must burn that, and have great double-walled flues to carry the stoves' heat up and out before it melted their frozen bakeries, their cook-shops, their apartments.

. . . A little white dog, sharp-muzzled and fluffed with fur, scurried out into the road to chase them, and followed for a considerable way, snarling, threatening to bite.

A comical little creature; Baj imagined the child who owned it huddling under furs with the dog for warmth. Imagined all the Boston people—those many without the Warming-talent—living with constant cold, their only relief coats of pelt and the grudging heat of those iron stoves found necessary. . . . All their days and nights spent in furs and southern wool, their children swaddled in defense against the glacier-cavern's killing air. A steady burden of suffering, where civilized men and women spent their lives—like the grimmest savages over-the-Wall—sheltered under snow and ice for warmth half-imagined. . . . Forever breathing out slight clouds of frost.

Reason enough for the Township's ancient oddness, its cold and merciless heart.

. . . All of them were very tired now. Baj found his mind being left a little behind. Only the stinging cold and his aching leg-muscles assured him he was where he was, and not dreaming of it in some Smoking-mountain glen. . . . His lungs ached with Boston's frigid air; his breath was bitter smoke. Nancy staggered beside him. Richard was panting, laboring just behind.

. . . They were out of the colonades, had left the streets of shops—with a woman suddenly screaming, pointing at them as they went—and were crossing a small square, fenced by four high ice buildings of windowed apartments. Baj saw, to the left and right, that those narrow frozen streets, their great apartment buildings, diminished into considerable distance—still gleaming bright under endless chains of hanging lamps.

The Walkers-in-air would tend those thousands of lights. Whale oil. Whale oil and captive little flames to pretend sun to the buried city.

Patience suddenly swerved left off the way, and led them stumbling after her into such a narrow high-walled close, an alley, that shoulders rubbed ice on either side, and they soon went single file, exhaustion's hoarse breaths echoing beside and above them.

Then she turned suddenly left again—and was gone.

There was a deep-stepped entrance, cluttered with frozen debris, with a low frost-splintered door in shadow at the bottom. Baj went down, shoved at the wood, and pushed through as it gave, Nancy and Richard behind him.

He stumbled into darkness and cold so absolute, so still, it seemed a sort of solid—freezing water made somehow breathable. Heard the Shrikes crowding in behind him.

"What is it?" Nancy said.

"Storage," Patience's voice, "for those living above. Now, *rest.*"

Rest . . . Baj reached out, found Nancy still beside him, and hugged her as they sat on what was either freezing stone or rough ice. Errol burrowed between them. Tongue-clicks . . .

It was difficult to take deep relieving breaths of air so frigid. Baj sipped his breaths, slowly drew them into his lungs as his cramped leg-muscles eased. . . . Warm-time minutes passing, he found it a great relief to sit still, and felt he would be willing to stay in the dark for awhile.

Nancy began to murmur something—then was silent as a sound came first whispering . . . then muttering . . . then roaring down the street past this building's front, a sound like an avalanche of stones, with shouting. It was a killing crowd—and certainly chasing them.

"This was a lucky rest." Dolphus's voice. "It seems that Boston has noticed us."

"When they pass," Patience said, "—we go."

That pursuing tumult, which had made even the ice building tremble, slowly seemed to drain away, passing . . . and in a little while, was gone but for occasional footsteps, men calling.

"Up," Patience said, from darkness. "Up and out!"

Up the ice steps behind the tribesmen, and into Boston's lamplit always day, Baj and Nancy jostled along the alley. At the street entrance, Patience half-skipped, half-sailed past them . . . drew her scimitar, and led them to the left—the way the mob had gone.

Four men—startled late chasers—were met there, and rolled under, transfixed by Shrike javelins.

Then Patience was away, running, bounding down the street. Baj, Nancy with him, galloped hard to catch up to her, with Richard, Errol, and the Shrikes coming up behind. The street lay empty and frost-white before them, its ice battered by the boots and bare feet of the crowd that had passed.

Coat-tails flapping, Patience reached the next intersection a little in the air . . . touched her left muk-boot to the ice, and spun to the right, leading away from the pursuers' tracks. Down a wider way, they ran walled high on either side by Boston's frozen apartments—shabby buildings, stained with rusty melt, their doorways, cornices, and corners blurred . . . poorly carved.

Someone threw something from a high window as they ran past. It smashed on the road. Then, more came down . . . and men appeared at the building entrances. Furred men, wool-clothed men, almost none naked. They had iron bars in their hands.

"Our windows are braced with iron." Patience, in a conversational way, while traveling fast. "—or they sag and crack." Baj, running almost beside, heard the "Our," felt the *Our* in her. However furious a lady for her stolen son, still Patience had come home. He heard it, saw in Nancy's sidelong glance that she had heard it too.

The men with iron bars began to come out as they passed. Baj and Nancy drew their swords. . . . Women were screaming from the high windows . . . throwing things. A wooden stool cracked onto the ice beside Richard as he ducked aside. Pottery was coming down, smashing in the street. More men had gathered, came out with their iron bars—and Shrikes ran to meet them. Baj saw Marcus-Shrike leading.

Patience drew the rest of them on, leaving behind the cries of the impaled and dying, the grunts as brutal blows broke bones.

It seemed to Baj that soon there would not be enough of them left, even to murder women. . . . And now came again the sound of many pounding feet—more pursuers—their distant voices a roaring and furious surf. The voices of Boston-in-the-Ice, a wonder, centuries old—and so long the source of sorrow for others. The Township, startlement over, was rising against them.

"We're almost . . . out of time." Richard, panting as he lumbered on.

Baj—tiring again, despite their cellar rest—turned to look back as he ran, and saw others doing the same, looking back for the first crowding shadows of enraged thousands coming after, to drown them in blood.

Patience—ground-running now, head down, arms pumping so her scimitar's blade flashed and flashed—brought them to the end of ice buildings, of windowed apartments . . . though the sounds of screaming still followed them from the street left behind, as women there saw their men fighting, dying on Shrike javelins.

She led them into a park, or what seemed a park. There were trees—the first they'd seen since they'd climbed the Wall— hemlocks planted in great carved-ice tubs of dirt set out in rows. They stumbled, faces and hands numb with cold, into that shade and shadow, relieved of the reflected sparkle and glare of Boston's myriads of hanging lamps, constellations crowded as starshine.

The surf sound . . . the crowd was coming behind them.

Richard, a weary Errol holding onto his hand, caught his breath, and called, "*Patience*—"

But she was already off, down a row of trees. There was a huge gate there—a true gate, it seemed to Baj, with bars of iron hinged and fixed into a low thick vault of ice. The ice-face had been sculpted into figures—seen clearer as they followed her—figures of a tree giving birth from its branches to a naked women . . . who, lying legs spread, gave birth to what seemed a goat, a goat presenting an egg on its out-thrust tongue. The egg, by the gate's right base, cracking to birth what seemed a partridge, but with a weeping baby's head.

. . . A man in blue-striped furs had come to the gate carrying, like the Constables, a staff weapon, but this a heavy single-bladed partisan. A sentry-guard of some sort, though not half-armored as the Constables had been. He spoke with Patience through the gate, stared at Baj and the others as they came up, and shook his head.

Patience said, "The Faculty's orders." But the man shook his head again.

Patience swung her scimitar blurring out from behind her back, struck between the gate's iron bars, and took him in the throat with the point. Then she shoved to swing the iron open, but the sentry's body, still thrashing, blocked it until Richard reached her, hunched, and drove the gate wide.

. . . As they crowded in, Baj saw that beyond this, there was another entrance—or exit. A round pit, its edge polished, was set in stone flooring. —A hole in the ice introducing only darkness, it seemed a small replica of the immense crater they'd stepped down, around and around, to enter Boston from the north.

Patience wiped her scimitar's blade on her coat-tail, then sheathed it. "Fall sliding," she said, stepped into the ice hole and was gone.

"For God's sake . . ." Dolphus-Shrike, and a WT phrase that would have gotten him burned in the south, some years ago.

"Perhaps." Baj scabbarded his sword. "Richard, throw the dead man after us, and swing the gate closed before you all follow."

"Yes."

Baj reached to gather Nancy in—as she, scimitar sheathed, gathered Errol—then took them with him into the pit.

27

They fell in darkness, tangled—arms, legs, scabbarded swords, and struggling Errol. They fell skidding, ice-sliding in swift sickening circles, Errol whining as they went swooping down and down.

"Be ready!" Baj called out—though ready for what he couldn't have said. They swung in such swift circles that he felt them floating for moments as they fell—floating, then a sickening pressure against slick ice as they flew round and round, so he swallowed vomit.

Finally, a long relieving slide straight—a blessing by Frozen-Jesus to be no longer spinning in circles—and a round of light growing before them.

"Be ready . . . !" The light grew and they slid into it and swiftly out along an ice incline, then stumbled and fell onto a frosted floor where low lamps were lit along a corridor.

Patience stood waiting with a dead man. He'd been furred, as the other sentry, in striped blue—now turned sticky crimson. A simple pole-arm, a glaive-gisarme, lay beside him, great blade and back-hook bright in lamplight.

"Get up," Patience said to them; her voice was shaking. Baj and Nancy scrambled to their feet as Errol ran little widdershins circles, tongue-clicking, apparently unwinding from his slide.

"We're . . . at the base of the gallery bridge to the Pens," Patience said—and a young man swung into the corridor down the way, and came sailing high off the ice floor, open blue coat fanning behind him. He called, "Ah . . . our *exile*—and come with the reasons for the bell!" A handsome young man, pale, and with a fine mustache, he held a drawn scimitar in his hand. Patience had just time to turn and say, "Jacob," and he was on her with swift slashing strokes—driving her back and back to steel's music. Other sentries, furs striped blue, came running behind him with glaives balanced in their hands.

The young man parried a cut, kicked Patience into the corridor wall, said, "Sad end for an Almost-Lodge," and struck to put her sword aside, then kill her.

Baj, rapier drawn, lunged past a sentry to them as Patience fell to the side, the young man turned to finish her. Baj would not have reached him in time—but his sword did, and half a foot of steel slid through the young man's coat and into the small of his back.

He arched, frozen for a moment—and as Baj tugged his blade free, Patience thrust up into the man's belly and killed him. "*Jacob,*" she said again, but sadly, after she'd done it.

Baj turned and struck at the sentry—certainly caught him with the edge—and saw Nancy backed along the corridor to the ice ramp they'd slid down, a glaive's blade-point riding in at her belly. She cut along the weapon's wooden shaft, caught the man's guiding hand there and severed fingers so the sentry recoiled, spattering blood—as the man Baj had slashed in passing turned, sliced face bleeding, and charged him, swinging his weapon's broad blade.

Baj ducked, and the sentry was on him, chopping. Too close for sword-work. Baj drove into him—struck weight and muscle greater than his own—but drove, *drove*, kept grappling close as the glaive's thick staff struck down, its hook caught behind his left shoulder. He drew his left-hand dagger and stabbed the man though fur, through scraping ribs, then deep.

The sentry, strong and older, coughed sudden blood into Baj's face, made a fist and hit him in the mouth as if they were brawling . . . then staggered back, plucking at the place the dagger had gone in, so the glaive's hook dragged Baj after him, then fell free.

Spinning away, Baj saw the man Nancy had wounded was kneeling, clutching a hand blurting blood—but another sentry was on her, driving her back, swinging his pole-arm's blade, through she struck at him high and low. There was blood on the glaive's steel.

Baj shouted as if a shout could save her—leaped to reach them, and was tripped so he fell . . . then rolled to his feet, slashing. Another of the sentries was on him—a man old enough to be his father, and strong, striking very fast, alternating his blade and the shaft's steel-capped butt. Baj, grappling him close as the other, was hit hard in the belly—and as they wrestled, saw from the corner of his eye, Errol, quick as a squirrel, climb up the back of the man Nancy fought, and stick a knife in his neck.

Then Baj was struck again. Where, he wasn't certain, perhaps at the side of his head, since the corridor's lamps went dim, and he woke that instant on his hands and knees, saw the sentry's booted feet shift to deliver a finishing stroke. —Obeying the Master's shouted command from years before, Baj lunged in full *passata soto* and thrust the rapier's blade up into the man's bowels.

Getting to his feet as the man went down—gripping his belly as if to hold life in—Baj saw a different dying man stumbling here and there, screaming, clawing up behind him where Errol still rode his back, eyes squeezed shut in pleasure, mouthing the knife wound, drinking.

Two more sentries had come. Baj faced one with wearied clumsy rapier strokes and dagger wards that rang left and right as he ducked first one way, then the other, to keep the glaive's point wavering.

Very tired, Baj urged the pole-arm's heavy blade a little aside, thrust for the man's face, drove the point through his cheek deep into the angle of his jaw, and backed him bleeding away as the second sentry rushed past, face convulsed with rage. This man raised his weapon high, then hacked it down.

Baj turned, intending to manage something, as Errol—eyes shut and still suckling, dreamy with pleasure on a shrieking mount—was struck at his back, and split. For an instant, the boy's snowy rib-ends showed, and the intricate chain of his spine . . . then flooded red.

Baj heard Nancy scream, turned to help—and was struck and knocked aside as the first of the Shrikes, in swift slipping thuds and scraping, came skidding, tumbling from the ice ramp, recovered, and charged with thrusting javelins.

Two sentries, still living, were lifted on those slender points, transfixed, kicking, making noises . . .

Baj looked for Nancy—and saw her alive and weeping, kneeling by ruined Errol, touching and plucking at the spoiled parts, as if she might heal him.

"Jumping Jesus." Dolphus-Shrike came away from the others, shaking his head. "Poor climbing boy . . ."

"Where *were* you?" Baj saw the place at the base of Dolphus's throat where the rapier's point would go.

The Shrike sighed. "Some Boston people came and forced the iron gate. There were . . . a number." One of the fallen sentries had still been alive. Baj heard the slice and gargle behind him as a Shrike cut the man's throat.

Richard, just off the slide, said, "*Fucking thing.*" Then, finding his feet, saw what was around him, ". . . Baj . . . we had no choice but deal with people up there—which cost us men—and no time to send the bodies down. So . . . they're left for anyone to see."

"Next time," Baj said, though he had no idea what "next time" that might be, "—next time, do as was done back on the streets. Leave a few men to hold, while the others go on to finish what must be finished."

"Right," Dolphus said, and Richard nodded. It was an acceptance that Baj found somehow expected, as if his fathers had spoken through him, their voices one in harmony. The plainsong "Obedience."

Nancy knelt in puddled blood, crooning as if the dead boy could still hear her.

Baj knelt beside, took her in his arms. "Sweetheart . . . sweetheart, he never knew he was struck, it came so fast." His left shoulder hurt where the glaive's hook had caught it . . . the same shoulder George Brock had hit with his hurled shield.

"I don't care," Nancy leaned against him, weeping. "I don't *care*."

Baj saw she was cut down her left forearm, sliced through leather and cloth. Slow bleeding . . . not serious. "He saved your life."

She shook her head, took the opportunity to wipe her nose on his sleeve. "He didn't mean to. He was only doing what he wanted to do." Then, lisping, "He was a *child*. Not like the rest of us, always scheming and wondering and . . . *thinking*."

"True," Baj said. His lip was sore, split and bleeding where the older man had hit him. His shoulder hurt. "True . . ."

He heard Richard saying, "Rest a minute," looked across the corridor, and saw him helping Patience to stand. She stood, but swaying. ". . . The boy was killed?"

"Yes," Richard said. "I should never have brought him."

Baj felt, and felt in the rest, exhaustion from the long run through Boston, the fighting—and more than either, from the task still before them. There was a great temptation simply to stay and rest awhile, consider further what must be done. . . .

The great bell's tolling of alarm—somehow unheard through the fighting—rang softly shivering down the corridor of ice. It rang its slow, ponderous periods, and Baj woke to them.

"Dolphus," he said, "have your people gather the sentries' glaives, chop notches in the ice ramp, and prop the pole-arms up so anyone coming down after us will run onto the points."

"Nasty." Dolphus smiled, and gestured his men to the work. There were only seven tribesmen now, Dolphus making eight. . . . All the others cut down, beaten down, holding the ice streets of Boston. Holding the pit-gate above. Marcus gone. Christopher gone, also.

"Patience," Baj raised his voice, since she seemed still dreamy from the fighting. "—where do we go? And who still defends?"

". . . We're in the tunnel to the bridge, entrance to the Pens."

"Defenders?"

She seemed to wake, shrugged Richard's supporting arm away. "Never many, only enough to keep order here and in the Pens. The guard roster was—used to be—a file of eighteen. There are locked gates for every tier, so more were never thought necessary, with Constable Formations in the town." She glanced at the scimitar in her hand as if surprised to see she still held it, then slowly wiped its blade clean on her coat's cloth. A bruise was beginning to stain the side of her forehead. "There may be . . . Talents working there, if the bell hasn't sent them all home."

"Sweetheart," Baj said to Nancy, "do you have cloth to bandage that arm?"

"Yes. It's nothing much—"

"Dolphus," Baj interrupted her, "leave two men to finish setting the glaives. You and the rest follow me. —Patience?"

"I'm well enough," Patience said, though, to Baj, she didn't look well enough.

"Then we go." He led down the tunnel at a trot—led as if a wind were blowing at his back, whispering *"Decide and move . . . decide and move, and they'll follow after."*

They followed climbing, soon enough, up an ice slope crosscut for better footing. There, Baj felt what the epics, Warm-time and after, never troubled with—the aches and stabbing pains in muscles, tendons strained in any desperate fight. As he climbed the slope, he felt even the injuries George Brock had inflicted, battering for advantage in the tundra circle. His cracked cheekbone. . . the left shoulder; that hurt again, of course. . . .

And if so for him, and young—how much more for Patience and those older others? But he didn't slow. *Time . . . time.* There was a quote from some Warm-time Great Captain. "Ask me for anything, but time."

Still, Baj came to a stop when he climbed into the open. Stopped and stood still in a steady, biting wind.

Before him, the slope—dazzling under distant lamps—became the steep bone-white rise of a great unrailed bridge of ice that arched up and up over a crevasse wide as a tributary river, fractured, and darkening blue to black with deepness. But both— grand, gleaming bridge, and the depthless coursing vacancy it spanned—shrunk to insignificance in the enormous chamber that contained them, miles from side to side, its riven ceiling certainly almost another mile high . . . all, with the city behind them, forming the glacier's immense and hollow heart.

The others caught up, and stood staring as he did.

"Wonderful," Patience said, "isn't it?" The whining wind caught her words and spun them away.

"The bridge," Nancy said.

"Yes." Patience smiled. The side of her forehead was bruised dark blue. "Great blocks of ice cut, then each drenched with heated water and frozen into place—and every course set a little farther out into the air. This was made by our many-times great- grandfathers . . . who were men beyond what is meant by 'men.' "

"It's a great work," Richard said, apparently relieved to stand a moment to catch his breath.

"And we," Baj said, "still have work to do." He set off climbing the bridge's gently rising arc, thankful for the grooves crosscut into its footing. Even so, it became uneasy as climbing through the air, since no railings interrupted view of the chamber's vast expanse at either side, so the bridge, seeming so grand and wide at first, appeared to narrow—and perhaps did narrow—as they climbed near the height of its arch.

And while they climbed, the cavern wind came stronger, thrumming over the span, cold and sharp as weapons, so there seemed nothing easier than to suddenly slip and slide away—off that arching height, and down through the great space of air into depth immeasurable.

Baj kept his eyes on the ice-way before him . . . climbed to its crest . . . then went even more carefully down a slope that ran like grand descending chords of music, falling . . . falling bow-shots away to lie at last, like some huge ice-beast's tongue, on a broad frozen landing. This an introduction to the fourth of five stories of pillared galleries, open-sided cloisters stretching at least half a Warm-time mile to left and right—a great hive of ancient blue ice, carved from the cavern's wall. Between each story, sculpted dadoes ran the galleries' lengths—of men and beasts walking hand in paw . . . and changing as they went along, as if the ice had melted them one into the other.

Behind the low rampart of the structure's roof, Baj saw what seemed a distant huge wing of leather rise . . . then fold down and away. There were soft, echoing calls, plangent as if from brass instruments.

"What . . .?"

"Occas," Patience said.

Baj had seen an occa, when Ambassdor MacAffee had come to Island—had seen two, earlier, when he was nine or ten years old. Those had been flying, bringing Boston Trade-factors up from Map-McAllen to the bund at Baton Rouge. . . . Huge brown things with angled awkward heads, and looking made of tanned hide, the occas had flown on wide wings with slow majestic flapping—and cried out just as these, in their rooftop roost, were hooting now.

Pedro Darry, standing beside him—they'd been watching Or-dinaries at foot-ball—had said, "There are great gifts, that still come too costly."

Baj had supposed Pedro meant that wonderful gift of riding flying—and couldn't imagine a cost too great for that. . . .

"Look there!" A Shrike—Paul-Shrike—pointed down to the

right, off the bridge's side. Baj and the others went near that edge cautiously, and saw, far below, hundreds of Boston's citizens walking . . . trotting along a frosted-ice road running west alongside the great crevasse. Some of those, blue-coated, were sailing the air.

"The Pens Staff, and Faculty people," Patience said. "Most live in West-buildings. They're running to their homes."

"Well done, Sylvia Wolf-General, to make matters easier for us," Richard said, and the distant alarm struck a deep, ringing, musical period for him.

"Yes, until they come back, and bring other citizens with them. —But still, good for us now. There'll be only a few sentries left in the galleries; none are ever allowed inside the Pens." Patience turned away, and trotted down the bridge's slope—lifting a little off the ice now and then, as if she were a winter crow, half-hopping, half-flying a pace or two, so the others had to run—some sliding, skidding perilously—to keep up.

Baj, breathing out dragon-breaths of frost, managed to stay beside her—and Nancy caught up. ". . . Patience, your son is here?"

"No." Patience answered her from a little height in the air. "Maxwell will be in Creche-solitary off River Street." She smiled. "He so frightens them by dreaming the truth of things— as I was frightened when he dreamed the truth of me."

"Then go to him," Baj said.

Patience shook her head, white hair breezing in the wind. "I promised—promised this first. . . ." Then there was no more stepping and half-flying, but she lifted and dove through the air, striped coat-tails flapping—and was down off the bridge and across the wide landing to the fourth-floor gallery, where she landed as Baj and the others followed, running over rough ice.

"That fucking flying," Richard said, lumbering along.

. . . Leaning against a huge, carved, gallery pillar for a moment, to catch his breath, Baj felt its frozen mass even through his parky's fur. "There are only the occas on the floor above—the top floor, and the roof?"

"Yes," Patience said. She was standing on one foot like a chimney stork, taking her own odd rest. "—Their home-roost and nursery."

* * *

"Do we go up?" Nancy's red crest of hair was powdered with frost, her narrow face pinched and pale with cold.

Patience shook her head. "The mothers who tend *those* daughters are . . . past killing." Boston's great bell of alarm tolled its distant regular stroke as she spoke. "—And in the cellars beneath the building, the big mampies are stabled—born only to be ground-ridden."

"Their mothers?"

"Their mothers die, giving birth to them."

The pillared corridors, one side open to the air, ran distant to either side of them, but Patience—apparently rested enough—turned to their right and trotted that way, small swift muk-boots crunching over floor-ice striped wavering by the columns' lamp shadows. Baj, Nancy, and the others trooped behind her, Richard humming to himself under his breath.

Baj saw, down the way, a naked young man standing to the left at the cloister wall, staring at them as they came. He had a roll of writing paper under his arm. . . . Patience ran past him, then Baj, Nancy . . . then Richard.

"*Who?*" the young man called. Perhaps meaning them—perhaps asking who threatened Boston's gate.

Baj heard a single shriek as one of the Shrikes, trotting behind them, speared that young man. Turning to look back, he saw him down, kicking, struggling in the crimson and blue coils of his intestines. His writing papers were unfurled, lifting on the cavern wind . . . shifting out between ice pillars into vacancy over the great crevasse.

"These stairs," Patience said, rose a little in the air, spun left, and seemed to fall away down steep frost-white steps, Baj and Nancy going after side-by-side, with Richard's heavy boot-steps and the softer *shush* and thud of the Shrikes' footfalls coming behind.

They reached a landing, turned and went the next flight down. Baj heard a Shrike slip on the steps behind him, fall, then scramble up. . . . Patience led to an iron gate set deep into the ice, and locked with a chain and heavy round mechanical key-turn. It stood sturdy for three clanging strokes of Richard's ax—then the key-turn's thick shank broke with a *snap*, the chain fell free, and Richard set his shoulder against the bars and shoved the gate squealing open.

They stepped into a wide inside corridor lit by hanging lamps swaying on their chains in a bitter breeze—a long corridor that seemed to run the building's breadth. Patience led the way down it. There were iron doors spaced well apart along both walls; the door frames, also iron, were set as the gate had been, into rounded, thick blue ice. "Inquiry," Patience called as they passed a door. "The Corridor of Inquiry and Advancement . . ."

Passing one door, then another, Baj saw their metal was smeared thick with black, pitchy grease—and supposed all Boston's iron must be, or rust away.

"Inquiry?" Nancy said, and as if a door had heard her, it clanked, groaned, then swung open as Baj turned to face it.

An old man in a long blue coat stepped though the doorway, leaving spacious rustling darkness behind him, and bringing the odor of babies' manure. He carried a leather parcel on his left shoulder. There was a soft chorus of "*Good-bye . . .*" behind him, as the iron door swung shut.

Apparently preoccupied, his head turned to the bundle on his shoulder, the old man started at the gleam of Baj's drawn rapier, and froze, standing still. A pale hairless chest, its flesh fallen, was revealed where the greatcoat fell open, and Baj saw the Boston man was naked beneath the cloth. Naked, and barefoot on the ice.

Astonished, the old man stared at Baj, at the Shrikes—now standing at ease, leaning on their javelins.

"Who are you?" A voice cracked with age.

"Visitors," Patience called, and turned back to join them.

"'Visitors.'" An echo from the leather bundle on the old man's shoulder. The bundle stirred, spread a veiny, delicate wing, and Baj saw it was a Mailman. He'd seen one once, at Island—and been told it brought a message from Map-New Mexico, concerning Roamer raids. But this was within arm's reach. He stared, and the Mailman stared back. Shriveled, an owl's size, it had a little baby's head, a baby's considering blue eyes.

"Willard Adams, Tenured," Patience said. "And still working wonders in the Mailman lofts. You haven't heard the bell of Enemy-at-the-Gate?" She cocked her head to mime listening, and the bell struck its regular note for her . . . its peal shivering softly through corridors of ice.

"I've heard the bell," the old man said, "—and assume these creatures and tribesmen are part of the reason, with friends no doubt pecking futilely at one of the city's entrances. . . . And I know you," he looked unpleasant, "a nasty exile booted from the Township, from Harvard Yard, for lack of cooperation. More than mostly Irish, I've always thought—well-named Riley—and no part Lodge at all."

"Kill him?" Dolphus Shrike.

"These savages," the old man stuck his tongue out at the Shrikes, "are fit company for an in-fact Moonriser exile, who brewed a gross and mind-rotten baby out of our best blood."

"Where is Woody Lodge, Willard?"

"Woodrow Cabot-Lodge is gone west to mention matters to ice-tribesmen in Map-Minnesota. Gone away for shame at what has sprouted from your spoiled belly. . . . Now, I have training to accomplish, and so leave you and the rest of these . . . Persons. . . to the Constables."

The old man put out his arm to set Baj aside, and strode into the corridor as if he were alone.

"*Constables*," the Mailman said from his shoulder.

Patience said, "Kill him."

A Shrike Baj had heard called Perry, struck the old man's spine with the butt of a javelin, and Willard Adams gasped, turned away—and suddenly rose up into the air as the Mailman called, "*Uh-oh!*" and flew from his shoulder. The old man thrashed higher, skinny naked legs flailing as he rose, and Shrike javelins—Perry's and two others'—flashed up to strike at him, sliced his legs so he screamed and mounted higher, almost to the corridor's blue-ice ceiling.

"*Bad*," Nancy said. "Badly cruel, and he so old!"

"Stay still." Baj held her arm—and glancing at Patience, saw nothing but satisfaction in her face while the Shrikes stirred in a swift whirl of lancing, as if in a dance, whipping bright steel up to catch Willard Adams as he flapped and crawled along the ceiling. A blade went in at his groin, and the old man screamed and tried to twist away—but where the Shrikes could not follow, their javelins could, and rose and struck him again, so he was silent but for grunting as the steel went in . . . then suddenly slid down out of the air and fell among them, choked on his blood, and died.

The Shrikes stood back as hounds stand back from a torn coyote.

"*Uh-oh . . . uh-oh . . .*" The Mailman, winging away, sailed up the stairwell they'd descended.

"*Cruel*." Nancy pulled her arm out of Baj's grip.

Baj said nothing, but the old man's death stirred nausea in him as if he'd eaten spoiled meat, so he felt he had to hurry . . . hurry to do what must be done before the sickness overwhelmed him. His own voice called "Faster!" to him, called for such speed in action there'd be no time for thinking, for imagination, no time for choices.

"Move," Patience said, and Baj was glad to do it. Glad that as they ran the frigid corridor, no more old men came out to die. . . . Though there was something that battered at a door they passed, smashing into the iron to be let out. No one opened that door to see what it might be.

Patience—skipping, then sailing just beneath the hallway's hanging lamps—led them fast. The walls' ice-blue and the hanging lamps' gold combined to send light wavering, flashing, settling in odd shadows as they went. It seemed to Baj that running to exhaustion had been most of what they'd done in Boston-town . . . was perhaps most of what all soldiers, all fighting people did.

Passing iron doors—though none presented signs or markers—Patience sometimes called back, "Birthing . . . Discoveries of Tiny Things . . . Considerations . . . Good-bye to Naughty Changes. . . ." No one paused at any of these doors.

Near the corridor's end, one iron door stood partly open, though no one could be seen, but only a single oil lamp shining down on a bench and a table glittering with blown glass vessels in odd shapes and sizes.

"Surprises Examined," Patience had called, tapping that half-open door with her sheathed scimitar when she went by. Then, reaching a stairwell, she whirled to the right and down it, coat-tails bannering.

Richard, galumphing down the ice steps after Baj and Nancy, puffing clouds of frost as he came, muttered "Frozen-Jesus . . ." apparently praying for a rest.

But Patience, as if she were young again and tireless—though the side of her forehead showed deeply bruised—gave them no rest, but bounded down and around through two turns of stairs and landings, all cut from ice mature—blue, and hard as stone.

Then there was a pause. Baj heard the ring and clash of steel—and he and Nancy, turning the stairway's corner, saw Patience, scimitar drawn, fighting with two stripe-coated sentries. Five . . . six more men were coming up the steps at her.

Still alive by virtue of such close quarters, where the men's pole-arms were awkward, Patience hacked a man down and was wrestling with the other as Baj and Nancy dove into the fighting. The landing, skidding slick and close-walled, was a gift to scimitar and rapier-and-dagger, a curse to long-staffed partisans. The sentries would have been wise to drop those, and draw their knives, but were given no time for it. Pierced and slashed—another down—they staggered bleeding back as Richard came, stepped over a dying man and struck another with his ax, the Shrikes flooding after to fight down the steps.

Patience, cut and bleeding at the back of her left wrist, and limping—led them down the flight of stairs over still-moving bodies, their blood crawling, wrinkling as it froze over blue ice. One of the Shrikes, Ned—silent, and tall for his tribe—was left dying as well.

No one else had been lost, or dangerously wounded, though many had been cut or hammered—and Nancy had been badly bruised when she'd slipped, fallen, and been kicked hard in the struggle. Baj had stepped back then to stand over her against a sentry gripping his glaive short—jabbing with the thing—until she got to her feet again to fight, snarling. Furious, she'd slashed out left and right, so both Baj and the sentry had stood away in almost comic agreement before the surge and striking drove all three of them apart—and the sentry into Shrike knives.

The stairs ended at a chained iron gate that stood sturdy under five swinging blows from Richard's ax—then broke by the keyturn at the sixth, and he drove through with the rest of them after.

One sentry, a man almost old and very frightened, stood waiting in a wide entrance hall, his glaive's heavy blade up to strike. He said, "Who are you?"

"You know me, Thornton." Patience took a step to him. "Put up, and come to no harm."

The man stared at her, then at the others. "No," he said, and stayed on guard.

Behind him, Baj heard Dolphus-Shrike say, "One chance is chance enough," then grunt with effort, and a javelin came hissing past—very close past Patience. The sentry had no time to see it before it struck him in the throat and sent him stumbling back to sit, then lie on his side as if to sleep in the shallow bed of his blood. Dolphus went to tug his javelin free.

"You might have hit me," Patience said to the Shrike.

"Embarrassing, but unlikely." Dolphus shook red drops from the javelin's blade. "Where now?"

"Down to second-floor gallery," Patience said, and led the way—slower now, as if she were tiring at last—across the hall and down a narrower stair than those before.

"One more gate," she said.

"Well," Richard grunted, "I'll have no ax-edges left." And at the foot of the stairs, with Patience standing aside, he beat at an iron gate again, a Shrike clapping his hands to the rhythm of five ringing blows before the gate broke open.

Patience going slowly now, they filed out onto the widest landing yet, that opened onto a broad stairwell to the left—and a long, open gallery to the right, its ice pillars fenced between with tall iron bars from rampart to roof.

Past those barriers . . . out and two stories down, the narrow west roadway lay carved in the ice. Running alongside it, the great crevass yawned deep blue, to darker blue, to black.

Voices rose from the stairwell, and Patience led that way, but in no hurry.

They came onto the staircase—its wide ice steps descending— and were met by silence absolute, and the eyes of many women. . . . Many women, and girls not yet women.

"The Pens," Patience said, into that silence.

Baj saw, within a huge high-ceilinged chamber—lamp-lit as all the city's spaces—four wide, barred corridors stretching away, each lined down either side with ordered pallets and stools. The corridor bars for some convenient separation, apparently, though all four entrance gates now stood open beyond the foot of the stairs. . . . There were artful little flowers of colored ribbon tied to the bars here and there . . . and on several of the nearest pallets, small rag dolls lay as if asleep.

There was the salt-sweet scent of many women—an odor warm, even in freezing cold. That scent . . . a growing murmur . . . and the eyes of hundreds, staring.

Dolphus-Shrike looked across the great room as the women and girls, crowding from their corridors, gazed back, some now calling questions. Tribe-talk . . . book-English. ". . . There must be almost five hundred," he said, and shook his head. "Boston will not give us time enough to finish this." He tapped his javelin's butt on a step's blue ice.

As if that soft tapping had been a signal heard, the women and young girls—all in furs, none naked in Warming-talent—fell silent again in their barred corridors.

"No *children*," Nancy said. "But I was a child, here. . . . I know this place very well."

"No." Patience shook her head. "The girls and women only. Now, what . . . children . . . they breed, are soon taken from them."

The women stirred—talking, calling out—some coming running down the corridors, and Baj saw tribal tattoos, scarring, long hair pigtailed or twisted into particular knots. . . . Below the steps, a young girl shouted a question in some clattering tribe-talk—then was shushed to silence as others were quieted, so only Boston's great bell of alarm sounded, dull with distance.

Baj felt a deeper silence close beside him. Nancy's silence, and Richard's. Patience's silence, and the Shrikes'. It was a silence that seemed to have been slowly descending upon him through the years, so now he must speak to fill it.

"Do . . . what we are here to do," he said, and gripping his innocent sword, started down wide frost-crusted steps, the others shuffling to follow.

As he went down, one of the women—leaving the others after

hugging, reassuring another—came up the stairs to meet him. She was tall, wore a torn, long sealskin cloak, and was smiling. Her teeth were filed to points, her braided hair gold and gray, and tribal tattooing laced her forehead. Her eyes were an older woman's, a weary dark brown.

"We heard the bell," she said, in fair book-English with a soft tongue-click to it. She stood an ice step down, but was so tall she and Baj were almost eye to eye. "Is there now a difference?"

"Yes," Baj said, but would not have known his voice.

"I have been here eleven years, and have been bred five times. . . . Young man, is it to be a great difference?" Baj saw hope rising in her eyes as the sun must have risen for Warm-time summers.

Other women began calling questions. Some in book-English, some not.

"My name is Mary-Shearwater," the tall woman said, "from the ice at Map-Roque Bluffs. My father is Elder Simon—" She stopped talking, and looked into Baj's eyes. "Have you come to take us free?"

"No, my lady."

She looked down at the rapier's blade. "You were sent. Did my father send you?"

"We were sent by . . . necessity."

"Ah . . . Now, I understand." She tried to smile. "You've come to take Boston's advantage from them. —Yes?"

"Yes."

She nodded. "As we would have done ourselves, and gone into the crevasse, but for the gallery bars. They have not allowed us means, though a few have hanged themselves. Though one swallowed sewing needles . . ."

"Dear lady," Baj said, "we have no time."

"Yes, the Talents will return, bring others, Constables. You have no time." She reached for his left hand, held it hard in both of hers, then let it go. "We of the Ice-coast are raised to necessity."

She turned and called out to the others. "Listen! . . . *Listen!* These who've come, have work to do—great, *great* injury to Boston-town! But they have little time in which to do it. So—" Baj heard her take a shaking breath, "the brave among us will help them accomplish it quickly. Remember that Pen-mothers past are watching from the sky."

She turned back to Baj, and touched the fur cloak at her breast. "Tell my father," she said, "for his peace."

"I will." Baj—though not the Baj he'd always been—drew his left-hand dagger to spare his sword's honor, and thrust Mary-Shearwater through the heart.

28

She fell away, fell down the ice steps, struggling with death. Baj saw her try to breathe, the fur at her breast soaking in blood from the ruined heart. She tried to breathe—then coughed blood, put her hands to her mouth, and died with red running through her fingers.

Screaming then in the Pens, a tumult of shouts and weeping. And although a number of women and a few girls knelt to await blade edges, some praying to the Jesus from their homes—others shrank back, withdrawing as a sea's tide falls away, crowding back into their corridors, calling for someone to help them.

"Baj—oh, my Baj." Nancy gripped his dagger wrist, made to force the blade sheathed again. "Wrong for you. Wrong for *you*."

Then Patience pushed past them and went down the stairs, calling, "Sorry! Oh, sorry, my sweet ones!"

Richard, muttering, lumbered down after her, his ax in his hand. The Shrikes rushed past, silent.

"Nancy," Baj said, and had to raise his voice over screaming, "—stay here."

"*No.*"

Below, Patience called again she was sorry, struck and killed a small brown-haired woman who'd knelt waiting. Richard and the Shrikes were among the women—all of those the bravest, who knelt or stood still for the steel.

Nancy, her face white as fine paper, started down after them, but Baj gripped her arm and held her. "No, my dear. You are not needed. I'll slaughter for both of us."

"*Not so.*"

"Obey me," Baj said, "so at least a part of us is saved." It seemed his fathers spoke through him, since Nancy, scimitar in her hand, stayed weeping on the stairs of ice while he went down.

. . . There was a difficulty in killing women. Their beauty, of course, and their value—so much dearer than a man's. Their very cushioned softness seemed to oppose the steel, making it appear so rude, so rough in what it did to them. Baj found, after the second one—the third, an older woman, had closed her eyes, bared her throat to make it easier for him—he found it a chore so odd, so dreadful as not to be real at all. It seemed no slender arms were actually raised to keep the dagger's long blade away. No delicate hands truly tried to guard, only to be struck aside. Certainly no lovely eyes were wide in terror, no screams sounded. . . . It was all imagined, though noisy, strenuous in its way.

What might have been blood, was only something like it.

Baj had a girl's white throat in view; she was backing frantically away, as if all were serious. The imagined dagger swung back to slash—when another blade, though unreal as his, blocked the stroke.

"Listen!" Patience forced his steel aside. "Listen . . .!" The great bell, that had rung its note so deep into them they hardly heard it, had been joined by a second sounding even through the screams. Another plangent shivering note, but higher, so the bells rang now in alternation, their sounds beating at the ear.

"The second!" Patience stood, mouth open as if for even better hearing. Her white hair was streaked red where blood had flung from her scimitar. She nodded, as if that tolling were some confirmation. "The second bell . . .! It has never ever rung. That call is Enemy-in-the-Town! It means defeat!"

Richard and the Shrikes, blood spattered, were still—held still, listening. There were the great bells, and the women's cries, their screams and weeping as they fled into their barred corridors.

"What . . .?" Baj said, speaking from his place of pretending, quieter than a dream. "What?" he said, but meant all questions he wished to ask. He and Patience, Richard and the Shrikes, stood bloody and quiet while the Pen's women, shrieking or silent, crowded back from dagger and scimitar, from ax and javelins, thrusting the youngest girls behind them as if sufficient softness, courage, or beauty might become armor adamant, and proof against the world.

"The Guard!" Patience spun in a circle as if dancing, her scimitar's blade flinging drops of blood. *"The Guard is in Boston Town!"* She turned, shouting at Richard and the Shrikes, *"Put up blades! Kill no more . . . !"*

If so, it seemed to Baj, as he roused, a miracle too late. Too late—and had been too late once his dagger thrust through Mary-Shearwater's breast.

"Not possible," Richard said, over a soft chorus of weeping, a shriek of agony from a woman wounded. "Not enough guardsmen to *do* it—not even with Sylvia commanding."

"The bells say so," Patience said. "—And have never rung together before." Distracted, she wiped her scimitar blade on her coat, wiping blood onto blood, and sheathed the blade dirty.

"What's happening . . . ?" Nancy came down the steps. She looked to Baj so like the women, the girls he'd been killing. . . .

"I hear drums." A Shrike named Porter cocked his head to hear better.

"I doubt it," Dolphus said. His furs were soaked, here and there. "Those bells are lying."

"Listen," Porter-Shrike said.

Then there was listening. Listening. . . . And softly through the sobs, the cries of women, softly between the distant sonority of the bells, came the faintest heartbeat thudding. And a trumpet's thready cry.

"Dear every Jesus," Richard said. "How is it *possible?* She hadn't the companies for it!"

Baj, awake, saw as if for the first time that girls and women were lying in little drifts of the dead and dying. There was an injured lady screaming, with Nancy kneeling beside her. . . . More than twenty-five. They'd slaughtered at least that many. More than thirty. . . .

Baj recognized his second murder. Then his third, in running blood. And no longer shelter-dreaming—seeing now so clearly that his eyes ached with seeing—found that one was missing. He drew a rapier stained only by the blood of fighting men, and turned to Patience.

"Prince," she said, started to touch her scimitar's hilt, then saw there would not be time. And not time enough for rising in the air.

Baj had not seen her frightened before. "You were half-expecting the second bell. Listening for it. This was your planning, your doing. And now we have murdered for nothing."

Patience put her hands together as several of the dead women had put their hands together, waiting. "Prince," she said, "how could I have known?"

". . . I think you knew because your child dreamed the future for you. You knew at least the *chance* the Guard would win."

She shook her head, watching the rapier's blade. "No, no. Only *perhaps*—but he's just a baby, and might have been wrong. There are bloodlines he has no knowledge of." She took a deep breath, looked away from the blade as if not seen, it wasn't there. "—I knew only what was *likely*, and saw no way for the Wolf-General to win the city! No way . . . our duty could be avoided."

Baj said nothing.

"—If I had believed my Maxwell, you know I would have harmed no girl, no woman, here." Patience tried to smile, as Mary-Shearwater had tried to smile. "Prince, don't kill me. My son . . ."

Nancy crouched silent by the wounded woman. Richard was silent, and the Shrikes. None said a word for her—and so saved Patience. That little rest, the quiet of no argument, and silence but for weeping women, saved her.

". . . For past kindness, past courage," Baj said, stroked his sword and dagger clean—criss-cross—on his parky's sleeves, and sheathed them. "How fortunate you are, that I am not my First-father . . . who, I believe, forgave nothing."

Then noise rose up as if it had been held down before. Injured women cried for help, girls for consolation for butchered friends. . . . Patience went to Nancy, and together they began binding, bandaging, pressing cloth to bleeding injuries, murmuring "There . . . there, dear," to a silent, dying lady whose intestines were out.

The men stood stupid, but for two Shrikes who went down the barred corridors calling to the huddled women, "Mistake . . . mistake! Oh, how *stupid* we were. And now, all safe!" They called like boys who'd been bad.

Richard set his ax down on the ice floor, and made a motion of washing his great hands. "But how could the Guard *do* it?" he said.

A hint . . . then the fact of bell-staff music softly jangled in the air.

"Too many fucking bells," Dolphus said.

Patience looked up from binding a wound. "Constables."

Baj led Richard and several Shrikes at a run up the ice steps to the landing, then out onto the gallery. He pressed close against freezing iron bars, looked down—and saw many hundreds of Boston soldiers, ranked in their formations, coming marching along the crevasse road, halberds swaying together on their shoulders. Bell staffs struck and sounded—nearer music than Boston's great bells. Nearer than the trumpets of the Guard.

"My God." Dolphus joined them, pressed his forehead against the bars to see better below. "I thought the cowards who ran from here, were to bring back only a *few*. If that fucking regiment comes into the building, we might slow them on the stairs, but not for long."

As if to confirm bad news, the cavern winds gusted hard along the ice gallery, so the carved pillars moaned a rising note with it.

"If they come into the building," Baj said, his breath clouding, "—we go back up to the crest of the bridge." Giving orders had become as easy as those orders were unimportant, considering the women who'd just been butchered. "The crest is narrow, and footing treacherous enough for us to hold them there a little while. Perhaps until a Guard company comes."

Richard shook his head. "Too many, Baj. They'll march over us, and hardly know it."

"*We*'ll know it—and deserve no better. If they come into the building, we go to hold them at the bridge."

"Well," Dolphus said, "this is terrible fucking luck. And I was just thinking to live forever."

"Where are they?" Patience trotted along the gallery, went to the bars and stared down. ". . . I know them. The West-Gate Constables, all four formations. But *here*—not at South Gate. They weren't at the fighting!"

"Where's Nancy?"

"Tending the women, Baj." Collected and herself again, as if there'd been no begging for her life, Patience stared down as the long columns, to called commands, came to a march, march—and halt, almost below the gallery wall. Halberds swung up, then were grounded on the road's ice with a thud and rattle like a hailstorm striking.

A number of men in the formation were naked but for bronze breast-and-backs. Three of those—standing together to the right of the ranks—looked up, searching the galleries . . . saw Baj and the others at the second-floor parapet, and pointed them out.

"They've come for us," Richard said. "And now they see how few we are."

"Yes," Patience said, "now they see. But the West-Gate commanders must have heard before, that some invaders were *already* in the town, and were going to the Pens."

"Panic . . . rumors." Baj watched the men below; the long ranks were shifting uneasily. He could hear voices over the cavern's wind.

"Yes." Patience nodded. "They must have feared to leave a

possible great number of us at their backs—so came the long
march here."

"Well," Dolphus said, "they've succeeded. We're not at their
backs—and hardly any number of us at all."

"Then why," Baj said, "aren't they coming up?" The two great
warning bells still rang over Boston—but drums and trumpets
sounded nearer, and faint howls of victory.

Below—despite commands, and one officer's threatening
halberd—the ordered files of Constables were becoming more
ragged. Their ranks now were only roughly ranks as, here and
there, men left formation to walk . . . then trot back the way
they'd come.

"They see—they hear—the city lost," Patience said, "and are
afraid for their families in Township-west. . . . Do you realize what
we've *done*? We've done an accidental wonder! Diverted these from
the defense, and so let Sylvia Wolf-General come into the city!"

"Perhaps," Richard said. ". . . I suppose the impossible might
have became possible, when these men marched here, instead of
to South Gate."

Below, even with filtering away, hundreds of the West-Gate
Constables of Boston still stood in their ranks, waiting commands for a battle already lost.

"They will not come up," Baj said.

"From your lips," Dolphus, with an apt and ancient quote,
"—to God's ear."

A woman cried out, back in the Pens. As if that cry had sent
her, Nancy came out onto the gallery. "Constables are here, but
don't come up?"

"Not yet," a Shrike said.

"We have a woman dying." There was blood soaking Nancy's
parky sleeves. "Another was, and so sick I cut her throat to ease
her away. Also there's one with the strings to her left leg cut so
she'll never walk again, but hobble."

"Do you need me, Nancy?" Patience said.

"No. There's no more good to do except by Guard-doctors." Nancy turned to go back to the pens. "Baj—call me if the Constables come up."

"I will, but they won't."

"No," Patience said, softly as to herself. "No, they won't."

Baj touched Patience's hand, where it rested on the ice parapet. "Still, sadness for you," he said, "even with winning."

"Yes . . . sadness." There were tears in her black eyes. Ice-chips melting on obsidian. "But this is nothing undeserved. If not now, then later—and if not Sylvia, then some other Moonriser general. The Guards, our soldier Persons, our sharpened edges, were bound to slice *us* someday. . . ." She turned to him. "And you, Prince. Do you forgive me?"

"I forgive none of us."

The silence following became oddly richer. "Listen!" a Shrike said, and all then heard the quiet of Boston's great bells tolling no more.

That quiet was filled with distant clamor and trumpet calls, an approaching rumble of kettle-drums—and below, the clatter of halberds dropped on ice as the last of the Constables' formations broke apart . . . and men ran the crevasse road, back to their homes.

Only several officers, naked but for half-armor, stood like statues on the ice.

"Run, you fools," Richard said, but softly.

"They won't." Baj shook his head. "Their blunder has brought their soldiers here, wasting battle time, when they would have made the difference at South Gate. They've marched their men—and their city, as it was—into only history."

Turning from the rampart, he felt a sudden knife-cut of disappointment, at being certain to live on as who he'd become. ". . . Now, everything is won, except the lives of the women we killed."

Richard muttered something—reached over suddenly to grip Baj's arm, and shook him hard. "We are not Weather-Greats, to know what was to come! You are *certainly* not." Another hard shake. "Don't be so proud of sorrow!"

". . . I promise," Baj said. "If you don't break my arm."

Guards Persons had appeared at the crest of the crevasse bridge. Banners, with steel glinting under. Moonriser trumpets called over the glittering city—and under their music, a rising chorus, the shouts, the howls of Person soldiers come at last into Ancient Boston-in-the-Ice.

* * *

Sylvia Wolf-General was bandaged. A wound, a slash at the side of her throat, had almost killed her. Just above the mail gorget, there was stained cloth against pale skin and blood-stuck gray fur.

She stood with her officers at a great blue-ice table in the almost transparent entrance rotunda of what had been the Township's Clear Hall of Perfect Justice, its polished floor, walls, and ceiling, gleaming wonders under lamps whose evening light was no different than morning's. The building's frozen perfection kept, apparently, by having no iron stoves vented near, so the cold was penetrating as knife points.

Baj and the others had passed, beside the entrance, a tall statue: a woman with a sword, sculpted in green ice, her eyes carved as blindfolded. They'd passed her . . . then, as they came in through massive iron doors, had seen a great mechanical clock built of wood and spring-machinery that whirred and clicked. A silver crescent moon was rising above its figure twelve.

Baj had assumed the machine's gear-cuts and wheels were fine-powdered with black lead—like ice-ships' rigging—rather than oiled, to ease their rubbing in such cold.

. . . The General's near-violet eyes were the beautiful same, but weary at the end of a fighting day. Her voice, still a rip-saw, sliced through the silence that had at last succeeded baying hunting calls . . . occasional shrieks down the long, frozen streets of Boston, where most citizens, stunned, huddled in their ice apartments.

"An accidental favor is no favor at all," she said, with a flash of fang in that murderous mask—to show Baj, Nancy, and Richard, to show Dolphus and his surviving Shrikes how little the luring away of the West-Gate Constables had mattered. "We would have won through, even with those other soldiers there."

"No," Baj said to her, "—you would not. You won barely, as it was." His shoulder, where the glaive-hook had caught him, hurt when he moved his arm. His injuries, all their injuries, kept modest by luck and sudden assault—also by sacrificed Errol . . . the sacrificed Shrikes—had been hastily bandaged and were reminding now, stiffening in clotted blood.

"You say she *lies*?" A wolf-blood officer took a step toward him, almost-hand on his saber's hilt. This was not the handsome officer; the handsome one was missing, as was the General's grim aunt—both, Baj supposed, lying with the mounds of dead piled at South Gate. Sunrisers . . . Moonrisers, now lying brothers in arms.

"Don't touch hilt to me," Baj said to the officer, "unless you want to die." Speaking out of disgust with killing, so one more seemed to matter not at all. Behind him, he heard Dolphus-Shrike murmur, "Uh-oh."

The Wolf-General said, "Leave it, Ronald," and the officer took his hand from his sword and stepped back. ". . . Very well," she said. "It was a possible *small* favor."

"I ask one in return," Baj said.

"And that is?"

"A woman I killed at the Pens . . . her name was Mary-Shearwater. She asked that her father be told how she died, and bravely. And that she loved him."

"Ah. And the father is . . .?"

"A tribal elder. Simon."

"I know the far-north Shearwaters." Another officer, scarred and short-muzzled. "Don't know this Simon, though."

The Wolf-General sighed. "Well, see the message is taken wherever to the man, with my gratitude and commendation for her courage. . . . As if there were nothing more important for us to do."

"Thank you," Baj said.

"I don't require thanks for acts of honor." Sylvia stood surveying them, her eyes improbably gentle, her gray crest stained where blood had spattered. The bronze breast-and-back she wore was dented, and chopped through in a narrow place at her left side, where a halberd's swing had struck her.

"Are you hurt at your side, there?" Baj said.

The question seemed to startle her—certainly startled her officers.

After a moment, she said, "Not badly."

"Your aunt . . . ?"

". . . Dead."

Baj saw in the Wolf-General's partly-human face, in her entirely human eyes, exactly what he had seen in Cooper's as the traitor king charged down upon him—a recognition of the mingled pride and sorrow of leadership. And he knew he would have seen the same in his First-father's face—his Second-father's too, if he'd been wise enough to look for it.

Sylvia Wolf-General licked her chops. "Where is the woman, Patience?"

"Gone to her son, ma'am."

"An oddity, I understand."

"As who is not?" Baj said.

Sylvia laughed, jaws wide and grinning—then shook her head. "Sunriser arrogance," she said. "But Moonrisers will rule in Boston now. And more decently than was the case under you Simple-bloods."

"To be hoped," Baj said.

The Wolf-General stared at him a moment more, then bent to her ice table, its sheaves and stacks of southern paper. "I have a year's orders to give," she said, and seemed to be talking to herself, her harsh voice softer. "—Victory is more trouble than defeat."

She said nothing more for a while, and Nancy tugged at Baj's sleeve to be going. Dolphus and his Shrikes shifted, restless.

Sylvia looked up. "Yes. It is time and almost past time, Prince, for you to leave us." Her breath frosted in the ice building's air. "—Leave this Township, and New England entirely." Her curved black nails tapped a sheet of paper. "With our thanks, of course. Our thanks, and generous payment to you and your companions for your service."

"I would be . . . an awkward guest?"

"You would be a guest who might someday encourage *interference* from your family's old friends in the Rule, from its fine navy come up along our coast. Interference I will not have."

"And so . . ."

"And so," Sylvia Wolf-General said, "the best of fortune attend you in your travels. In yours," she glanced at Nancy, "and your companions'."

"A day?"

"Oh, Prince," Sylvia smiled, "take two days. Rest . . . enjoy a hot bath. Did you know these people have a public bath? An icehouse with many iron tubs over iron stoves—burning black-rock like their others."

"Good news."

"Yes. *Civilization*, and I intend to enjoy it. A bath-house open to the ice-cavern's air, I understand, to prevent heat and steam from melting matters, but still wonderful."

"Then," Baj bowed to her, "since baths and travel preparations will take up our time, I'll say farewell, General."

"Farewell," Nancy said.

"You've found luck, Nancy?" the General said.

"I've found luck."

Sylvia Wolf-General nodded. "And to you," she glanced at Richard, "I return a deserter's honor, so you may style yourself 'Captain' again, and not wince for shame."

". . . Thank you, ma'am."

"So, you—you three, I assume, with any of these tribesmen who care to join you—may have your two days' rest. But if I ever see you after, Prince, I will have your head. . . . A matter of state."

"Understood," Baj said, and as he turned to leave, paused. "Both my fathers would have enjoyed meeting you, General."

Sylvia bent to her papers again. "As to enjoyment, I can't say. But I believe they would have found themselves . . . occupied."

29

Baj knew he had the left-shoulder thing, and another, bandaged, but was surprised—as Nancy, Richard, and perhaps the Shrikes were surprised—by minor wounds they hadn't known they'd received, until weapons were racked, and bloodstained and sweat-stiffened furs peeled off and laid on wooden benches at the baths.

The porticoed row of huge iron tanks—braced over stoves holding seething trays of coals—was already filling with bellowing guardsmen given temporary passes. Scarred, their knot-knuckled hands splashing, they thrashed and rolled in steaming water, some skins sleek and shining, some matted with soaked pelt.

Baj led the others, naked—Nancy uniquely beautiful, Richard very different, the Shrikes only pale heavily-muscled human—to a far tank still empty. Roiling clouds of steam were rising even to Boston's high-hanging lamps, so they glowed misted-gold. There, the great cavern's freezing wind pulled the steam to pieces, streamed it away under vaults of blue and diamond ice.

They balanced at the walkway's edge, and plunged in. Dolphus and his Shrikes, strangers to bathing except at rare hot springs, jumped last and reluctantly—but then were most pleased, yelling loudest as they thrashed and sputtered in deep, milky, hot water, the tank's iron bottom too hot to touch toe to for more than a moment.

Smelling of the glacier's mineral skirt, the water licked gently at bruises and sprains, soaked bandages, opened clotted injuries, and brought out tiny plumes of blood as they bathed. . . . Most of those slashes had been to wrists and forearms, though here and there a steel point had pecked through furs unnoticed, only bloody-marking instead of deep enough for death. The hot water opened all those shy places, and took strained muscles in its soft hands, gently stroked and twisted them to ease. . . . They all, bobbing together in mineral lather and steam, moaned with pleasure as if at sex.

Just surfacing from a peaceful underwater kingdom, stretching and turning in ringing pressing heat, Baj rose to vaporous air to find Richard, a soaked and shaggy monument, floating like an island beside him. The dark, bear's eyes examined Baj through drifting steam. ". . . We are alive," Richard said, took a fanged mouthful of milky water, and spit it to the side. "We are alive, Baj, and have won. None of our dead fighters—and none of the ladies who died—would begrudge us."

"I hope not," Baj said, to shouts and splashes from tanks nearby.

"Hope not what?" Nancy busily swimming to him. Determined swimming in a Vulpine style, pretty head held high, red crest drenched dark, her slender hands thrashing before her.

"Hope not to be drowned by a fox-girl."

"Liar," she said, splashed to him, grappled, and kissed his nose.

"I have to teach you to swim Austral."

"I know how to swim."

"Yes, sweetheart—and you're beautiful, but Austral is faster through the water. And in Kingdom River, it was swim fast or freeze."

"I *am* pretty." She lay back, floating in his arms.

"Very pretty. . . . Let me see where you were hurt."

She lifted a slender arm with only a faint fringe of wet fur to her elbow—and displayed a soggy bandage above the wrist, oozing red. "See?" She made a small fist. "No strings sliced."

"What else?"

"Little cuts . . . nothing. And I was kicked; somebody kicked my leg when I fell."

"The arm needs to be cleaned with vodka, and perhaps sewn."

"We all need sewing. I saw where you were hurt." She hugged him closer, touched his shoulder's soaked bandage with a finger, and stared at him so near her golden eyes went slightly crossed.

"—What's funny?" Lisping her *s* a little.

"*We're* funny." . . . Perhaps funny, Baj thought, as they floated together—and certainly, except for poor Errol, very lucky. Luck and surprise had kept them alive, though bruised and whittled.

Nancy sighed and lay back into his arms. "Sad child Errol," she said, as if she'd read his mind. "He was always with us, yet not with us. I miss him, gone only this morning. I look around, here and there, to see that he's behaving. . . ."

"He saved your life, comb-honey. May Lady Weather warm him for it."

"You bad man." She nipped the side of his neck. "You do not pray to any Great!"

"I make a Thanks-exception, for the gift of your life."

. . . Baj was first out, climbing from the tank to the wooden walkway—dripping, with fine threads of blood lacing down his forearms—and down his back from the left shoulder.

"A duty call, sweetheart," he said, to Nancy's questioning look. And to all of them, drifting—wallowing, in Richard's case—he raised his voice over the guardsmen's racket. "*Meet at the troopers' mess . . .*"

His wounds—no bone chipped, no tendon or spurt-artery sliced through, though one had been slightly nicked on his right forearm—were unbandaged and cleaned at one of the bath-house tables with vodka (the shoulder-cut stinging worst), then sewn and rebandaged by a Guard medic with a dog's dark and sympathetic eyes.

Treated, then passed along for new issue to a grumbling quartermaster of the Guard—advantage apparently being taken of soldiers and commanders actually clean—Baj was surprised to be directed to the senior officers' benches. "Staff's orders for you an' yours, Sunriser. —Travelin' goods."

There, he was clothed in underthings, foot-wraps, and buckskin. Then fitted with a light, superbly wrought mail hauberk and its

Corinthian helmet, and dressed in rich furs (lynx, fisher-cat, and wolverine) from a great heap of all sizes of luxury plate and mail, fine cloaks, trousers, and jackets—treasures no doubt courtesy of Boston's plundered shops and storerooms. . . . And, with some difficulty finding a fit, was presented new muk-boots as well.

Washed, injuries stitched, dressed so well and warmly—and impressed by the Guard's attention to such matters, with a desperate battle won only hours before—Baj went down the bath pavilion's carved-ice staircase, his new fisher-cat cloak thrown back as he buckled his sword-belt. He noticed, among the several sewn-cut pains and muscle strains, a deep ache in his left hip, bruised by some blow he couldn't recall.

A bath attendant—Sunriser-human, elderly, and frightened—had given him directions to what he'd called "A Grand Unusual, well-known, and kept in C-Creche Solitary." The old man had told the way, then ducked as a trooper with odd ears surfaced grinning from a tank beside, and splashed him.

As he walked, helmet under his arm—and noticing even the so-fine hauberk's weight—Baj traveled the ice paths and narrow streets of a city silent and waiting. He saw faces at iron-framed apartment windows, men and women shocked by the sudden loss of what had always been. Now, having to accept a future unimagined only the day before.

. . . Baj encountered several Guards patrols—menacing, then recognizing him—armed Persons pacing along the frozen streets. They were swiftly weaving the binding cords of the Wolf-General's rule, while the citizens of Boston, so many more thousands strong, still huddled, stunned, in their homes. —And doing so, of course, were completing their defeat. Walking, Baj had so far met only nine of Boston's people passing, hurrying by. None had looked him in the face, as if not to see, was not to be seen.

The bath attendant's directions seemed to have been certain enough, though distance hadn't been mentioned. It took more than a glass hour for Baj to reach the river—first trudging down

Court Street (its sign in wrought iron on a post), then turning right onto Cambridge, to walk a very long way past many-storied buildings frosted white as celebration cakes.

As he went, the Township's heaven of high lamps shone their golden ever-daylight, throwing his shadow multiple. And it occurred to Baj that the Wolf-General would have to keep the Talents to sail up and serve them. Would keep the Talents, perhaps, for other chores as well. . . .

From Cambridge Street, at last, onto a pleasant, pillared bridge—built of strong blue ice-blocks, and signed *Longfellow*. A shallow stream of glacier water wended below, white as goat's milk—melted perhaps by Boston's close breath, perhaps by the warmth of earth not so far beneath its bed.

Over the bridge, at River Street, there was a very small church, polished clear as best glass, and sculpted along its walls with Warm-time matters: ships with no sails, carriages with no horses drawing, planes in air and supported by nothing, or by whirlers, pro-pellers. Prayers in ice, it seemed to Baj, for those times' return—though he thought that Frozen-Jesus must dislike prayers intended to melt the Great they addressed.

As he passed this chapel, Baj saw through open iron doors that it held only one Boston citizen. A woman in handsome middle-age stood naked, her breath frosting in bitter air. She was praying amid a forest of small wonderfully-carved trees of ice, their perfect leaves scintillant under mirrored lamps.

Baj considered calling to her to go home. The Guard was certainly under discipline, but perhaps not perfectly at the end of this constantly-lit day of triumph. . . . Then he decided not, and left her to her prayers.

At the end of River Street, past four quite-elegant ice-brick buildings—perhaps the homes of notables—Baj came to the Township's edge at a looming barrier of ice, cracked and fissured, that rose in gleaming blues and greens to shadowed heights where no bright lamps hung.

In that uneven shade, a relief from lamplight constant, Baj found the large letters *A*, *B*, and *C*, posted in iron on a narrow, uneven path running along the base of the ice. *A* and *B* were indicated left. *C*, to the right, and he went that way.

There was a droning whistle sounding . . . sounding louder the further he went—climbing the steepening path, and annoying his sore hip. . . . That noise, the vibration of a single deep note, made his rapier buzz in its scabbard like a short-summer bee. Made him slightly sick with the sound—and perhaps from the long day's weariness, and sting and ache of his injuries. He stood still on the ice path, taking deep breaths so as not to vomit.

He saw sudden brightness, though his eyes were closed— brilliant as sunshine, so he thought for an instant that frozen Boston burned. But the light was in a dream, a dream while awake and standing, of the sun shimmering over an endless ocean of ice.

Baj staggered . . . opened his eyes only to the wonderful silent city—and as he did, felt illness fall away, so he was able to climb on up the path, though tired, and yawning.

He turned a corner to the left—edged around it—and saw a cut cave-mouth making that deep droning as the wind blew past it. There was a neat iron gate set into blue ice, but its key-turn and chain hung free.

Baj stepped down the path, gripped cold black grease on the iron—frigid even through new fur and leather gloves—and shoved the gate open on almost silent hinges.

Warmth . . . and warm darkness immediately. He drew his sword—when would that begin once more to seem hasty, odd?— and walked onto something less slippery than ice. Cut stone. He went on into darkness, the rapier's blade questing before . . . until what might have been faint lamplight ahead, became certain.

Still, he kept the sword drawn into richer and richer warmth. Off to his left, in what seemed an iron chimney vault of its own, the rumble and shuttered glare of a double-vented furnace heated itself to the dullest red. There was a soft splash of melt-water running through an ice-cut dug deep beside it.

Here was the warmest air Baj had known in weeks. Warmth at first, then becoming heat almost sickening, so he sheathed his rapier, tugged his gloves off, swung his cloak free and folded it over his arm . . . then kept moving, furred boots grating softly on graveled stone.

"Did you know . . ." A soft, echoing voice.

Baj stood still, hand on hilt.

"Did you know, Prince?" Patience. "Did you know that you stand where once a world wonder—the Mass-Into-Tech—once stood?"

Her voice had come from the right, and Baj went that way into lamplight brighter and brighter. Warm wind pressed gently at his back.

Patience waited outlined in an iron doorway by golden light, carved ice glittering beside and above her. "Dear Baj," she said, and stepped aside. Her white hair tied back with a leather string, she wore only a long, stained, white apron, and stood otherwise naked in lamplight, her body pale and slender as a young girl's, though softened, hollowed by age. "Dear Baj—in fine furs and mail, as a prince should be. And how stands our day's victory?"

"It stands, so far tonight." Baj walked with her into a huge round chamber, a sort of oubliette, shaped like a wild-bee hive. He'd seen the same spaces on Island, sunk deep under North Tower.

This room's roof, as with those much smaller, grimmer, donjons, came together into a round funnel shape—though here almost a bow-shot high, and lit spangled as all of Boston was, with clusters of hanging lamps. A faint odor of hot oil drifted on the air.

The chamber was warm, heated by the corridor's furnace draft flowing in and up through its roof. A roof, Baj saw, lined with iron sheeting framed away from the ice beneath it. Though still, runnels of milky melt-water trickled down carved drains.

There were wooden benches spaced around the room, with fat embroidered pillows drifted on them—and at the room's center, a stepped dais, heaped with more cushions. The encircling ice-block walls were rich with pegged bright decorations—polished copper moons and suns and stars—and four wide cord-hung tapestries spaced evenly around, all telling tales of pleasure in gardens Boston hadn't seen for many centuries. Beside each, a doorway into other rooms.

Two women—Boston women, gray-haired and sturdy in woven shirts and sealskin trousers—stood in one of those across the chamber, watching.

"Eleanor Potts," Patience said, "and her sister, Verity—an ancient New England name."

"I've never heard it," Baj said, and bowed to the women, who nodded back. "It means . . . truth?"

"Yes," Patience said, "and might as well have meant fidelity, loyalty, friendship. These have tended my Maxwell, and with wet-nurses, since he was born—and tend him still."

"Maxwell," Baj said, and looked for a child—perhaps already taking first steps.

"You've come to meet him."

"Yes, I've come to meet him. . . . And to ask his mother if she and her son will accompany us. Leave Boston."

"Leave Boston?"

"The Wolf-General has more than suggested I go—with any who choose to go with me."

"Ah . . ." Patience smiled. "Concerned the Rule might make you a cause to interfere here?"

"Yes. —Where's your boy?"

Patience took his hand. "Come meet my dear dreamer." She led him to the dais, and up a wide step.

For an instant, Baj saw only big satin pillows, pale pink. Pillows over cushions, and half-covered by a white-bear's fur. Then he saw the pillows lived, and were the round arms and chest of a sleeping child. A baby—plump, perfect, its eyes closed by lids almost transparent, its hair a wisp of glossy brown. A baby the size of a man.

Bigger than a man. Richard's size.

Baj's voice caught in his throat for a moment, then he whispered, "Maxwell . . . are you sleeping?"

There was, perhaps, a deep murmur in response.

"Yes, he's sleeping. . . . See how he's grown?" Patience smiled down at her child. "Well, you wouldn't know that—but he has grown." She bent to kiss a huge, soft, dimpled hand. "My darling came as other babies came, but has grown and grown . . . though not grown older."

"He's beautiful," Baj said. And the child *was* beautiful. Perfect, though so mighty. There was the odor of all infants about him— of newness, pee, oat powder . . . of shit, and sweetness.

Patience stretched sinewy, scarred arms yearning to the child as if to seize him, size or not, and haul him to her. But instead, gently stroked the huge round head, its fine drift of hair . . . gently traced the tender pouting lips so the baby shifted, tickled by the touch. ". . . Has any woman on the frozen earth a son like this?"

"Should he choose to grow older," Baj said, 'choose' seeming the proper word, "then a Great will certainly stand over Boston."

"And they haven't hurt him. Eleanor says the Faculty studied long, argued, considered foolish correctives—but hadn't yet decided." She smiled. "And now, I think the Talents will take the greatest care of us, hoping that Maxwell might someday twist the future as once they twisted the unborn—and so dream Boston back to itself again."

Baj stepped back a little, as if the baby were too large to stand close beside. "Even so, you and your son should come with us—

and likely be safer than here with Sylvia Wolf-General."

" 'Likely' be safer?" Patience stroked her son's round cheek, bent over to kiss a dimple. "And where would that be?"

"I know ice-rigged boats; I've sailed since I was a boy. We can go east to the coast, to Boston's harbor. Choose a vessel there, and if loot and our pay suffice," he smiled, "buy it."

"And then?"

"Then, across the frozen Ocean Atlantic, to Atlas-Europe."

"But thousands of Warm-time miles, Baj, if any of the maps are true! And for what reason?"

"For . . . whatever reason awaits us there."

"And Maxwell and I?"

"Come with us."

Patience smiled. "Do you not think, dear, dear Baj—do you not think Maxwell might be too large even for the journey to the coast? And then too large for comfort in a fishing boat?"

"We will make do. We'll take him, and see him comfortable."

"And if still he grows? Grows, and then grows slowly older to become what he must become? . . . Do you know what warmed goats, what willing women must be milked for him every day?"

"We'll bring goats—bring women."

"Sweet Baj, you're speaking of The Book's ark of Noah—not an adventuring barque with an exiled prince and whatever fighting friends." Patience reached over to fold the white bearskin coverlet back. "Too warm; he gets a rash." Maxwell stirred, cooed to himself, a deep, blurred, string-instrument note.

"—And of course, Nancy goes with you."

"Yes."

"I knew you two would love each other. I knew because I'm a woman—and what else would an exile prince and a pretty fox-girl do *but* fall into love. Inescapable. . . . But I knew also, because Maxwell dreamed it into a dream of mine in the Smoking-mountains. We saw you together—though you were both older—together at Island, on the Bronze Gate's landing." She shook the southern-cotton sheet out billowing, then covered the baby again. "Richard goes as well?"

"I believe he will. —Think again, Patience. Will you both be safe with the Guard ruling Boston?"

"Oh, Sylvia minds honor. Minds it the more for the wolf in her blood. She won't disturb me or my child—and besides, she must rule gently, with a triumph so rawly new, so unexpected . . . and half her Guard companies dead at South Gate." Patience tucked the sheet, saw to it a plumply massive arm was covered. "This room is sometimes too warm, sometimes cool. Drafts by the walls . . ."

She tucked and arranged until satisfied, then stepped back and observed her child as if he were a loved landscape. "—Baj, the Wolf-General holds here by her fingernails. If the people of Boston recover their courage, grow angry enough, she and her soldiers might still be overwhelmed."

"Formidable fingernails."

"Yes, but not sufficient for comfort. So Sylvia will rule gently for a long while . . . and will not allow the Talents' changes, anymore, their use of women's wombs."

"Will not," Baj said, "unless, in the future, she finds a need for guardsmen created perfectly fierce, perfectly obedient."

"A prince's thought, Baj." She smiled at him. "And like most such, unpleasant."

"Yes. Unpleasant.—You will not go?"

"No." Patience shook her head. "The Faculty . . . the Talents, will see us well-cared for, here. They will imagine Maxwell's gift a secret hope for a Sunriser Boston reborn." She sighed. "Besides, no baby—not even a wonder—should wander an ice ocean to *perhaps*, or *maybe*. That's a journey for a young man with a sword. . . . And what others?"

"I think Dolphus-Shrike may go with us—and his few men remaining—since their tribe will be living in peaceful dullness for some time, with the Wolf-General's Boston to deal with."

"Yes . . . And if they go, you will remember they are savages, however clever and well-read their chieftain?"

"I'll remember."

"They live by signs we never see."

"I know it. . . . And Nancy—all of them—will come to say good-bye to you and the baby."

Patience led him down from the dais, stood looking at him for a moment, a cool regard. Then she said, "I will never see you again, unless in Maxwell's dreams," and swept into his arms like a lover, hugging him close. Her body was startlingly small and slight. There was no human odor, not even of her breath, only the white scents of ice and stone. "I have *two* sons," she said, looking up into his eyes, her own dark as dug coal.

"Yes," Baj said, and kissed her forehead. "And I, a Third-mother."

"And would you have killed me at the Pens?"

". . . Yes, if not for that little time to consider."

"Then you are Sam Monroe's son, more than Toghrul Khan's."

"Perhaps."

"Prince," Patience sighed, and left his arms, "I remember the boy I first saw fleeing through a windy day in the southern mountains, afraid, exhausted. But still, the man he was to become rested waiting in him like a shaft of stone. —The boy now is worn away by Lady Weather, and the man revealed. . . . Do you understand that the brave woman you killed at the Pens—the women *we* killed—were soldiers as much as any swordsmen, any halberdiers? They died of necessary war; and you—like the rest of us—simply an instrument."

"And no tragic figure?"

"Only if you're foolish enough to choose it."

"Oh," Baj said, "—I doubt if I'm done with foolish choices." He stepped up to the dais again, to the side of Maxwell's massive bed, leaned over and kissed the great warm round of the baby's cheek. "Farewell, my brother. Dream safety for our mother . . . and luck for me."

The giant child sighed, its eyes slowly opened, a pale wondering blue and soft with sleep. Perhaps seeing Baj, perhaps not, but only the vaulted lamp-spangled ceiling of its crèche.

30

Captain Pruitt, Sunriser and almost sixty, styled himself "Commodore"—though only to himself to ward the laughter of other fisher and sealer captains. At what was considered on the coast an advanced age, he owned three boats clear of debt. Sloops to sail blue sea or white ice—though ice-rigged now, as usual off New England. Ice-rigged to run days out to the great storm-split leads, with wet-rigging ready—once skates were up and stowed—to fish them.

Three boats and decent crews for every one—bits of seal-stuff born in two bosuns, though only evident in their odor.

Pope was at sea. *Parson* in the yards with cracked strakes, but *Priestess*—all ancient sacred names—*Priestess* was afloat, fresh scraped, caulked, and sounded, cord lines and hook-wire spooled, and provisioned for many weeks on sea ice to sea leads, for whenever came the cod.

. . . Buzz and buzz had sounded at the coast—with Bostonians in flight from their disaster. Pigeons also had come flying. But the city—under Sunrisers *or* Moonrisers—still must eat, and more and better than occasional musk-ox or caribou. Cod was the matter. And seal meat. And whale. So bitter buzzing beside the point—and history turned on its back—still the coast would fish, the coast would hunt and whale, and the men and women of the coast would be paid for it.

Captain (Commodore) Pruitt, a hard-hander but fair enough to his crews, had come down *Priestess*'s gangway, still considering the luck of being necessary—*and* almost thirty frozen miles from unlucky Boston-town—when he saw an odd group waiting down the dock in day's-end light.

Waiting—with two caribou sledges just swinging away through fine blowing snow, leaving them standing with nothing but their bundles. And their weapons.

. . . As he was no fool in finding fish, so Captain Pruitt was no fool in avoiding ugly weather. He had a nose for it—and therefore turned back to climb aboard *Priestess* as if he'd recalled further business on her.

"*You!*"

It was one of those *You*'s—this called in a young man's voice—that brought bad news with it. Pruitt sighed, signaled a seaman by her rail to keep sorting hooks by sizes, then turned to walk down to them.

". . . I have work to do. What's your business?"

A man—undoubtedly the caller of "You"—said "Good evening," and smiled at him, a smile that made Captain Pruitt no easier. This was a young man, scarred and weary, perhaps also injured in the Boston fighting. He wore rich furs, and—hinted gleaming at his throat—apparently fine chain-mail under them. Wore those and a wicked rapier, also a long-blade knife.

Bad enough, but his company was worse. Some sort of Moonriser girl—likely a little fox or coyote in there—also armed. Still grimmer, a Person the size of a small berg, with an ax to match, and six . . . seven Shrike tribesmen grinning, file-toothed.

Bad weather.

"I have to attend my work, so say what you have to say."

"You are the captain, the owner of that boat?" A nod to *Priestess*.

It occurred to Pruitt to lie to this young man—and he might have, but there was a look in those dark and slightly slanted eyes that said, "Don't trouble. I know command, and you were giving orders to that crew."

"Yes, I own her. And so what?" A fine little WT phrase.

"The boat seems sound. . . ."

"*Is* sound," Pruitt said. "The best." Then uneasily regretted the boast.

The young man nodded. "People told us so at Bay Dock. . . . We are ordered out of Boston, and wish to leave this coast."

"Then hire a vessel to skate you down to Map-Carolina, and do not trouble me."

"We wish to own, not hire, Captain. We've been shown what's to buy along these piers, and were told to come see this boat—smart, just stocked for weeks of fishing—and it does suit us."

Pruitt was so startled, he was silent for a moment. " 'Suits you' for what?"

"For crossing the Ocean Atlantic. For going to Atlas-Ire and England, then perhaps the supposed Europe."

It seemed a speech in a dream, and took Captain Pruitt a moment to accept. ". . . Well, not in *my* boat. Not in my *Priestess* in any way at all! Our people fish or hunt the ice, and always have—and any gone past the Banks are never heard from after. But not in my boat in any case."

The big Moonriser—some bear in there for certain—muttered something, and the young man looked at Pruitt in a concerned, almost a sad sort of way. It was not reassuring. "Captain," he said, "we will buy your boat."

"No, you will not."

The Shrikes appeared to grow restless, shifted so like a pack of wolves that it was striking.

"Forgive me for insisting," the young man said, bowed as if out of a story-book, then held out a heavy jingling pouch. "Here is part of our very generous pay from Sylvia Wolf-General, the same who orders us gone. Thirty-seven Boston golds." He held the pouch out—and when Pruitt didn't take it, let it fall to the dock planking.

"You fucking seal-pup." Pruitt kicked the pouch a little way—but not out onto the ice. "I sell no boat to you at all!"

The young man shook his head. "Think again, sir." The sea wind blew his breath in frost. "I believe that pouch would buy you the building of even a better. And I do know boats; know them well. I've sailed and skated for years on Kingdom River."

"Then build your own." Captain Pruitt wished—oh, how he

wished—that *Priestess* lay at Bay, or East Dock, where seamen, captains, and salters came and went, weighing fish and selling fish. There would be more than a hundred hard-handers there to see these people gone. . . . Here, at Pier Point, there was no one else seen through the last, light, sun-filtering snow. Only his crew—and only one or two fighters among them. ". . . I sell you *nothing.*"

The girl—fox-bits in there for sure—lisped in the young man's ear. He sighed like someone older, and said, "We haven't time for this, and allow Sylvia to change her mind to execution. Not the time, Captain—nor, frankly, the patience. Take this as the last unfairness of a war . . . and not that unfair after all." Another of those damned smiles. "Considering we might simply butcher you, leave you lying, then go send your crew ashore. . . . I'll make a crew of my friends."

"And I say fuck you! I do not sell my—" Pruitt would have continued, but the Fox-girl had drawn a nasty curved sword.

"You are troubling my Baj," she said, "—who has had enough trouble." The girl's odd yellow eyes as disturbing as her blade.

Captain Pruitt noticed one of the Shrikes, apparently amused, smiling at him. The Shrike raised his javelin a little, so the steel head glinted.

"Well, Salt-Jesus drown you all. . . ." Pruitt's heart was thumping. "You are pirates, and will have sinking luck on the ice and off it!" He went and stooped for the pouch of gold. "You come back to this harbor," he counted minted coins into a trembling palm, "and I'll gather men to stake you out for the crabs!"

"We won't be back," the young man said. "We skate and sail across the sea."

"And will never reach what's there—if there's anything at all." Pruitt finished his count.

"Build a lucky new boat, Captain," the young man said, hoisted his bundle, and led his odd company away down the dock to *Priestess* . . . then up her gangway.

Soon enough, her crew of seven came down confused, and over the dock to Pruitt with questions.

"Don't fucking ask me! Don't ask me about a robbery—which is what this is. I've been robbed here by armed trash from Boston's fighting, that paid me poorly for the best sloop on the coast!" Though he had good copybook English, Pruitt—now they were needed—could recall no sufficient ancient curses.

"Do we fight 'em, Cap'n?" This from a line-hauler who barely knew a hake from a cod.

"Why, yes, Freddy—we certainly fight a bad man, two bad Persons, and seven worse Shrikes. And you go first, you fool!"

And damned if the man didn't start, and had to be collared.

"Oh . . . stand still, all of you," Pruitt said, "and wish those thieves the worst of luck."

He and his fishers stayed put, and watched the lubbers—such a fine old word—wrestle lines free . . . then slowly pole *Priestess* out from the dock, shoving her sliding clear, skates scraping. None of that done as true sailors would have. All very unsteady.

Came time to raise her big mainsail for the wind—a little past time. Walter-bosun, seal-blooded, said "Slow . . ."

Sail shaking out, now. Better late than never. Setting the canvas . . . and, to Pruitt's satisfaction, clumsy getting it hauled taut. *Moonrisers and tribesmen, just the seamanship you'd expect. A fine southern linen sail—and almost new!—gone. I'm a robbed man, and the gold makes no difference in it. They've taken my Priestess!*

And though he hadn't meant to, Captain Pruitt ran to the dock edge and shouted after, shaking his fist. "Don't you wreck her, you young son of a bitch!"

"Poor Cap'n," Freddy said.

. . . Out in the offing under a gray-ribbed evening sky—mainsail slatting in offshore gusts, then firming as her jib came rising—*Priestess* swung hissing on her skates to a sea heading, a single gull gliding in company. Her starboard steering-blade raised a plume of powdered ice as she steadied, jolting a little over pressure creases where the frozen harbor had cracked and mended.

Then, going faster, she sailed away sweetly ... running east by east, chasing her sunset shadow out onto the frozen ocean.